DAW Books presents the finest in urban fantasy from Seanan McGuire:

The October Daye Novels:

ROSEMARY AND RUE
A LOCAL HABITATION
AN ARTIFICIAL NIGHT
LATE ECLIPSES
ONE SALT SEA
ASHES OF HONOR
CHIMES AT MIDNIGHT
THE WINTER LONG
A RED-ROSE CHAIN
ONCE BROKEN FAITH
THE BRIGHTEST FELL
NIGHT AND SILENCE

The InCryptid Novels:

DISCOUNT ARMAGEDDON
MIDNIGHT BLUE-LIGHT SPECIAL
HALF-OFF RAGNAROK
POCKET APOCALYPSE
CHAOS CHOREOGRAPHY
MAGIC FOR NOTHING
TRICKS FOR FREE
THAT AIN'T WITCHCRAFT*

The Ghost Roads:

SPARROW HILL ROAD
THE GIRL IN THE GREEN SILK GOWN

*Coming soon from DAW Books

SEANAN McGUIRE

THE BRIGHTEST FELL

AN OCTOBER DAYE NOVEL

DAW BOOKS, INC.

DONALD A. WOLLHEIM, FOUNDER

375 Hudson Street, New York, NY 10014

ELIZABETH R. WOLLHEIM
SHEILA E. GILBERT
PUBLISHERS

www.dawbooks.com

For Julie.
You told me Toby wanted a novel.
I never knew how right you were.

ACKNOWLEDGMENTS:

We've reached the point in the series where I am paying off debts I created five and six books ago. It feels like a miracle. Thank you all so much for trusting me to lead you down this twisting garden path into the woods, and for believing that I would be able to lead you out again. I will always do my best to be worthy of your faith in me.

No matter how many times I do this, it's always a little daunting to sit back and realize how much work it is. My thanks go, forever, to the Machete Squad, for their tireless attempts to make my books better, and to the entire team at DAW, where they have become old hands at putting up with me. Thanks to everyone who's hosted me while this book was being written, from one side of the country to the other and back again.

Thank you Vixy, for loving these people and this world as much as I do; Amy, for keeping me focused and moving forward; Brooke, for being herself in the face of infinite frogs; Shawn, for axolotls and X-Men; and the Crowells, for everything. Thanks to Margaret and Whitney, for spaghetti and sanity, and to Carrie, for the infinite greenness of salad.

Sheila Gilbert remains the best of all possible editors, Diana Fox remains the best of all possible agents, and Chris McGrath remains the best of all possible cover artists. While we're on this track, my cats are the best of all possible cats. So are yours, if you have them. All hail the pit crew: Christopher Mangum, Tara O'Shea, and Kate Secor.

My soundtrack while writing *The Brightest Fell* consisted mostly of *Hadestown*, by Anais Mitchell, *We Are Who We Are*, by Vixy and Tony, the soundtrack of *Waitress*, endless live concert recordings of the Counting Crows, and all the Ludo a girl could hope to have (still waiting for a new album). Any errors in this book are entirely my own. The errors that aren't here are the ones that all these people helped me fix.

Come on. We have so much deeper to go.

OCTOBER DAYE PRONUNCIATION GUIDE
THROUGH THE BRIGHTEST FELL

All pronunciations are given strictly phonetically. This only covers races explicitly named in the first eleven books, omitting Undersea races not appearing or mentioned in book eleven.

Aes Sidhe: *eys shee*. Plural is "Aes Sidhe."
Afanc: *ah-fank*. Plural is "Afanc."
Annwn: *ah-noon*. No plural exists.
Bannick: *ban-nick*. Plural is "Bannicks."
Barghest: *bar-guy-st*. Plural is "Barghests."
Blodynbryd: *blow-din-brid*. Plural is "Blodynbryds."
Cait Sidhe: *kay-th shee*. Plural is "Cait Sidhe."
Candela: *can-dee-la*. Plural is "Candela."
Coblynau: *cob-lee-now*. Plural is "Coblynau."
Cu Sidhe: *coo shee*. Plural is "Cu Sidhe."
Daoine Sidhe: *doon-ya shee*. Plural is "Daoine Sidhe," diminutive is "Daoine."
Djinn: *jin*. Plural is "Djinn."

Dóchas Sidhe: *doe-sh-as shee*. Plural is "Dóchas Sidhe."

Ellyllon: *el-lee-lawn*. Plural is "Ellyllons."

Folletti: *foe-let-tea*. Plural is "Folletti."

Gean-Cannah: *gee-ann can-na*. Plural is "Gean-Cannah."

Glastig: *glass-tig*. Plural is "Glastigs."

Gwragen: *guh-war-a-gen*. Plural is "Gwragen."

Hamadryad: *ha-ma-dry-add*. Plural is "Hamadryads."

Hippocampus: *hip-po-cam-pus*. Plural is "Hippocampi."

Kelpie: *kel-pee*. Plural is "Kelpies."

Kitsune: *kit-soo-nay*. Plural is "Kitsune."

Lamia: *lay-me-a*. Plural is "Lamia."

The Luidaeg: *the lou-sha-k*. No plural exists.

Manticore: *man-tee-core*. Plural is "Manticores."

Naiad: *nigh-add*. Plural is "Naiads."

Nixie: *nix-ee*. Plural is "Nixen."

Peri: *pear-ee*. Plural is "Peri."

Piskie: *piss-key*. Plural is "Piskies.'

Puca: *puh-ca*. Plural is "Pucas."

Roane: *row-n*. Plural is "Roane."

Satyr: *say-tur*. Plural is "Satyrs."

Selkie: *sell-key*. Plural is "Selkies."

Shyi Shuai: *shh-yee shh-why*. Plural is "Shyi Shuai."

Silene: *sigh-lean*. Plural is "Silene."

Tuatha de Dannan: *tootha day danan*. Plural is "Tuatha de Dannan," diminutive is "Tuatha."

Tylwyth Teg: *till-with teeg*. Plural is "Tylwyth Teg," diminutive is "Tylwyth."

Urisk: *you-risk*. Plural is "Urisk."

LORD, WHAT FOOLS THESE MORTALS BE . . .

THE WORLDS

The Faerie and human worlds have always existed side by side, sometimes aware of one another, sometimes not. Ruled by their King, Oberon, and his two Queens, Titania and Maeve, the fae fought to protect themselves when necessary, finally fading entirely into myths and legends when, five hundred years ago, the Three vanished and left their descendants to fend for themselves.

Humanity forgot. The fae did not. And some overlap between the worlds continued, wreathed in lies and illusions to keep the humans from understanding what was happening. Most of the purebloods remain in the Summerlands, last and nearest of the accessible realms of Faerie. The deeper realms, from Annwn to Avalon, were sealed by Oberon before his disappearance, and have proven as yet impossible to reopen. Without them, heroes and monsters who might never have met are forced to share space with not only the human world, but with each other. It's a volatile mix, and one that seems destined to lead to tragedy.

In order to prevent the Summerlands from becoming a prison, the purebloods have divided the human world among themselves, creating unseen kingdoms ruled over by their unwavering hands. In Northern California, young Arden Windermere is Queen in the Mists, trying to keep her home and people safe. But she is a young regent, and San Francisco seems to be a magnet for those who would cause trouble in both worlds, no matter how much danger it puts them in . . .

THE PEOPLE

The children of the Three take many forms, borrowing aspects from their parents and shaping them into something completely new. From the ethereal to the monstrous, they are all born of Faerie, and they are kin, even as they stand against their own relations.

Greatest and most terrible among the remaining children of Faerie are the Firstborn, the immediate descendants of the Three, from whom the rest of Faerie descends. Their powers are as varied as their faces, and make them virtually unstoppable in the absence of their parents. Most are dead or missing, but those who remain—the Luidaeg, better known as the sea witch; Eira Rosynhwyr, who some claim was the inspiration for Snow White; even their youngest sister, the Liar, who wanders alone, rattling at unseen doors— are terrifying to any who would stand against them.

The purebloods, for the most part, treat themselves as rulers of their constrained world, clinging to a system of crowns and titles, refusing to entertain any possibility of modernization. The Daoine Sidhe control most of the higher positions, including the High Crown of North America, currently held by the Sollys family. The Duchy of Shadowed Hills in the Kingdom in the Mists is also held by a Daoine Sidhe, Duke Sylvester Torquill, a former hero of the realm.

Under the purebloods are the mixed-bloods, whose

fae parents descend from different Firstborn: their magic is sometimes unpredictable, and can refuse to follow the supposedly immutable rules. They might rebel if not for the fact that they aren't at the bottom of the pecking order. That role is reserved for the changelings.

Changelings—the children born when fae and humans reproduce—spend their lives balanced between the two sides of their heritage, helping their fae parents to understand the challenges presented by the constant changing march of human technology. Without them, Faerie would doubtless have been discovered centuries ago. Sadly, this truth does nothing to elevate their status among the purebloods, who treat them as nuisances and servants, hating the taint of mortality in their blood. It's a hard line to walk, and it should be no surprise that many changelings will eventually flee to the human world, concealing their true natures as they play at fitting in among people who would hate them if they only knew.

October Daye is one of those changelings, the first to be knighted in over a century. She has lived in both the fae and mortal worlds, and now, with the ground shifting under her feet, she is trying to hold onto her heritage, even as the rules are rewritten all around her.

THE STORY SO FAR . . .

Eighteen years ago, October "Toby" Daye was performing a service for her liege lord, Duke Torquill, when his brother Simon enchanted her and transformed her into a koi fish, leaving her for dead in Golden Gate Park's Japanese Tea Garden. She would be lost to the world for fourteen years, finally rising from the water when his spell was worn away by sunlight and time. She returned to find everything she thought she had gone: her human fiancé had married another woman, her daughter had grown up without her. She was starting over.

Quickly, Toby found herself in a web of mysteries and contradictions, monsters and complications. Through her efforts, the false Queen of the Mists was dethroned and Arden Windermere was elevated; the Kingdom of Silences was returned to the Davies family; even the position of changelings in the Mists was improved.

Of course, it isn't over yet. And who knows what's going to go wrong next?

The Luidaeg, probably. But she's not telling.

ONE

October 9th, 2013

Angels are bright still, though the brightest fell.
—William Shakespeare, *Macbeth*.

THE FETCH IS ONE of the most feared and least understood figures in Faerie. Their appearance heralds the approach of inescapable death: once the Fetch shows up, there's nothing that can be done. The mechanism that summons them has never been found, and they've always been rare, with only five conclusively identified in the last century. They appear for the supposedly significant—kings and queens, heroes and villains—and they wear the faces of the people they have come to escort into whatever awaits the fae beyond the borders of death. They are temporary, transitory, and terrifying.

My Fetch, who voluntarily goes by "May Daye," because nothing says "I am a serious and terrible death omen" like having a pun for a name, showed up more than three years ago. She was supposed to foretell my impending doom. Instead, all she managed to foretell was me getting a new roommate. Life can be funny that way.

At the moment, doom might have been a nice change. May was standing on the stage of The Mint, San Francisco's finest karaoke bar, enthusiastically bellowing her way through an off-key rendition of Melissa Etheridge's "Come to My Window." Her live-in girlfriend, Jazz, was sitting at one of the tables closest to the stage, chin propped in her hands, gazing at May with love and adoration all out of proportion to the quality of my Fetch's singing.

May has the face I wore when she appeared. We don't look much alike anymore, but when she first showed up at my apartment door to tell me I was going to die, we were identical. She has my memories up to the point of her creation: years upon years of parental issues, crushing insecurity, abandonment, and criminal activities. And right now, none of that mattered half as much as the fact that she also had my absolute inability to carry a tune.

"Why are we having my bachelorette party at a karaoke bar again?" I asked, speaking around the mouth of the beer bottle I was trying to keep constantly against my lips. If I was drinking, I wasn't singing. If I wasn't singing, all these people might still be my friends in the morning.

Of course, with as much as most of them had already had to drink, they probably wouldn't notice if I *did* sing. Or if I decided to sneak out of the bar, go home, change into my sweatpants, and watch old movies on the couch until I passed out. Which would have been my preference for how my bachelorette party was going to go, if I absolutely had to have one. I didn't think they were required. May had disagreed with me. Vehemently. And okay, that had sort of been expected.

What I hadn't expected was for most of my traitorous, backstabbing friends to take her side. Stacy—one of my closest friends since childhood—had actually laughed in my face when I demanded to know why she was doing this to me.

"Being your friend is like trying to get up close and personal with a natural disaster," she'd said. "Sure, we have some good times, but we spend half of them covered in blood. We just want to spend an evening making you as uncomfortable as you keep making the rest of us."

Not to be outdone, her eldest daughter, Cassandra, had blithely added, "Besides, we don't think even you can turn a karaoke party into a bloodbath."

All of my friends are evil.

As my Fetch and hence the closest thing I had to a sister, May had declared herself to be in charge of the whole affair. That was how we'd wound up reserving most of the tables at The Mint for an all-night celebration of the fact that I was getting married. Even though we didn't have a date, a plan, or a seating chart, we were having a bachelorette party. Lucky, lucky me.

My name is October Daye. I am a changeling; I am a knight; I am a hero of the realm; and if I never have to hear Stacy sing Journey songs again, it will be too soon.

Danny, who was looming beside me at the bar, nudged me with his shoulder. "It ain't so bad," he rumbled, in a voice deep enough to sound like it had bubbled up from the bowels of the earth. It was in proportion to the rest of him: he's a Bridge Troll. When not wearing an illusion to make himself look human, he's more than seven feet tall, with skin like granite and hands that can punch through walls. Take the rest of him into account, and his voice is kind of dainty.

At the moment, he looked like any other wall of a mortal man, wearing a brightly colored Hawaiian shirt that somehow wasn't any more garish than the décor. His hand dwarfed the cocktail glass he was holding. Its contents were an impressively virulent shade of pink.

"They're going to make me sing," I said.

"Probably," he agreed, taking another sip of his cocktail. "But you know what?"

"What?"

"We've been here for three hours and you ain't had to bleed on *nothin'*." His grin was broad enough to show his back molars. "If we can make it another hour, you and I set a new personal best, and Quentin owes me twenty dollars."

I lowered my beer bottle in order to gape at him. "You're *betting* on me?"

"Oh, please. As if you didn't know that going in."

"I suspected, but I didn't think any of you would be stupid enough to admit it to my face."

Danny kept grinning, unrepentant to the last.

We weren't the only people in The Mint. Aside from the bar staff—mortals all, although given where they worked, they probably saw weirder groups than ours on a regular basis—and the karaoke DJ, there were about twenty regulars who had yet to give up and surrender their places in the karaoke rotation. May had planned the party for a Tuesday night because of the bar's popularity: if it had been a Saturday, those twenty regulars would have been fifty or more, and it would have been a lot harder to get to the bar for a beer.

I needed my beer. I needed a *lot* of beer. Thanks to my specific flavor of fae heritage, I heal at an incredible rate. Sadly, that means I can't get drunk without really putting in an effort, and even if I manage it, I can't stay that way; my hyper-efficient liver sobers me right up. By drinking almost constantly, I could stay mellow enough not to flee screaming into the night. If I stopped, sobriety would reassert itself, along with the true horror of my situation.

All things considered, I might have been happier getting covered in blood, the betting pool be damned.

May finished her song to scattered applause, some of it more sincere than the rest, and hopped off the stage to sweep Jazz into her arms and kiss her deeply. That got more applause from the regulars, who clearly appreciated a good floor show. I took another swig of beer.

"Next up, we have . . ." The DJ squinted at the slip of paper in his hand. "Diana, come on down."

I choked on my beer.

"No," I said, refusing the evidence of my own eyes as Dianda Lorden got up and took the microphone, to general cheers from the people at her table. She was wearing a short blue-and-green–sequined dress that showed off the legs she normally doesn't have. It was weird. I didn't like it. "How does she even know what karaoke *is*? I call shenanigans."

Danny smirked.

Dianda is several things. Cheerfully violent. The Duchess of Saltmist. A frequent ally of mine. And, oh right, a mermaid—specifically, a Merrow—which means she lives under the Pacific Ocean and doesn't have that many opportunities for exposure to human culture. I'd been surprised when she'd shown up at all. I certainly hadn't been expecting her to *sing*.

I definitely hadn't been expecting her to sing Phil Collins.

"I really don't know how to deal with this," I said, staring at the stage.

Danny plucked the empty beer bottle from my hand and replaced it with a fresh one. One nice thing about being the bachelorette: even if I was being forced to watch essentially everyone I knew play pop star while wearing illusions designed to make them look human, at least someone else was picking up my tab. I could drink until I forgot why I needed to keep drinking, let myself sober up, then do it all over again.

"So don't deal with it," he said. "She's pretty good. Have another beer."

"All my friends are awful and I hate you," I said,

handing the beer back to him as I slid off my stool. "Save my place. I need to pee before I do any more drinking."

"You got it," he said, and settled in to loom menacingly over my stool. The few people who'd been looking at it thoughtfully backed off, recognizing a lost cause when they saw one.

The Mint is designed to prioritize karaoke over alcohol, with the bar dividing the entryway—which served as a space for the serious drinkers to do their serious drinking—from the stage and performance space. The entryway side is narrow to the point of being a claustrophobic panic waiting to happen, and naturally, that's where the bathrooms are, since that makes a poorly-timed flush less likely to disrupt someone's Sondheim medley. I pushed through the crowd toward the back of the bar, feeling my buzz dwindle with every step I took.

Sometimes it's nice to have a Timex watch for a body—I can take a licking and keep on ticking. But when I can't stay drunk for more than ten minutes, or get enough of a jolt from a cup of coffee to actually wake myself up, it sort of sucks. It would be nice to be impossible to kill *and* capable of reaping the benefits of caffeine, but alas, we can't have everything in this world.

There was a short line for the two unisex bathrooms. I took advantage of the opportunity to check my phone. It was barely past midnight. We'd been here for three hours, and May had stated, several times, that she intended to close the place out.

Swell.

Dianda hit a high note; someone whooped. It was probably her son, Dean, who was refreshingly not embarrassed by everything his mother did. They have a remarkably solid relationship, one that has only been strengthened by him moving out to take over the County of Goldengreen. His father, Patrick, is Daoine Sidhe, and Dean takes after his father's side of the family, which means he can't breathe water. Dianda clearly misses him, and every time I see her, she's just as clearly relieved not to have to spend her time worrying about whether he's going to drown.

Faerie makes families complicated. Mermaids have sons who can't breathe water. High Kings and Queens send their children into hiding to keep them from being assassinated before they reach their majority. Fetches become sisters.

People like me, who mix their fae blood with human ancestry, wind up standing on the outside looking in, wondering what it's like to have two parents who know and accept them for who—and what—they are. My father died a long time ago, and he died believing that my mother and I had been killed in a house fire. My mother . . .

Well, it's complicated.

The bathroom door opened, and Kerry came wobbling out, a broad grin on her face. "Bachelorette party, woo!" she cheered, before pressing a wet kiss to my cheek and weaving away into the crowd. I smiled after her and slipped inside.

When I emerged from the bathroom several minutes later, Dianda had finished her song, and Quentin and Dean were on stage, gamely making their way through "One Week" by the Barenaked Ladies. I stopped to stare for a moment. Then I pushed my way back through the crowd to my stool, which Danny had managed to hold open during my absence.

I sat. He handed back my beer.

"This is a good time," he said. "Stop looking like you expect to be ambushed."

"Have you met me?" I asked. "I'm always expecting to be ambushed, and I'm rarely wrong." I looked around the crowd. So many of the faces were familiar, even under the veils of their human disguises. "But we'll probably have them outnumbered."

Danny smirked.

Four years ago, after I woke up naked, confused, and freezing in the Japanese Tea Gardens, I would have sworn I didn't have a friend left in the world. My human fiancé had moved on with his life after my unexpected, unexplainable disappearance had stretched into fourteen years; my two-year-old daughter had grown up calling another woman "Mommy." I'd tried to go home to them. Neither of them had wanted me there. They had moved on, and I still couldn't give them any answers about where I'd been. When the fae and mortal worlds collide, someone always suffers.

The changelings I'd known on the streets of San Francisco had viewed me as a lapdog of the nobility, thanks to my service to Duke Torquill of Shadowed Hills, while the nobility had viewed me as a failure, thanks to the circumstances of my disappearance. Everyone had gotten on with their lives while mine had been on hold . . . or at least that was how it had seemed at the time.

I was never as alone as I'd believed myself to be. If I had been, I wouldn't have needed to work so hard to isolate myself from the people who still cared about me. But that didn't change how I'd felt at the time. I'd thought my life was over. I'd thought I would die alone.

Instead, I was in a jam-packed karaoke bar, listening to my friends whoop and laugh while my squire and his boyfriend belted out a late-90s pop hit. Most of the people here were here for me. To celebrate the fact that I was getting married—finally—to the man who'd taught me that moving on was possible, no matter how improbable it had seemed, once upon a time. They were here because my life was moving on, and I was moving with it.

"I'm still not going to sing," I said, and took a swig of my beer.

Danny laughed.

When May had informed me that I was going to have a bachelorette party whether I wanted one or not,

I'd drawn the line at one very important point: it was going to be open to any of my friends who wanted to attend. I wasn't going to lock out the men in my life just because she wanted to throw me a party out of a Miss Manners handbook.

To my relief, she had agreed to my demand, in part, I think, because she knew Quentin would kill her if he didn't get to come. Technically, he and Dean were both too young to be here, but they had human disguises that made them look like they were in their mid-twenties, and no squire of mine was going to walk around not knowing how to get a fake ID. Given that Dianda is at least two hundred years old and still using an ID that says she's twenty-two, it seemed like one of the lesser lies of the evening.

Raj, Tybalt's nephew and heir, would normally have been present, since he and Quentin are functionally joined at the hip, but he was staying with his uncle for the night, keeping Tybalt company and learning more of what he'd need to know when he became King of Cats. Once Tybalt and I were married, he'd need to step down in order to avoid a situation where his family and his crown came into conflict. Raj was only eighteen. He was still ready to serve his people. Thank Oberon for that. I don't know if I could have handled the guilt if he'd been taking the throne unwillingly.

The rest of the room was a weird cross-section of the local fae courts. In addition to Dianda, we had Queen Arden Windermere in the Mists and her Seneschal Madden, both of whom were pureblooded fae, and both of whom had been recognized by the bartender when we arrived; my changeling friends Stacy and Kerry, and Stacy's daughter, Cassandra; Danny, who was pureblooded but associated with no noble courts; Jazz and May, and a good dozen others.

The only person who'd refused the invitation was Sir Etienne of Shadowed Hills, who sent his regrets, enough money to buy two rounds for the whole party, and his human wife Bridget. She was sharing a table with Marcia, both laughing as they pored over the book of song options. Thick rings of faerie ointment surrounded their eyes, letting them see through the illusions around them. They may as well not have bothered. For once, everyone was on an equal playing field, and everyone was enjoying it.

Quentin and Dean finished their song. The applause was more enthusiastic than it had been for May, probably because both boys had managed to stay within a reasonable distance of the right key for the entire song. It wasn't that we were musical snobs. We just enjoyed our ears not actively bleeding.

"All right, all right," said the DJ. "Next up, we have Annie. Annie to the stage!"

"Arden's going to punch him in the nose for getting her name wrong," I said, and took another swig of my beer.

"Uh," said Danny. "That ain't Arden."

I turned. A dark-haired woman in tattered jeans and a white tank top was walking toward the stage. She didn't look familiar. I shrugged.

"We're not the only people here," I said. "Everybody gets a chance to sing if they want it, right? She'll be done in a few minutes."

"Don't you recognize her?"

"No. Should I?"

Danny looked frustrated. "I dunno. She looks familiar, but I'm pretty sure I've never seen her before."

I frowned, first at him and then at the woman. There was no sparkle in the air around her; she wasn't wearing an illusion. She was, however, wearing one of May's glittery red-and-silver "Bachelorette Backup" buttons pinned to the left strap of her tank top, marking her as either part of our group or as an opportunistic stranger who was hoping to get some cake.

The music started. I felt the blood run out of my face, leaving me cold.

"Oh, oak and ash," I said. "This isn't happening."

I wasn't the only one to have that thought. Quentin pushed through the crowd to stand on my other side, trying to snatch the beer away from me. I slapped his hand. It wasn't that I specifically objected to underage drinking—especially since he was of legal age in Canada, where he comes from—it was that I really, really needed my beer.

"That's the Luidaeg," he said, sounding dazed.

"Uh-huh," I agreed.

"That's the Luidaeg, singing 'Poor Unfortunate Souls.' In a karaoke bar. In front of other people."

"Uh-huh," I agreed again. Doing anything else seemed impossible. Well, except for maybe drinking my beer. Drinking my beer, I could do. I drank some of my beer.

The Luidaeg did not disappear. The Luidaeg remained on the stage, belting out the sea witch's song from Disney's *The Little Mermaid*. Given that the Luidaeg *is* the sea witch according to every legend I've ever heard, the overall effect was more than a little jarring.

"We're gonna need more beer," said Danny.

May flounced through the crowd and wedged herself between us, beaming from ear to ear. "Didn't I tell you this would be the best place to hold your bachelorette party?" she demanded. "Tell me I'm a genius. Go on, tell me. I promise not to argue with you."

"The Luidaeg is singing," I said, in case she hadn't noticed. May can be a little flighty sometimes. It was possible she'd been too focused on her need for another cocktail to realize that we were witnessing one of the portents of the apocalypse. "The Luidaeg is singing *Disney songs*."

"Because I'm a genius," said May. She leaned over the bar, waving to the bartender until he nodded and flashed her a thumbs-up. Then she rocked back to the flats of her feet, looking obscenely pleased with herself. "You can say it."

"I didn't even know you invited her."

"Uh, duh, I had to? It's the Sleeping Beauty principle. You always invite the biggest badass on the block, or they show up later and curse everybody just to make a point. Besides, she's having fun. We're all having fun."

"Not all of us," I said, nodding toward Dianda.

The Duchess of Saltmist was staring at the Luidaeg, hands clasped so tightly around her beer bottle that I was worried about her crushing it and getting broken glass everywhere. The Luidaeg used to spend most of her time in the Undersea, which only makes sense for someone whose most frequently used title is "sea witch." She stopped after the slaughter of the Roane—better known as her children and grandchildren. So far as I know, she's lived on the land ever since.

This might have been the closest Dianda had ever been to the Undersea's most powerful, most legendary Firstborn. She was looking at the Luidaeg the way I would have expected her to look at Oberon himself, if he'd still been around to be seen.

May sighed. "She needs to take a deep breath and remember that you and the Luidaeg are friends." A fresh cocktail appeared by her elbow. This one was as green as Danny's was pink, and garnished with several wedges of fresh kiwi.

I eyed it. "I'm not sure what's more disturbing. This party or that drink."

"Both. Neither. Everything." May grinned. "You're having *fun*, October. Just relax and let yourself enjoy it. You never go out and just have *fun* anymore, and I'll be damned before I let you march off to your own wedding like it was your execution."

"I've been sentenced to death before, and I assure you, nothing I do with Tybalt is nearly as unpleasant," I said.

Danny laughed. "I don't wanna know what you and the kitty-cat get up to when I'm not around," he said.

"That's the sort of thing that should be between two consentin' adults, and not their designated driver."

"I don't need a designated driver," I protested. "My body burns alcohol so fast I can't even stay drunk for more than five minutes at a time. And the house is barely more than a mile away."

"Don't care," said Danny. "I have a taxi for a reason. Driving the bride-to-be around is part of it."

I considered pointing out the ridiculousness of a man who'd consumed six pink cocktails claiming to be my designated driver, and decided against it. Danny probably weighs upward of six hundred pounds, and most of his body is made up of something close to, if not identical to, granite. I'm not sure he *can* get drunk. I'm absolutely sure that if he can, he wasn't going to manage it on less than several gallons of straight whiskey. He was still perfectly safe behind the wheel.

Instead, I said, "I'd prefer it if you'd drive the bride's drunk friends home."

Danny grinned. "That's a compromise I can live with."

The Luidaeg finished her song. Everyone clapped. If the applause from the other members of our party was a little more enthusiastic than her performance warranted, well, who could blame them? Failure to properly appreciate one of the Firstborn was probably bad for silly things like "continuing to have a pulse."

The DJ called a name. An actual stranger this time, someone whose song choice wasn't going to make me choke on my drink or otherwise lose my composure. I took advantage of the break to turn and smile wryly at May.

"All right, you got me," I said. "You were right, and I was wrong: I *am* having a good time. This is a good party. I bow before your infinite wisdom."

May preened. "I told you you'd have a good time if you'd let yourself. Everyone else is having fun, too."

She was right about that. Walther and Marcia were

carrying their song selections to the front, while Bridget—possibly the only person here aside from me and Quentin who wasn't over-awed by the Luidaeg— was congratulating the Luidaeg on her performance. Arden was laughing so hard that she looked like she was going to hurt herself, while Madden grinned and took a drink of his own beer.

So many of my friends and allies were here. So many people who trusted me, and who I trusted to have my back, no matter what. It was an odd thing to realize that I was outside my house and utterly relaxed, but I was. Maybe for the first time in a year, I felt like I could drop my guard and just exist.

The stranger finished his song. Stacy jumped up onto the stage without waiting for the DJ to say anything, grabbing the microphone.

"We're here tonight because our friend Toby is getting married!" she shouted. The bar cheered, even the parts of it who weren't with us.

I groaned. "Oh, sweet Titania, no."

"Yes," said May, taking my beer away.

"Yup," agreed Quentin, and pushed me off my stool.

Kerry and Cassandra were suddenly there to grab me by my wrists and haul me to the stage, where Stacy had produced a headband that looked like a cross between a bridal veil and one of those ridiculous "fairy crowns" hippies like to sell at open-air farmer's markets. They pushed me up the stairs. She plopped it onto my head and shoved the microphone into my hands, turning me to face the karaoke screen as the lyrics for "White Wedding" began to appear.

"I am going to kill you all," I said, and lifted the microphone, and sang.

My life's not so bad these days.

TWO

THE MINT STOPPED SERVING alcohol at two; the karaoke DJ left at two-thirty; thanks to some reservation magic on May and Stacy's part, they didn't kick us out until three, by which time everyone was well on their way to sober, or at least competent to get home without passing out on somebody's front step.

We thronged on the sidewalk, hugging, laughing, and saying good-bye one by one, like we wanted to make the party last as long as possible. I realized, with some surprise, that I was doing just that: I didn't want the night to end. For once, nothing was trying to kill me or complicate my life. I didn't have any quests to finish or problems to resolve. I got to exist, with no qualifiers. It was nice. I wanted it to continue.

Arden walked over, offering an awkward smile and a fist-bump to the shoulder, which was about as close as the two of us were prepared to come to hugging. "I need to get back," she said. "Nolan gets anxious if I leave him alone for too long."

Nolan is her younger brother. He's technically Crown Prince in the Mists now that she's Queen, and most importantly, he's awake. That part's new. He spent more than eighty years asleep, courtesy of the usurper who'd been sitting on his family's throne. He's a nice guy. A little flustered-looking every time I've seen him so far, but that makes sense, given how dramatically things have changed—both in the mortal world and in Faerie—during the years he missed.

"May invited him," I said. "We would have been happy to have him."

Arden's laughter was bright and sincere. "Oh, no. He's not ready for The Mint. I'll try him on a piano bar first, someplace nice and calm where they serve wine and sing old standards. We'll get there. It's just going to take time."

"Well, I'm glad you came," I said.

"Me, too."

Madden was less restrained. He walked over and hugged me hard, the action lifting my feet off the ground. "Bye, Toby," he said.

"Good-bye and put me down," I replied.

He laughed.

That was enough to break the seal on the party. Arden and Madden walked around the corner of the nearest alley; the scent of redwood sap and blackberry flowers drifted through the air, erasing the normal mortal scents of gasoline and stale beer, and I knew they were gone. Danny loaded Kerry, Stacy, and Cassandra into his cab, promising to get them home safely, all while trying to lure me into the cab for a ride that I neither wanted nor needed, but appreciated all the same. Dianda, still in her sequined cocktail dress, ruffled Dean's hair, waved to me, and started walking down the street toward the Bay, her shoes dangling from her hand.

Quentin stepped up next to me. "She's going to get mugged," he said.

"And that will be very educational for the muggers," I agreed. Dianda fought to win. Anyone who tried to get in her way was going to have a bad night indeed. "Dean coming home with you?"

"Not tonight." Quentin yawned. "He has stuff to do at Goldengreen, so he's escorting Marcia home. Bridget parked there."

"Then it's down to family." That was nice, too. There's something to be said for returning to a quiet house after a night out with friends.

May and Jazz waited a few yards away, arms around each other. I waved to the remaining party-goers one last time before walking over to join them. May smiled at me.

"I told you you'd have a good time," she said.

"Yes, you did," I agreed. "Let's go home."

Walking through San Francisco after last call is like stepping into a different world. Sure, there will be a few drunks on the streets, but they tend to disappear once the bars close, retreating to their homes or slipping into the nearest alley to look for someone who can provide them with a drink. It was late enough that the homeless population had mostly pulled back into the parks and their tent cities under the freeway overpasses, trying to get a good night's sleep before the day people woke up and started complaining about them ruining property values by daring to exist.

Humans can be surprisingly cruel to their own kind sometimes. The fae may be terrible, but at least we largely don't pretend otherwise.

"We." That's an interesting word choice. My father was human: my mother is fae. Not just fae, but Firstborn, barely removed from Oberon himself. That makes me a changeling, and for years, my human heritage was the only thing I wanted to acknowledge, like the things I'd inherited from my mother were just inconvenient tweaks of biology that would eventually go away.

They haven't gone away. They've gotten stronger, thanks to my talent for winding up in situations where blood is the only answer. I've been sliding farther and farther from my humanity, burning it out of myself one drop at a time in exchange for the power I need to survive. Coffee used to wake me up. Alcohol used to stay in my system for more than fifteen minutes. I used to stay hurt, instead of healing so fast that my skin has been known to heal around the weapons used against me. My body has become a locked-room mystery only I can solve, and every time I feel like I've figured it out, something else changes.

The commercial streets dropped away, leaving the four of us to wander down residential streets, past quiet brownstone homes with their Victorian facades and tiny, artfully tended gardens. This was the old San Francisco, far-removed from the tech boom consuming downtown. Most of the people who lived here had been in the city for generations, clinging to their family homes with all their might, refusing to let go, refusing to be moved, despite increasing pressure to sell to millionaires who liked the idea of living in a classic home.

Some of the millionaires are baffled by how hard it is to buy into this neighborhood. They keep accusing tenants of collusion, of conspiracy, of snobbish insistence that only the "right" people should live in the area. They're sort of right. There *is* a conspiracy to keep them out. It's just that the conspiracy is a lot less human than they assume. Fully half the rental properties in the neighborhood are owned by fae landlords like my liege, Duke Torquill, who bought them for a song when they were newly-constructed and still smelled like fresh wood and paint.

Pureblooded fae have a thing about land. They like to own it. In the Summerlands, the last of the fae realms accessible to us, the king *is* the land, and a demesne will thrive or fail based on the health of its ruler. They like owning land more than they like having mortal money, especially when owning the land makes them rich without needing to do anything more than refuse to give it up. Those tech millionaires could offer forever, but the fae landlords of San Francisco would never sell.

Sylvester and I have had some rocky spots recently, starting when he lied about some life-changing details of my mother's past and progressing from there. I'm working on forgiving him; he's working on being honest with me. But even when things were at their worst, he'd tried to look out for me the best way he knew how; that much, at least, has always been true. Among other things, he's the reason my little band of weirdoes has a place to live in one of the most expensive cities in the mortal world. The tech millionaires might not know how to get into this neighborhood. All I'd had to do was ask.

Our house is one of the few on the block that was never split into a duplex. It's painted in eye-searingly bright colors that seem garish and aggressive during the day, but are beautiful at night, which is when fae eyes are most likely to see them. I smiled wearily as we started up the walkway to the front door, already digging in the pocket of my leather jacket for the keys.

Quentin stopped one step from the top. May and Jazz stopped below him, and I took the last step on my own, raising my hand to tap the air in front of me. It flashed red, a tingle running through my fingertip as the wards reacted. I relaxed a little. Nothing had tried to break in while we were all out of the house.

"Not to rush you, but some of us need the bathroom," said May.

"That *is* rushing me," I said. I tapped the air again, and chanted, "Life's but a walking shadow, a poor player that struts and frets his hour upon the stage." The wards flared more violently before dissolving into the smell of cut-grass and copper.

May wrinkled her nose as she pushed past me, snatched the keys out of my hand, and unlocked the door. "Most people don't use *Macbeth* to seal their wards, you know."

"Most people are boring," I said. I took my keys back, following her into the hall.

The lights were on. So was the television, the sound drifting out of the living room. May and I exchanged a glance. Then she smirked, patted me on the shoulder, and said, "It's your problem," before heading for the bathroom.

"I'm going to make some tea," said Jazz, and ducked into the kitchen, leaving me alone with Quentin.

"Cowards," he said amiably.

"Yup," I agreed. "But we love them anyway."

"Why is that?"

"I'll be honest. I don't really know."

He laughed, and walked with me to the living room door, where we peeped inside. One of the recent BBC versions of *Much Ado About Nothing* was playing on the television. Tybalt has his reservations about much modern technology, but the discovery that he could order DVDs from England and watch Shakespeare performed in London in the comfort of my own home had been a revelation to him. I was pretty sure he'd forgive humanity for almost anything if it meant he could have his Shakespeare.

I love him for a lot of reasons. The way he looks in leather pants is surprisingly far down the list.

Nothing moved apart from the TV. I stepped into the room, walking around the couch and stopping to smile. Besottedly, if the look on Quentin's face was anything to go by. He could cope. I had just come from my bachelorette party, and if I wanted to take a moment to be soppy, that was my prerogative.

Tybalt was asleep, slumped against the armrest. The reason he hadn't stretched out was easy to see: Raj was taking up the rest of the couch, head in his uncle's lap. It was a beautifully domestic moment, and I would have been tempted to take a picture if not for the fact that neither of them was wearing a human disguise. The stripes in Tybalt's hair were visible, black against the darker brown, as were the sharp points of his ears. Raj's hair was long enough that his ears were hidden. Nothing, however, could hide the black ticking on his otherwise russet hair, a color pattern that doesn't naturally occur in anything except for Abyssinian cats.

I took a moment to stand there and appreciate the two of them, my Cait Sidhe boys, both comfortable enough to go to sleep in my house and stay that way through the sound of the door opening. It was no mystery how they'd gotten in: Cait Sidhe have access to the Shadow Roads, one of the hidden routes through Faerie, and the wards were designed to let the two of them through. It wouldn't make sense to lock my fiancé, or my squire's best friend, out in the cold.

Finally, I walked to the couch, knelt, and touched Tybalt's hand, releasing the illusion that made me look human at the same time. The scent of it perfumed the air around me. "Hey, Sleeping Beauty," I said. "Don't make me kiss you in front of the boys. I'd never hear the end of it."

Tybalt opened his eyes and smiled. My chest seemed to get tighter and lighter at the same time. It wasn't a strange sensation anymore. I felt that way every time he smiled at me like that, like I was some sort of miracle.

"October," he said, voice still hazy with sleep. "If you do not wish to kiss me in front of our charges, I'm afraid our wedding will be a dull affair." He paused, smile fading into a puzzled frown. "What in the world is that thing on your head?"

"Party hat," I said, reaching up and whisking the offending veil away. "Blame May."

"A sentence with merit in almost all situations," he agreed. He sat up, stretching languidly, before shaking Raj brusquely by the shoulder. "Up, kitten. It's time for napping somewhere that is not atop your King."

Raj made a grumpy noise, and didn't move.

"Awaken, Prince of Cats, or suffer the consequences."

Raj made a grumpier noise, and didn't move.

"Alas, you did not heed my warnings, and now you must pay," said Tybalt, before reaching over and hauling me into his lap, a gesture which planted my butt atop Raj's head.

That was enough to wake Raj. He squawked in startled disapproval and sat up, leaving me to drop the final few inches into Tybalt's lap, where I fit comfortably. It was a position I had a lot of practice with.

"You *sat* on me!" Raj protested. His hair was ruffled, sticking up in all directions.

It was all I could do not to laugh as Tybalt slid an arm around my waist, looked serenely at Raj, and said, "No, she did not. I placed her atop you, when you refused to wake and move. This is why you should listen to your betters."

"I'm a Prince of Cats," said Raj.

"And I am a King, and she is my consort. You see? There are two people in this room who are better than you. Go and torment Quentin, if you wish to match wits with an equal."

"I heard that," said Quentin from the doorway.

"I intended that you should," said Tybalt, without rancor.

Raj glowered at us both before running a hand through his hair to smooth it and hopping over the back of the couch. A few seconds later, I heard him talking to Quentin in the hall, voice pitched low enough that I couldn't tell what he was saying. Their footsteps moved down the hall.

"At last," said Tybalt. "We're alone." With that, he leaned in, and kissed me.

Kissing Tybalt is an activity I used to fantasize about, back when repression and denial were my only bedfellows. These days, it's something I get to *do*, and reality has never disappointed. He kissed me slow and languid, like he was in no hurry, like there was nothing in the world he would rather be doing. I knew that wasn't entirely true—there were plenty of things he liked to do with me that didn't involve kissing, largely because our mouths were otherwise occupied—but that sort of focus was undeniably exciting. I shifted in his lap, pulling myself closer, easing my arms around him, until we were necking on my living room couch like a pair of teenagers.

That was nice, too, and definitely a point in favor of my increased alcohol tolerance. In the old days, I would either have passed out already, or be nursing my third cup of coffee as I attempted to combat the impending hangover. Instead, I was awake, alert, and raring to go.

Tybalt was smiling when he broke away, leaning forward just enough to rest his forehead against mine. "I take it the party went well?" he asked.

"The Luidaeg showed up."

He blinked. "That raises more questions than it answers, I think."

"She sang. It was possibly the weirdest thing I have ever seen. But she was pretty good. It was fun. I wish you could have been there."

"The entire point of the bachelorette party is for the bride-to-be to get out and explore the nightlife without her betrothed on her arm. My presence would have confused the issue. Besides, I have no doubt your lovely Lady Fetch would have demanded I sing also, and I had no desire to make a public spectacle of myself." He settled back into the cushions, smiling at me languidly. "Well, then, bride-to-be? Did you find yourself a finer suitor during your night of freedom? Am I to be cast aside, never again to know the safe haven of your arms?"

"You're a nerd," I said, and swatted him in the arm. "You seemed all cool and mysterious back when I was afraid of you, but I'm not afraid of you anymore, and I can see clearly that you are a nerd."

"I never denied it," he said, and leaned in to kiss me again.

The doorbell rang. We both froze.

The doorbell ringing isn't that unusual. In addition to serving as a knight errant and hero of the realm, I still work as a mortal P.I., handling cheating spouses, small thefts, and the occasional custody dispute. Since I don't have an office, my clients come to the house, and people who want to hire a private investigator aren't usually bound by normal business hours. I've had human clients show up as late as one o'clock in the morning. Fae are largely nocturnal and have been known to show up at two or three, apologizing for the proximity to dawn, but fully expecting me to be awake.

The trouble was the time. It was after four. That's late for anything short of a Kingdom-wide emergency, and if it had been a Kingdom-wide emergency, someone would have called.

"Let May handle it," said Tybalt, hands moving to encircle my waist. "The hour is late. You need your rest."

"This isn't my definition of 'rest,' exactly," I said, and leaned in for another kiss.

The doorbell rang again. This time, the sound was followed by footsteps—May's, from the tempo of them. I resumed my lean.

My lips were about to touch Tybalt's when I realized the house had gone silent. May wasn't saying anything. The doorbell had stopped ringing; I'd heard her open the door. She should at least have said hello. But she hadn't said anything.

Tybalt met my eyes and nodded. As quietly as I could, I climbed off him, wishing my knives weren't upstairs in my room and my sword wasn't in the trunk of my car. Only a few minutes before, going unarmed in my own house had seemed like the most reasonable thing in the world. Now, it felt like the sort of oversight that could get me and the people I cared about killed.

The hallway ran in a straight line down the length of the house. As soon as I stepped out of the living room, I turned to get a look at the visitor who had silenced May so conclusively.

May was between me and the open door, giving me an excellent view of her pink denim jacket and the bright red steaks in her otherwise colorless brown hair. My Fetch never met a garish color combination she didn't want to put to use. She was standing rigid, her shoulders locked into a hard line, and every inch of her radiated fear and confusion.

The smell of pennyroyal and musk drifted from the living room. Tybalt had stepped into the shadows. If I knew him as well as I thought I did, he was using the Shadow Roads as a shortcut to my bedroom, and my knives. He didn't like leaving me undefended. He liked me being functionally defenseless even less.

"May?" I called. "Everything okay?" I started toward her, doing a quick inventory as I went. Tybalt would be back in a few seconds. In the meantime, there was an aluminum baseball bat in the umbrella stand. Sometimes blunt-force trauma is a girl's best friend.

May didn't reply. May didn't move. This was bad.

Anyone who could freeze my Fetch like that either wasn't human or wasn't going to live to see the morning. I didn't bother recasting my illusions as I hurried down the hall, nudging her to the side in order to face our unexpected guest. "Can I help—" I began.

The words turned to ashes in my mouth. Serene to the end, my mother tilted her head, accenting the swanlike line of her neck. Everything she did was beautiful. Every move was designed to show her to her best advantage. I loved her. I wanted to impress her. I wanted her to be proud of me.

I wanted her to go away.

She wasn't wearing a human disguise; she didn't care whether my neighbors saw her. There was no car on the street. I had no idea how she'd reached the house. It didn't really matter—she was there, whether

I wanted her to be or not. Amandine of Faerie, Last among the First, on my doorstep.

There's a reason humans called the fae "the Fair Folk" back when they admitted we existed. Some of us take beauty to the kinds of extreme that can be painful to look at. My mother put most of them to shame. She stood a few inches shorter than either me or May, her figure lithesome and flawless. Time had no hold over her: she was as beautiful now as she'd been when I was a little girl. I hadn't seen her much since then. She had been slipping away from me for a long time before I'd disappeared, and even my return hadn't been enough to bring her back. When my mother didn't want to be found, no one found her.

She wore a dress spun from flower petals and sweet drifts of Queen Anne's lace, still blooming and perfuming the air around her. Her hair was a cascade of white gold tumbling to her hips, held out of her eyes by a pair of thin waterfall braids that started at her temples and ran along the crown of her head, finally meeting at the back. Her skin was so pale that I wouldn't have been surprised to hear she hadn't seen the sun since her disappearance. Her face was still somehow accented by a faint dusting of freckles across the bridge of her nose. They weren't imperfections: they were a reminder that she was real, and hence proof that no one else would ever be as flawlessly constructed as she was.

Her eyes were a foggy shade of gray-blue, like mist in the morning rolling across the San Francisco Bay. They weren't human eyes. They never could have been. And they were so much like mine that it hurt. Without those eyes, it might have been possible to pretend I was a changeling in all senses of the word: not just part-human, but someone else's child entirely, foisted on Amandine when she failed to prevent it. Those eyes . . . there was no way I could have belonged to anyone else.

There was a soft sound behind me, accompanied by

the scent of pennyroyal and musk. Tybalt was back. Tybalt was back, with my knives, which she might take as either an insult or an attack, depending on what kind of mood she was in. Amandine was Firstborn. She could hurt him. I needed to stop this.

"Hello, Mother," I said, loudly enough for Tybalt to hear.

Amandine's perfect lips twitched at the corners, in what might have been the beginnings of a smile.

"Hello, October," she said. "Aren't you going to invite me in?"

THREE

THE URGE TO SAY "no" and close the door was so strong that I had to bite my lip to keep from blurting it out. My mother and I haven't had a good relationship since I was seven years old and chose Faerie over the mortal world—not knowing, as a changeling child who just wanted my mother to love me, that choosing the other way would have meant her killing me on the spot. Apparently, choosing to live, however accidentally, was a crime in her world.

She'd been pulling away from me ever since. Oh, she fed me, housed me, and clothed me when I was a little girl and an adolescent. My adolescence had lasted well into my twenties, since we'd been living in the Summerlands. Time runs oddly there under the best of circumstances, and its oddness tends to become concentrated in changelings, who age slowly in Faerie, or in reverse, or not at all.

I suppose I was one of the lucky ones. I'd grown up enough to run away to the mortal world, where I could try to make a life for myself. Whether it had been a good life, or the right life, was irrelevant. It had been *mine*, and Amandine had had no part in it. She hadn't wanted any part in it. Once I'd run away from her, I might as well not have been her child.

But the first time someone had decided to use elf-shot to get me out of the way, I had still been mostly mortal, and fully capable of dying from the poison. The arrow had pierced my skin and I'd fallen where I stood. My heart had stopped. Technically, I *had* died, maybe for the first time. And Luna Torquill's rose goblins had run to find my mother and bring her to Shadowed Hills, so she could save me. She *had* saved me. I could still remember the way she'd smiled and called me her darling girl, and maybe it had all been an illusion and maybe it hadn't, but she could have let me die, and she'd chosen to come when I needed her most.

Maybe she was ready to be a mother after all. Who was I to blame her for needing a few years to think it over? It wasn't like she was running out of time, being immortal and all.

"Come on in," I said, stepping to the side.

She stayed where she was. I blinked. She lifted one eyebrow, and I realized what she was waiting for. I fought to suppress a groan. Leave it to my mother to be the one person in Faerie who expected me to stand on protocol.

"By the root and the branch, you are welcome here; by the rose and the thorn, no harm will be offered to you while you stand beneath my roof," I said. "Our weapons are bound, our hands are spread, and our hospitality is open to you. By oak and ash and rowan, I swear."

This time, the twitch blossomed into a proper smile. "Your form is poor and you forgot to require the same promises of peace from me before swearing, but at least you haven't forgotten *everything* I ever taught you," said Amandine, and she stepped inside.

The air in the hallway seemed to chill and change with her arrival, like the house didn't know what to do with her. That made two of us. I made a quick review of the available rooms. The living room was a mess, as always, and the TV was still on; the dining room was mostly okay, except for the part where Jazz was doing one of her big decoupage projects on the table, and Amandine had never shown much appreciation for construction paper. That left . . .

"Follow me, Mother," I said. "The kitchen's this way. I can make us something to drink, and you can tell me why you're here."

"Your manners are lacking," she said. "Hopefully, your selection of teas is not."

She fell into step behind me, leaving May frozen by the door. I was starting to worry that she'd thrown some sort of whammy on my Fetch when May shivered like she was shaking off some deep enchantment and turned to follow us. Tybalt was next to her. He had hidden my knives somewhere, probably inside his jeans or the burgundy Oregon Shakespeare Festival sweatshirt he was wearing.

A pang of irritation lanced through me. A modern, casual Tybalt is something I don't get to see very often. Mom's arrival suddenly felt like a robbery. I quashed the feeling as quickly as I could. I hadn't spent any real time with my mother in years. The fact that she was getting in the way of my morning make outs really shouldn't matter.

Jazz was in the kitchen when we stepped inside, standing at the stove, stirring a pot of hot chocolate. She turned toward the sound of the door opening, a smile on her face. It froze when she saw my mother, turning puzzled. I realized that she had no idea who Amandine was.

"Mother, I'd like you to meet Jasmine Patel, my housemate," I said.

"My girlfriend," said May. Her voice was shaky, but there was steel at its core.

As a Fetch, as *my* Fetch, she remembered Amandine as her mother, even though Amandine had no reason to remember her. That had to feel like rejection, however blameless my mother was in the situation. For once. If we were looking for things to actually blame Amandine for, I was sure we could find plenty. Starting with "why have so many of the Firstborn I know called you 'the Liar' like it was your title?" and going on from there.

"A Raven-maid? How quaint." Amandine looked around the kitchen, a small frown on her lips. "Really, October, when you rejected your mortality, I didn't expect you to turn around and embrace it quite so enthusiastically. This place is positively shameful."

"We like it," I said, tamping down my annoyance again. Amandine was Firstborn. Amandine was a pureblood, centuries old, who didn't have as much contact with the mortal world as most of the purebloods I interacted with. Of course, her standards were going to be different. Losing my temper wasn't going to do any of us any good.

Maybe if I told myself that enough times, it would somehow magically stop me from getting angry. I didn't think so, though.

"Would you like some hot chocolate?" asked Jazz hesitantly. "I made it myself. It's quite good."

"Is the cream from the Crodh Sith?" asked Amandine.

"No, Mom, we don't travel all the way down to Golden Shore to get our milk," I said. "It's ordinary milk, from ordinary cows, bought at the ordinary store."

"Actually, it's from Whole Foods," said Jazz.

Amandine sniffed. "Remind me, October: why, when Sylvester came to you, did you not choose a mortal life? Since that's so clearly what you're trying to create for yourself here. You could have saved us both ever so much trouble."

"You were the one who tried to choose mortality for me, Mom," I said, before I could think better of it.

Silence fell, broken only by the soft bubbling of Jazz's cocoa. Then Amandine smiled.

"Yes, exactly," she said. "When I had the chance, I tried to choose mortality for you. If Sylvester had arrived to find a human child, he wouldn't have offered you the Changeling's Choice, because there would have been nothing to choose. He would have walked away. I could have been with you every day of your life, the best and most loving of mothers, until I laid you to bed in a blanket of earth, with a pillow of stones for your head. I *tried*. You tied my hands. To have you going back on your choice now, it's . . . well, it's shameful, October. You should at least have the courage of your convictions."

I stared at her for a moment, stunned into silence. Tybalt moved to stand behind me, not looming, not threatening my mother, but lending what support he could through his sheer presence.

Finally, I took a deep breath and asked, "Why are you here, Mother? I'm assuming it isn't to criticize my interior decorating."

"I've been informed that you're continuing to play at being a detective." Amandine sniffed. "It seems an odd thing to spend your time doing, as we both know you have no native talents in the area, but if you will persist, then it seems you are equipped to do me a boon."

I blinked. "What?"

"I wish to hire you."

This time, the moment of silence lasted a lot longer. Then, almost despite myself, I started to laugh. Once I started, I discovered that I couldn't stop. I bent forward, one hand pressed against my stomach, trying to make the laughter end. It refused.

Tybalt put a hand on my back, steadying me. May looked alarmed. And Amandine . . .

Amandine looked resigned, like she had expected nothing better from me, her changeling daughter. That killed my mirth right quick. I stopped laughing and straightened, taking some small comfort in the weight of Tybalt's hand against my spine. I wasn't a child anymore. Amandine might be my mother, and one of the Firstborn, but so what? I'd stood up to Firstborn before. I'd killed one of them. I didn't want to kill my mother, but it helped to know that she wasn't invincible.

"I'm sorry," I said. "It sounded like you insulted my profession and then said you wanted to hire me."

"Yes, because that's exactly what I did."

"Mom . . ." I reached up and pinched the bridge of my nose. "Okay, what do you want to hire me to do? Did you lose something?"

"Yes," she said. "Your sister."

I lowered my hand, staring at her once again. It felt like the air had just been sucked out of the room, replaced by something hot and stale and difficult to breathe.

"What?" I finally squeaked.

"Your sister. I know you know about her. Your foolish father is bound to have told you, when he was struggling to make his amends." She sniffed again. "I married him for many reasons. His brains were not among them. Be more careful, should you ever decide to marry. Choose a man who can think for himself, and not be led astray by every dainty dame who comes walking down the lane."

"My . . . father?" The blows just kept coming.

Amandine waved a hand dismissively. "Your *legal* father, not the man who sired you. Humans have no claim over any part of Faerie. Simon may not have been in my bed when I got you, but he has the responsibility for you in our world. Given your seeming determination to shed as much of your mortal blood as possible, it won't be long before he becomes the only father you have."

The thought made my stomach turn. Simon Torquill is my liege's twin brother, and the man responsible for my fourteen-year disappearance. Without him, my life would have been very different. Not better, maybe . . . but in some ways, absolutely, because without him, I would never have lost my little girl.

I can like everything else about my new life better than I like the memory of my old one. Not that. Losing Gillian will haunt me until I die—and there's so little mortality left in me that I'm going to live for a long, long time. Long after my daughter is dust, I'll still be here, and still mourning for the fact that I never got the chance to be a parent to her. I gave her life. Other people gave her everything else.

Simon is also my mother's husband. Since Faerie doesn't acknowledge the validity of marriages between humans and the fae, she wasn't even cheating on him when she went off to spend a decade in the mortal world. To have a daughter. In the eyes of our law, such as it is, he's my father and always has been.

Sometimes I wonder what it would feel like to have a normal family. Not that anyone I know actually has one.

"Mom . . ." I paused; took a breath. "Yes, Simon told me about August. He told me she disappeared decades before I was born, and that he wound up working for Evening because he was trying to find her. He's a pure-blood. Evening's Firstborn. If the two of them working together couldn't find her, what makes you think I can?"

"You have a gift for doing the impossible," she said airily. "The things they tell me you've done! You killed Blind Michael. You brought his stolen children home. You stopped Oleander de Merelands, after everything she's done. You found the lost Princess in the Mists, and chased a pretender from the throne. They tell me you're a hero now, my October, and who am I to question the word of what seems to be all of Faerie? Heroes undertake impossible quests. Heroes complete them. I want my child back. You stole yourself from me when you chose wrongly. The least you can do is return the daughter I lost before I had you."

I stared at her again. Our conversation had been more defined by silences than by sentences, in part because every other word out of her mouth made me want to turn around and leave the room. She was my mother. She would have been good at insulting and belittling me even if she *wasn't* my mother—that seems to be a trait shared by all the Firstborn—but because she was, she knew exactly what to say to cause me pain.

"Mom . . ."

"Do this for me, and you will be forgiven."

"*Forgiven*? Forgiven for what?"

"For refusing to be the child I needed you to be," she said. "I tried to save you, my father knows I tried. I tried to do it without hurting you because you fought me when I went too quickly. I had already unwound more than half the damage I had done to you when my foolish brother-in-law came to carry you away. If you had been less recalcitrant, if you had been willing to let me have my way, when I knew better for you than you knew for yourself, you would have been human by the time he arrived."

That was the second time she'd implied that things would have been better if I hadn't held onto my fae blood. "Are you seriously saying things would be better if I were mortal? Mom, that was sixty years ago. I'd be lucky to be *alive* now!" Mortals can live to be sixty and beyond, but my luck has never run to the good, or to the safe. If it hadn't been for my changeling resilience, even before I started healing at an accelerated rate, I would have been dead a long time ago.

"I know," she said serenely.

That was the last straw. "If you wanted me to be human, why the hell did you save me when I got elf-shot?"

"Because the roses begged," she said. "It seemed a shame to disappoint them, when they asked so sweetly."

"Right," I said. "Okay. No, Mother, I will not be taking the job. I'm sorry. It's been too long, and I don't want to deal with you, and I need you to leave now." I felt bad even as I spoke. It wasn't August's fault that our mother loved her more than she loved me. Maybe my sister was out there somewhere, trapped, suspended in some terrible limbo, like Luna and Rayseline had been after Simon orchestrated their kidnapping. Maybe she needed me.

But I didn't need Amandine. I could refuse to work for her and go looking for August anyway, on my own terms. I could bring her home without ever involving our mother.

"I was afraid you'd say something like that," said Amandine. She slipped a hand into the froth of petals on the side of her dress. When she pulled it out again, she uncurled her fingers to show me two long, slender seeds, like something I might dig out of an orange. "I would ask you to change your mind, but that would be very much like begging, and I do not beg my own children to do what they should have done willingly. You *will* learn your place, October. I only regret that I have failed you so completely that the lesson is necessary."

"Get out of my house," I snarled. I stuck my hand behind myself. Tybalt dropped a knife into it. I wasn't going to attack my own mother—I didn't think I was going to attack my own mother, especially not when I had formally granted her the hospitality of my home—but I'd be damned before I went unarmed for another minute.

Amandine sighed. "No," she said, and tossed the seeds into the air. The blood and roses smell of her magic was suddenly everywhere.

The seeds germinated instantly, bursting into tangled masses of thorny vines that whipped through the kitchen, wrapping themselves around everyone who wasn't Amandine. There was a splash as Jazz's pot of cocoa hit the floor. Jazz yelled, as much in surprise as from the pain of the hot liquid hitting her feet. Then the thorns were breaking our skins, and there was something more important to worry about than a little spilled milk.

The pain was hot and intense, racing along my nerves like lightning. I inhaled, preparing to scream—

The pain stopped. Completely. It was replaced by a soothing numbness, and by absolute immobility. I couldn't even move enough to squeak. I tried to look for the shape of the spell, to unweave it as I had other bindings, but it slipped away from me like water.

Of course it did. Amandine is Firstborn—*my* Firstborn. My magic is a pale imitation of hers. Any tricks I know how to perform, I inherited from her. No matter how powerful I become, how much practice I get, her spells will probably always be the only ones I can't unwind. I was caught.

We all were. Tybalt was behind me, outside my frame of vision, but I could see May and Jazz. They looked terrified, wrapped in their cocoons of calming thorns. Only Amandine was free to move around the room.

She walked to the kitchen table, clearing it of mail, newspapers, and dishes with a sweep of her arm. Something smashed when it hit the floor. She didn't appear to care. "Even as a girl, you were willful," she said. "You never wanted to listen. You never wanted to mind me, even when minding me would have been the proper thing to do. I thought it was the humanity in you, so I forgave it—I was making it worse, wasn't I? That meant it must be what I wanted. But look at you now. Barely clinging to your mortality, and still you refuse to mind me. It's a flaw in your nature. You're a part of my punishment. Well, I'm sorry, October, but you need to learn how to mind your mother."

Amandine reached into her dress again, this time coming up with a handful of thorny twigs that looked like bits of briar. She placed them on the table in two tidy piles, stacking them on top of each other like she was preparing for a game of pick-up sticks. Then she snapped her fingers. The twigs writhed and stretched, weaving together until they had grown into two small wicker cages.

"You think me a monster, I'm sure. Heroes always think the people who tell them 'no' are monsters. Heroes and children have a great deal in common." She plucked two bunches of Queen Anne's lace from her skirt and tossed them into the cages, where they expanded and fluffed out, becoming blankets thick enough to protect the eventual occupants from the thorns under their feet.

Nothing would protect them from the thorns in the walls. Whatever she intended to shut up there would be cramped, and confined, and unable to move.

I strained against the thorns binding me, reaching again for the shimmering threads of her magic, wishing I could scream when they flowed away from my mental hands. I was starting to see the terrible shape of her intentions. It couldn't be real. I refused to let it be real. I couldn't do a damn thing about it.

Amandine walked across the room, stopping to caress my cheek with one hand. Part of me—the part that was still her frightened, abandoned little girl—relished the touch. She hadn't touched me like that since I'd made the Changeling's Choice, all those years ago. The greater part of me raged. She had no right to touch me like that. No right at all.

"My poor child," she said. "You really have no idea how outmatched you are, do you?"

She stepped past me, out of sight. There was a snapping sound, and the smell of blood and roses grew stronger, suddenly underscored by the mixed scents of pennyroyal and musk. When she came back into view, she had a struggling tabby tomcat by the scruff of his neck. The spell of the thorns had broken when she transformed Tybalt against his will: he spat and writhed, digging his claws into the alabaster skin of her arms over and over again. It didn't do him any good. She was healing as fast as he could hurt her, and only a few drops of blood were able to escape and fall to the floor.

Amandine walked calmly back to her cages, the purpose of which was suddenly, terribly obvious. She dropped Tybalt into the larger of the two and slammed the lid before he could leap out. A knot of thorns wrapped itself around the latch, sealing it.

"No Shadow Roads for you, cat," she said, a smug smile on her face. "My magic is greater than yours, at least while you stand within my ring of roses. Best calm yourself, or it will not go well for you."

Tybalt's response was an infuriated yowl before his paw lashed between the bars, claws cutting lines down her cheek.

Amandine sighed, the scratches already healing. "Or you could choose to be trouble, and learn what waits for recalcitrant cats. It's entirely up to you."

I struggled against the vines that held me—or rather, I struggled to find the strength to struggle. No matter how hard I tried, I couldn't move a muscle. I couldn't even blink. All I could do was watch in mute horror as Amandine turned her back on Tybalt and walked across the room to where Jazz was pinned by her own encircling cage of vines.

"Skinshifter," said Amandine, looking back at me. "Your Fetch is a reflection of yourself. I would have thought any child of mine would have slightly better taste than to love someone who keeps their ties to Faerie on the outside—but then, you dallied with that Selkie boy before you moved on to better beasts, didn't you, darling? I blame myself. With a human for a sire, there was nowhere you could go but down."

She grasped Jazz's chin firmly in her hand. The spell weakened enough for Jazz to widen her eyes in terror before Amandine was holding the beak of a vast black raven. She moved quickly, sweeping her other arm around to pin Jazz's wings against her sides.

"Struggle, and I'll shred the pretty bauble you call a cloak of feathers. I'll leave you on two legs forever. How do you think you'll care for that, hmm?"

It was difficult to read Jazz's expression when she was in raven form, but she didn't fight against Amandine, and I suppose that was answer enough. She held perfectly still, seemingly frozen with fear, as Amandine walked across the room and dropped her into the second cage. She sealed it the same way she had sealed the one containing Tybalt.

"Nothing sensible keeps its magic outside of its body," said Amandine. "It's one weakness too many. Find another lover, Fetch of my child; this one is beneath you."

She picked up the cages, one in each hand, and looked over her shoulder to smile at me thinly. There was no kindness in her expression, no love; she was looking at a servant, nothing more.

"I'll take care of these for you while you find your sister," she said. "Don't fail me, October. You won't care for the consequences."

She walked to the back door. It swung open at her approach. Then she stepped outside, taking Tybalt and Jazz with her. The door slammed shut.

They were gone.

FOUR

THE VINES DIDN'T DISAPPEAR when Amandine did: they remained as tight as ever, and the stasis lingered with them, holding me and May in place. Then, bit by bit, they seemed to loosen. I could blink. I could breathe. I hadn't even realized I wasn't until I started again. That was alarming.

The vines loosened more. I strained against them, feeling the thorns bite deeper into my arms—and now there was pain, sensation beneath the numbness. May still wasn't moving. I didn't know whether Mom's magic had less of a hold over me because I was Dóchas Sidhe and May wasn't, or whether I was just more willing to hurt myself, but it didn't matter. All that mattered was getting loose.

Amandine had frozen us right after Tybalt handed me my knife. I had a knife. Carefully, I began working it back and forth, sawing it against the vines. The position of my pinned hand meant I was *only* sawing it against the vines, and not against my own leg, but that wouldn't have made any difference to me. Not now. I needed to get free. I needed to save them.

The smell of Amandine's magic hung in the air, blood and roses, getting fainter all the time. For the first time, my own magic was strong enough to sketch out the subtleties of those two elements, the crisp brightness of the blood, the woody wildness of the roses. They had a strong perfume, but they were wild things, the sort of roses that grew rampant in wooded places, never tended by a gardener, nor planted by a human hand. I filed the details away in the part of my mind that was always documenting the magic of others. It might matter someday, and if it didn't, at least it was a small distraction from what she had done. I needed the distraction. I needed to keep sawing, and I needed not to drop the knife. If I lost that, we could be trapped here until the boys came to cut us loose.

The boys. Amandine had come here with the intent of taking hostages—the presence of the seeds in her skirt had proven that. They'd been enchanted before she came to the house, requiring only a small amount of magical effort to trigger them. Why? It wasn't like anyone who lived here could stand against her.

But the Luidaeg could. And the Luidaeg had been at my bachelorette party. Ridiculous as her presence had seemed at the time, it was probably the only thing that had stopped Amandine from making her visit in the middle of a mortal karaoke bar. Everyone in Faerie is supposed to help maintain the secrecy of the whole. For someone like Amandine, that could mean transforming every human in the place into rabbits and leaving them to be eaten by urban predators. A few missing persons cases have never been a big deal for the purebloods. There are always more mortals to abuse.

Which brought me back to the boys. They'd been in the house when the doorbell rang, or at least they should have been. Had Amandine taken them as leverage before coming to offer me the chance to work for her? Or had they somehow missed the sound of everything going terribly wrong in the kitchen? There was no way they were sitting idly by while this went down. It wasn't possible.

My knife finally sliced through the vines pinning my arm. I began cutting the rest of them away, faster now, the numbness receding more and more as the vines fell. When I pulled my legs free, the numbness dispersed entirely, leaving me physically fine. Mentally . . .

May rolled her eyes, silently pleading with me to hurry.

"Sorry," I gasped, running across the room to her. I was halfway there when I tripped, stumbling into the nest of thorny vines. They barely punctured my skin. They'd been sharper before, hadn't they? They had felt so much sharper, so much more dangerous.

More of Amandine's magic. We couldn't trust a thing she did—or said. For all I knew, she was already hurting Tybalt and Jazz. I hadn't included her in my offer of hospitality. Faerie would offer no consequences for what she'd done. If she killed them . . .

If she killed them, I was going to show her what I'd shown Blind Michael. Firstborn are hard to kill, harder than purebloods, maybe even harder than me. That doesn't mean they can't die. It just means I have to work a little harder.

May started sobbing as soon as I sliced through the first layer of vines and freed her from enough of the stasis to let the tears come. My own eyes were dry. Shock and fear had chased my tears away. I kept thinking of the look in Jazz's eyes when Amandine had forced her to transform, of the way Tybalt had yowled. Tears would have been a luxury. I could cry when they were safe. When they were home.

The vines fell away. May collapsed into my arms, hanging bonelessly against me for several seconds before she pushed herself back to her feet, grabbed my shoulders, and exclaimed, "We have to save them!"

"I know. I know we do." I felt a surge of shameful gratitude. Jazz had been taken along with Tybalt.

Much as I wanted to fall to pieces with worry, I couldn't do that. She needed me. May needed me. I could stay strong, because someone else's heart was at risk.

I've always been better at being strong for other people than I am at being strong for myself. Maybe it's the way I was raised—or maybe it's the way I was made. Either way, I guiltily shoved the gratitude to the back of my mind, pledging that May would never know about it. Ever.

May's fingers dug into my shoulders until it hurt. I didn't welcome the pain, exactly, but I was grateful for the distraction it offered. "Well?" she demanded. "Go! Get them back!"

"I can't."

She stared at me like I'd just confessed to summoning Amandine to the house myself. "What?"

"I mean, not yet. The boys—"

Her eyes widened. "Oh, oak and ash, where are they?" She looked around the kitchen like she expected them to appear. "They should have heard . . ."

"Maybe they did. Hang on." I pulled my cellphone out of the pocket of my jeans and swiped my thumb across the screen. Quentin's name was at the top of my "frequently called" list, which made sense. Tybalt doesn't have a phone, and the Luidaeg's number is the very definition of unlisted.

She was going to be my next call. Just as soon as I knew the boys were safe.

The phone rang twice before Quentin answered, sounding breathless and hesitant. "Hello?" he said, cautiously.

"It's me," I said. "Where are you?"

"Prove it."

"Last week you tried to convince me to help you make a sushi pizza for your boyfriend, and I laughed until orange juice came out of my nose. Not my most dignified moment."

"You don't *have* dignified moments," said Quentin,

sounding profoundly relieved. "Is it safe? Can we come home?"

That confirmed my impression that if he had been in the house, he would have at least tried to come to my rescue. "Where are you?"

Silence answered me. I pulled the phone from my ear, and saw the call had dropped, just as the smell of pepper and burning paper filled the air, mercifully washing away the last of the blood and roses. I turned. Quentin and Raj were in the corner next to the fridge, Raj with his body positioned to block Quentin from the rest of the room. It was a protective gesture. It was also a sensible one. If anything tried to touch them, Raj could shove Quentin backward, onto the Shadow Roads, before either of them was hurt.

I lowered my phone. "Hey," I said.

"Where is my uncle?" demanded Raj. He raked his eyes across the chaos in the kitchen, glaring at the wilting vines littering the floor and the bloody pinpricks on May's arms. His gaze finally settled on me. Only the faint tremor in his lower lip betrayed how frightened he was. "Where is he?"

"Amandine has him," said May, stepping forward before I could speak. "She took Tybalt and Jazz. As collateral."

"Collateral against what? Wait—Amandine? She was *here*?" Quentin shoved his way in front of Raj, starting toward me. "Toby, I'm sorry, we were coming out of my room when Tybalt appeared in the hall upstairs and told Raj to get out of the house, I didn't want to go with him, I wanted to stay and fight for you like a squire is supposed to, but once we were in the Court of Cats, I didn't know how to get back—"

"Stop apologizing," I said. To my great relief, he did, and stood there looking at me mutely, waiting for me to tell him how I was going to fix this. Waiting for me to tell them all.

I couldn't, because I didn't know. Instead, I rubbed

my eyes with one hand and said, "I didn't ask Tybalt to give that order, but I would have if I'd been thinking. Raj did the right thing getting you out of there."

I couldn't see Raj through my hand. I could picture his expression. He would be sagging slightly with relief. Relief that I wasn't angry at him for grabbing Quentin and running; relief that I hadn't expected them to stand and fight. Quentin is officially my squire, but Raj frequently falls into a similar role. Somewhere between our first meeting in Blind Michael's lands and my slow courtship with his uncle, I had come to matter very much to the kid, and he had come to matter very much to me. That doesn't mean it's his job to risk his life for mine.

"I should have stayed," said Quentin. "I should have fought."

I lowered my hand. "You're my squire. You're also the Crown Prince of the Westlands," I said. "We were up against one of the Firstborn. None of us knew what she was capable of. Tybalt gave the best order possible, under the circumstances. I'm just glad Raj was able to follow it."

"Amandine was really *here*?" Quentin shook his head. "I thought . . . I don't know what I thought. I didn't think she knew where we lived. Why did she come *here*?"

"Because she wants me to find my sister." I closed my eyes, taking a deep breath. I could do this. I could find August; I could save Tybalt and Jazz. I could.

I just needed to figure out how.

"Why did she take them? They're not going to help you find anyone when they're not here." Raj sounded very small. With my eyes closed, it was easy to remember the skinny, terrified boy he had been when we met, the one who had been convinced that he was never going to make it out of Blind Michael's lands. I had been the one to tell him to be brave, then. I had been the one to promise him that he was going to make it home.

I opened my eyes. "Because she wanted leverage

against me," I said. "I told her I wouldn't work for her. She got mad."

"It wasn't your fault," said May.

"Maybe it was!" snapped Raj. "One of the Firstborn came here and asked you to do something, and you said *no*? October. Why? Why would you do that?"

"She's not 'one of the Firstborn,' " I said. "She's my mother. She's the reason I am . . . well, she's the reason I am just about everything I am. She knows how to push all my buttons, because she was there when they were installed. I said 'no' because I didn't think she'd hurt me." But that wasn't true, was it? She had confessed to doing exactly that. Try as I might, I couldn't think of turning someone human against their will as anything *but* hurting them.

"And it wasn't her fault," said May again. Her voice shifted, taking on traces of the strange, nameless accent she had when she was touching her night-haunt roots. She was a part of their flock for centuries untold before she became my Fetch. It was easy to forget that sometimes. "Amandine may be your mother—I may remember her as my mother—but she was planning to take collateral as soon as she stepped through that door. I know enough about her to have no question about *that*. She came here intending to take something to guarantee your good behavior."

"Why?" Quentin asked.

"Because that's how Amandine is. That's how she's always been." May shook her head. "I can't remember much more than that. The memories aren't mine—I got them from the dead—and those get fuzzy after a while."

"I know someone who will remember," I said. I wanted to run out the door and start looking for Amandine. I had a pretty good idea of where to start: she was likely to have taken Tybalt and Jazz back to her tower. But I couldn't best her magically, and she might hurt them if I showed up without having even started looking for August. I needed help.

There was only one person who could give me that.

Raising my phone again, I called up the keyboard and tapped the numbers in a decreasing spiral, moving from one to eight. As I dialed, I chanted, "Cinderella, dressed in yellow, went upstairs to kiss a fellow; made a mistake, kissed a snake, now they're happily married with a dental practice outside Marin." The smell of cut-grass and copper rose in the air around me, my magic gathering for the attack.

The copper smelled bloody, arterial. The more of my humanity I lose, the more my magic smells like my mother's. I have never hated that fact more than I did in that moment.

The spell coalesced, drew tight, and finally burst, drifting down around me. I lifted the phone to my ear, waiting as patiently as I could.

The death of the dial tone has not been kind to me. I can have trouble telling whether a call has been successfully completed when I'm calling someone like Quentin, whose phone actually exists. The Luidaeg's phone isn't connected to the exchange. She doesn't have a cell, and her landline doesn't have any wires; the jack is stripped, the cords cut off close to the body of the phone to keep her from tripping over them when she gets out of bed for a midday snack. The fact that I can call her at all is pure magic, and the spell doesn't always work.

There was a long pause—long enough that I started to think I was going to need to cast again—when there was a click and a sound like a bottle smashing to the ground before the Luidaeg asked wearily, "What the hell do you want? Isn't it enough that I came out in public for you? You know, in my day, people were grateful when I blessed their events with my presence. They didn't go expecting me to answer the fucking phone to boot."

She sounded tired, and annoyed, and a little bit glad to hear from me, although she would never admit it. She sounded, in short, normal, and somehow, that was the last straw. The dam broke and I started to cry, great, racking sobs that shook my entire body. Quentin looked alarmed. Raj looked embarrassed, like this was something he wasn't supposed to see. May . . .

May looked relieved. She wasn't the only person crying anymore.

"Toby?" The weariness dropped away from the Luidaeg's voice in an instant, replaced by confusion and a small amount of dread. "October, what's going on? What's wrong?"

"M-Mom," I managed, before I started sobbing again. It felt like once I'd started, I couldn't figure out how to stop.

There was a long pause. Finally, the Luidaeg said, "She's not dead. I would know, if she were dead. What did she do to you?"

I couldn't answer. My tongue seemed three sizes too large for my mouth. The Luidaeg sighed.

"Fine. Tell your kitty-cat to come and get me, and you can explain in person. I swear on Dad's guts, October, I wouldn't go to half this much trouble for most—"

"He can't."

"What?"

"He can't come and get you. Because she took him." I took a shuddering breath, not bothering to wipe the tears from my cheeks. "She came here, she came into my home, under the auspices of my own hospitality, and she took him, Luidaeg, she *took Tybalt*." May was looking at me, stricken. I amended, "Jazz, too. She's using them as collateral."

"Collateral for what?"

"She wants me to find my sister."

There was a long pause before the Luidaeg said, almost hesitantly, "She wants you to find August?"

"Unless I have another sister out there that I don't know about." I paused. The urge to ask the Luidaeg whether I had another sister was almost overwhelming.

The trouble was, the Luidaeg was bound by a complex web of geasa that kept her from answering everything I asked even as they prevented her from lying, and more, could bring this whole conversation to a halt if I asked the wrong thing. Much as I wanted to know, I couldn't afford to get distracted. I resumed: "She named August specifically. She wants me to find her, and when I said 'no,' she took Tybalt and Jazz to make sure I'd do it."

"I'd ask you why you tried to defy her, but I've met you, so I don't need to ask, and anyway, it wouldn't have made a damn bit of difference. Amy would have taken prisoners just to make sure you wouldn't let yourself get distracted. So if you're beating yourself up, you need to cut that shit out and focus on what matters."

I glanced at May, who was watching me with wide and worried eyes. "May said pretty much the same thing. That Mom would have taken them no matter what."

"We ruined Amy. We didn't mean to, but done is done, and we can't take it back now. She doesn't know how to be refused." The Luidaeg sighed. "Fuck, Toby, I'm sorry. What do you want from me?"

"I want you to help me."

"I can't."

Somehow, that wasn't a surprise. It hurt all the same: "Why not?"

"Because she's my sister. No matter what she may have done to you or anyone else, I can't stand against her. Not without breaking rules I don't even have names for. More than that, though, she is our father's daughter. If she faced me on the sea, or even near it, I'd win. On her ground, on her terms? There's no guarantee. She might be able to defeat me."

That was a chilling thought. I shoved it aside as best as I could, asking, "So what am I supposed to do? She has my people—and she didn't tell me how long she'd keep them. Do I have three days? A week? What's my time limit?"

The Luidaeg chuckled, dark and mirthless and terrifying. It was the laughter of a woman being led to the gallows, already knowing what comes next. "Oh, October. Sometimes I forget how *young* you are. Don't you understand? We say 'three days' or 'a week' or 'in a fortnight's time' because otherwise, we would never stop."

I went colder than I already was. "What are you saying?"

"I'm saying Amandine doesn't care about anything as petty as time. She didn't tell you how long you had because she's planning to keep them forever. Bring August back to her, and she'll return her hostages. She took the shifters—may I assume they weren't in their human shapes when she left?"

"No. She forced them to transform, and then she put them in cages."

Raj hissed at that, his lips drawing back to reveal teeth that were larger and sharper than the human norm, and larger and sharper than they'd been only a few seconds before.

"There's your answer. Amy always did like pets. She'll keep them as long as she has a use for them, and when she breaks them—and make no mistake, she *will* break them—she'll say she'd forgotten they were originally fae, and not just vermin. No one will believe her, but that won't matter. She'll be above reproach."

"I have to save them."

"You do. But I can't help you."

"So who can?"

"Talk to the people who remember August. The people who knew her before she went missing. Maybe one of them will be able to do something."

I paused. "I need to ask you something, and I need you not to get angry with me."

"For Dad's sake, Toby . . ." The Luidaeg sighed again, angrily this time, like she couldn't believe I was making her say this. "No. I don't know where August is. I've never known where August was. If I did, I would have told Simon when he came to me, and I would never have let him do what he did in the name of saving his daughter. I may be a monster, but I know the meaning of mercy. Now go and bring your people home."

The line went dead. I slowly lowered the phone. My tears were drying on my cheeks, leaving itchy trails behind. I stood frozen, not wiping them away. Not doing anything.

"Well?" said May, finally.

"I know what we have to do," I said.

Oak and ash preserve me, but I didn't want to. And I didn't have a choice.

FIVE

"**T**HIS IS A TERRIBLE idea," said May.

"I know," I agreed, and kept my eyes on the road.

We were rocketing toward Pleasant Hill at what would have been an unsafe speed even without the don't-look-here spell I'd asked Quentin to throw over the car. As it was, if I let my attention veer for a second, somebody was going to get seriously injured, and it probably wasn't going to be me. Predawn traffic is vicious in the Bay Area, as commuters try to beat the rush to work, and succeed only in moving commute hours earlier every year. Luckily for us, we were going against the grain. Getting back into San Francisco was a nightmare for later.

It had taken us less than ten minutes to get out of the house and on the road, which was a record I might have been proud of under other circumstances. As it was, those ten minutes had felt like ten too many. We would have gone faster, but leaving without grabbing weapons, supplies, and my leather jacket had been out of the question. I didn't know when we'd be coming back. I wasn't going out there unarmed. Not when Tybalt's life was at stake.

"It's not the worst one she's ever had," said Quentin, from the back seat. He was taking his exile well. It would have been difficult for him not to, considering the situation. If Mom had taken Dean, he would have been baying for blood as loudly as the rest of us, and their relationship wasn't even that serious yet.

"Top ten," snapped May. "You don't know Simon like I do. You don't remember what he did to us."

"No, but I heard the stories, and I remember what he tried to do to Jazz when she got in his way," said Quentin. "Sometimes the enemy of your enemy is your friend."

"He's not Amandine's enemy! He's her *husband*!" May twisted in her seat to glare at my squire. "This isn't going to work."

"The Luidaeg can't help us, and I can't think of anyone who'd know August better than her own father," I said, tightening my hands on the wheel. A compact car zipped by, coming a little too close for comfort. I hit the gas harder. They couldn't hit us if they couldn't catch up with us. "We're doing this."

"I don't like it, but I'm not trying to stop you, because you're right," said May. She twisted back into her original position, staring at the road ahead of us like a condemned woman. "We have to do the impossible and find a missing person who disappeared so long ago that the trail isn't just cold, it's fossilized. Refusing to let someone help just because they're an asshole won't do us any good. It won't do Jazz and Tybalt any good, either."

Quentin's phone beeped. He picked it up, scanning the screen.

I glanced at the rearview mirror, watching him. "What's the news?"

"Raj tracked Walther to his apartment and woke him up, and he's got the countercharm. He's taking the

Shadow Roads, and he'll meet us at Shadowed Hills."
Quentin paused before adding, "Walther says good
luck."

"We're damn well going to need it," I said grimly.
"Is Raj still with him?"

"Yes."

"Good. Let Walther know that we may still need
him, and ask if he can head for his office. I'll call him
there if there's something he can do." I might have felt
bad about my high-handed assumption that Walther
would help, if the situation hadn't been quite so dire—
but then again, I might not have. As Walther himself
has pointed out, more than once, I have a tendency to
grab for whatever tools were handy when there's a job
to be done. Sometimes those tools are my friends. In
my line of work, saving lives is more important than
asking nicely.

Quentin nodded and resumed texting.

Walther Davies is a chemistry professor at UC Berke-
ley. He's also one of the best alchemists I've ever known.
That, combined with my freakishly precise ability to
identify the magical signatures of the people around
me, recently enabled him to do the impossible: he cured
elf-shot. The spell that purebloods used for millennia to
cast their enemies into centuries of sleep is no longer a
binding sentence. Oh, elf-shot can still be used, and no
doubt will be; it's just a shorter term of slumber.

Or a quick and reasonably painless death, for changelings and mortals. Because even a cure can't make Faerie become kind.

We were drag racing our way toward the mortal city
of Pleasant Hill and the fae Duchy of Shadowed Hills
for one simple reason: Amandine's husband, my stepfather, Simon Torquill, was there. Sleeping. He had been
elf-shot in the process of saving me from Evening Winterrose, also known as Eira Rosynhwyr, also known as
"my mother's oldest sister, who sort of wants me dead
for reasons that I do not fully understand."

Sometimes I wish my life came with a flow chart.

Simon was not my ally. Simon was not even my friend. Simon was the man who'd transformed me into a fish and abandoned me in the Japanese Tea Gardens to dream fourteen years of my then-mortal life away. Simon had done worse things than that over the course of his time in Evening's service. How much worse, I didn't know . . . but for much of that time, he'd been involved in some sort of relationship with Oleander de Merelands, an assassin and poisoner who had definitely killed Lily, the Lady of the Tea Gardens, and had probably killed King Gilad Windermere in the Mists, Arden's father and our rightful King. Simon could have been complicit in all of that. There was no way to be sure, save for asking him.

Traditionally, once someone has been elf-shot, it's a little difficult to have a conversation. My niece, Karen, is an oneiromancer, and could carry me into his dreams, but that wasn't good enough. Dreams are funny things. Even lucid dreams, guided by an oneiromancer, could be more symbols and ideas than actual facts. I needed information. I needed guidance.

I needed Simon to wake up.

The parking lot at Paso Nogal Park was empty. It was also locked, with a heavy chain holding the lot's wooden gates together. I stopped the car and glared at the chain, as if that would be enough to bust it open.

"What in the name of the root and the branch is *that* doing there?" I demanded.

"Parks Department," said Quentin, unbuckling his seatbelt. "Kids from the local high school were driving up here at night to smoke and drink, so they started locking the gate again."

"Park on the road," said May.

"I've got this," said Quentin. He got out of the car, walking to the gate, and produced a key from his pocket. It fit the lock exactly, and in a matter of seconds, we were driving through.

I took the spot nearest to the trailhead that would take us up the hill to the knowe. Quentin was standing next to the car when I got out.

"You have a key?" I asked.

"You'd have one, too, if you'd been here recently," he said. "Etienne will probably give you one today."

"Today" was the operative term. The sky was getting light; we had less than twenty minutes before the sun came up and all our illusions came tumbling down. The Parks Department would probably assume that one of their own had unlocked the gate, since the lock had clearly not been tampered with in any way, but they wouldn't be nearly so accepting of a bunch of inhuman hikers found running around the place at dawn. We needed to get moving.

"Come on," I said, and waved for May and Quentin to follow me as I turned and started walking up the trail. The gravel turned and shifted underfoot, adding gripping surfaces to what would otherwise have been a treacherously slippery climb. That was nice, while it lasted: in no time at all, we were scrabbling up the dirt hillside, grabbing at clumps of dew-slicked grass and fighting not to slide back down to the beginning, where we'd have to start all over again.

Most fae holdings are hidden in the Summerlands, anchored to the mortal world by enchanted doors. Those places—those directly connected places—are called hollow hills, or knowes, and they can be a bear to access. The people who control them get to decide how difficult the doors will be to find or open. Sylvester Torquill was a generally kind man, thinking the best of people, encouraging them to think the best of him. Somehow, that translated to his knowe having an entrance that could double as an obstacle course.

Quentin pulled ahead. I didn't try to stop him. He'd been here more recently than either May or I, and he knew the exact permutations of the current lock, leading us over, under, around and through the hawthorns and the fallen logs and the great sandstone boulders. We played ring-around-the-roses with a wild rosemary bush, whipped twice around a lighting-blackened oak, and stopped as a door appeared in the largest of the old oak trees in front of us.

May was wheezing. She waved me forward, and Quentin hung back, both acknowledging that this would go better if I were the one to do it. Swell.

I stepped up to the thick oak door and knocked, the sound echoing into the stillness beyond. I stepped back, glancing nervously at the sky. The sun was almost up. We had five minutes, maybe less, before dawn, and then I was going to be in a world of hurt if I was still in the mortal world.

Dawn is painful outside the Summerlands. The only reason it isn't painful *there* is that it never happens. The Summerlands exist in a perpetual twilight that grows deeper or brighter according to the whims of the purebloods who control the individual slices of territory, but which never quite yields to day. Somehow, crops still grow there, even mortal ones, and no one suffers from a Vitamin D deficiency. It must be something in the water.

I live in the mortal world. Dawn is part of the price I pay for my freedom from noble oversight, for being able to have things like cable television and midnight trips to 7-11. But I was normally paying that price in the safety of my own home, where I could stick my head under a pillow and wait for the air to come back. I raised my hand to knock again.

The door swung open to reveal Sir Etienne, who was—for once—less than perfectly polished. His dark hair was in ruffled disarray, and his gray tunic was barely belted, creating the impression that he'd grabbed it off the floor. The air around him smelled of limes and cedar smoke. He must have opened a gate to bring himself to the door, possibly because dawn was so near. His eyes widened at the sight of us.

"Get inside," he snapped, stepping to the side to make room. "The sun is almost up. Hurry!"

It wasn't the most polite of invitations, but he didn't need to tell me twice. I rushed inside, trying to ignore the way the world tilted around me at the transition, marking the demarcation between the human and fae worlds. May and Quentin were close behind.

Etienne slammed the door, sealing the mortal world and the mortal sunrise safely on the other side. Then he turned to me, surprise fading, replaced by wariness. "October," he said. "What's wrong?"

"Who said anything was wrong?" The question sounded frail and strained, even to my own ears. I still had to ask it. If I didn't keep up appearances, I was going to break down. My conversation with the Luidaeg had proven that much.

"You're here," he said simply.

For a moment, I couldn't think of a reply.

There was a time when it felt like I was driving to Shadowed Hills every ten minutes, looking for answers, looking for help, or just looking for a hot meal. Sylvester was my liege. His wife, Luna, had been my friend once, before things had gotten so strained between us. But they were just the tip of the iceberg. I'd grown up running around the knowe, giggling with the household staff, sleeping in the guest rooms. This had been my home during a period of my life when I'd felt like I didn't deserve to have one, and I had walked away from more than just Sylvester when he'd broken my heart by lying to me.

My heart was healing. The bridges between me and my liege were in the process of being mended. And once again, I needed help.

"I don't know how many times I can tell this story without losing it, and I need to ask Sylvester for a favor," I said, all too aware of May and Quentin at my back. May was in even worse shape than I was. I had always known that Tybalt lived a dangerous life. Jazz ran an antique store. She wasn't supposed to be a target. "Is he up?"

"For you, he will be," said Etienne. "I'll fetch him. I trust you can find the receiving room on your own?"

"Pretty sure," I said.

He nodded, traced a circle in the air with his hand, and vanished through the portal of his own making, leaving the smell of limes and cedar smoke hanging once more heavy in the air. I didn't wait for it to dissipate before I started walking again.

Quentin pulled up next to me. I glanced at him.

"Does Raj know how to get around the wards?" I asked.

"He can't come straight into the knowe, but there's a spot in the woods we always use when he needs to meet me here," he said. "He can walk from there."

"Because Raj will be *thrilled* that we made him walk," I said.

Quentin smirked.

Raj was a Prince of Cats, but he wasn't a King yet. Once he was crowned, his power would expand, making him the anchor to the Shadow Roads in San Francisco, and—more importantly, in some regards—opening the wards of the local knowes to him. It's considered incredibly bad form to ward against Kings and Queens of Cats, just like it would have been considered bad form to ward against Arden. Princes and Princesses are fair game, but the monarchs? They can come and go as they pleased.

Would Tybalt still be a King when he stepped down? It seemed likely. Power doesn't like to let go once it has hold of someone. Tybalt would be a King without a throne. An enviable—and dangerous—position to be in.

It helped a little to think about the future. What he was going to be after I got him safely back from my mother, after he'd recovered from whatever she did to him, and most importantly, after he'd been able to step down from his throne. Abdication was a funny wedding gift, but under the circumstances, I'd take it.

The receiving room doors were unguarded. Another sign of how late, or early, it was. The people who would normally have been standing by to let us in were probably already in bed. I was grateful that Etienne hadn't felt the need to wake them just so they could stand on ceremony. Fatherhood really was mellowing him.

The doors were heavy, but Quentin and I were able to get them open, revealing the spacious cavern of a room on the other side. We started across the black-and-white checkerboard marble floor, toward the dais on the far side. Everything smelled of roses. Not my mother's roses, thank Maeve; these were cultivated things, pampered garden flowers, trained and raised up by a loving hand. Luna is one of the best gardeners in the Westlands, and she specializes in roses, which makes sense, since technically she *is* a rose. She's of the Blodynbryd, a form of rose Dryad, and where she walks, flowers bloom.

That wasn't always how I'd known her. Luna is Blind Michael's youngest daughter. When we'd met, she had been claiming to be a Kitsune, wrapped so tightly in the stolen skin of one of her father's victims that the change had run all the way down to the bone. The magic she used to make the change was similar to the spell the Luidaeg used to create the Selkies, but unlike the Selkies, Luna had never been able to put her Kitsune skin aside. She'd been trapped, wrapped in hot, mammalian emotions and biology, until her own daughter tried to kill her and, in the process, stripped the stolen skin away.

The Torquills are a complicated family. I'm still not sure how I feel about being legally one of them.

A door opened behind the dais, and Sylvester rushed out. He was wearing tan pants and a white muslin shirt, and nothing else: for a Duke, he was barely presentable. I didn't care. Relief washed over me, coupled with a sudden hope that maybe, just maybe, we could find another way. Sylvester had loved his brother, once. Who was to say he hadn't truly known his brother's daughter?

"October," he said, hurrying toward us. "What's wrong?" He scanned our small group, and frowned. "Where's Tybalt?"

There's no love lost between my liege and my lover, but he still noticed when Tybalt wasn't there. That made me feel even more hopeful. Sylvester noticed things.

"Is Etienne coming back?" I asked. "I don't want to repeat this more than I have to."

"I'm here," said a voice behind me.

I turned. There was Etienne, with a yawning Grianne standing next to him, her Merry Dancers bobbing sleepily in the air to either side of her head. I'd been so distracted that I hadn't even noticed the scent of his magic. That wasn't good. This was *not* the time for me to start losing my focus. Not if I wanted to bring them home alive.

"Good," I said, and looked back to Sylvester. "Amandine came to my house and demanded I find August for her. She took Tybalt and Jasmine as collateral against my doing what she says. The Luidaeg can't help me. I need someone who knew August to help me figure out where she could have gone, before my mother does something that can't be undone. Can you help me?"

"I . . ." He stopped, looking stricken. "I don't know where my niece is. I'm so sorry. I tried to find her when she disappeared. I was still a hero then, I thought I could save her, but I couldn't. I couldn't do anything but watch my brother break himself against walls that I couldn't even see. I tried to help him. He pushed me away. He said it was my fault his family had been broken, that if I . . . if I hadn't encouraged August to heroism, she would never have wandered from the path he had charted for her. I don't know where she went. I don't even know if she's alive."

Everything seemed to freeze. My breath caught in my throat as I stared at him, absorbing the true enormity of his final words.

What if August was dead?

What if she hadn't just disappeared, all those years ago: what if she had *died*, and was no longer out there to be found? Would Amandine take proof of death as my bringing her daughter home, or would she say that I'd failed to do the one thing she had ever asked of me? Would she punish Tybalt and Jazz because I couldn't raise the dead?

"I need to talk to Simon," I heard myself say. It seemed impossible for me to be speaking, since my entire body was numb, but I was doing it. Good job, me. "He's the only person left who might be able to help me find her."

"If you wish to enter his dreams, I'm sure—"

"No." I raised my head slightly, meeting his eyes and refusing to let myself look away. "I need to *talk* to him. Not in a dream. Not in a blood memory. I need to wake him up and make him help me find her, before Amandine hurts our people. Please, Sylvester. Please, I am begging you. Let me wake your brother."

His face was stone. He didn't speak, and so neither did I. I just looked at him, silently pleading.

Sylvester Torquill is Daoine Sidhe, like Quentin, like his brother: the descendants of Eira Rosynhwyr, daughter of Titania and Oberon. Daoine Sidhe trend toward the beautiful, with dramatic coloration and perfectly sculpted features, and Sylvester is no different. His hair is russet red, like fox fur, and his eyes are the clear gold of wildflower honey. He wore his face with kindness, and his twin brother had always seemed to wear it with cruelty . . . at least until I'd seen Simon elf-shot for my sake. Until I'd traveled through his memories, and seen how much he loved his family. The brothers have more in common than they might ever admit, and I needed both of them to be willing to help me.

Sylvester looked away first. "He hurt my child," he said, voice thick with loathing. "He took her from me, damaged her in ways that may never heal. He stole my wife. Why? Because he was alone, and wanted me to be alone as well? Because he thought I didn't deserve to be happy if he couldn't be?"

"Sylvester—"

"He took *you*!" Sylvester spun back to face me, grabbing my shoulders and shaking me once, for emphasis. "You, who should have been my daughter, for all the care your mother offered you, for all the love I showed you! He stole the child of my blood, and then he stole the child of my heart, and I still don't have either of you back! Why should I let you wake him up, when he deserves to suffer for eternity for what he's done to me?"

"Because Jazz doesn't deserve to suffer," I said softly. "Because Tybalt doesn't deserve to suffer. Because my mother has stolen *my* family, has stolen my friend and my husband-to-be, and I need them back, Sylvester, I don't know what I'll do if I can't get them back. You can help me. You say I should have been your daughter? Well, be a father to me now, and help me. Give me what I need."

"Luna won't approve."

"Luna doesn't approve of anything I do anymore." I paused. "But there *is* one thing I can offer to make her feel better about the idea."

He frowned. "What's that?"

"We haven't woken Rayseline because she killed Connor. If we wake her, she has to stand trial, and she broke Oberon's Law. You know what Arden will have to do."

Sylvester's frown became a grimace. "I do."

"But the Luidaeg is technically the Selkie First. I can talk to her. I can talk to Arden. We can try to find a way to pardon Raysel for what she did." It burned, talking about Connor's death like it was a bargaining chip. At the same time, I didn't think he'd mind.

All he had ever wanted was for me to be happy, and for us to have the chance to be together. We were never going to get the second. Why shouldn't I do whatever I could to achieve the first?

Sylvester looked like he was wavering. I pressed on. "High King Sollys was able to pardon me for what I did to Blind Michael. That was only a few years ago. I can testify on Raysel's behalf. I can tell them the combination of her biology and what was done to her as a child meant she wasn't in her right mind when she killed Connor—she didn't know what she was doing, she just knew that she was in pain and needed it to stop. She won't do that again."

"How can you be so sure?"

"Because I took the Blodynbryd out of her. Her blood isn't at war with itself anymore. She's going to need counseling, and honestly, we should ask Karen if she'll help Raysel audition therapists before we wake her up, so she'll already have somebody standing by to give her a helping hand, but she isn't going to do what she did again. Please. I can help you help her, but I need you to help me first."

Sylvester was still. He looked at me impassively, and for a moment I thought I had pushed too far. Then, wryly, he smiled.

"You are your mother's daughter, no matter how much you may hate me saying that, especially right now," he said. "You know what I want most in the world, and you'd offer it to me if it meant I gave you what you wanted."

My stomach churned. Was he right? Was I doing to him what Amandine had done to me, taking hostages against his heart for the sake of my own desires?

Yes. And no, because if he'd ever asked me to help with Raysel's defense, I would have done it, no strings attached. It was just that we hadn't really been speaking, and I hadn't really been thinking about it. I had been selfish, but not cruel.

"I'll help you with Rayseline's defense no matter what, Sylvester; you only ever had to ask me," I said, fighting to keep my voice level. "But I need Simon now, and I need you, my liege, to help me. Will you help me?"

Sylvester closed his eyes. "Yes," he said. "I will."

I didn't say anything. I just stepped forward and put my arms around him, resting my head against his chest, and waited for Raj to come with the potion that would change the world.

SIX

ELF-SHOT HAS BEEN A problem in Faerie for so
long that some knowes, like Queen Windermere's in
Muir Woods, have dedicated rooms for its victims, places
where sleepers can dream away the century of their sentence without getting dusty or being shoved into a closet
and forgotten. Others, like the now-deposed King Rhys
of Silences, kept their elf-shot sleepers in the dungeon,
which to be fair, was a large, often unused space, but was
not the nicest place for a hundred-year nap.

Shadowed Hills split the difference. They don't have
a dedicated room, but they have plenty of space, thanks
to the eccentric and unpredictable geometry of the
place. I knew Rayseline was asleep in a glass coffin in
one of her mother's greenhouses. The imagery of it
made me a little uncomfortable, especially since the
inventor of elf-shot, Eira Rosynhwyr, is sometimes considered the progenitor of the Snow White story.

Sylvester led us through a maze of hallways and
empty rooms. A few looked like they'd been sealed for
decades; dust coated the floors, a stain on the normally

impeccable work of the housekeeping staff, marked with footprints along the path from door to door. Most of the prints were clearly Sylvester's. He didn't say anything, and so neither did the rest of us. We just followed.

May looked even shakier than I felt. Her eyes were red, and she flinched from every sound like she no longer had the ability to process danger. She'd lived for uncounted centuries as a night-haunt, feeding on the memories of others, her face and thoughts ever-changing to fit the parade of Faerie's dead. I had no doubt that she had loved before, but always secondhand, always borrowed from someone else's life and death. In many ways, Jazz was her first love. I was as scared as she was—maybe more, because I had lost lovers; I knew that I could fail and they could die—but I at least had the cold comfort of knowing this wasn't the end of the world, no matter how much I might wind up wishing it had been.

Only Quentin looked halfway like himself. Sad, yes, withdrawn, yes, but still himself. He was going to have to be the levelheaded one through what came next . . . and I was the one who'd done most of his training.

May Oberon have mercy on us all.

Etienne and Grianne brought up the rear. Neither had said anything about the fact that we were on our way to wake Simon, who had betrayed Shadowed Hills and Sylvester more conclusively than anyone else in the world. Maybe they didn't feel it was their place. Or maybe they just understood that making this harder than it had to be wasn't going to do anyone any good, and might lead to me breaking somebody's nose.

Sylvester opened another door. The hallway on the other side looked like something from a haunted house, all rickety, splintering wood and cobwebby corners. The floor was scuffed, a threadbare runner rug stretching down the center like a pathway to doom. I blinked.

"I honestly thought Melly would skin anyone who let part of the knowe get this bad," I said.

"The staff is not allowed in this area," said Sylvester

stiffly. "I don't know how much you know about how a knowe is built."

"Not much," I admitted.

He walked through the door. We kept following.

"It begins with intent," he said. "Intent and power. The maker must convince the Summerlands to yield, as a gardener convinces the soil to yield before the seed. That was part of what drew me to Luna, when we met. I was building my garden walls, and she already had the spade in her hand. She seemed perfectly suited to understanding what I would face—and she did. Oh, she did. She didn't know much about the process of construction, but she forgave me when the foundations took me away from her. She tended her roses, and she waited for me."

This seemed to be less about knowe construction and more about his relationship with Luna. I didn't say so. We were still moving, and he wasn't stalling; he was just filling the silence, an impulse I understood all too well. The instinct to whistle past the graveyard is standard to everything I've met with enough intelligence to understand what it is to dread the consequences of their actions.

"You walk into the Summerlands, you find the place you're going to stake your claim, and you mark it. You go into the mortal world, and you find the place where you want the intersection to occur. You gather your magic and your strength, and you cut a hole between the worlds for the sake of what's to come. Then you build. You build a beginning. So much of the beginning has to come from your own hands." He touched a wall, trailing his fingers along it as he walked. "I was never a carpenter."

Suddenly, the shoddiness of the hall made a lot more sense. "You built this?"

"With my own two hands, and with the help of the man I loved most in all the world." We had reached a small door. Sylvester pushed it open.

The room on the other side was as shabby as the hall. The walls were papered in lilac brocade that peeled in places, revealing the plaster beneath. The window had no glass; instead, the panes held sheets of oiled paper, no doubt enchanted to stand up to the elements, turning the world outside into a blobby impressionist painting. A single twin bed was pushed up against the wall, and in the bed was Simon Torquill, my old enemy, my last hope.

Asleep, with all the hard lines and worry eased from his face, he looked more like Sylvester than ever. They had the same bones: it was the way they wore them that differed. They were even dressed similarly, although Sylvester's clothes were faintly medieval, while Simon's were more "I stopped keeping up with mortal fashions somewhere in the 1920s." He was wearing shoes. I guess when there's no chance the sleeper will roll over, it's less about dressing them for comfort, and more about dressing them for display. Like a funeral.

His cuffs were frayed. I realized that every time I'd seen him without Oleander there to put on a show for, his cuffs had been frayed. He was holding on tightly to the few things he had, mending them when he had to, never letting go.

That was his problem, really. He'd never figured out how to let go.

I turned, looking to Etienne. "You know where we are now," I said. "Can you go check the grounds for Raj? He's supposed to be coming with the countercharm."

Etienne frowned. "I thought the stuff was too delicate to be exposed to magic."

"Walther's still tinkering with it. Every batch is more stable than the last, and cold is good for it. Helps it settle. According to him, carrying it through the Shadow Roads is actually beneficial—the magic may do a little damage, but the cold repairs all that, and more."

"Fine," said Etienne. He looked to Sylvester, who

nodded minutely, granting permission. With that formality observed, Etienne turned, sketched a portal in the air, and was gone.

Grianne remained behind. Her Merry Dancers spun around her, betraying an unusual degree of agitation.

"Is he not to be bound?" she asked.

Ah.

For Grianne, that was a speech—she doesn't talk much, and when she does, it's always to make a point. Unlike the rest of us, who will probably go to our graves yammering wildly away. This time, her point was a valid one: Simon, for all that I needed him, and for all that I was embarking on a quest that was to his personal benefit, had run away before. He'd betrayed everyone in this room, to one degree or another, at least once. What was going to stop him from doing it again?

"He will be," said Sylvester. He looked at Simon as he spoke, and his words were filled with a mixture of regret and longing that hurt my heart to hear. "His punishment does not end because I must wake him. For what he's done, his suffering has just begun."

Oberon's Law forbids us to kill each other. That's it: that's everything. The rest of the crimes we commit, the rest of the times we transgress, there's no law to describe what happens next. There's tradition, and there are punishments, but the basic judicial system of Faerie is "I do what I want."

Simon Torquill was a landless Count who had committed crimes against a landed Duke in his own home. He had committed treason by kidnapping his brother's wife. He had imprisoned Luna and Rayseline for years, in a place we had yet to identify or find. He had assaulted another noble's vassal by transforming me against my will. No one would question Sylvester for taking his revenge, whatever form that revenge might take.

Sometimes, revenge could take some pretty vicious forms. The former King of Silences had been using his rivals for spell components, cutting them apart one piece at a time. While he had been elf-shot for his crimes against the Crown, he wasn't specifically being punished for that. In the eyes of fae law, he had done nothing wrong. Also in the eyes of fae law, Queen Siwan—who was now back in her rightful place as ruler of Silences—would be doing nothing wrong if she ordered him sliced to bits, as long as he didn't die.

When Faerie decides to hold a grudge, the ramifications can echo for centuries.

"Your knife, please, October," said Sylvester. He held his hand out, making it clear that this was not entirely a request.

Feeling uneasy, I pulled the silver blade from its sheath under my jacket and passed it to him. "Do I need to bleed?"

"For once, no. Your blood is not required." He leaned forward, grasping Simon's left hand and turning it so the palm was facing toward the ceiling. With a quick, decisive motion, he sliced the ball of Simon's thumb lengthwise. The smell of blood filled the room.

I could smell Simon's magic in his blood, the smoke and rotten oranges tracery that marked him now, and the smoky mulled cider scent that had marked him once, before things had gone so wrong for him. It was complicated all out of proportion, that mix of scents: people's magic isn't supposed to twist to such a degree that it actually *changes*. I couldn't imagine what it would take to rewrite a person's essential nature like that. If there was any kindness left in the world, I would never have to learn.

The world is so rarely kind. Sylvester drew the blade of my knife across his own thumb, making a cut identical to the one on his brother. The daffodils and dogwood scent of his magic rose, stronger than Simon's, which was—after all—still slumbering, unable to rise in his defense.

The true horror of elf-shot kept revealing itself, like

a terrible flower opening one petal at a time. Simon could no more defend himself against his brother than he could wake of his own accord. I'd known that, I'd always known that; the sleeping monarchs of Silences had been the proof, if I'd ever needed any. Yet physical damage can almost always be healed, in Faerie. Losing a leg is a tragedy and an inconvenience, but there are healers who can rejoin severed flesh, artisans who can craft replacements from enchanted wood, or stone, or living fire. There are *options*. Magic, though . . .

Sylvester could bind Simon's magic into his bones, and it might take him a hundred years or more before he could find someone capable of unweaving his brother's workings. He could turn Simon to stone and leave him there, to wake one day in the dark and the cold, frozen, awake but still captive, forever.

I reached out before I could think better of it, grabbing Sylvester's arm. He turned to look at me.

"Don't . . . don't hurt him," I said. "Please. I need him to help me."

"He will," said Sylvester, and there was no warmth in his tone.

"I want him to help me *willingly*." I'd been the person forced to embark on someone else's quest before: I hadn't enjoyed it. Maybe I wasn't ready to forgive Simon; maybe I still wanted him to pay for what he'd done to me. I hadn't figured out my own feelings quite yet. None of that meant I wanted to drag him, unwilling and fighting me, into my problems.

Sylvester was still for several seconds before he sighed heavily and said, "I will bind him only enough to keep him from hurting you."

"Quentin—"

"Is not family. I am sorry, but I can protect only one of you in this specific fashion."

"I'll be fine," said Quentin.

Sylvester continued to look at me gravely. "Trust me?" he asked.

"I do," I whispered, and took a step back, letting him go.

He nodded once, accepting my implicit permission to continue, and turned back to his brother. Leaning forward, he pressed his cut thumb against Simon's. The smell of daffodils and dogwood flowers was suddenly everywhere, filling the air until it should have become cloying. Somehow, it wasn't. Somehow, it was exactly right.

"Simon Torquill, I bind you," said Sylvester. Each word was a brick slotting into a wall, building it high and strong against the world. "By my blood and my bones, I bind you."

I clapped a hand over my mouth. I had heard those words before. Not spoken by him, no: spoken by Evening Winterrose, when she cursed me to find the person who'd attacked her—supposedly killing her—or die trying. It was a traditional form. It only made sense that the mother of the Daoine Sidhe would have taught it to her children, who would have taught it to their children, all the way down to Sylvester. But oh, it hurt to hear.

"By the root and the branch, the rose and the tree, I bind you," he continued, not seeming to notice my dismay. "By our mother, by our father, by the name we share, I bind you. For the crimes you have committed against me, you owe restitution, and this is what I ask of you. Raise no hand against Sir October Daye, daughter of Amandine. Break no blade and cast no spells against her, lest your tongue be stilled and your hands be silenced. Harm her not, or know no peace. By all that I am and all that you are and all the mercies of our missing Lord and Ladies, I bind you, brother. May Oberon have mercy, for I will not."

The spell gathered tight in the air above Simon, filling the air so completely that for a moment, I couldn't breathe. It was almost visible, a haze of white and pale gold, like the flowers that comprised it. The spell twisted, growing thinner and thinner, until it was a thread, before wrapping itself tightly around Simon's body.

This was what a geas looked like when it was cast. This was how a person was bound. I gasped again, this time dropping my hand.

Sylvester straightened, pulling his thumb from his brother's. Both wounds had healed. Somehow, that wasn't a surprise.

The door opened.

I turned to watch as Etienne stepped into the room, with Raj close behind him.

"The Prince of Dreaming Cats," Etienne said, formal to the last.

Raj looked like he had regressed years, becoming the twitchy, arrogant child he'd been when we met. Like May, he flinched from every sound. Unlike her, he glared at the world, daring it to challenge his authority, wrapped in his own self-importance like a veil. With Tybalt missing, he was in charge of the Court of Dreaming Cats, at least until someone came along and challenged him. He wasn't a King yet. Their succession didn't work that way. But if someone else figured out that San Francisco's cats no longer had a King, he might have to take the crown, and all our careful plans would be disrupted. So would his life. And none of that accounted for the fact that Tybalt was all the family he had left. If he died . . .

Tybalt wasn't going to die. Neither of them was going to die. We were going to get them back, no matter what it took. No matter what I had to do to accomplish it. We were *going* to get them back.

"Hey," I said. "Did you get the stuff?"

Raj pulled a glass vial out of his pocket, holding it up for inspection. The liquid inside was pink, purple, and gold, like something a small child would think looked delicious.

"Good," I said. "Bring it here."

"You don't get to give me orders," he said, but he brought the bottle anyway, dropping it into my outstretched hand with a quick, sidelong glance at my face, like he was looking for my approval.

He already had it. I allowed myself the flash of a smile, holding it just long enough for him to see, and said, "Yeah, but I'm so good at it." I looked around the room. There was no one here who was wholly unfamiliar to Simon. More importantly, there was no one here that he would see instantly as an enemy, except for maybe his brother—and he had to know that if his brother was there when he woke up, he was probably going to live. Sylvester could hate him. He couldn't kill him, or watch while someone else did it. He wasn't that kind of hero.

"Do you want me to do it?" asked Sylvester.

"It should be me; I'm the one who's forcing you to let this happen," I said, and turned to Simon, crouching down enough to put myself on a level with his prone form. He looked so much less dangerous like this, when he was unconscious and not in a position to ruin anybody's day. And I was about to wake him up.

A hand landed on my shoulder. I glanced back. Sylvester was standing there, ready to defend me.

That helped. Gingerly, I raised the bottle to Simon's lips and tipped it until the liquid trickled into his mouth. He swallowed, an automatic reflex not normally found in elf-shot victims. That was the magic in Walther's work, already starting to reactivate the body.

I pulled the bottle away, stood, and waited. Not for long. By the time I had counted silently to ten, Simon's breath had quickened, moving from enchanted sleep onto the borders of wakefulness. I counted five more, and he twitched, his previously injured hand opening and closing.

He opened his eyes.

Silence reigned for several more seconds before Simon said, in a perplexed tone, "Is this the old knowe?

Root and branch, it looks like it's going to collapse at any moment."

No one answered him.

He pushed himself into a sitting position, moving easily, without any visible aftereffects from his enchanted nap. He was still looking at the ceiling, maybe because he didn't want to see who else was in the room. I couldn't blame him for that. He had to be half-wondering whether he was experiencing his last moments of freedom for another hundred years, before Sylvester had him seized and thrown into the nearest available dungeon.

"I think it is," he said. "I remember doing the joins in that ceiling. Terrible work. I was never meant to be a carpenter. Anyone who said I was, well, they were lying. Hello—" He finally looked down, and his voice caught, hitching before he finished, barely above a whisper, "—brother. And October. October, what are you doing here?"

"Simon," said Sylvester, and his voice was ice, his voice was a killing frost sweeping across the land. There was no love there. Listening to him, it seemed impossible that love could ever live there again. "Look at me."

Simon went still, the brief animation draining from his face. He shifted until he was fully facing his brother, shutting me out. "Hello, Sylvester," he said.

I flinched. Simon was a chameleon, in many ways. He was a man who had traded his freedom to his Firstborn for the chance to bring his daughter home, who had done things so terrible that they'd twisted and tainted the smell of his magic. But he was also the man who had loved my mother, who had loved his daughter, and who had tried, in his own misguided way, to save me from Evening. His methods were terrible. His intentions were, in their own way, pure. How did he contain that many contradictions without breaking himself?

By becoming someone else. The Simon Torquill who had taken an arrow to save me, even knowing that it would put him to sleep for a hundred years, at least remembered what it was to care. But the Simon who had turned me into a fish and left me was someone else, someone colder, who didn't care about anything but himself.

It was the second Simon who was speaking now. He wasn't going to beg for forgiveness or explain himself. If he was about to die, he was going to die with dignity, and if he had any regrets, he wasn't going to share them with the likes of us.

"Your century is not up," said Sylvester. "If it had been my decision, you would still be sleeping, and I would be hoping every hour of every night you lived was filled with the foulest of dreams."

"My only nightmare in this moment is the quality of the mattress you saw fit to place me on," said Simon. "Really, brother, have you never heard of lumbar support?"

"Kinda surprised you have," I said.

Simon glanced my way, his icy demeanor cracking for an instant. Once again, I was struck by how similar the brothers were, and how different. He looked at me the way Sylvester did, like I was something he needed to nurture and protect. But while Sylvester's protection had always been built on a foundation of love, Simon's looked like it was built on regret. Odds were good that not all of it was for me. Whatever his motives, he had been a very bad man for a very long time.

"Literacy in the ways of mortals has been important this past century," he said. "Things change so quickly where the humans are concerned that sometimes even they get lost. Unless I wanted to start disguising myself as one of their elders, I needed to maintain my understanding of current trends."

"In lumbar support," I said blandly.

Simon shrugged. "It was a factor."

"Your vanity will be the end of you yet," snapped Sylvester.

"No, brother." Simon turned back to him. "If I make myself over to look like an eighty-year-old human man, and am forced to flee, to run, to do something physically beyond the reach of what I appear to be, what then? Vanity would be making myself the most beautiful of men. Sanity is preventing myself from betraying that I am something more than I appear by maintaining all aspects of a good disguise. Why am I awake?"

"Because Oberon has no mercy," said Sylvester.

A hand grabbed my arm and yanked. I glanced to the side. Raj was standing there, eyes narrowed, looking like he was about to start biting people. It would have hurt, too. He was currently sporting the kind of dentition a tiger would envy, and when he spoke, it was with a faint lisp, words distorted by the size of his teeth.

"Make them stop talking and start finding," he snarled. "My uncle is *missing*."

"I am the last person in the world who is going to forget that, believe me," I said, voice low. "I'm letting Simon get his bearings back. If we rush this, he might refuse to help."

"Excuse me?" The voice was Simon's. I turned. He was looking at me, a small frown on his face. "I'm right here. I can hear you both, and as my brother seems intent on being the least pleasant conversationalist in the room—and that includes you, Sir Etienne, don't think I can't see the way you're looking at me, like you'd enjoy nothing more than the chance to crop my ears—I'm inclined to listen. What's going on?"

"I was thinking more of gelding you," muttered Etienne.

I took a deep breath, ignoring him. Ignoring everyone except for Simon, because he was the one I needed to convince. "Mom came to see me," I said.

Simon's eyes lit up. "Amandine is here? *My* Amandine?"

He sounded . . . younger, or less tarnished, at least,

when he said my mother's name. There was a light in his eyes that I'd only seen in memories of him, like he suddenly believed the world was a kinder place.

"No," I said, and watched that light go out again. "She didn't come to Shadowed Hills: she came to my house. You remember, the house where you attacked my friend?"

Simon grimaced, looking abashed. "I am sorry about that. I needed to make my exit without being delayed, and I knew you would be able to care for her. Is she well?"

"Care for her *how*, by putting her in a bucket?" demanded May, shoving her way forward. I remembered belatedly that the memories she'd taken from me when she was "born" included my transformation—our transformation, since we both remembered it like we were there—and abandonment. What Simon had tried to do to Jazz was even more personal for May than it was for me. "You tried to turn her into a fish, you sick asshole!"

"It's a spell I've woven enough times that I don't have to prepare it," he said, not flinching away from May's rage. Maybe he wasn't afraid of her. Or maybe he thought he'd earned it. "I said I was sorry."

"Sorry isn't good enough," she said, and burst into tears.

Oh, this was going well. I put my arm around her, pulling her against me, and said, "Simon, Mom has asked me to find August, and she's taken our loved ones as collateral against her request. Please, will you help me?"

Simon sighed heavily. "I can't tell you how long I've been waiting for this," he said.

SEVEN

FOR A MOMENT, EVERYONE froze. It felt like the room was holding its breath. Just as quickly, the moment passed, and I had my hands full keeping May from lunging for Simon's throat, while Quentin fought a similar battle with Raj. If the Prince of Cats transformed into his feline form, he could escape my squire, but he seemed to be too angry to think of that: he twisted and spat, held back by a solid arm-lock and Quentin's greater mass.

Simon put a hand over his eyes. "Oh, sweet Titania. I apologize. I was *not* intending to say it was time for Amy to kidnap your friends. I can see why you would take insult at the insinuation."

"If you'd ever learned to watch your words, you would spend less time apologizing," said Sylvester.

"If you had ever learned to say anything of relevance, you would spend less time swinging a sword at people like it was a substitute for intelligent conversation," said Simon. It sounded automatic, almost, like he'd been insulting his brother for so long that he no longer knew how not to.

"Can everyone please stop taking swings at each other for a second, and *listen* to me?" I demanded. May wasn't fighting anymore. I let her go, trusting her not to lunge at Simon. "Amandine has taken the local King of Cats and a representative of the local Raven-may flock captive. She's forced them to transform into their animal forms, and she's said she won't give them back until I find August and bring her home. I need help. I need someone who knows August. I need you."

Simon actually looked surprised. "That's why you woke me—because you want me to help you? After everything I've done? What's to stop me knocking you out and running away?"

"Try it," suggested Sylvester, almost sweetly.

"Ah," said Simon. "You've laid a geas on me. Clever thinking, brother, although I didn't think you knew how."

"I had the same training you did."

"In the beginning, yes, but you never focused on your magic. Too busy playing knight in shining armor. What are my limitations?"

"You cannot raise a hand against October, nor a blade, nor your magic," said Sylvester. "If you try—"

"I get the picture," said Simon. "Why only her?"

"The family connection," said Sylvester stiffly.

"And your blood magic has never been what it should have been, because you refuse to practice," said Simon. "Why not bind me to help her?"

"Because I wanted you to come willingly," I said. "August is your daughter. I thought you'd want her back."

Simon went still, all the false arrogance draining from his face, leaving only a sad, lonely man behind. "Want her back?" he asked. "Everything I've done has been in the name of getting her back. Every line I've crossed, every crime I've committed, every atrocity I have allowed to unfold, has been in the name of bringing my August home. Don't question, even for a second, how much I want her brought back to me."

"So you'll help me," I said.

"I have conditions," Simon replied.

Raj hissed. Quentin tightened his grip.

"I'm not sure you're in a position to set conditions," I said.

"Perhaps not, and yet here I am, setting them," said Simon.

I clenched my teeth until my jaw ached. He was right. Damn his eyes, but he was right. Sylvester hadn't compelled Simon to help me, because I had asked him not to. I wanted Simon to come willingly, to give me the kind of help that only happened when it was unforced.

He had a better self in there. He had to. I wanted him to find it again.

"What do you want?" demanded Sylvester.

Simon smiled. "First, I stay awake. I'm not going on some mad quest with your darling protégé only to return here and be put back to bed for a century. I don't know how you woke me early, and I don't entirely care, so long as you understand that when the first of you comes near me with an arrow, I'll stop playing nicely."

"Done," said Sylvester.

"Your lovely lady wife no doubt wants my head on a platter, and while I can't say I blame her, I need my head where it is, especially if we're bringing my daughter home. August will want her father close at hand to help her adjust to the way the world has changed. So that, then, is my second demand: that you not allow the lovely Luna to seek revenge against me."

"You, who have never once been able to control your wife's actions, would tell me to control mine?" Sylvester asked.

Simon shrugged. "A demand's a demand."

"I promise to try."

"Swear it. On our sister's name."

Sylvester narrowed his eyes. "In September's name, I swear."

"That will be good enough for me. I trust the mercy of our courts much more than I ever could have trusted hers." Simon turned to me. "My third demand is simpler than it seems. If I am going to help you—if we are going to undertake a ludicrous quest for the most precious of prizes—you must try to forgive me. I did what I did in the name of saving you, however it may have looked at the time, and your bad opinion of me smarts. I won't ask you to promise that you will. I try never to deal in the impossible when there's another choice. But I will ask you to try."

"I will," I said.

"Then we have an accord." Simon slid off the bed, to his feet. May flinched. He looked at her and sighed. "The Fetch. You are lovely, lady, and I am grateful for your existence."

May frowned, wary and confused. "Why is that?"

"Because on the day Oleander came to me and told me Amandine had got herself a changeling girl to ease the sting of what we'd lost, I knew that one day, that girl would cease to be. Changelings always do, and a changeling of Amy's descent, well. For such a child, the Choice would be a real one. But you wear the face October was born to, and you wear it with undying grace, that one changeling in all of Faerie should not be forgotten."

May stared at him. I stared at him. Sylvester rolled his eyes.

"Your silver tongue does you no favors here," he said.

"My tongue is golden, as befits a man of my standing," said Simon. He turned his attention to me. "I am at your service, Sir Daye, and I hope that by the time we find what we seek, I will have earned that forgiveness from your lips."

"I don't even know where to start," I said.

"Then, if I may be so bold as to offer suggestions, start by assessing your resources," said Simon.

"Whatever you need is yours," said Sylvester.

"I know. I know. I just . . . hang on." I took a deep breath, pinching the bridge of my nose. Too often, I rush into things half-cocked, not planning for what I might face along the way. In my defense, that's usually because everything falls apart so fast that I don't have a choice. When the ground is crumbling beneath your feet, you don't look for the right path. You just jump and hope you land safely.

Finally, I lowered my hand and said, "I have Simon. He knows where August was seen last. He knows her magic. I have Quentin. He can watch my back in case Simon finds a way around the binding, and I can watch his, since the binding doesn't cover him at all."

"You have me," said Raj.

"No, I don't," I said.

He stared at me, eyes wide and pupils narrow, until they were almost lost in the glass-green depths of his eyes. "What?"

"Raj, you're the Prince of Cats, and your uncle is missing," I said. "If someone attacked the Court right now, there wouldn't be anyone there to defend it. Honestly, I shouldn't have let you come here. Your people need you."

"But . . ."

"When I agreed to marry your uncle, we both knew there'd be times when his position would come between us. Times when he had to put the needs of the Court of Cats before me. It hurt. It still hurts. Right now, it feels like it's killing me." All that time we could have spent together, and hadn't, because he'd had a duty to uphold. I had my own life, my own job to do, but suddenly it all seemed like such a waste. "While he's gone, the Court of Cats needs you."

Raj's shoulders drooped. "I don't want to," he said.

"I know."

"Bring him home." He darted forward, flinging his arms around my waist for one heart-rending moment. Then he tore himself away and ran for the door, shifting into feline form as he went. He was faster on four legs. He would reach the edge of the wards and disappear, heading back into the shadows, back to the Court of Cats.

I let out a shuddering breath. "All right," I said. "All right. We should—"

"If I may," interjected Simon. "As this seems to be the time when you set the members of our party, I recommend your fair Fetch remain here." He nodded toward May.

She recoiled. "What?" she demanded. "No! Why? No!"

"There are spells that can be woven—spells I can weave, and you can trust, so long as my brother's binding limits the damage I can do—to let blood call to blood."

May and I blinked in unison. I was the first to speak. "Okay, first, I'm not sure what that means, and second, if blood can call to blood, why can't you use that to find August? We could all go home and actually get some sleep."

"I've been sleeping for some time," said Simon.

"Not long enough," muttered Sylvester. Louder, he said, "We tried blood charms to bring August home. Wherever she is, she's outside their reach, or something is blocking them. My brother is proposing using your Fetch as an anchor. Your blood calls to hers, no matter how far apart you are, and if we make that calling . . . louder . . . she will be able to know more of where you are. She would know immediately if you were in danger, and we could send aid."

"Why not just, I don't know, take aid with her in the first place?" asked May.

"There are many reasons, but the simplest is that a smaller force moves faster," said Simon. "Send a hundred knights and all you'll do is slow us down. But that doesn't mean I'm refusing to be sensible. Anchoring her to you, and leaving you here with my brother to serve as an early warning system, only makes sense."

May looked at me, silently pleading for me to disagree. And I wanted to—sweet Maeve, I wanted to. May had as much right to bring her lover home as I had to go racing after mine.

At the same time, May's combat experience was all borrowed from my memories, and while she had knowledge, she lacked muscle memory. She couldn't drive—not well, anyway—couldn't sharpen a knife, couldn't do anything that required her to have actually *done* the things she remembered doing. All my sword training had come after her creation. She didn't have any of it. She was indestructible, but she healed as slowly as I had before my blood was shifted.

"I need you here," I said, and my words were a betrayal: I could see it in her eyes.

"Okay," she whispered. "But you bring them home. You bring them *both* home. If I find out you saved Tybalt over Jazz—"

"I won't," I said. "You know I won't."

"But I won't be there," she said, and burst into tears.

I put my arms around her. She buried her head against my shoulder, weeping loudly. Looking over her head to Simon, I asked, "Is this really necessary? Can't she come?"

"We are going to travel to places that are not safe," he said. "There's no one else to serve as anchor to your blood."

"Sylvester can serve as anchor to yours, can't he?" I felt May stiffen in my arms, waiting for his response. This could be the solution: a way for May to come with us while still having an early warning system on the ground at Shadowed Hills.

"Yes, and you could slit my throat in a fit of pique," said Simon. "It's safer if we're both anchored."

"I don't care. She needs to be there." May was a liability in every sense imaginable, except for the one that counted: she loved Jazz more than she loved anyone

else in the world. If I had been left behind while someone else went to rescue Tybalt, it would have devas-
tated me.

May pulled away, sniffling. "No," she said, voice
thick with tears. "He's right. I can't help. I can't fight, I
can't pick locks, all I can do is get between you and anyone who wants to stab you, and you don't really care if
you get stabbed."

"I'm getting used to it," I said dryly.

She laughed, voice unsteady. "See? You'll be all right.
Let me be the anchor, so we can find you if things get
bad. Can I do that?"

"You can." I leaned in and kissed her forehead,
murmuring, "I *will* find them," before turning back to
Simon. "All right. Do what you need to do."

"Fortunately, I do not need to enchant you directly;
my brother's binding recoils at the very thought," said
Simon. He took a step forward, holding out his hands.
"If my brother and the Lady Fetch would be so kind?"

Sylvester narrowed his eyes before sliding his hand
into Simon's. After a pause for breath, May did the
same with Simon's other hand. Simon smiled. It was not
a kind smile. It wasn't a cruel one, either. He looked
sad, almost, like he understood the enormity of what
they were both doing, and regretted that they couldn't
trust him more.

"We begin," he said, and started chanting in a language I vaguely recognized as Irish Gaelic. The smell
of candle smoke and rotten oranges swirled through
the room, underscored by Sylvester's daffodils and
dogwood and May's cotton candy and ashes. Simon
kept chanting. The air thickened, growing heavy—and
then the spell burst, sending the unmingled perfumes
skittering into the corners.

Simon stopped chanting and dropped their hands.

"It's done," he said. "If harm comes to either one of
us, you'll know it. You'll know where we are. It's down

to you to find a way to reach us, if we are beyond this realm."

"I'll find a way," said Sylvester.

Simon looked at his brother, and this time there was no disguising the sorrow in his expression. He looked like a man who had never been able to count on the ground beneath his feet, but who had set his own anchors against that instability, only to have them all crumble in the first stiff wind.

"I wish you had been able to say the same when it came to saving me," he said softly. He turned away before Sylvester could reply, focusing on me. "Well, Sir Daye? Are you ready to save my daughter?"

"I'm ready to save Tybalt and Jazz," I said. "Everything else is secondary."

Simon grimaced. "I can understand why you would feel that way, but I'll need you to rein in your tongue, at least until we've finished with our first stop."

"Why?" I asked warily. I already had some idea of what he was likely to say. I was hoping to be wrong.

"We'll be starting at your mother's tower."

"Oh, right," I said. "Of course." Well. Crap.

EIGHT

AMANDINE'S TOWER ISN'T A knowe: it isn't anchored to the human world, and there's no mortal way to get there. It's a freestanding structure in the Summerlands, built of fae stone under a fae sky. The most mortal thing ever to exist there was me, and I fled as soon as I could, choosing the streets of San Francisco over a place that seemed determined to erase everything I knew to be true about who I was and who I was meant to be.

So not the most warm and fuzzy of childhood homes, is what I'm saying here. Walking back to it in the company of a man who had been my personal bogeyman for years didn't particularly help. Worst of all, Simon *chattered*.

"I remember when this forest was all acorns and pinecones and other such rubbish," he said grandly, indicating the trees around us. The fact that none of the trees were oaks or evergreens didn't stop his cheerful misidentification of the seeds they'd sprouted from. "Sylvester was absolutely determined to have some sort of demarcation between his land and my lady's. As if the fact that it was always high summer in Shadowed Hills, with the roses growing rampant, wasn't enough? Luna refused to entertain the idea of any other season in those days."

"What season was it at the tower?" I was ashamed of how eager I sounded for the answer. Amandine had done something terrible to me. We were here because of what she'd done. And yet, she was still my mother, and part of me yearned to know more about her, who she'd been before she had me, who she'd been when she was happy.

"Spring, usually, but my Amy has always been mercurial. Sometimes it would change overnight, from spring to the depths of winter, and we'd all put on our coats and grit our teeth against the chill." He smiled fondly, distantly, like he was looking at a memory. "August preferred the fall. Amy used to say it was a consequence of her name. I think our girl enjoyed how calm it was. The growing time was over, and the gathering time was just beginning. For her, it was a chance to breathe."

"Why are we starting at Amandine's tower?" asked Quentin. "That's the one place we know absolutely for sure that August *isn't*."

"Because that's also the one place we know absolutely for sure that August *was*," said Simon. "The walls will remember her. We can start to follow her trail from there."

"You looked for years without finding her, and you were starting from the tower." Quentin was making no effort to hide his distrust. That was actually sort of soothing. No matter what happened here, he had my back.

It was difficult to believe that less than six hours ago, I'd been laughing and happy, and feeling like the world was finally starting to go my way. That would show me not to relax. It was just an invitation for life to kick me in the teeth as hard as it could.

"I was starting from the tower, but I didn't have October to help me." Simon shook his head. "I was in a rare position for a long time: a man, married to one of the Firstborn, raising the first known daughter of her descendant race. Everything August did was a surprise and a revelation. Amandine's magic was similar, of course—the First are always similar to the fruit their branches will bear—but it wasn't exactly the same."

"What do you mean?" asked Quentin.

"I mean that you are not just a watered-down copy of your parent and original. How could you be? The Dryad and the Blodynbryd descend from the same woman, and neither has wings. I've always wondered how the Mother of the Trees felt about that. For her children to not only be anchored to the earth, but bound to it, *rooted* to it . . . it was either a punishment or a reward, that they couldn't be blown away by the wind."

"I never thought about it that way," I admitted. Acacia—the Mother of the Trees, and Luna's mother—has skin the color of flower pollen, and moth's wings growing from her shoulder blades. She's magnificent, but she doesn't look anything like her children.

Amandine and Evening, on the other hand, look so much like their respective descendant races, and so much like each other, that they'd both been able to pass themselves off as Daoine Sidhe for decades, maybe longer.

"Wait," I said. "How many people actually *knew* Mom was Firstborn?"

"Some," said Simon. "I knew before I married her, as did Sylvester. Our parents told us when Amy was sent into Fosterage with our household. It was our job to help her pass for one of the Daoine Sidhe—we were her protective coloration. We moved as a mob of four, she, my brother, my sister, and I, and we seemed enough alike that when she couldn't quite perform a trick as one of us would, we could cover for her. It was made very clear to us that we needed to maintain her masquerade until it was safe to do otherwise."

"Who brought her to you?"

Simon shook his head. "That, I don't know. I was a child when she arrived. To be honest, I can't remember a time before Amy. She was always there, part of daily life, growing more beautiful with every passing night. It was inevitable that my brother and I should both fall in love with her—but that's not the story you want to hear right now."

"Not really," I said, feeling slightly sick to my stomach. The thought that my entire life, my entire world had hinged upon my mother choosing between twin brothers was ridiculous enough to be difficult to swallow. "You were talking about the differences between Mom's magic and mine."

"Yes," he said. "I'll admit, I'm not entirely sure your magic is a match for your sister's. You have different fathers, after all, and that could have changed things slightly. Not by enough to make you something other than Dóchas Sidhe, but enough for you to have different strengths. It's happened before."

"Faerie is weird, film at eleven," I said. "What could August do that Mom couldn't?"

"Magic has a scent," said Simon. "It's there for everyone. For most of us, though, it's a whisper, a secret, a sigh. We're better at picking up the magical scents of those we feel strongly about—family, lovers, close friends. For years, my best friend was a man who smelled of cranberries in bloom, but all Sylvester could say for sure about his magic was that it was some sort of small white flower. Magic *adapts*. For Amandine, the scents are secondary. She barely notices them. All her focus is on the bloodlines they identify. She could take one sniff of your squire and know how many generations removed he was from his First, where those generations branched, and how many of his ancestors had been Daoine Sidhe."

"Uh, all of them," said Quentin.

I said nothing. His mother, Maida, was born a changeling, the daughter of a human woman and a fae man. The mortality had been pulled out of her before she became High Queen; it had been long, long gone by the time Quentin was born. That didn't change the fact that he had a direct human ancestor. I could see the watermarks in Maida's blood when I looked at her closely. I could see their echoes in his.

"Maybe," said Simon, with surprising charity. "Some of us carry secrets even we don't know. A world where blood can be changed is a world where what's beneath the surface is unknowable by many of us. August could see who someone *was*, not what their blood wanted them to be. She could follow the trail of a spell for miles. Amy couldn't do that. Still can't, I suppose, or she would have gone after our daughter long since."

The forest was growing thinner. We stepped out of the trees, and the season shifted, melting from high summer into early spring. The meadow where we stood was an endless explosion of wildflowers, some familiar from my time in the mortal world, others bright and impossible and utterly fae. A patch of what looked like glowing poppies had attracted a swirling storm of moths, which danced above the light, not seeming to notice the predatory flock of pixies that was picking off the ones flying at the edge.

Simon grasped my arm and steered me around the glowing flowers. "There are a remarkable number of toxins native to the plants in this area. The pixies have no doubt taken advantage of them."

"Right," I said. I would heal quickly enough not to lose much time. Simon and Quentin wouldn't.

The shape of Amandine's tower appeared between one step and the next, rising white and pristine from the landscape. It looked almost organic, like it had grown rather than being built. I shivered. I couldn't help myself. I might have lived there once, when I was too young and too eager to please to know better, but it had never been my home, not really. It had never been *mine*. It was only recently that I had started to understand all the reasons my mother had held herself apart from me, refusing to love me more than she was absolutely required to. As long as there had been anything fae about me, I had been nothing more than a pale reflection of the daughter I had been intended to replace. She didn't want another August. She couldn't understand how a child who shared her eyes could be anything else.

Simon's hand touched my shoulder. I turned, startled, to find him looking at me with a surprising degree of understanding.

"Sometimes the places that should be home aren't," he said. "Sometimes there's no one we can blame for that, and so we blame ourselves, because aren't we the easiest targets? It's not like anyone will come to our defense when all the loathing and finger-pointing is happening in the privacy of our own minds."

"Aren't you supposed to be the bad guy here?" I asked.

Simon paused before taking his hand away. "My apologies," he said. "I forgot my place for a moment." He resumed walking, striding ahead toward the gate to Mom's garden.

I stood where I was for a few seconds longer, trying to reconcile everything I knew about the man with the urge to apologize for hurting his feelings. "This was easier when I was allowed to hate him," I finally muttered, and took off after him.

Quentin followed me, silent, wary. He'd had as much sleep as I had, which was to say, none, and the fact that he was still standing was a testament to how much he cared about protecting his family and standing by his knight. He wasn't going to drop until I did.

When the hell did I wind up needing to do right by so many people? What could I have possibly done to deserve them?

Simon didn't wait for us. He reached the garden gate, pushed it open, and stepped through, into Amandine's world of springtime snow. Every flower she grew there was white. White roses, white daffodils, sprays of Queen Anne's lace, and beds of snowdrops and white crocuses. There were even white violets, which seemed to defeat the purpose of having a flower named after a color. Some of the leaves and stems were green, but even they seemed less vibrant than the plants growing outside the garden walls.

We caught up with Simon at the center of the garden. He was crouched, sniffing a large, bell-shaped lily. Turning at the sound of our footsteps, he smiled, wry and sad and something else that I couldn't put a name to, and said, "My mother, Oberon rest and keep her, always said a lady's garden should be an ornament for the lady it contained. Amy grew everything white when we met, because she felt ashamed of how little color she had. She wanted to set herself against a blank canvas, so as to look like she existed."

It made a certain amount of sense, especially since she'd been raised among the Daoine Sidhe. They don't have a "look," the way the Tylwyth Teg or the Tuatha de Dannan do. Instead, they tend toward bright, dramatic coloration, like Simon's red hair and golden eyes, or Quentin's brilliant blue eyes and bronze hair, complete with a razor's edge of growing patina. I've met Daoine Sidhe with hair in every color the rainbow had to offer, and a few the rainbow would have rejected for being overly garish. Compared to all that, Amandine's palely golden hair and virtually colorless eyes would have made her stand out, and not in a good way.

Thinking about my mother—who had always seemed like the most beautiful woman in the world to me when I was a little girl, the person I could aspire to be, but never become—as feeling like an outsider was a bit surreal.

"After I married her, I convinced her to add some

color to her flowerbeds, for the accent it provided," Simon said, and straightened. "And when August joined us, she planted such flowers . . . oh, October, you should have seen it."

"I have," I said quietly. "In your memories, remember? When you let me ride your blood."

That wasn't all I'd seen. I had seen August herself, wearing a dress the color of corn husks and holding a white candle mottled in calico patches of black and gold, walking into a forest. I had seen those trees before. I couldn't remember where, but it would come to me; I was sure it would come to me.

"Oh, yes," said Simon, looking pleasantly surprised. "I had forgotten all about that. Come on, then." He started for the front door, steps light, stride almost casual.

It hurt to watch him. Not because he was supposed to be my enemy, and he was walking toward my childhood home: because he was a man whose entire family was gone, one way or another, and he was walking toward his own home, the one he had lost through a combination of bad luck and his own actions. Through his own failures. Based on what little I understood of what had happened after August disappeared, it wasn't so much that Amandine had objected to the methods he'd resorted to in trying to recover their daughter: it was that they hadn't worked.

Simon Torquill had been carefree once, the sort of man who would no more turn a person into a fish and walk away from them than he would go outside without his trousers on. Here, in the shadow of my mother's tower, the ghost of that man still lingered, and it made me ache for what he had become.

To my surprise, he didn't walk straight in, but raised his hand and knocked, waiting patiently on the steps as Quentin and I caught up with him.

"She hasn't been home in ages," I said.

"Perhaps not, but it's always better to start with an

excess of civility and then move toward breaking and entering, rather than attempting to go in the opposite direction," said Simon. "There's no one to apologize to if a knock goes unanswered. There's quite a lot of apologizing to do if, upon picking a lock, the owners of the place turn out to be having breakfast in the parlor."

"I know how to pick locks," said Quentin. "Toby taught me."

"Good," said Simon. "A boy your age should have useful skills, or else no one is ever going to think of you as anything more than a dilettante, and where's the fun in that?"

I groaned.

The door began to open.

I snapped to immediate attention, posture straight, chin up, fear and muscle memory propelling me into the posture of a scared teenager who knew her mother would never approve of her. Quentin's posture almost mirrored mine, although there was more formality in it; he'd learned from the best etiquette tutors his parents could find, rather than snatching knowledge from the shadows and spackling it as thick as he could over the rough edges of himself.

Then the door finished swinging wide and Amandine was there, still in her gown of white flowers, a frown on her pretty face. The only sign of her activities from earlier in the evening was a single red drop on one of the petals of her skirt. She must not have noticed the blood. I couldn't notice anything else. It was screaming for my attention, as blood always did.

Amandine's frown melted into a look of surprise. "Simon," she said. "What are you doing here? They told me you'd been elf-shot."

"They woke me up," he said, and smiled, open and earnest and bright as moonrise. "Hello, Amy. It's been a long time."

"Not nearly long enough," she said. "I said I didn't

want to see you until our daughter came home, and she's not with you. Just the other one, and her little pet."

Hearing my own mother call me "the other one" stung less than I would have expected. Maybe I was finally growing up. Or maybe the desire to punch her in her pretty nose was keeping me from feeling like I wanted her to be proud of me. "We're here because we're about to go looking for August," I said. "Remember, Mom? You hired me?"

"I remember that you refused me and forced my hand, and I remember that you're a devious, sneaky little thing. If I let you inside, you're likely to try freeing your other pets, and then where will I be? You won't help me willingly. I have to compel you."

"I'd work better if I weren't worried about them," I said. "You have my word that if you give them back now, I won't rest until I find out what happened to my older sister."

Her frown became a scowl. "She's no sister of yours," she snapped. "Simon had no part in making you, and I claim no responsibility for the blood you bear. August is my heir, and I shall have no other."

"I don't want anything that belongs to you," I said. "I just want Tybalt and Jazz back."

"Then you're a liar, dear daughter, because right now, they belong to me. You can't have things both ways. Either you want nothing of mine, or you want my most prized possession. Which is it?"

"How can they be your most prized possession when you just stole them from me?" I asked, too frustrated to mind my words. "You're the one who's trying to have things both ways."

"They're the pretty pets that bring my August back to me, as she should always have been," said Amandine. She smiled serenely. "There's no way out of the circle you're stuck in, October. I won't give them back. You won't give up wanting them. So find my daughter."

"That's what she's had me woken to help her do," said Simon, stepping in before I could start yelling. There was a soothing note in his voice, calm, like this was a perfectly reasonable conversation. "Amy, remember how I used to laugh and call August our little wolfhound, from the way she could follow a person's magic from one side of the tower to the other? I suspect October can do the same. May we enter?"

"October grew up here," said Amandine. "I think I would have noticed if she had wandered off one afternoon and returned with August."

I saw my opening. "Yes, but I was more human then," I said. "That was how you wanted me to be, remember? I could always detect magic, but it's only been recently that I've really been able to understand it. I can follow it a lot farther than I used to. Let me try."

She looked at me with open disgust. "Of course you would embrace the part of your heritage that left you sniffing at the corners like an animal. Fine. Do as you like. Only be aware that I am watching you, and you'll be punished if I think you're trying to trick me."

She turned on her heel then, stalking back inside, leaving the door open so we could follow. Quentin blinked.

"Your mom is sort of terrifying, and I don't think I like her very much," said Quentin, looking at me.

"Yeah, well, she stole my fiancé in order to blackmail me into doing my chores, so I don't like her very much either right now," I said, and stepped inside.

Now that I knew what I was looking for, I could see Simon scattered all through the décor of the tower, which hadn't changed since I was a child—or, I suspected, since the first time Amandine had walked away from it, fleeing out into the mortal world to escape the shadows which haunted this place. The floor was polished stone, smooth enough to be pleasant underfoot, rough enough not to become slippery when wet. There was a fireplace in one wall. It shared a flue with the other fireplaces in the tower, one to a floor, all their smoke combining to emerge from the same chimney. The furniture was simple but elegant, rustic and timeless, and chosen with a care that my mother had never shown when dealing with material possessions.

Simon stopped at the middle of the room, drinking it all in with hungry eyes. Amandine was gone. So were Tybalt and Jazz, if she had been keeping them here at all. I looked around, finally spotting a single black feather on the floor near the rear door. They had been here. She had taken them away.

"What room did she give you?" Simon asked, turning toward me.

"Fourth floor," I said.

"That makes sense," he said. When I raised an eyebrow, he explained, "We slept on the sixth, where she could watch the moonrise from our window. It soothed her. August's room was a floor below ours."

I blinked. "That's not possible."

"Why not?"

"Because the tower only has five floors."

Simon looked almost amused. "Ah. Because of course, one of the Firstborn, in her own home, would not be able to manipulate the architecture to her own ends."

I resisted the urge to groan. Of course Amandine could change the place around to suit herself. I had always known she had the capability: she had expanded my room at least once, when I was a child, and had outgrown my available space. I just hadn't expected her to erase an entire floor. Instead, I asked, "How are we supposed to get there?"

"Unless she's changed the place more than I expect she has, I know the way," said Simon, and started for the stairs with me and Quentin at his heels.

The stairs wound around the body of the tower in a gentle curve, never steep enough to become a strenuous climb. I kept looking around with new eyes, imagining this place full of life and laughter, occupied by a family, not a woman and the daughter she had never intended to save. It was hard. It hurt. That didn't matter, because I couldn't stop myself.

We climbed past my old bedroom, until we were halfway up the stairs leading to my mother's chambers. Simon stopped, crouching and studying something on the floor. He pointed.

"See that?" he asked.

I squinted. "No," I said.

"Yes," said Quentin, sounding faintly bemused. "What is it?"

"It's the edge of the fold Amy made when she sealed August's room away," said Simon. "It's no wonder you can't see it, October; this is an illusion, a powerful one, and the Dóchas Sidhe have nothing of Titania in them. You'll never be the illusionist your mother is, and only the fact that she was Firstborn allowed her to pass for Daoine Sidhe."

My illusions have never been my strong suit. There have been times when I had to lose my temper before I could even raise the magic necessary to cast a human disguise. It still rankled to hear him dismiss my capabilities so cavalierly.

"Look," he said, focusing on Quentin. "If you want to dispel this sort of illusion, it helps to have a tie to the person who cast it—in this case, Amy is my wife, and so I am familiar with the way she spins a spell. Every illusion is different. I could punch through the center of this one, but that would be difficult, and it might do me harm, as she can work quite a bit of power into a casting. So what I want to do is find the thread, and pull."

What he was saying made sense, especially when I compared it to the way I perceived other people's spells. I tilted my head, watching intently as Simon twisted his fingers through the air, finally hooking them over some invisible thread and beginning to pull. The smell of blood and roses, faint, like it had been bottled up and was only now being released, began to permeate the air. The stairs wavered, shimmering, before there was a distant shattering sound, and they seemed to extend, growing longer.

Simon sat back on his haunches, clearly winded. "Oh, she meant for that to last," he said, rubbing the back of his neck with one hand. "Best get up and move along, before she comes to ask why I've started breaking her things."

He didn't need to tell me twice. I started moving, pausing only long enough to offer him a hand and help him up. I wanted to see what was up this new flight of stairs, what my mother had hidden from me in my own home for my entire childhood. And I called myself a detective.

There was a new landing. At the new landing was a new door, closed but not locked, like the occupant of the room on the other side had expected to be back soon. I opened it, gingerly.

August's room was a mirror image of mine, and nothing like mine at all. Her furnishings were of the same school, all oak and ash and princess canopies, but they were visibly mended in some places, like they'd been used hard and repaired by an unpracticed hand. One wall was devoted to bookshelves, stretching from floor to ceiling, and there was a cartographer's desk under the window, with a half-finished map still weighted down at the center of it, waiting for August to come back and resume sketching the lines of its terrain. It didn't feel like a place that had been shut off for a century. It felt like it had been shut off for less than a day. Good. That meant Simon's plan just might work.

I moved to the center of the room, closed my eyes, and breathed in deep.

Everyone's magic is different, but everyone's magic takes something from their parents. I inherited the copper in my magic from Amandine, which I suppose is why the less mortal I become, the less it smells like metal, and the more it smells like blood. The cut-grass . . . I can only think that's my magic interpreting what I got from my father, because it didn't come from her. Quentin's magic was steel and heather, and his father smelled of heather and celandine poppies, while his mother smelled of fresh-cooled steel and dry hay. We carry our past in our veins, and we reflect it in our magic.

August's room smelled, at first, like any other lived-in bedroom: clean, but with a faint undertone of sweat, the smell of hot days and tangled sheets, of striving for sleep when it didn't want to come. That smell has been baked into the walls of every bedroom I've ever occupied, no matter how clean the house was, no matter how often we bleached the sheets or repainted the walls. It's the smell of being alive, and while it's normally a welcome one, I couldn't help but feel a little uneasy. We didn't know whether August was alive or dead. We wouldn't know for a long time yet . . . and if she was dead, I didn't know what Amandine was going to do.

Focus. I needed to focus. My own magic was trying to rise in response to my distress, and I damped it down again, refusing to let it complicate matters more than they already were. I needed to find old magic, not new.

Amandine was the first person I identified. Her magic was the strongest, as befit a Firstborn, and it was everywhere, touching and tracing every surface. She had spent so much of her time here, with the daughter she actually wanted, never dreaming that one day, a daughter she didn't know what to do with would sleep one floor below.

Simon came next—or rather, the Simon I'd seen in his own blood-memory came next, all mulled cider and sweet smoke, with no hint of taint or rot to complicate matters. I inhaled and tried to push past it, digging deeper, looking for the unfamiliar.

And then, between one heartbeat and the next, I found it. The scent of sweet campfire smoke, close enough to Simon's candle smoke to be a kissing cousin, but distinct enough that there was no question of whether it belonged to him. It was wrapped with a ribbon of rose. Not Amandine's wild, woody roses: something small, cultivated, sweet, the sort of rose that would grow in a princess' walled garden. August.

"Smoke and roses," I said, and opened my eyes. "She smelled like smoke and roses."

"Yes," breathed Simon. "Can you follow it?"

I looked at him and nodded. "Yes," I said. "I can."

NINE

WE DESCENDED THE TOWER steps with me in the lead, all my concentration focused on teasing out the often-thin, always-faded scent of August's magic. Only the fact that it had been so concentrated in her room had allowed me to find it at all, and if I lost it, I was going to need to start over from the beginning. Mom was nowhere to be seen. I was grateful for that. She was a distraction, and if there was anything I didn't need, it was to be distracted.

At the same time, if she'd been there, maybe I could have used the fact that I had the trail to convince her to return Jazz. One hostage was enough. Tybalt was better equipped to take care of himself. More importantly, he would understand why I had saved Jazz first. He would forgive me.

Maybe if I told myself that enough times, I would believe it, and stop being faintly grateful that I hadn't been forced to put the theory to the test. We walked to the tower door and out into the garden, which was a riot of perfumes that should have made my task even harder. Instead, having so many things that *weren't* the scent of August's magic narrowed my focus more and more, until the trail was the only thing that mattered, like a thin ribbon road stretching out to the horizon, shimmering, intangible, and *mine*.

We stepped through the gate and out of the garden. The trail divided, heading toward Shadowed Hills and heading away at the same time, and with equal strength. I frowned, pointing down the line of the second trail.

"Where was she going, Simon?" I asked.

He followed my finger before adopting a frown of his own. "There's not much in that direction. September and Malcolm discussed breaking ground there for a home of their own, but abandoned the idea when they decided to return to Londinium."

"September," I said. "Your sister."

"Yes." A shadow crossed his face. "She's long dead and gone now, and the rose has fallen from the tree."

There was real pain in his voice. I put the rest of my questions aside. September was a matter for later, if ever. Purebloods rarely want to talk about their dead. "If no one built there, what *is* there?"

"Well, there's a stretch of marshland, mostly. A flock of pixies lived there the last time I checked; they probably still do. That sort of terrain makes a perfect kingdom for the little things. I used to visit them sometimes with Patrick, after the pixie population from his workshop relocated, and—"

"Wait," I said. "Patrick?"

"Yes. Baron of Twycross, although he set that title aside when he married a mermaid. I believe he's Patrick Lorden now."

A memory flashed by, of Patrick standing in Arden's knowe, ordering Sylvester never to say Simon's name again: calling himself "more a brother to him than you ever tried to be." I'd been distracted with murders and a major political conclave at the time, but . . . "Patrick Lorden is your friend." It wasn't really a question, more a statement waiting to be confirmed.

Simon chuckled wryly. "He may not be anymore, given everything that's happened. But once, he was the dearest person to me in all the world, outside of my own family."

"Huh," I said thoughtfully. "So he knew August?"

"Yes."

"Would she have gone to see him, maybe, before she disappeared? Since we know she didn't go to Shadowed Hills." I was pretty sure Sylvester would have said something if she had. He knew better than to keep secrets from me these days, especially where *my* family was concerned. Simon was an uneasy ally and August was a stranger, but Tybalt was the one in danger, and Tybalt?

Tybalt was the cornerstone of my new family, the one I'd constructed for myself, and Sylvester had been working too hard at rebuilding the bridges between us to let them be broken again. Especially by Amandine. We had been over that ground, and I trusted him not to betray me there.

"Possible," said Simon, slowly. "She was never a gregarious child—or I suppose, if she had wanted to be, that she never had the opportunity. Amandine worried about her, you see. She kept her close to home, and August didn't seem to mind. She doted on her mother, and her mother doted on her."

If there had been time, I would have sat down and asked Simon to explain, exactly, what the dynamics of their little family had been. I was starting to draw a picture, and I wasn't sure I liked it. But there *wasn't* time. Every minute that passed was another minute where Tybalt and Jazz were at my mother's mercy. Both of them were purebloods, immortal unless something came along to kill them. That didn't matter. Having a lot of time didn't mean they deserved to have it stolen from them like that.

"This way, then," I said, and started following the second trail, the one that led away from Shadowed Hills and my mother's tower at the same time.

Quentin stuck close by my side, while Simon lagged behind, hands in his pockets, looking at the landscape with the grave, regretful eyes of a man who had seen too many things change to be truly comfortable anywhere.

The meadows surrounding the tower gradually gave way to forest. Not the tame, almost decorative forest that divided the tower from Shadowed Hills: this was a dark, overgrown, tangled thing, a forest that belonged in either a nightmare or a fairy tale. The trees—which had some aspects of oak and some of elm and some of nothing that had ever grown in the mortal world—rose around us like giants, their branches clawing at the sky, their trunks heavy with strange burls. Red shelf fungus dotted with white spiraled around the bodies of the trees, while glowing blue-and-white toadstools grew among their roots, filling the air with a strange, lambent light.

Bushes laden with berries I didn't recognize grew on all sides, clogging the underbrush. They smelled like candy and Christmas and all good things. I shuddered, sticking to the thin trail someone else had beaten through the wood.

Simon saw my discomfort and said, "It's not goblin fruit. Try as people might—and people have tried—goblin fruit refuses to grow wild in the Summerlands. The soil isn't right."

"The soil people use to grow the stuff has to be imported from deeper Faerie, doesn't it?" asked Quentin. "I always sort of wondered what kind of person found out that Oberon was about to lock the doors and went for buckets of dirt instead of something useful."

"Ah, but you see, the buckets of dirt *were* something useful. They still are." Simon's smile was fleeting. "I was born in fair Londinium, along with my siblings—our parents were among the first to feel that their children should be born to the Summerlands, close to the mortal world, where so much was *happening*. It's difficult to express how boring things could be in deeper Faerie, when the mortal world was not close at hand and providing points of interest. I've heard humans speak of 'the golden afternoon,' those days when the sunlight stretches out like taffy and the time seems to go on forever. Well. That sort of thing starts to feel less like a blessing and more like a curse when it's every day, for centuries without end."

"That doesn't explain the dirt," I said.

Simon actually laughed. "You see? I talk like what I am, because I expect to have forever to get to my point. The dirt, then. When Oberon said he was going away, and that we were all to move ourselves to the Summerlands, because he couldn't trust us unattended in the deeper lands . . . oh, it was an exodus the likes of which I can scarce describe. Worlds upon worlds, some large, some small, all pouring into the bounds of one small realm. Deeper Faerie is not all of a size. Some of the realms are more properly considered islets, islands where the local rules of engagement have been established to benefit one race of fae over another. Avalon held no more than five hundred hearts when it was turned inside out and wrung dry for the sake of Oberon's order, and it was one of the larger single holdings."

"So deep Faerie is more like a bunch of really big knowes?" asked Quentin.

"In a sense, yes. If you took all of my brother's land, not only the part which forms the knowe proper, but the gardens and the forest and every other scrap of it, and if you dropped it into empty space, out beyond anything, with only a thin channel of power to clasp the nearest anchor, it would become a seed, and from that seed would grow another realm, one large enough to house all those who dwelt there, slowly drawing power from them to fuel its own expansion. With no one living in them, the deeper realms can grow no greater."

"Will they die?" asked Quentin.

"No. But they may slumber. The dirt." Simon clapped

his hands, not seeming to notice how I flinched away. "There are crops which only grow in certain soil, things that various of our newly homeless citizens couldn't imagine doing without. The more entrepreneurial among them realized that with greenhouses and buckets, they could corner the market on those little tastes of home. People who carried dirt away from their abandoned lands are richer now than those who carried only gold and jewels."

"So what *are* the berries around here?" asked Quentin.

"Something that arose in the Summerlands. I doubt anyone has eaten many of them, save perhaps for the local pixies: they're as likely to be poisonous as they are to be delicious, and why should we take risks when we have so many of the fruits of home yet to enjoy?"

"Snob," I said, almost fondly, and Simon looked pleased.

The trees were getting shorter and twistier, becoming almost parodies of themselves, while the mushrooms and toadstools were becoming taller and broader, casting umbrella-shaped shadows over the land. The glow came from their gills, and as the size of those gills expanded, so did the intensity. The earthy smell of fungus pervaded everything, sometimes almost obscuring the scent of August's magic. I had to close my eyes a few times, trusting Quentin to guide me as I clung to the thread I was trying to follow.

Part of me was rebelling at the ridiculousness of the entire situation. I was following a magical trail over a century old, and I didn't have the training to know whether it was the *right* one. Maybe I was on my way to discover August's favorite mushroom-picking spot, and we should have been heading for Shadowed Hills after all. Or maybe there were a hundred trails like this one, a thousand, all leading somewhere different, a child's map of the land surrounding Amandine's tower. I had never really explored that much. My world had consisted of the tower and the woods between home and Shadowed Hills, where I had run night after night, looking for companionship, for warmth, for welcome. Amandine hadn't made a home for me, and so I hadn't felt like it was safe to use her as my compass.

It was hard not to be jealous of August. She had been the one to enjoy our mother's attention when Amandine was present and focused, not mourning for the child she'd lost and resenting the one she had. It felt weird, yearning for my mother's love when she was the reason I was hiking through a creepy toadstool forest instead of tucked safe home in my bed, but that's the thing about parents: they're never simple. They're never straightforward. And try as we might, we can never quite be free of the shadows they cast over us.

The ground was getting marshy, tugging at our shoes and slowing us down. I scowled. "Next time Mom decides to ruin my night, I hope she does it after I've had time to change my clothes."

"I wasn't going to say anything, but your footwear is quite unsuitable," said Simon.

I glared at him. It was almost a relief to have a person to glare at. Glaring at a situation is possible, but it's never as fulfilling as we want it to be. "These sandals were totally appropriate for a karaoke bachelorette party," I informed him.

Simon blinked. "I understood perhaps three words of that."

"Time marches on," I said airily. "I was at a party, these shoes were fine, then I was dealing with a home invasion and the abduction of my fiancé, and now these shoes are not fine. I don't want to be barefoot in the middle of the creepy mushroom forest, I'll deal." There was a time when I would have been worried about blisters and chafing. Thankfully, that time was past. Any blisters that tried to form would heal as quickly as they'd come, and I would keep on going.

"I can try to improve them, if you don't mind," said

Simon, with surprising delicacy. "You would need to remove them first, as I am forbidden to use my magic upon you, but I know a few tricks."

I eyed him. "You want to transform my clothes?"

"Yes."

"The old Queen used to do that to me all the time. Generally without my consent. Illusions weren't good enough for her."

Simon grimaced. "I won't make excuses for her. Her ascension came at the cost of a good man's life, and destroyed the lives of his children for far too long. I didn't know the full scope of the plan before it was too far along for me to change a single thing in how it unfolded."

"Wait," I said. "You were *there*. I mean, a lot of people were there, but you were—were you already with Oleander? Do you know?" Everyone said Oleander had been responsible for King Gilad's death. No one had ever been able to prove it.

"Shoes, please," said Simon. He held out his hand.

It was clear that I wasn't going to get any answers until I gave him my sandals. I sighed and bent to undo the buckles before stepping out of my shoes and handing them over. The soft earth squished between my toes. Quentin looked entirely too amused. That may have been the sleep deprivation. He normally had more sense than that.

"To answer your first question, no, I was not yet with the Lady de Merelands, although I had made her acquaintance a time or two. Enough that—and I say this not to boast, but with the resignation of hindsight—she desired me. She disliked your mother for reasons of her own. The thought of stealing and corrupting a Torquill boy from his lawful wife appealed to her. She was already in Eveni—in *her* employ. I've asked myself, more than once, whether what happened may have been triggered by Oleander asking her mistress for a puppy."

Simon's fingers moved as he spoke, plucking twigs

from the bracken, blades of grass from the base of nearby mushrooms: anything, in fact, save for the mushrooms themselves. He began to weave his pile of pilfered ingredients into a small wicker loop.

"And my second question?" I asked.

"Yes." Simon shook his head, not looking at me, still weaving. The smell of smoke and rotten oranges began to rise from his pores, tainting the air around him.

I took a step backward. He didn't seem to notice.

"King Gilad Windermere was a good man. I think that may be what people say about him the most. Not that he was a brilliant ruler, not that he was a kind king, but that he was a good man. Good men with crowns are difficult to find. The fae soul was not meant to have so much power over others without becoming harder, colder, less capable of charity. We have too much time to spend. It makes us miserly with it, in a way all out of proportion to its plenty. But he knew time was short. His parents had been assassinated when he was young, you see, and the throne thrust upon him. His prince-hood was a brief, cruel thing, not long and rich and palatial. He understood that things change. He understood that brief was not the same as nonexistent. So he encouraged the acceptance of changelings in his Court. He allowed mixed-bloods to inherit from their parents—before him, titles passed only along purified bloodlines. So far as he knew, the Mists possessed no hope chest, and my Amy refused to reveal herself solely for the sake of becoming someone else's tool, and so when love rose between fae of different worlds, their children were allowed to exist untampered with. My niece, January. You met her, I believe?"

"I did," I said quietly. It hadn't been a long acquaintanceship: Jan died shortly after we met. I hadn't been able to save her. Oh, I had tried, and sometimes it still ached to know that I had failed.

"There are places, even still, where the fact that her

mother was Daoine Sidhe and her father was Tylwyth Teg would have worked against her. Where she would have been expected to live as one thing or another, forsaking half her heritage." His fingers continued moving, tying smaller and smaller knots. "But it was her mixed blood that gave her the alchemy that enabled her to do the marvelous things she did. Tylwyth Teg are more resistant to iron than many of us. She used that to her advantage, and she was happy. She was always such a happy girl."

"She has a daughter," said Quentin, and watched Simon to see how he would react.

To my surprise and relief, Simon smiled. "I know. I hope I have the opportunity to meet her someday." He used his little loop of woodland rope to tie my sandals together. "Regardless, there were those who did not care for Gilad's egalitarian approach to the monarchy, and feared he was making those changes because he thought to take a wife who did not share his bloodline. The woman who would become my keeper, she already disliked having a Tuatha de Dannan family sitting upon such a prominent throne. All thrones, she felt, belonged to her."

"But the false Queen was a mixed-blood," I protested. "She had at least three different Firstborn."

"Yes. That was my keeper's little joke that no one else understood, perhaps because it wasn't funny. The imposter was the worst possible manifestation of certain peoples' fears: someone whose heritage was so mixed that she couldn't possibly bring stability to the land, whose magic was unpredictable, too weak and too strong at the same time. Someone they couldn't judge based on the slope of her ears."

"That sounds sort of racist," said Quentin.

"It is, and it isn't," said Simon. "Similar fears fuel it. But in the case of Faerie, the blending is not so much race, although we use the word, as it is species. Some of us are not meant to mingle." He waved his hand above my sandals, focusing the scent of his magic. Then he snapped his fingers.

The wicker rope expanded to cover my footwear, wrapping it tight before falling away to reveal a pair of black leather ankle boots, the sort that seemed designed to wade through lava without being scorched. Simon offered them to me with a flourish.

"This will do you better," he said.

"I hope so," I replied, dodging the forbidden "thank you" as I took them. They fit my feet perfectly. "These are great."

Simon beamed. In Faerie, praise is often a suitable replacement for gratitude. "The spell should hold, if you don't pick at it before it has a chance to settle."

"Swell." We started walking again. "Do you really think Oleander killed the king because she wanted your body?"

"No. She killed the king because she was ordered to. But the timing . . . it was an intricate thing, the timing. August announced that she was undertaking a quest, that she was going to find the doors to the deeper realms of Faerie and open them. That Oberon had always wanted us to find our own way home, and she seemed to know what she was talking about—she seemed to know a bit more than she should have. She had been speaking to someone. When I asked if I could help, she said no." Simon took a deep breath. "She said I wasn't a hero, and I wasn't Firstborn, and I couldn't help her."

"I saw her with a candle in your memory," I said. "Do you know why?"

"She was going somewhere," he said. "On the Babylon Road."

That was a road I had taken myself. I frowned. "Do you think maybe the woman you worked for told her where to go?" August could be a tree in Acacia's forest, enchanted to save her from Blind Michael. That would explain why she had never come home. Trees aren't all that migratory.

"Maybe," said Simon. "I'd rather not wake her up to ask."

I shuddered. Then I sneezed.

"What the . . . ?" I looked down. My foot was buried in the heart of a puffball mushroom, filling the air with glittery spores that swirled around us in a silver-and-blue cloud. I blinked. That didn't help. My vision seemed to get more blurry every time I closed my eyes, even if it was only for an instant.

I yawned. So did Quentin.

"Uh-oh," I said, and fell down.

The last thing I saw before I closed my eyes was a figure coming toward me through the glittering cloud. It was either very small or very far away, and it didn't really matter either way, because I was gone.

TEN

IWOKE IN A DARK ROOM. My hands were tied behind my back, my feet were weighed down by some heavy, enveloping substance, and a sugary-tasting gag had been stuffed into my mouth, blocking off both speech and a distressing amount of my air. I bit down, and the gag yielded, releasing more sugar into my mouth. Suddenly, breathing was an exciting race to see whether I could chew faster than I choked.

The worst part was, this wasn't the strangest wake-up call I'd ever had.

I was swallowing my third mouthful of the gag when the part of my mind that was constantly cataloging and storing away the labels for magical scents finally decided to come to the party, and informed me that I was chewing on a violet. That made sense, as far as flavor went, while simultaneously making no sense at all. The gag was exactly that—a gag, a single strip of material pulled tight around my head. It wasn't a mash of pressed flowers, or anything ridiculous like that. Although I supposed it *could* be the petal from a gigantic violet, turned to a unique and somewhat antisocial application.

There was another option there, one that probably made a little bit more sense, but I didn't want to think about it until I had myself unstuck. All it would do was upset me. That was bad no matter what I was currently chewing on; I needed to keep my wits where they were.

One nice thing about getting knocked out: it substitutes pretty well for sleep a lot of the time. I felt more alert than I had in a while. Eating my gag, bizarre as that sounds, was also helping. My blood sugar had not been in a good place.

I took a last hard bite, swallowed a last sugary mouthful, and felt the gag drop away. Good: that was step one. I still couldn't see anything, which was unusual. Fae have excellent night vision. We're like cats, able to see in the slightest trace of light. For it to be this dark, there had to be no light at all—that, or something had been done to my eyes. The thought caused a brief spike of panic, until I blinked several times and confirmed that I could still *feel* my eyes. No one had removed them or sealed my eyelids shut.

It says something about my life that this was a concern.

If my gag had been edible and organic, maybe whoever tied me up had made the same mistake with whatever was tying my wrists. I twisted them inward as much as my bones allowed, until I could get the nails of my right hand against the bonds. Holding that position ached but didn't actually hurt, which was a pleasant surprise. Gritting my teeth against the strain, I began digging my nails into the "rope." It definitely *wasn't* rope. It tore like an organic thing, yielding under my hand until I began to feel like this was some sort of perverse joke. Maybe whoever it was who had tied me up didn't have much experience, or maybe they hadn't actually been intending to hold me; maybe they just wanted to slow me down.

The world narrowed to my nails against the vines— I was almost sure they were vines—and the sticky green smell of sap that rose from them. *Sweet pea*, murmured the cataloging part of my mind, not as an endearment, but as an identification. Someone had gagged me with a violet and tied me up with sweet pea runners. This day just kept getting stranger and stranger.

When the last vine broke, I pulled my hands from behind my back, massaging my wrists for a second before bending and feeling for whatever was covering my feet. To my dismay, if not surprise, my questing hands encountered what felt like the largest glob of hardening pine resin in the world. It hadn't reached the "hard enough to shatter when you hit it with a hammer" stage yet, but it was well on its way. Swell.

Pine resin is sticky, viscous, and greedy, if such a thing can be said about an inanimate substance: what it catches, it likes to keep. Still, it's a liquid until it hardens, and it's possible to pull things free, if you move slowly and don't yank. Yanking is bad. Yanking increases the resistance of the stuff, and increased resistance means increased hardness. I would recover if I broke half the bones in my foot, but it would hurt, and it would slow me down. Better a little slowness now than a lot of slowness later.

Carefully, I began to pull my knees to my chest, tugging against the sap. It tugged back, but as it wasn't alive, and didn't know what I was doing, it couldn't fight as effectively as I could. It was like challenging a sleeping giant to a slow-motion wrestling match—and honestly, I would have been a lot more comfortable with an *actual* sleeping giant. At least then I could have screamed until it woke up and turned things into a more standard sort of fight. As it was, I had to keep pulling steadily but constantly, never varying the amount of pressure I was putting on, until finally my left foot came free, quickly followed by the right.

Both my feet were covered in a thin layer of pine resin, all the way up to the middle of my calves. I scraped as much of it off as I could before standing.

My head hit the ceiling.

"Oof," I said, without much vigor. The ceiling, low as it was, was also soft and spongy, like it was made of foam rather than wood or stone. I reached up with sap-sticky fingers and pushed against it. It yielded. A faint, earthy smell pervaded the room. I closed my eyes for a moment, out of sheer frustration. It wasn't like having them open changed anything. The room was still totally dark.

The room was also carved out of the living body of some enormous fungus. The urge to make terrible jokes about mushrooms was strong, and born at least partially out of panic. I don't have issues with claustrophobia, but I don't think you *need* to have issues with claustrophobia to be unhappy about being encased in a living structure with no windows or doors.

Sometimes violence really is the answer. I punched the wall, feeling it break under my hand. It was like punching foam: bloodless, painless, and remarkably cathartic. I opened my eyes, smiled, and went to work.

On the fifth punch, my fist went through the wall. When I pulled it back, moonlight poured through the hole I'd created, warm and bright as day in comparison to the dark. I stopped punching and started rending, ripping away great fistfuls of mushroom, until I had created a hole large enough for me to walk through. I burst triumphantly into the moonlight—

—and stopped as the woman in front of me leveled her wickedly pointed spear at the tip of my nose. Weapons tend to have that effect on me. Normally, my freeze would only have lasted for a few seconds. Normally, the person holding the spear wouldn't have been glowing. Everything about her, from skin to hair to long gossamer wings, radiated a bright shade of lilac. It was like she'd swallowed a basket full of Christmas lights.

Or like she was a pixie.

Once I had the thought, the evidence became impossible to ignore. Her hair was dark purple under the glow: her ears, while pointed, didn't match any breed of fae I knew, maybe because I wasn't used to seeing them at this scale. Maybe most tellingly, her clothing appeared to have been made from enormous flower petals, held together with cobweb stitches. There was even a fishbone in her hair, holding her messy bun in place. The spear, while dangerous, was made of a sliver of glass glued to a pine twig. She was a pixie.

She was also taller than I was. Oh, this was bad.

I raised my hands, palms outward, in what I hoped would be taken as a gesture of peace. "Uh, hi," I said. "Sorry about your, uh, toadstool." I would not call it a mushroom, I would not. If I said the word, I would start making architecture jokes, and I wasn't sure I'd be able to stop. "I don't like closed spaces."

"Make no moves, prisoner," she said, wings vibrating as she spoke, like they were amplifying her voice. That wasn't as surprising as the fact that I could understand her. Normally, the speech of pixies was like the high ringing of bells, fast and shrill and impossible to follow.

My surprise must have shown. She scowled and said, "Oh, didn't think pixies could talk, did you? Maybe it's because you don't know how to listen, do you? Ears the size of a grown man, and they can't hear a damn thing but themselves jawing on for nights without end."

"It's less you talking and more me being the same size as you that has me a little off-balance," I said, lowering my hands. She didn't seem inclined to stab me at the moment, although Oberon knew, that could change. I have a gift for making people want to see me bleed. "I had two men with me before I passed out. Where are they?"

"Making demands already? Cheek." The pixie woman waved her spear in a threatening manner. Lights were beginning to appear at the edges of my vision, daffodil yellow and clover green and a surprisingly violent shade of blue. More pixies were coming. Because what

I always needed was to be shrunk, menaced, and then surrounded by hostile people who could fly.

"Not cheek, concern," I said, fighting to keep my voice level. "They're my responsibility."

"You should've been somebody's responsibility," said the woman. "Then you might've known not to go walking in our woods."

The giant mushrooms. Naturally. I should have taken them as the warning they were, but I fell into the trap of thinking "I've seen this before, in movies intended for human children, which means it can't be true." It's easy to forget that those human legends and stories were based on real things they had encountered and somehow survived, back in the days when Faerie and the human world collided more often. When the deeper realms linked straight onto the mortal world, and not just the Summerlands. Things like the pixie fondness for mushrooms, and for shrinking intruders when they thought they could get away with it.

"I apologize," I said sincerely. "I didn't know this was your territory. I'm just trying to find my sister."

"She's not here, unless you've got wings strapped under that leather jacket," said the woman. The other pixies laughed. It wasn't an unpleasant sound. Being reduced to their size had taken the shrillness from their voices, dropping them to a register I could deal with.

"My sister's not a pixie," I said. I hesitated, considering my next words carefully. This wood didn't quite border on Amandine's tower—we'd walked too far for that—but it was close enough that the odds were good the pixies would know who she was. Would invoking her name help me, or get me locked in the nearest toadstool for the next hundred years?

Caution isn't normally my strong suit, and had I been weighing the risks for myself, I might have gone ahead and done it. I wasn't. I was weighing the risks for

Simon and Quentin, and more, for Tybalt and Jazz. I couldn't take the chance of getting them hurt.

The woman seemed to take my silence for fear. She laughed. "Oh, look at you, all scared of a *pixie*," she said snidely. "What's your name, wingless?"

"October."

Her eyes went wide, the tip of her spear dipping toward the ground—which was actually a tree branch, judging by the rough brown surface beneath our feet. "October?" she echoed.

I tensed. This was usually where the stabbing started. "Yes."

"Once Countess of Goldengreen, who kept her word even to us, even where so many others would not? Who freed our captives, and filled our stocks?"

I blinked. Then, more slowly, I said again, "Yes."

The woman dropped her spear and flung her arms around me, wings suddenly vibrating so fast that they became a blur of color. The rest of the pixies did the same, and I found myself the recipient of a pixie group hug, which was something like being trapped in the middle of a carillon of bells, all of them ringing at the same time in their own keys. It was surprisingly soothing, for being so incredibly loud.

A bright orange hand reached through the crowd and grabbed the collar of my jacket, dragging me out. I found myself in another hug, this one singular, but somehow even tighter.

"I thought I was going to *die* in there!" cried the hugger, a pixie woman whose body was lit up like a jack-o-lantern. She shoved me out to arm's length, beaming in every sense of the word. "Hello!"

"Er, hi," I said. "I'm . . . sorry. Have we met?"

"Not properly!" she said. "You let me out of a jar once!"

I blinked.

There was a trend among the purebloods at one time—or maybe more than one time; fashions have a lot of time to come and go when you live forever—for lights made of living pixies trapped in glass domes or stuffed into lanterns. No food or water, of course. Those would encourage excrement, and what kind of delicate, decorative lantern was covered in its own shit?

Pixies are considered somewhere between monsters and vermin by most people, which means they aren't covered by Oberon's Law. Killing them isn't a crime, even though they're intelligent beings. The end result of that loophole was a lot of dead pixies, left to starve in their glass prisons and then discarded when their lights went out. Oberon's Law doesn't cover changelings, either. If I ever meet Oberon, we're going to have a long, long talk.

When I had accessed the shallowing at Muir Woods, following Rayseline, the kidnapped sons of the Duchess of Saltmist, and my own stolen daughter, the place had been lit by lanterns filled with captive pixies. I had freed them, choosing mercy over expediency, and the pixies had rewarded me by helping me save the missing children.

They hadn't saved everyone. The face of the orange pixie fell as I watched, and she said, "I'm sorry about your friend. We couldn't turn the arrow aside."

Connor, who had died of elf-shot in front of me. I forced a sad smile. "It wasn't your fault. You did more than I could have asked."

"That you asked at all was a miracle to us. We still owe you life debts a hundred times over." The pixie woman hugged me a second time before finally, mercifully letting go. "What are you *doing* here?"

"Honestly, I don't know," I said. "I was following the trail of my sister's magic when I kicked this big puffball mushroom, and woke up in a dark room with no doors."

"Ahhh." She smiled knowingly. "You triggered the sentries. Got yourself ensmallinated. Fun times!"

"Yeah, maybe, but I don't have time for fun right

now. I need to find my sister. Do you know where the other people with me were taken?"

She cocked her head to the side. "Don't you want to explore? Most people don't ever get to come here, and when they do, they don't ever get to look around."

August's trail had led through here . . . I stiffened. "How long have you lived here?"

"Me, or everybody?"

"Both."

"Me, I don't know. A while. I go to Human sometimes, to hunt and scavenge, when it's my turn, but mostly I stay here. Help with the kids, see my family, all that stuff you do when you're not questing. The flock has been here for days and days and days."

Right: this wasn't getting me anywhere. I decided to try another approach. "Do you remember the big earthquake? The one where the old King died?"

"We don't have a King," she said. "You do, but we don't."

The question of whether pixies were part of the Divided Courts seemed like it was best left for another day. "Okay," I said. "But do you remember when *my* King died?"

"It was bad," she said. "Lots of things burned, and it even shook here, in Faerie, not just in Human."

"In . . . wait. You call the mortal world 'Human'?" It was oddly charming.

She looked at me like I'd just said something unbelievably stupid. "What else should I call it? The wingless call this 'Faerie,' so of course we'd call that other place 'Human.' The names go together."

"They do," I agreed. "But you remember the earthquake."

"Yes. Why?"

"Did someone like me—one of the wingless—come here around that time? She would have had red hair, but looked a lot like I do, otherwise. She might have been wearing a yellow dress." August, in her dress like corn husks, walking into the woods by the light of a candle.

To my surprise, the pixie woman shied away. "We saw her, we saw her, but we didn't take her, no, we don't have her, not then and not now, we've never had her, I promise. Tell the sea witch we didn't interfere."

"The sea—what are you talking about?"

"We saw her, yes, we saw her. I was here, helping to hold the walls up while the world fell down, and she had just gone by, walking down *our* paths, in *our* place. Some of us wanted to interfere, until they saw the candle in her hand. You know about the candle?"

I nodded. "I do."

"She was already on the Babylon Road, following it to somewhere that wasn't here, and if she was on a road to a place that wasn't here, she wasn't ours to take. You understand? You see? We knew someone else held claim, and so we let her pass us by. We didn't interfere." She grabbed for my hands. I let her. "We didn't."

"I believe you," I said.

Relief flooded her features. "I knew you would. You were kind when you didn't have to be. Of course you would be kind now."

"But I need to find her. My lover and my sister's lover have been taken by someone who will only give them back if I can find my other sister." Explaining the actual structure of my family tree would take too long and complicate matters too much. This was the bare bones of it. It would serve. "Please. Can you convince whoever's in charge here to give my people back and let us go?"

The orange pixie looked disappointed. "You really won't stay."

"Look, I'll—I'll come back, okay? You have my word. I will come back and stay for a couple of days. I'll let you show me around, introduce me to your friends—honestly, if I didn't have to do this, I would be really interested. I didn't even know for sure whether pixies could speak English before tonight. Today. What time is it?"

"It's after moonrise in Human, if that's what you're asking," she said. She grinned. "The sentries picked you and your friends up hours and hours and hours ago, and you're the first to wake. Sleep must have wanted the lot of you *very* badly."

I went cold. Simon had only been awake for a few hours. Walther's elf-shot countercharm would still be in his blood. Who knew how it was going to interact with whatever the pixies had used to knock us out?

"Can you take me to them?" I asked.

She nodded. "Follow," she said, and started walking.

Her pace was quick but not too fast. She walked like she was accustomed to it, which made me think that pixies must not fly much when they were at home. Which reminded me . . . "I don't actually know your name," I said.

"You're the first of the wingless to ask a pixie's name in days and days," she said, slanting a smile in my direction, like light cutting through clouds. "Should be a monument to say it happened."

"Sorry," I said, feeling vaguely responsible for the rest of the people built on my scale.

"Oh, don't be. Not your fault. I'm Poppy." She waved a hand, indicating some of the other pixies watching us from nearby paths and rooftops. "That's Dandelion, Parsnip, Lilac, and Stoplight. His mother flew into one while she was carrying, and it was green at the time, and he's green, so . . ." Poppy shrugged, the gesture made somehow more expressive by her wings.

"Huh," I said. "Some of those are pretty common flowers."

"Makes for pretty common names," she agreed easily. "There's a Poppy in near every flock within two days' flight of here, and probably more beyond that."

"Wingless fae—not that we're all wingless, although

I guess most of us are—tend to frown on reusing names. So it's just unusual, is all."

"Wingless fae live longer," said Poppy matter-of-factly. "Lilac's the only one left who was little when I was who still has her parents living, all three of them, and they've made it this far because they used to have a wingless patron who'd give them good things when they needed. Set them up solid, kept them out of danger until she was big enough not to need keeping, and then they brought their luck home. Sometimes only way to remember our dead is by naming babies after them, to keep flying when they're gone."

Pixies are fae, which means they're immortal. But they're also small, and relatively delicate, and people think of them as pests and thieves and nuisances. Even I did, before I got to know them better. Shame swept through me like bleach, leaving everything washed-out and pale.

Poppy gave me a sidelong look. "Not your fault. You're wingless, but you've never hurt us a'purpose, and that's all we'd ask from you. Chin up, shoulders back, wings straight, like my mama always used to say. As long as you don't fly into anything you shouldn't, you're probably doing all right."

We had reached a large toadstool, the sides smooth and white, the cap bright blue and spangled with silver spots. Poppy leaned in and knocked.

"Open-open, harvest's come," she said.

The sides of the toadstool rippled before splitting to reveal the room inside. Quentin was sprawled on the floor, bound with the same combination of plant materials and sap as I had been. I rushed inside, crouching down to remove his gag and check his pulse, which was slow and steady.

"The fresh air will wake him," said Poppy. I turned. She was standing in the "doorway," the glow from her skin easily compensating for the loss of moonlight. "We don't have strong magic for the most part, not like you wingless, but what we have, we have a lot of practice using. Your other person is in the toadstool on the next branch over."

"That's Simon," I said, turning back to Quentin. "I'll wake him when I'm done here."

There was a sudden loud ringing behind me, like the pixie alarm system had just been activated. I turned again, this time reaching for the knife at my belt.

Poppy was staring at me, eyes wide, hands clasped over her mouth. "Simon *Torquill*?" she squeaked.

"Um, yeah?" I said.

She didn't say anything after that, just launched herself into the air and flew away, still ringing like a five-alarm fire.

"That can't be good," I said, and stood, and ran after her. Quentin would have to wait until I was sure that Simon wasn't about to get himself murdered. If anyone was going to do that, I was pretty sure that it was going to be me.

ELEVEN

POPPY WASN'T KIDDING ABOUT Simon's toad-stool being on the next branch. Pixies might be content to walk when they were at home, but that didn't prevent them from building without concern for petty little concepts like "gravity." Their homes—most of which appeared to have been built from chunks of wood and bark, unlike our organic toadstool prisons—extended both up and down from the level where I stood, and spanned multiple trees.

It wasn't hard to know which one contained Simon, as it also appeared to contain every pixie that had been present when I woke up, and several dozen more on top of that. It was like watching a Christmas tree rave in the process of getting started, since they were all glowing, and some of them were flashing, giving the whole thing an unsettling strobe effect.

There was what looked, at my current scale, like at least a twenty-foot gap between me and them. Whatever magic they had used to reduce us all to pixie-size hadn't been kind enough to give us wings, or otherwise equip us for life in a pixie-scaled environment.

Since I couldn't fly, I settled for the next best thing, cupping my hands around my mouth and shouting, "Hey!"

A few pixies turned in my direction, looking surprised to see me standing there. I had time to wonder how many unwitting guests they had wandering around the place, if I could be such a shock, before two of them launched themselves across the gap, wings working furiously, grabbed me by the arms, and flew back the way they had come.

At first, I was too surprised to struggle. Then I was slightly too smart to struggle, since being dropped would have been . . . bad. I've fallen from a great height before, great enough to break every bone in my body, including a few that Jin—our resident healer—said she hadn't been sure *could* break. Being roughly six inches tall would probably make the landing less traumatic, but I wasn't willing to bet on it, not when the pixies didn't seem to be acting in a malicious way.

They set me back on my feet at the other branch, where a conscious, groggy-looking Simon was standing in the mouth of his own toadstool, awkwardly patting a sobbing Lilac on the shoulder. The purple pixie's wings were flat against her back, making her stand out in sharp relief from the rest of the pixies, whose wings were in constant, chiming vibration.

Simon met my eyes across the crowd of diminutive onlookers and grimaced apologetically.

"I forgot," he said. "Their colony was much smaller the last time I came through this way, and they didn't have the resources to defend themselves against travelers. Or to set traps."

"Thought you were dead," wailed Lilac, and went back to sobbing.

"I know, dear, I know," said Simon. He stopped patting her shoulder and began stroking her wings instead, the way he might have stroked a cat. The motion seemed to soothe her. "I'm so sorry. I couldn't come to see you, any of you. I would have, if I could."

Lilac looked mollified. That didn't mean she stopped crying.

"Okay, wait, I missed something." I pushed my way through the crowd of pixies. They let me by easily. Apparently, the fact that I'd been captured in the company of Simon Torquill, of all people, meant I was owed deference now. "Why would you have been visiting the local pixie colony? What *possible* reason could you have had for visiting the local pixie colony?"

"Ah," said Simon, looking relieved. I'd asked him something easy. "I helped them establish it."

I stared at him. I didn't say anything. Saying anything would mean acknowledging what he had just said as something that made sense, and I wasn't ready to do that.

Simon sighed. "Before Patrick married his mermaid and moved to the Undersea, he cultivated a remarkably large colony of pixies in his workshop. As an unlanded Baron, he was afforded a certain amount of courtesy by the other noble households, and if he wanted to keep, ah, 'pets,' they weren't going to stop him, even if they *were* going to laugh at him behind their hands. The fashion then was for—"

"I'm going to stop you there, because I'm pretty sure I know what the fashion was."

Simon nodded, looking relieved. Lilac's sobs were slowing. That may have contributed to his relief. "Patrick didn't want to leave them defenseless, but he couldn't take them to the Undersea. This land was unclaimed, and close enough to Amandine's borders that it seemed likely to stay such. He asked me to help them resettle."

"You carried an entire pixie colony from San Francisco to here."

"Yes."

I paused. "Poppy was in Muir Woods. They're moving between the Summerlands and the mortal world. How . . . ?"

"They use the knowes, as a rule, or they use the door I opened for them."

I stared at him again. "You opened a door. For the pixies."

"Yes. It's in a tree in the Golden Gate Park botanical garden. It's quite small. No one larger than a squirrel is even likely to notice that it's there."

"Best door," said Poppy proudly. "Most colonies haven't got one. We do lots of hunting through it."

"I'm sure you do," I said, looking at Simon in confusion. It was getting harder and harder to reconcile the things I knew about him—that he'd kidnapped his own niece and sister-in-law, that he'd spent years in the company of a woman who killed for fun as much as for money—with the things I was learning.

People are complicated. That's the problem with people. It would be so much easier if they could all be put into easy little boxes and left there, never changing, never challenging the things I decided about them.

Lilac pushed away from Simon, wiping her eyes. "He used to always come, and then he never came, and we thought—*I* thought—he had died. And if he was dead, who would tell Patrick where we were? Who would tell him we were all right?"

"Patrick's fine," I told her. "I'm sure he'll be pleased to hear that you're all doing so well. But Simon and I need to go, and we need to take my squire with me." If Quentin was awake by now, he was probably going to be pissed about the fact that I hadn't untied him before running after the pixies.

A little discomfort is good for the soul. I'd managed to get myself free, and he could do the same, given the proper incentive. A giant blob of pine resin on his feet was pretty good incentive.

The pixies exclaimed in dismay, their words lost

under the din from their buzzing wings. Simon put up his hands. The pixies settled down.

"We *will* come back, but October is right. We have things we need to accomplish, and we can't do them while here—or while shrunken to this scale."

"We do fine at this size," shouted one of the pixie men.

"You have wings," said Simon. "That expands your range rather a lot."

"We can't give you wings," said Lilac. She sounded genuinely sad about it.

Simon offered her a warm smile. "That's all right, dear. A safe trip back to ground level and our original sizes will suffice."

"And my squire," I added hastily. "I really do need him back."

"I'll get the other one," said Poppy, and launched herself into the air. Seen at this size, the way the pixies took flight was really impressive. She bent at the knees, jumping straight up from a standing start, and somehow snapped her wings open with sufficient velocity to continue propelling her, never allowing gravity to catch hold. The muscular structure behind her wings must have been incredible; otherwise, not even magic would have been enough to support her.

Simon and Lilac were speaking animatedly when I turned back to them, their voices low, their postures a curious mix of old friends and total strangers. This might have been the first time they had been able to speak as equals. Before, he had been too big and she had been too small, so they had existed in the curious mix of pantomime and patience that had always defined my interactions with the pixies.

Lilac looked at him like he was a hero. To her, he probably was. And Simon . . . Simon looked at her like she was a revelation he had never expected to have. She didn't know what he'd done. She didn't know that he was the villain in so many other stories. She didn't care.

Maybe when this was all over, if Sylvester didn't have Simon thrown into the dungeon to think about what he'd done, I could convince them both that exile among the pixies was the perfect punishment. Sylvester would see it as a way to get his brother out of his life forever without actually killing him. Simon . . .

Simon might see it as a way of going home.

Poppy flew back, landing in front of me and letting go of Quentin at the same time, so that he pitched forward. I grabbed him before he could hit the ground. He blinked at me, looking stunned.

"We're *pixies*," he said, tone implying that he couldn't decide between amazement and offense.

"No, we're pixie-*sized*," I corrected, setting him back on his feet. "No wings for us. We triggered one of their automatic defenses, and they took us prisoner."

"But we're well sorry now, honest we are," said Poppy brightly. "Can't make an omelet without killing a few chickens."

Quentin turned his confusion on her. "What do you think an omelet *is*?" he asked.

Poppy laughed. "I like this one," she informed me.

"I do, too," I said. Raising my voice, I called, "Simon, it's time to go."

He leaned in and kissed Lilac on the forehead before stepping away from her and walking over to join me and Quentin. "A pity," he said. "I was just starting to enjoy myself."

"You've been enjoying yourself since you woke up," I said.

He shrugged, expression guileless. "Can you blame me?"

"I guess not." I looked back to Poppy. "Can you put us back the way you found us now, please?"

"You said you'd come back," she said. "You and he both. You *will* come back?"

"A promise is a promise."

She grinned broadly. "Omelets for all," she said. Reaching into a pouch at her waist, she pulled out a fistful of glittering pixie dust and blew it in our faces.

Then, before any of us could react, she stepped forward and shoved us out of the tree.

We fell as gracefully as could be expected—which was to say, not at all. The three of us plummeted like rocks, Quentin flapping his arms like he thought he could suddenly learn to fly, me straining to grab hold of him before we got too far apart, and Simon just falling, dropping like a rock as the ground came up to meet us with incredible speed.

Wait. Too much speed. Our fall couldn't account for how quickly the ground was gaining, or for the way the landscape was shifting around us, everything becoming smaller, including the pixies, who were dwindling not just due to distance, but due to a shift in scale.

Then my feet hit the ground, knocking the air out of me with the force of the impact, but not breaking any bones. I bent my knees to keep from toppling over. Quentin wasn't so lucky. He went sprawling, narrowly missing another of those huge puffball mushrooms.

Simon landed on his feet, a pleasant smile on his face. "Well," he said. "Wasn't that fun? We should really make it a point to bring gifts when we come back. I seem to recall the pixies in Patrick's workshop being exceedingly fond of preserves and—" He stopped midsentence and toppled forward, the smile still on his face.

"Simon!" I rushed to catch him, grabbing him by his shoulders and hoisting him up as best I could. There was no tension left in his body. He was dead weight, hanging against me like a doll made in the shape of a man. "Quentin, help me!"

Quentin rushed to my side, helping me lever Simon into a position where we could lower him to the ground and brace his back against the nearest tree. He didn't wake up. Even when I lightly slapped his cheeks, his eyes stayed closed and his breathing stayed steady, betraying no sign that he was aware of our presence. Quentin and I exchanged a wide-eyed, terrified look.

"This is bad," he said.

"Give me your phone," I said.

Quentin didn't argue, just pulled the phone out of his pocket and passed it to me. There was a new picture of him and Dean on the lock screen, this time of the two of them riding the carousel at the Yerba Buena Gardens, looking disgustingly cute. I barely glanced at it before swiping my thumb across the image, pulling up the keypad, and dialing.

I had no idea what time it was. Quentin's phone, despite being modified to work in the Summerlands, didn't seem to know, either; the time on the display was eighty-nine o'clock, and I was pretty sure that was wrong. Walther might not even be in his office.

The phone rang once, twice, and I was resigning myself to trying to find a way to leave a neutral but urgent voicemail when there was a click, and Walther said, "Professor Davies here."

"Walther, it's me."

"Toby! Did Raj get the formula to you in time?"

"He did. That's sort of the problem. We got hit by some kind of pixie knock-out powder and shrunk down to their size, woke up, got re-enlarged, and now Simon's asleep again and I can't wake him up. Is there any chance their knock-out dust interacted badly with your elf-shot cure?"

There was a long pause. Too long.

"Hello? Walther? Are you there?"

"All those things were words, and they all left your mouth, but I'm having trouble with the idea that they form any sort of coherent sentence." Walther took a deep breath, the inhalation clearly audible through the phone. "Okay, first question: is he alive?"

"He's breathing."

"Good, that means it's not the sort of spell interaction where you need a resurrection to fix it. What do his pupils look like?"

I leaned forward and pried Simon's left eyelid carefully open. His iris had been reduced to a thin ring of honey gold around the enormous black circle of his pupil.

"Dilated," I said, letting go.

"Right. Last question. What does he do when you cause him pain?"

"I slapped him. He didn't wake up."

"Cause him more pain."

"I'm not going to knee him in the nuts just to see what happens."

"So stick him with a pin or something. I need the sort of shock that a normal person couldn't sleep through."

I sighed. "Hang on. Quentin, hold this." I handed the phone to my squire and pulled the knife from my belt. Leaning carefully forward, I dug the tip of it against the skin of Simon's hand until it broke the surface, sending a trickle of smoke-scented blood running down the channel between his knuckles.

Simon didn't stir.

I leaned back, reaching for the phone. Quentin returned it to me. Bringing it to my ear, I said, "He didn't wake up."

"Okay. It's a bad interaction. Based on his pupils, I'd say he's basically stoned. It may wear off on its own. It may also mean he's out for a while."

"How long?"

There was a pause before Walther said, "I don't know. If he doesn't wake up soon, bring me a blood sample and I'll see what I can find. Try not to let him get exposed to anything else."

"Right. I'll talk to you soon." I hung up the phone and handed it back to Quentin.

"What did he say?"

"That we're screwed. Hang on, I'm going to do something stupid." I stood, cupping my hands around my mouth, and called up to the tree, "Hey, Poppy, can you come down here for a second?"

A bright orange mote of light zipped from one of the high branches and descended to hover in front of my face, where it resolved into the pixie woman who had been so happy to show me around. She waved, expression shy.

"Hi," I said. "You can understand me, right?"

Poppy nodded, wings chiming.

"Great. So here's the deal. Simon was elf-shot. I had him woken up to help me find my sister, but the countercharm was still in his system, and I think the stuff you used to knock us out is interacting poorly with it. I can't carry him the way he is right now. Is there any chance you can shrink him again, so I can stick him in my pocket until we figure out a way to wake him up?"

Poppy clapped her hands over her mouth, looking alarmed. I shook my head.

"I'm not mad, I just need to get moving. So can you?"

She hesitated before nodding and zipping away, back into the trees. I waited impatiently until she reappeared, and started flying circles around me and Quentin, trying to move us away from Simon's body.

I took a big step back, reaching forward to haul Quentin after me. Poppy gave one approving ring before she darted forward, pulling something from her belt, and threw it into Simon's face. There was a burst of bright orange glitter.

When it cleared, Simon had dwindled to the size of a pixie. That was expected.

Poppy, standing there, still barefoot and glowing bright orange, but suddenly built to human scale, was less so. I blinked. She blinked. Then, looking absolutely delighted, she did a little jig step and clapped her hands together.

"It worked, it *worked*, oh, I'm a miracle and no mistake! Look what I did! Look what I've done!"

"I can see what you've done, I just don't understand it," I said. "Why are you big?"

"Because your friend's small," she said matter-of-factly.

"Not a good enough answer," said Quentin.

"We don't have big outside magic like you wingless do," said Poppy. "If we did, you wouldn't go in for swatting us half so often, because we'd swat you right back. Pow!" She paused to giggle before adding, "We make an inside magic. All of us together, we can small the wingless down by all giving a little. If you want someone to be small without you calling on the whole flock, somebody has to give a lot. That's me! I'm giving a lot!"

I blinked. "So you can make someone else small if you use, what, *all* your magic?"

"Not *all*," she said. "Most, though. Not too much left for me. If you said 'Poppy, make yourself to look like a human-kind,' I couldn't do it."

"What about your natural magic?" asked Quentin. Pixies normally have a sort of passive "you can't see me" field that keeps them from being noticed by mortals. It's handy. Sometimes I wish I had one.

Poppy shook her head. "Not that neither, which is why we don't do it for much anymore. Used to be, someone kicked our mushrooms and squished our children, we'd small them right down for a while, maybe let a cat bat them about. Teach them a lesson and send them back to their parents not believing. Ha! But now, looking like we do . . ." She indicated herself, glowing skin, wings, and all. "If I smalled somebody down out in Human, I'd get found straightaway, and taken for a freak, or arrested by the wingless for endangering us all. I can't hide myself from human eyes when I'm the same size as they are."

"Hopefully, it doesn't come to that," I said. "This is a very big favor, Poppy. I won't forget it."

" 'Course you won't, because I'm coming with you,"

she said blithely. She laughed at my blank look. "You don't think I'd be letting you walk off with all my magic, do you? I'll want it back as soon as he's awake, no mistake of that. But this is an adventure, and we don't have so many of those."

"Right," I said faintly. Because a human-sized pixie in need of shoes was exactly what this quest needed.

There was no sense in arguing with her, and she was right about one thing: it was unreasonable to expect her to let us walk off with her magic. But if Simon was his usual size, there was no way we'd be able to transport him.

Sighing to myself, I walked over to where he was lying in the dirt and picked him up as gingerly as I could, all too aware of the size difference between us and how fragile his body was in comparison to mine. If I accidentally crushed his rib cage he wouldn't recover; he'd just die.

"You want as for me to carry him?" asked Poppy blithely. I turned to blink at her. She offered me an understanding smile. "We don't big ourselves up too often, because it's hard and it hurts and we need to small somebody down to do it, but I know how it feels to have somebody lots bigger carrying you. I know how to hold."

"That would be great," I said, and let Simon's body slide into her waiting hands. She made him vanish into the bodice of her dress—where, I realized, pockets had been stitched to almost every seam. It made sense. Pixies are scavengers, taking whatever they could get their hands on. Of course they would need as many pockets as they could fit into their clothes.

We had wasted enough time. I stepped away from Poppy and closed my eyes, trying to filter through the myriad scents surrounding me until I found the campfire smoke and climbing roses trail of August's magic.

The fact that it was still there for me to find said something about how long the pixies had been alone here. Under normal circumstances, all traces of August would have long since been buried under the magical trails of a hundred other spells, a hundred other passing fae. But pixie magic is different. It manifests as sparkling, scentless dust, and it hadn't obscured her passage.

I opened my eyes. "This way," I said, and started walking.

Behind me, I heard Poppy ask, "We just follow?"

"We just follow," confirmed Quentin.

They did.

The ground grew marshier under our feet, until we were picking our way around the edges of a swamp, surrounded by trees that looked something like mangroves, and something like magnolias, and something like nightmares given vine-encrusted branches and leaves that blocked the sky. Sometimes those vines seemed to slither, implying the presence of snakes. I hurried on, not looking around more than I absolutely had to. If something attacked us, then I would care about it. If not, we could live and let live.

There was a path in the mud if I watched for it carefully. It bent and twisted, all but tying itself in knots, and August's scent was all along it. She had come this way. So long ago that time had smoothed her footprints from the mud, but still—my sister had walked here, and now I was following her. Something about it seemed inevitable, almost, like life was always going to bring me to this point eventually.

A grassy mound rose out of the swamp ahead of us. Turtles in impossible colors, crystal blue and pine green and daisy white, basked on the shallow sides. They didn't slide away at our approach, only looked at us with slow, curious eyes.

The mound had a door, rough-hewn, sunk into the earth alongside a circular window holding panes of thick, bubbly glass. I looked back. Quentin shrugged. Poppy, busy goggling at the strange turtles, said nothing.

"Right," I said, and raised my hand, and knocked.

The door opened.

The woman on the other side looked barely old enough to deserve the title: she was sixteen at best, with the ghosts of old acne scars still haunting her cheeks, and long, dark hair that fell over her shoulder in a profusion of semicombed curls. She was wearing a blue tank top and jeans, and she looked wearily unsurprised to see me standing on her doorstep.

"All right, you found the back door," said the Luidaeg. "I suppose you might as well come in."

TWELVE

"LUIDAEG." QUENTIN PUSHED PAST me and threw his arms around the sea witch, first among Firstborn, monster under the collective bed of Faerie, in a way that would have been suicidal coming from virtually anyone else. From him, it was nothing more than a genuine expression of relief at seeing a friendly face. "You're *here*."

"You found the back door," she said again, ruffling his hair. Her hand came away faintly glittery. She looked at it, then at Poppy, who was doing her best to disappear behind me.

It might have been easier if Poppy hadn't still been lit up like a Christmas tree. The normal pixie glow is reasonably bright. On a pixie the size of a human being, it was virtually blinding.

"Toby, why is Quentin covered in pixie dust, and why is there a giant pixie behind you?" Somehow the Luidaeg made that question sound almost reasonable. She has a gift for that sort of thing.

"We met the local pixie colony," I said. "They knocked us out. Didn't you invite us in?"

"I wondered if you were going to remember that," she said, and stepped to the side, disentangling herself from Quentin in the process. Eyes on Poppy, she said, "Enter and be not afraid, for you have been invited."

"You're never that formal with *me*," I said.

"You're rarely invited," she replied.

I smiled wearily and stepped inside.

There was no sense of transition between one side of the door and the other; we were still in the Summerlands. We were also standing in the Luidaeg's apartment, which I knew for a fact was located in the mortal city of San Francisco. The illusions that sometimes made the place look like an EPA disaster zone were down, revealing clean walls, a sparse, vaguely nautical décor, and a carpet the color of fresh kelp. The air smelled like the sea, the clean, sweet sea, when the tide was high and all the darker aspects of it were safely out of sight beneath the waves.

The Luidaeg waited until Poppy was through to close the door. Her attention on the transformed pixie, she said, "I am the sea witch. I am the maker of bargains and the granter of dreams. Speak carefully to me, if you must speak at all, because if you put yourself into my debt, you will have to pay. Do you understand?"

"Might be," said Poppy, sounding dazed. "Never thought I'd meet you proper. Normally too small to notice."

"I notice everything," said the Luidaeg wearily. She turned to me. "How'd you find the back door?"

"I followed the trail August left when she came to see you."

The Luidaeg raised an eyebrow. "You followed a hundred-year-old trail no one else has been able to find? You're good, but you're not *that* good. How did you even know where to start?"

"Simon showed me." I looked to Poppy. "Can I have him back, please?"

Poppy dipped her hand into the pocket of her dress,

coming up with the diminutive, still-sleeping form of Simon Torquill. She held him out to me, a goofy smile on her face. "He's cute when he's this much smaller'n me," she said. "Pixies seem this cute to you?"

"When they're not trying to stab me, yes." I put my cupped hands under hers, and she gently tipped Simon into them, careful not to shake him too much. I turned back to the Luidaeg, presenting him like a trophy. "Simon Torquill."

The Luidaeg's eyebrows made a valiant attempt to climb to her hairline. "So it is. I'm assuming he swapped sizes with your pixie friend because . . . ?"

"Because I woke him up using Walther's counter-charm, and it was still in his system when Poppy's colony knocked us out. I think the magic is fighting. I can't keep him conscious."

"I . . . see." The Luidaeg gave Simon a dubious look. "What do you expect me to do about it? He can't make a deal with me. He's not awake. You have to be awake before you can promise me anything."

"To be fair, I wasn't *looking* for you," I said. "I didn't even know you had a back door. As far as waking Simon, I could—"

"Don't finish that sentence." The Luidaeg shifted her gaze to me, and her eyes were green as the shallow edge of the sea. A person could drown there. "You're already so deep in my debt that there's no seeing the surface from where you are, and you weren't careful when you acquired it. I'm not saying I blame you for that—you had people to save—but you may never finish paying me back. I'm not letting you go any deeper before you've started working it off."

"I can do it," said Quentin.

This time, I was the one to shake my head and say, "No. You're not going into debt over Simon Torquill, not if there's any other way."

"Then you've got a problem, Toby, because this isn't one I can give you for free."

"Pardon." We all turned to Poppy, who was twisting her hands in front of her, watching us anxiously. "Pardon, but why not do debts over Simon? He's good folks. You're good folks. Shouldn't good folks help each other?"

"It's not that simple." Simon was a hero to the pixies. The sentence still felt strange, but there it was. "Simon did . . . some things, after he stopped coming to see you. Things he probably shouldn't have done, that I don't think he'd want me to tell you about."

Poppy blinked. "Why not?"

"Because you'd look at him differently if you knew."

"Oh." Poppy frowned for a moment before she turned to the Luidaeg and said, "I don't know the things you won't tell me. I don't look at him differently. So I'll do debts for him. Can you do what needs done to wake him up, for please?"

The Luidaeg's frown was slow and serious. "You understand that I will take payment from you for doing this, and you may not like what I decide to claim."

"He was awake before we made him not to be," said Poppy. "We didn't know hitting him with our sleeping would mean he slept for longer than he should. Simon helped us once. He helped us so much. The only people who've helped as much as him are Patrick and her," she pointed to me, "and now we've hurt two from the three of them, because she needs him and we took him away. So please, let me do debts. Wake him up."

"Pixies," said the Luidaeg—but there was a note of fondness in her tone, like she couldn't believe she was dealing with this. She tilted her head, attention now fixed on Poppy. "Do you know where you come from?"

"Um," said Poppy. "There was Maeve, and there was some sad, and she wanted some happy where she could see it. So she cut some of the happy out of herself, and she made it into pretty stones that sparkled in the sun. All different stones, blue and red and green and silver. Only they weren't stones, they were eggs, and when they hatched, they were pixies."

"One drop of blood for each of you," said the Luidaeg. "That's why your magic works the way it does. That's why it's so all-or-nothing. Because you've never had the size to master anything larger. My mother made you to make herself happy, and you did your jobs very well."

"Sorry, but I wasn't there," said Poppy, with what sounded like genuine regret. "I didn't start for generations after that."

"Doesn't matter. You still get the credit for making my mother smile. I'll be right back." The Luidaeg walked out of the room, heading for the kitchen.

I knew what came after the kitchen. Usually, it was a lot of blood, and we hadn't even gotten to the question of August's candle yet. I turned to Poppy.

"If you want to change your mind, this is when you run," I said. "Take your magic back, return to your real size, and fly away as fast as you can, because when the Luidaeg makes a bargain, you pay what she asks of you. Do you understand?"

"We owe him," she said gravely. "The whole colony, we owe him. I wouldn't even have been living long enough for you to save if not for Simon. How can I repay you for what you've done if I don't start with the repayment of him?"

I didn't have an answer for that. I wasn't sure there was one.

Footsteps from the hall told me that the Luidaeg was returning before she stepped into the room. It didn't matter that we didn't have an answer, because there was no longer time.

"We like to talk about the Firstborn and the Three like there was always a clear chain of creation through Faerie, even though five minutes in the real world will tell you there wasn't." The Luidaeg walked to the middle of the room, stopping when she reached the coffee table. She knelt, placing three objects atop it: a shallow bowl made from an abalone shell, a long bone needle, and a glass flask filled with something that twisted and swirled like captive moonlight. "Maeve created pixies with no Firstborn to call their own. Acacia gave birth to the Blodynbryd, and when they cut their hair, rose goblins are sown. The Selkies were born in slaughter, the Raven-mays in sacrifice. Sometimes the rules break. Poppy."

"Yes?" said Poppy, in a hushed voice.

"Do you agree to pay whatever I ask in exchange for my removing the magic your people placed in the body of Simon Torquill? Do you understand that I am the sea witch, the mother of nightmares, and once I have taken what I want from you, you may never be able to buy it back, no matter how hard you try?"

"Yes," said Poppy.

The Luidaeg looked at her gravely. "Do you understand that I cannot refuse you, but I cannot give this to you for free?"

"Yes," said Poppy, more confidently.

"Then here we go. Toby, put Simon on the couch and step away."

"Right." I walked over to the couch and rolled Simon's sleeping form onto the cushion. I didn't think I'd broken him. It was hard to tell, with him refusing to wake up.

"Quentin, go stand against the wall," said the Luidaeg.

He looked startled. "Why?"

"Because I said so." She grinned, showing a mouthful of viciously pointed teeth. "Move."

Quentin moved. I moved to stand next to him. When the Luidaeg needed me to bleed, she'd call me. She always did.

"Mother didn't leave room for anything but herself when she made the pixies. That's part of why you're so small. She was never good at allowing things to become complicated. Poppy, give me your hand."

Poppy, not yet aware of the danger of listening to the Luidaeg when she said that sort of thing, stuck out her hand. The Luidaeg picked up the bone needle and drove it into the tip of Poppy's index finger.

The oversized pixie yelped and tried to jump back. The Luidaeg grabbed her wrist before she could, moving it so that her fingertips were positioned above the shell bowl.

"You promised," said the Luidaeg, and squeezed.

Poppy didn't bleed. Instead, something as thick and viscous as maple syrup began dripping from her finger—assuming maple syrup was bright orange and glowed like it was radioactive. She made a soft squeaking sound, half surprise and half dismay. Her wings rustled, but they didn't chime.

"Keep your hand exactly where it is," said the Luidaeg, and let go of Poppy's wrist. She reached for the glass flask, pulling out the stopper. The smell of blood wafted from the silvery contents. It was . . . thin, diffuse, impossible to identify, except in the sense that I knew I *couldn't* identify it. Whatever it was, it was something I had never encountered before.

"I don't feel good," said Poppy. The glow from her skin was starting to dim, leaving her pink and pale, save for the high spots of hectic color in her cheeks.

"Drink this," said the Luidaeg, forcing the flask into her other hand. "You'll feel better."

Poppy looked grateful, too innocent or too confused to sense a trap when one was springing shut on her—or maybe she just didn't care. Maybe she had already accepted that this was going to happen, and saw no sense in fighting. Whatever her reasons, she raised the flask to her lips and drank its contents without hesitation, gulping them down in three long mouthfuls.

Her eyes widened. Her jaw went slack. The flask fell from her fingers and landed on the floor with a sound like a single bell chiming. The stream of orange light was falling faster and faster, until it should have overflowed the shallow bowl. Somehow, the bowl seemed to keep expanding, growing broader, deeper, becoming wide enough to hold every drop.

The couch springs groaned. I shifted my attention to Simon, who was suddenly back to his original size. Still asleep, but no longer small enough to fit in the palm of my hand. That was almost a pity. He would have been so much easier to deal with if he'd stayed portable.

"Simon Torquill, whatever am I going to do with you?" The Luidaeg picked up the glass flask and walked over to him, crouching down and bringing the lip of it to his mouth. "Exhale," she commanded.

Simon did. A glittering swirl of pixie dust filled the flask.

"Good boy," she said, and slid the stopper home before slapping him, hard, across the face.

Simon opened his eyes.

The Luidaeg smiled, showing him a full mouthful of razor-sharp teeth. "Hello, failure," she purred.

Sensibly, Simon recoiled, slamming himself up against the arm of the couch. When he couldn't go any farther, he froze, eyes wide, as still as a mouse confronted with a cat.

"You know, if it were up to me, I might have left you as you were," said the Luidaeg. "The Davies boy concocted a clever counter for my sister's work, but he didn't account for the brute simplicity of pixie magic. The two were battling for dominion in your blood, and your body elected to go back to what seemed safest: sleep. I don't know whether elf-shot's protections would have kicked back in and kept you from withering away. You could have died and taught me something at the same time, but someone was willing to ransom you. Earn this second chance, *failure*."

"October, what have you—" began Simon, turning

to face me. Then he froze, eyes going even wider, which should have been impossible. "No."

I followed his eyes to Poppy. The light had almost stopped falling. The orange glow of her skin wasn't fading anymore: it was gone. Her hair was still orange, the color of maple leaves in the fall, as were her eyes. Her wings had changed shape, becoming longer and thinner, more equipped to her current size. They were no longer transparent, but had taken on a dozen shades of sunrise, so that if she spread them against the light, they might mimic a little of the glow she'd given away.

"Yes," said the Luidaeg. "This is what it costs when you're not careful. When you fail again."

"Luidaeg, what did you do?" The last drop of light fell from Poppy's finger. She wobbled. I rushed to catch her and hold her up, keeping her from falling. It felt like the bones had gone out of her legs, leaving her limp and unresponsive.

The Luidaeg met my eyes over Poppy's head. "What she asked me to do," she said. "Simon needed to wake, but Simon was under a pixie charm. The only way to dispel it was to unmake it, and unmaking it required unraveling it at the root. I would have needed to take apart a pixie no matter what. I just happened to have a volunteer."

"What did you do?" This time the question came from Quentin, and was underscored with a wounded confusion that hurt my heart.

The Luidaeg was a monster to me for years before the first time I realized I could see her as a friend. She was a story that local fae parents told their children. "Better watch it, or the Luidaeg will get you." Quentin, though. He had been born in Toronto, where they had other monsters to warn their kids about. He had made his first bargain with her when he was little more than a child, and she had always treated him fairly, and with kindness, and with her own strange brand of love. She was one of the people he trusted most in the world.

This wasn't the first time he had seen her be monstrous, but it was the first time he had seen her do something that could be construed as cruel.

"We say every kind of fae has a Firstborn, because it's easier than explaining that the truth is complicated and sometimes things aren't what they seem," said the Luidaeg. There was a new hurt in her eyes. She was reading Quentin's discomfort as clearly as I was, and she didn't like it. "My mother made the pixies because she was lonely and sad. She didn't count on the fact that anything made will start wanting a life of its own. Will want to be more than a drop of blood and an idea. So she told them 'come to me if you want more, and I will give it to you.'" She switched her attention to me. "Remember the Aes Sidhe?"

"They all died," I said automatically. Then I blinked. "No."

"Oh, yes." She waved a hand, indicating Poppy. "This is where they come from. No Firstborn. Just a pixie and a promise. They're related to the Piskies, actually—another family line without a true Firstborn. Some Aes Sidhe missed their families, went home to visit, got frisky, and wound up with size-changing babies. I think that may be part of why the Aes Sidhe died out. Why stick to your own kind when your offspring can be something better?"

I gaped at her, Poppy a warm weight against my shoulder. "She'll be alone."

"She'll have friends, and this isn't why you came to me. Why are you here, October?"

"We didn't come to you." I scowled. "You keep acting like we're here on purpose, and we're not. This is just where we wound up."

"Even so. You must have been looking for something."

"Amandine told me to find August."

"I knew that part. You followed her trail."

"Yes." Poppy still wasn't standing on her own. I gathered as much of her as I could into my arms and half-dragged, half-carried her to the couch, where Simon stood and helped me lower her down onto the cushions. We had to position her carefully, so as not to crush her wings. They twitched as we let her go. Still there was no sound of bells.

Light, and the sound of bells: those were the things that Maeve had given to the pixies when she made them, intending for them to make her happy. Light and the sound of bells. That was what the Luidaeg had taken away.

I turned back to her. "Is she going to be all right?"

"It depends on who you ask," said the Luidaeg. "Ask your questions."

I took a deep breath. "August walked the Babylon Road. Where was she going?"

The corner of the Luidaeg's mouth twitched. "That's not the right question. I already told you that I don't know where she is or where she went. Ask the right question."

"Luidaeg, why did my sister, August Torquill, ask you for a candle?"

"Now *there's* the right question." She stood a little straighter. "Amandine's line—your sister, your mother, yourself—is responsible for the loss of our King and Queens, and there are those who say that only Amandine's line can set right what they made wrong."

"Are you one of the ones who says that?"

The Luidaeg's eyes flashed black for a moment before returning to green. "I think there may be other ways, but your line is the cleanest of them. The fewest deaths will be lain at the root of the oak and the ash if you fix what once was broken. Your mother never wanted to be a hero. She *hated* what her mother's actions and our father's blood had lain upon her, hated the expectation that she would sacrifice herself for the sake of others. She wanted to be a rose in a walled garden, and not one growing wild by the side of some crumbling, half-forgotten well. So she refused. She could have ended this centuries ago, and she refused."

"You can't blame Amy for the actions of her mother," said Simon, stepping up beside me. "It's not fair."

"Oh, and do you know who her mother was? Did she tell you, *failure*, when she took you to her bed and promised to be true?" Simon looked away. The Luidaeg laughed. The sound was bitter. "I thought not. She may have loved you—my sister *is* capable of love, even if she spends it like a miser—but she's not so capable of trust. I don't blame Amandine for what her mother did. I blame her for what she, herself, chose not to do. I blame her for leaving us to clean up her mess. And I blame her for not preparing her daughter for what had to be done."

The Luidaeg turned to me. "August came to me and asked me for a candle. She asked to be set on the Babylon Road, because she'd heard Blind Michael had in his keeping a changeling child powerful enough to be capable of opening doors into the deeper realms. She was convinced that Oberon had sealed himself in Mag Mell. Had all the scraps of prose and prophesy to prove it to herself, to be *certain* she was on the right trail. Had the burning need to prove herself to her mother."

"What did she pay you?" asked Simon.

The Luidaeg looked at him calmly. "She gave me her way home."

"You—" His eyes widened, and he lunged.

Fortunately for him, he was positioned so that I was able to grab him and keep him from getting to her. He was taller than me, but he wasn't stronger; he'd never been a fighter. I, on the other hand, have always had pretty good upper body strength, on account of all the stabbing.

"Let's not attack the immortal sea witch today, shall we?" I said. "The Luidaeg has to give you what you're willing to pay for. *That's the deal.* She doesn't have a choice."

"When I asked for it, I didn't think she'd give it up," said the Luidaeg. "Sometimes my prices are set to serve as a deterrent. She was supposed to go home. You were supposed to have taught her never to undertake that sort of quest alone. You were supposed to have been clever enough to counteract my father's heroism."

"You took my daughter!" shouted Simon. "You left her with no way back!"

"If she'd managed to find Oberon, she wouldn't have needed her own way home. His would have been strong enough for the both of them, and then I would have been allowed, by the law of the exchange, to return her own. Really, it was her failure that doomed her, and not me." The Luidaeg sighed, looking briefly regretful. "I screwed up. I thought she'd go back to you and find another way."

"Instead, she went into the woods, and she didn't come back," I said. "Luidaeg, we need to follow her."

The Luidaeg frowned. "That's not something I can give you for free."

"I know."

"It has to cost."

"I know that, too."

"You're too deep in debt to be let off lightly; if I had a choice, I wouldn't bargain with you at all. Think hard before you do this, October, or—"

"Are you kidding?" I cut her off, taking a step toward her. In that moment, it didn't matter that she was the sea witch, or that she was Firstborn, or that she could probably have killed me with a flick of her wrist. I didn't care. "Please tell me you're kidding, because I can't *believe* you would think I hadn't already thought about this. My mother has *Tybalt*, Luidaeg. She has Tybalt, and she has Jazz, and she's going to keep them until I bring August back. Me. So, yeah, I am going to do whatever is in my power to find August, because without August, I'm dooming two members of my family to eternity in a cage. Do you understand? I haven't got a choice. I have to do this."

"And I'm her squire, which means I have to do it with her," said Quentin, stepping up next to me. His jaw was set. In that moment, there was nothing of the child I had mentored and worried about for all these years; I was looking at the man.

"I want my daughter back," said Simon, stepping up on the other side of me.

The Luidaeg looked between us, focusing on each of us in turn, and finally said softly, "You're fools, all of you. Fools and heroes, and I don't know if there's a difference."

"Sylvester used to say there wasn't a heroic bone in my body," said Simon. "I suppose I'd enjoy proving him wrong."

"Mother preserve me," muttered the Luidaeg, bowing her head for a moment. When she lifted it, her eyes were black. "Here is the cost of a candle, if a candle's what you desire: I can't close the way back, because you owe me, and I don't give up on what's mine. So I'll give you what Amy didn't. I'll give you a deadline. Seven days out and seven days back, a fortnight to learn if you're on the right track, and if by then your path's not clear, you'll come to me and stay a year."

It took me an embarrassingly long time to hear the binding in the rhyming cadence of her words. They wove over and around us, tying themselves tight before I could protest. Not that I was going to. If this was the only way to get Tybalt and Jazz back—to bring August home— then it was what I was going to do.

"Fourteen days. At the end of it, you'll have your sister, or you'll be my servants, unable to deny or defy me, doing whatever I ask. All of you." The Luidaeg held out her hand, palm upward. "Swear."

"We swear," said Simon, putting his hand in hers. Either he didn't recognize the danger, or he didn't care. She dug her suddenly hooked nails into the back of his hand, raking the skin open and pinning him in place so he couldn't pull away. Blood gushed from his wounds. Somehow, she grabbed hold of it, sculpting it like wax, until she was holding a long red taper streaked with bronze and gold.

"Mine required saltwater," I said.

"Yours was kinder," said the Luidaeg. She handed me the candle. The wick lit as soon as the wax touched my hand. "This will let you follow August's trail, as long as you keep your feet pointed in the right direction. You have to follow her, or all is lost. Fourteen days, October."

"We'll find her," I said.

"You'd better."

Fog was starting to fill the room, swirling around me, smelling faintly of blood and ashes and cinnamon. The spell was taking hold. "Grab onto me," I called to Simon and Quentin. "The Road's opening."

"You can get there and back by the candle's light," said the Luidaeg, and the fog came down, and she was gone, leaving the three of us alone in the unending gray.

THIRTEEN

"I SEEM TO BE BLEEDING quite a bit," said Simon. He sounded pained. That was understandable. The back of his hand was so much raw meat, and it wasn't like the Luidaeg had offered him an aspirin before she finished the spell. "I don't suppose either of you has a bandage on you?"

"You'd think so, with as often as October gets herself hurt, but no," said Quentin. "She heals too fast for bandages, and I'm pretty good about dodging before people cut me open."

"The implied insult is taken as read," said Simon. "If neither of you has a bandage, do you have a ribbon or other article that I can transform into one? I'm afraid I won't do you much good if I pass out from blood loss."

"Is this what it's like hanging out with me?" I asked, looking at Quentin through the fog.

"Sort of," he said. "You whine more. Also, you'd have lost a lot more blood and already be unconscious. Raj and I usually use that as an excuse to get something to eat while we wait for you to wake up."

"Liar," I said, and pulled the elastic band from my hair, offering it to Simon. "Will this work?"

"Better than nothing," he said, and took it, muttering something under his breath. The smell of smoke and oranges rose, and when it dissipated again, it took some of the fog with it.

We were standing on what looked like the road out of a Gothic thriller: a narrow, hardpacked dirt trail winding through black, empty moors on all sides. The sky was still mostly obscured by clouds; what I could see was spangled with too-bright stars. It was like the air was no longer thick enough to break up their light, allowing it to shine down on us with the force of a halogen beam. It was bright enough that we could easily pick out every detail of the nothing that there was to see in every direction, at least when the fog wasn't blocking everything.

Quentin was still taller than I was, and his hair was still bronze, rather than the dandelion gold it had been in childhood.

"Oh, thank Oberon," I muttered, earning myself curious glances from both Quentin and Simon. "This is the Babylon Road. Last time the Luidaeg set me on it, I wound up regressing into childhood, because it was part of the price of passage. With Blind Michael gone, I guess the rules are different."

Quentin looked horrified. "I forgot about that," he said.

"Yeah, well, you were young enough at the time that the road didn't mess with you the way it messed with me." I raised my new candle, turning until the flame leaped up and brightened, telling me that it had found its equivalent of magnetic north. "This way."

I started walking. The others followed. For a while, that was all we did. I walked, and they followed, and the moors unspooled around us without end, bisected by the dusty ribbon of the road.

After a time, I looked back at Simon. The smell of blood still hung in the air around him, bright and coppery, promising to tell me all his secrets, if I wanted to know them. I did. I wanted to know very badly. I didn't want to know at all.

"Simon," I said.

He lifted his head, looking at me. There was a wariness in his eyes. It occurred to me that there were a lot of unasked questions between us—questions that would change everything once I asked them. *What did you do to Luna and Rayseline? Why did you leave them there for so long? What part of losing your child made you think it was right to be so cruel?*

Those were questions for later, when I could afford to hate him without reservation. Right now, I needed to be able to tolerate him. So much depended on it.

"Why does the Luidaeg call you 'failure'?" There: that was a safe enough question, if there was such a thing. There was too much bad blood and stony ground between us for any question to be truly *safe*. Everything could have consequences.

"Ah." He sighed, relieved and regretful in the same breath. "She came to the wedding. Not in the form she wears from day-to-day. She looked like a Roane girl, with eyes the color of kelp and a smile like a breaking heart. People didn't know then that Amy was First-born, you see, and so disguises were required, but I knew who she was, and Amy knew. She was the only one of Amy's sisters to attend, or at least the only one I know of, and she made a toast after the ceremony. 'All I ask is that you keep her safe, and grounded, and stay by her side,' that's what she said. I thought I could do all three. As it happens, I couldn't do any of them."

"What happened to August wasn't your fault," said Quentin.

"It didn't have to be. I made the wrong choices after it was done. I thought if I could bring my daughter home by leaving my wife alone, that she would understand, and forgive me. Instead, all I did was make her a widow as well as a woman in mourning. Amy may forgive me someday, despite everything, but the Luidaeg? The Luidaeg never will."

The moors had started giving way to forest around us, the hills turning thick and bristly with trees. Their branches reached ceaselessly for the starry sky, their leaves rustling in the wind. The fog had all but dissipated, its purpose fully served. We were truly on the Babylon Road. No turning back now.

"A lot of people seem disinclined to forgive you," I said.

"I know, and I agree with them," said Simon. "What I did, I did for the best of reasons. That doesn't forgive it. If anything, that makes it worse, that a good man might become a villain thinking himself a hero in his heart. Take care, October. Your current quest . . . this is the road that broke me."

"I'll take that under advisement," I said, trying not to show how much his words struck home.

Amandine had Tybalt. There wasn't much I wouldn't do to get him back. If she had asked me to kill someone instead of sending me to find my sister, would I have considered it? Would I have agreed to do the things Simon had done? All she had asked me for so far was something I would have been willing to do anyway—but what if this wasn't the end? What if I found August, brought her back, and was greeted with a smug "for your next task . . ."?

I didn't know. That scared me.

"We are the sum of our actions," said Simon. "When desperation sets our course, those actions can blacken with remarkable speed."

"I know this place," said Quentin.

I stopped walking.

The forest had closed in around us completely, obscuring the moors. Many of the trees around us had probably been people once. The lady of this land, Acacia,

had attempted to transform me into one of them the
first time we met, stopping only when I revealed that I
knew her daughter, Luna Torquill. The last time I'd
checked, Acacia had been in the process of rehabilitat-
ing and restoring the victims of her husband's Rides . . .
but Blind Michael had been almost as old as the Luidaeg, and his Rides had spanned centuries. He had
stolen hundreds of children. Some of them had died.
Others had been broken so completely that their only
peace had been found in the forest.

I wasn't sure whether all of those children could be
brought back to their original forms, or whether they
would have any place to go if they were. Sometimes
lost is lost, even in Faerie. Maybe especially in Faerie.

"This is where we ran," said Quentin, the color
draining slowly from his face. He began, almost imper-
ceptibly, to tremble. "They were following us, and we
ran."

"Hey." I put a hand on his shoulder. "It's okay. Blind
Michael is dead. I killed him. He's never going to hurt
you again. You understand? You're safe."

A hunting horn sounded somewhere in the distance,
like the world was trying to make a liar out of me. I
flinched. So did Quentin. Only Simon, who had never
been on the receiving end of one of Blind Michael's
Rides, remained calm, looking toward the sound with
a speculative expression.

"August came through here," he said. "Do you think
she lingered?"

"I think she ran like hell, if she knew what was good
for her," I said. "Lingering is not a good plan when
those horns are sounding. Come on."

I started walking faster, following the flickering
light from my candle. It hadn't gotten any shorter since
this journey began. The Luidaeg might have to charge
for her help, but she didn't cheat: when she said she
would do something, she did it. This candle was good
for fourteen days of travel, and as long as the Babylon

Road could get to where we needed to be, it would take us there.

The Babylon . . . "Oh, hell," I said, and blew the candle out.

Quentin's eyes went wide. "Toby . . ."

"Why did you do that?" asked Simon, voice suddenly low and dangerous.

"Because we can't keep walking the Babylon Road without a destination," I said. "The Luidaeg said she sent August here because there was a changeling who was punching holes in the world. We've seen that before, and I've heard about that changeling." Not by name, but when Chelsea had been manifesting the same uncontrolled magic, he had been referenced as part of the reason she needed to be stopped.

The Luidaeg had told me about how my mother had been involved in sealing the hole that changeling made before it could grow wide enough to destroy Faerie. August had been looking for him. I glanced uneasily at Simon.

Suddenly, a lot of things were starting to fall into place, and I didn't think he was going to like the picture they made when they finished.

"He died," said Quentin. "The Luidaeg said he died."

"Right. But if August isn't in the forest here, it might be because she had him open a door for her."

"Then all is lost," said Simon. "We can't walk up to Oberon and ask him to please unlock the doors, sir, my daughter is on the other side and I need to bring her home. Finding him will be the work of far more than a fortnight."

"Maybe," I said. "If Acacia knows something, though—the Rose Road got us to the deeper lands once. I'm willing to bet that the Babylon Road can do the same, if that's *really* where we need to go."

The hunting horn sounded again, closer this time, startling me into flinching.

That was the last straw for Quentin. He'd been hold-

ing himself together as well as he could, and he was a
brave kid—but he was still, for all that he was tall and
broad-shouldered and clever, a kid. This place, that
sound, they were the things that haunted his nightmares. I flinched, and he bolted into the forest, running
as hard as he could to get away from the sound of
everything going wrong again.

"Quentin!" I shouted, and plunged into the trees
after him, not bothering to tell Simon to follow. He
would, or he wouldn't. Either way, we were all going to
wind up in the same place. I just needed to catch up
with Quentin before my squire ran off a cliff or fell
down a hole or something equally unhelpful.

The branches tore at my clothes and hair as I ran,
slowing me down. They seemed to put themselves into
my path on purpose, moving with a slow, malicious intent. That wasn't as far-fetched an idea as it might
seem. Acacia was the Mother of Trees, Firstborn to the
Dryads and the Blodynbryd. In her presence, even ordinary trees might have more of a consciousness than
the usual.

Quentin was somewhere up ahead, and I could hear
Simon crashing through the branches behind me. At
least we were staying together.

"Quentin!" I shouted. "Come back!"

The horns sounded a third time, so much closer that
it felt like I should have been able to turn around and
see the Riders bearing down on me. Which didn't make
sense. The Riders avoided the forest. When Blind Michael had been alive, they had steered clear because it
was Acacia's territory. Even now that he was dead and
everything was her territory, there were good reasons
to stay out of the trees. It was virtually impossible to
ride a horse there, for one thing. The branches blocked
too much of the light, making it hard for even fae eyes
to see what was going on.

Would the Riders even *have* horses now? The ones
they'd had originally had been transformed children,

mortal and changeling kids who hadn't been suited to join the Ride as anything other than transportation.

The forest ended abruptly, sending me stumbling as I ran onto the open plain. Quentin was less than ten yards ahead of me, backing up, his hands raised in a useless gesture of defensiveness.

Around him, in a loose semicircle, were Blind Michael's Riders.

They were hulking figures, dressed in mismatched leather-and-silver armor, sitting astride vast, strong-legged horses that pawed at the ground and snorted as they waited for the signal to run. None of the Riders belonged to any clear and obvious fae race: they were as patchworked as their armor, blending claws and talons and scales and fur. Some of them had horns. Others had fangs that barely fit inside their mouths, leaving trails of drool to run down their misshapen chins. All of them had weapons: spears and swords and crossbows.

"Quentin, get back here," I said quietly, hand going to the knife at my belt. It wasn't enough. It could never have been enough, not against this nightmare army. But if we were going to go down, I was going to go down swinging, protecting the people I loved.

Tybalt, I'm sorry, I thought. Maybe someday Amandine would have mercy and let him go.

The Riders looked toward me. One of them raised a horn and blew, sending a long, loud note cascading across the waste. It gained strength and volume as it traveled, seeming to feed off of its own echoes, until it was loud enough to fill the entire world. Quentin clapped his hands over his ears, legs shaking as if they were on the verge of buckling.

That was the last straw. I bolted forward, stepping in front of him, knife already drawn, like one silver blade the length of my hand could hold off the Riders for more than a fraction of a second.

"Back off!" I snarled. "If you want him, you'll have to go through me!"

"You never change, do you, October?"

The voice was Acacia's. I whirled, and there she was, Blind Michael's widow, the Mother of the Trees, standing between us and the forest. Simon was somewhere behind her, a pale smear at the edge of the shadows. I couldn't spare him much attention. Acacia was a much more pressing issue.

Her skin was daffodil-yellow, and her hair was a root-like mass of green-and-yellow strands that snaked over her shoulders and continued down her body, vanishing in and out of her clothes. She no longer wore a cloak, and her wings were exposed, enormous and green, marked with bright yellow circles like eyes. The scar that ran down the side of her face kept her from smiling with both sides of her mouth, but still, she looked kind.

"When I felt the Babylon Road seeking an anchor, I'll admit, you're not who I expected," she said. "You know my doors are always open to you. But it would have been a good idea to call first."

"Tell your people to stand down, Acacia," I said, voice tight with adrenaline. Quentin was still shaking, still terrified. I needed that to stop.

Acacia blinked, looking genuinely surprised. Then she shook her head and said, "They were looking for the Road. They're not here to hurt you."

"Could've fooled me," mumbled Quentin.

"My apologies," said Acacia. She looked to the Riders. "Go home. I'll be there soon, and you'll be rewarded for your work."

The Riders lowered their weapons and their horns, some quickly, others looking like they had been hoping for a fight. Then they turned their horses and rode away across the waste, kicking up dust and debris in their wake.

Quentin relaxed further, head hanging. I turned to face Acacia, putting a hand on his shoulder to steady him.

"Sorry," I said. "Turns out Quentin and I still have issues with the sound of that horn. I thought you were going to help them recover."

"I am," she said. "Some of the horses refuse to return to any other form. They're too broken to want to go back to what they were. They're treated kindly now. Fed and watered and rested. I'm looking toward acquiring Kelpies or Each Uisge for the Riders to use after these horses are gone."

"Oh," said Quentin, and shivered under my hand.

Acacia looked at me calmly. "Can you tell your friend to leave my trees? It's hard to believe you come in peace when you keep someone at my back."

"Sorry," I said. Raising my voice, I called, "Simon, it's safe now. You need to come out."

"I doubt that most sincerely," he said, and emerged from the trees, walking slowly across the open ground to stand at my other side.

Acacia tilted her head, looking at him. "You are not my daughter's husband, but you look like him," she said. "Are you his Fetch? Is my Luna to be a widow?"

"I'm his brother," said Simon. "My name is Simon."

"Interesting," said Acacia. "The two of you could be buds from the same branch."

"So I've been told," said Simon. "We're looking for my daughter."

"Her name is August," I said. "She would have come through here about a hundred years ago, via the Babylon Road, looking for a changeling boy that Michael had stolen on one of his Rides."

"I remember her," said Acacia, and frowned. "She crashed in as if she had every right, and she stole from my husband. He told me she was dust and bones. Did he lie?"

She didn't sound like she'd be surprised if he had. My heart sank anyway. I had been more than half-hoping August had spent the last hundred years as a tree, growing peacefully in Acacia's woods, waiting for me to come and take her home. "I don't know," I said. "We're trying to find her."

"Why?"

"Because she's my sister, and because our mother decided to take my lover as collateral against my bringing her back."

Acacia's eyes widened again. "Amandine spoke to you? A second child of Amandine's line yet lives?"

"I don't know, but I need to find her," I said. "You said she stole from Michael. Did she find the changeling she was looking for?"

"Yes. Grabbed the boy out of the stables and vanished into the night."

I did not want to go back to Blind Michael's stable. More, I did not want to take Quentin there. This place was a nightmare walking for him, and he deserved more than the traumas I was heaping on his head. We didn't really have a choice, considering the circumstances.

"I need to see where they disappeared from," I said. "Can you take us there?"

"For the woman who murdered my husband?" asked Acacia, with a hint of amusement in her voice. "Anything. Please, follow me."

She began to walk across the wastes, wings fanning at the air. Lacking any better options in the matter, the rest of us followed her, while the fog curled in to block the sky above us.

FOURTEEN

IF I HADN'T BEEN to Acacia's lands when they still belonged to her husband, they might have seemed utterly bleak, without any hint of life or recovery. But I had been there before. I had fled across them when they belonged to her husband, when they were nothing but thorn and stone and suffering. Now . . .

The ground was still hard, stony, and unforgiving. It was also dusted in a thin layer of delicate green, weeds and grasses starting to take root as they found a way to thrive in a place that had never welcomed them before. The thorn briars were still thick, almost impenetrable knots dotting the landscape, but now they were dotted with the occasional white flower the size of my hand, almost—not quite—like blackberries in bloom. Life was coming to Blind Michael's kingdom, and once it fully arrived, it wasn't going to agree to leave again. Life so rarely did.

Acacia walked beside me, watching as I reacted to everything around us. Smiling a small and secret smile, she asked, "What do you think?"

"I think it's going to be amazing."

"I think it already is." She tilted her head back, until she was sending her smile to the three pale and distant moons that dotted the blackness of the sky. "They've come so much farther than you can see from a distance. I've sent so many of them back to their people, and the ones who have chosen to stay—it was a *choice* for most of them, not the only option they had remaining."

There was a word there that said everything: "most." What Blind Michael had done to the children he stole was more than just a crime. It was a monstrosity. It was no surprise that some of them hadn't been able to recover, either because his magic had bent them too far from what they had been, or because they had no longer been able to imagine themselves as anything other than what they had become. This was their home now.

"How have the families of the ones who've gone back received them?"

Acacia grimaced. "Some well; some not. It had been centuries for some of the Riders. Their families had . . . moved on, I suppose. It can be hard to bring someone back to something they left so long before."

I glanced toward Simon. He was walking beside Quentin, looking around with calm curiosity, seemingly unbothered by the strangeness of his surroundings. This place didn't hold any deep-seated nightmares for him.

"I get that," I said.

Quentin was a lot less relaxed than Simon. That wasn't a surprise. He kept looking around, eyes wide and a little wild, like he expected to be attacked at any moment. The occasional blast of a hunting horn in the far distance probably wasn't helping any.

The land was malleable before the wishes of its mistress, even as it had once been malleable before Blind Michael's wishes. We walked toward the stable, and the plains bent themselves to suit us, reducing the distance without changing the shape of it, so that we walked over the crest of a shallow hill and were suddenly confronted with the low, boxy shape of the hall and its outbuildings, like a child's toys left carelessly scattered across the yard.

Quentin stepped closer to me, pale and a little shaky. I reached over and took his hand. He glanced at me and laughed uneasily.

"This was the first place I was taller than you," he said.

"I thought you didn't really remember that," I replied.

He swallowed hard.

"I lied," he said.

I gave him a sidelong look. There were lines in the skin around his mouth and eyes, drawn deep and cruel by an unseen hand. He was terrified. That wasn't so unreasonable. This was the first place that hadn't cared who he was or what he wanted—only what it could do to him.

There are days when I honestly wish I could kill Blind Michael all over again. Murder is wrong, but what he spent centuries doing to children . . .

Acacia was still walking. We followed her, rapidly catching up with Simon, who still looked like he was taking a casual walk in the park.

"Fascinating," he said, not looking at us. "Building an islet of this size while the deeper lands were sealed must have taken an incredible amount of power. Building it *well*, so that it would endure past the life of its creator—it's almost unbelievable."

"My husband was a clever one; he knew the power of ritual," said Acacia. "There are so many bones buried here that the islet will never crumble. It's been bought and paid for with the blood of the innocent, every inch of it. If you were considering the virtues of becoming a lord in your own land, I recommend you find a better way. Stronger men than you have been corrupted by the lure of empire."

Her tone was mild, almost bored, like she was remarking on the weather or talking about what she was going to serve for dinner. I stared at the back of her head, so much suddenly making sense. Blind Michael had borrowed the eyes of his Riders, but there had always been elements in Faerie who would have been delighted, even honored to join his Ride. People for whom a few extra teeth and claws would have seemed like a gift instead of a punishment. Instead, he'd taken children, snatching them from their beds and twisting them to his own ends. Why?

Because there is power in blood, and there is power in suffering, and for centuries, Blind Michael's lands had been a constant source of suffering. He had carved the islet with his own two hands, and stabilized and expanded it on the backs of the children he destroyed.

This was a graveyard that stretched from one end of the horizon to the other. No matter how far we walked, we would still be walking in the footprints of the dead.

Acacia looked over her shoulder, smiling sadly at the expression on my face. "Now you understand," she said. "My mother set her children against us—against *me*, who had the audacity to love a son of Maeve. She would have killed us both for our crimes, slaughtered our children in their cradles, and all for the sin of loving. He Rode with the best intentions, once. What he took, he thought the world could spare."

Simon turned his face away, but not fast enough to keep me from seeing the profound discomfort in his eyes. Good. He needed to remember that monsters were made from the best of intentions—and I needed to remember that Simon, despite being polite and friendly and beloved of pixies, was also the man who had taken me away from my family and Luna and Rayseline away from Sylvester. He claimed to have done it all with the best of intentions. Well, Blind Michael had claimed the same thing, and look what that had done. Some of his victims—most of his victims, when I counted the dead— were never going to recover.

Quentin was still holding my hand, clenching tightly enough that my fingers hurt. I didn't try to pull away, not even when we turned a corner and there it was: the stable, so close that I could smell the straw and horse-sweat scent of it. I tried to breathe shallowly, but I couldn't stop the scent from creeping in and filling my nostrils, bringing too many memories along. This was where nightmares were born.

The tangled thorn briars that had once locked the stable doors were gone; the doors stood open, allowing the inhabitants to come and go as they pleased. That wasn't the only change. The walls were still dark wood and stone, but they had been scrubbed at some point, and were no longer caked in several centuries of filth. The floor was clean. Everything smelled of horse, but not of urine or feces. Just hot skin, and fur, and all the other scents that were unavoidable when there were animals present.

Given more time, given more changes, this place might stop making my skin crawl. But I wasn't going to count on it.

"The changeling boy was kept here," said Acacia, indicating the stable.

"Wait," I said. "Blind Michael snatched a changeling powerful enough to rip holes in the world, and stuck him in the *stable*?"

"He was mortal," said Acacia, like that explained everything—and maybe, to her, it did. "Rider or ridden. In all the years I watched my husband working, you were the only changeling I ever saw him treat as anything other than a beast of burden."

"Lucky me," I said bleakly, looking at the stable. I pulled my hand out of Quentin's. He didn't fight me. He knew what I was about to do, and he wanted no part of it.

Might as well get this over with. I turned and offered him the candle. To no one's surprise, it burst back into flame as soon as it was clear that I intended to give it to someone else. "Hold this," I said.

He blinked. "What—?"

"It's going to be hard enough to find August's magic under everything in here. I don't need to have the Luidaeg's candle confusing me." The Babylon candle didn't smell of blood. It didn't really smell of anything, not even smoke. That didn't mean it couldn't confuse things. The Luidaeg is a sledgehammer in a world of scalpels, and when she gets involved, it leaves a mark.

"Okay," said Quentin uncertainly. He took the candle and pulled it close to his chest, so that the light of it bathed his face, making everything golden and wavering.

I offered him the most sincere smile I could muster, clapped him on the shoulder, and turned away from him. What came next was something I would have to do alone.

Blind Michael's stables—and they would always be *his*, Acacia could be lady of these lands for a thousand years, could do everything in her power to erase the stain of his legacy, and this place would still belong to him, drenched in the effects of his good intentions, of his monstrosity—loomed like an empty eye socket, black and bleak and dripping with menace. I took a deep breath and forced myself to step inside, past the threshold. I didn't look back. If I had, even once, it would have become impossible to continue on.

With every step, the shadows got deeper, and the smell of horses got stronger, even though most of the stalls were currently empty. I shivered. This was the real reason I'd given the candle to Quentin. If the shadows had danced when the flame flickered, I would have run screaming.

Some wounds never really heal. They just scab over enough to let you keep on going.

When I reached the center of the building, I stopped, braced myself against what was about to hit me, and closed my eyes.

Your name is October; you are doing this to save the man you love, I thought, and breathed in deeply.

Magic is distinctive. No two people have the same magic, no matter how superficially similar they may seem. Amandine's roses are not Evening's roses are not Luna's roses. My copper is not my mother's blood, no matter how similar the two might eventually become. Magic echoes. It does not repeat.

Magic is ephemeral. It fades with time, with distance, as other scents and other footsteps blur and rub it away. Even the strongest spells were never intended to last forever. In the mortal world, dawn chips away at magic with every sunrise, erasing it from the world, making space for something new.

This wasn't the mortal world. This wasn't even the Summerlands, where a thousand competing local regents wrote and rewrote the land according to their own desires. This was an islet, so far from the places most of us knew that the rules were different. For Blind Michael's lands, the time between August's arrival and mine had been nothing more than one long, unending night. Acacia had softened it, finally allowing it to die, but there was still a chance.

I breathed in, and the magic of hundreds of stolen children washed over me, screaming. Here were the illusions they had spun, desperate to hide themselves from the man who had stolen them, who was *still* stealing them, breaking their minds and bodies in order to remake them in his own image. Here were the transformations they had attempted—and, in some cases, achieved. One child's magic had smelled of bluebells and meadowsweet, and when I breathed it, I could taste the moment he had burst into a whole warren of rabbits, each holding a single piece of his heart. They had fled for the trees, and for all I knew, some of them were living there still, mute and unaware of what they had once been, but free.

August, I thought. *I am looking for August.*

Flowers and fruits and minerals and ideas, the smell of spilled cream drying in the sunlight, of fresh-milled grain, of ripe tomatoes, of sunlight on a bird's wing. All the shades of magic washed over and through me, choking me, bringing tears to my eyes. Most of these children had died here. The ones who hadn't . . . they would never go home. All this magic had been lost, harvested like wheat to reinforce Blind Michael's own aspirations.

And under so much of it—not at the bottom; I didn't think I could find the bottom if I spent a year trying—I found a ribbon of rose wrapped in smoke, all but buried under magic fueled by panic and agony and fear. August hadn't been in emotional distress when she'd arrived here. She had been on an adventure, doing something bright and brave.

Had she even paused to realize how many children she was leaving behind? Had she promised them she would come back, and died a little inside when she broke her word? Or had she seen them as just one more obstacle between her and the goal of fulfilling the prophecy about our bloodline? I didn't know. I didn't even want to guess. It was impossible not to wonder.

"Quentin, bring me the candle," I said, holding fast to the traceries of August's magic. I didn't want to let go. If I did, I might not find them again.

"Coming," he said, and then he was beside me, pushing the candle into my waiting hand.

The flame began to smoke, wreathing me in gray. "Simon!" I shouted. "I think we're leaving!"

"You found her?" He was suddenly beside me, looking at me with wide, anxious eyes. "Where are we going?"

"No idea," I said. The Babylon Road is a path between two points. It could get us there and back by the candle's light, but where "there" was going to be was anybody's guess. "Wherever August went."

"Come back when you can," called Acacia, from somewhere in the fog. I couldn't see her anymore. Maybe that was a kindness. "I'm always happy for your company."

"I'll try," I called, and I didn't hear anything from her after that. The fog was too thick, obscuring the stable walls entirely.

But it didn't obscure the path that seemed to unspool beneath my feet, leading off into the distance. I started walking, cautiously at first, and then—when I didn't slam face-first into the stable wall—faster, Simon and Quentin following behind. Quentin looked eager, relieved even. We were on an adventure, and we were leaving his nightmares behind. Simon looked distant, his face settling into an expression of neutral contemplation.

I glanced at him. "I thought you would have seen Blind Michael's lands before." It was as close as I could come to accusing him of using some forgotten, forsaken corner of the islet as a prison, back when Luna and Raysel had been in his custody.

Simon jumped a little, shaking his head. "No," he said. "It was too dangerous to tempt the attention of two of the Firstborn. I shared my bed and my heart with the youngest of their number, the one who understood the least about her own strength, and there were times I thought Amandine might kill me by mistake. I avoided them whenever I could."

"Oh," I said.

"I would have thought that if anyone would understand the inability to keep out of the path of the Firstborn, it would be you," he said, and attempted a smile. It fell flat. He could tell, because he gave it up quickly, and said, "My . . . eventual employer was always there, watching, but as she seemed content to maintain her personal masquerade, I felt it was safe to go about my business, despite the proximity of two of my wife's sisters. Had I brought Blind Michael and the Mother of Trees into the matter, I might have expired from sheer nervousness."

"Oh," I said again.

He sighed. "You'll have to ask me eventually. You might as well stop dancing around the topic and have your answers given to you."

"I don't want to hate you more than I already do when I still need to work with you," I said.

Quentin said nothing, but he stepped a little closer to me, matching his steps to mine, so that it was clear that whatever Simon said next, I wasn't going to be dealing with it alone. That was a good thing. Simon had been bound not to act against me, but there was nothing that was going to stop me from breaking his nose if I thought it was necessary.

Simon sighed. The sound carried through the fog, seeming to echo across whatever landscape we were now walking through. The light from our candle was the only constant, and it wasn't strong enough to give us any sense of presence or place. We were somewhere, and we were in the process of transitioning to some-place else. Everything around us was inconsequential. Or maybe it was very consequential, and a dragon was going to come charging out of the fog to devour us all. We wouldn't know until it happened.

"Everything I did, I did for August," he said. "I lacked your skill at asking the right boons of the sea witch—or perhaps I merely lacked her goodwill. I was the brother-in-law she never asked for, the failure who had married her youngest sister when Amandine deserved so much better than a landless younger son whose only aspiration was to own the nicest vest in the Westlands. When I asked her to aid me, she said she could do it, but that the price would be more than I could bear. I would have done it anyway, if she had been able to promise August would be safe. The woman I wound up pledging myself to, she was willing to make that promise."

"Yeah, well, the woman you went to work for lied."

Simon grimaced. "I know that now."

The Luidaeg can't lie. She's incapable of it. Every-thing she says is carefully considered and sounded out, to avoid possible contradictions. Evening, on the other hand, is a liar born and bred, and she had probably been willing to tell Simon whatever she thought he wanted to hear, especially if Oleander—her favorite pet—had been asking to keep him. Upset Amandine, make sure August stayed lost, and placate Oleander, all at the same time. It was elegant and efficient, two things Evening loved.

"At first, I was trying to find a way to open the doors," said Simon softly. "I was learning alchemy and mixing potions and making deliveries. I was transforming her enemies. It all started so *small*, and everything we did seemed to take us a step closer to finding the door August had walked through, to prying it open and reaching the other side. Amandine had her own ways of looking. She wanted nothing to do with me. She *blamed* me, and my brother, for giving August the example of heroism. With time, it became less about the immediate results, and more about keeping my mistress happy—and keeping Oleander happy, of course. I doubt our mutual owner would have been more than mildly annoyed if Oleander had slit my throat one day. She would have made Oleander clean up the mess, but Oleander was always the more productive of the two of us. I was a prize. The fallen Torquill, the bad brother, the one she'd lured astray. Oleander, she made things *function*."

Quentin started to open his mouth. I shook my head, cutting him off. Simon's voice dripped with bitterness and loathing, almost all of it self-directed. If we interrupted him now, he wasn't going to resume.

"I am . . . very sorry for what I am about to say," said Simon slowly. "When my mistress saw that Sylvester had taken an interest in the latest scion of Amandine's line, when she saw that there was going to be another chance for the prophecy to be fulfilled, when she *understood* that being partially mortal didn't make you harmless, she decided the best way to act without breaking her own bindings, which forbid her to directly harm the children of Amandine's line, was to task me to destroy my brother. And I am so sorry, but I went along willingly, because he hadn't been there for me when I lost my daughter, when I lost my wife as a consequence. I hated that he was happy and I wasn't. I wanted him to suffer. I thought that after you disappeared, presumed dead, she would let me bring them home. I was wrong."

I stopped walking to stare at Simon. "You're telling me you kidnapped them because of *me*? Because you didn't want Sylvester to be there to take care of me?"

"She wanted you gone and believed my brother might present an obstacle to your own self-destruction; she wanted him distracted before you were removed from the board," he said, voice barely above a whisper. "I'm so sorry, October. I would lie to you, if I didn't think you were tired of being lied to."

There were no words. I stared at him, unable to decide whether I was more furious with him or with Evening. In the end, he won the coin toss. He was there for me to rage at, and Evening was still asleep, sealed off in a forgotten Road, where she could rot for all I cared.

"You stole them because of *me*," I hissed. "You destroyed your own brother's life—you destroyed *my* life—you shattered Rayseline's mind, and you did it because Evening *told* you to."

Simon flinched when I said Evening's name, actually flinched, like he'd been slapped. "Please don't help her find us."

"What did you do to them? Where did you leave them?"

"I made a bubble," he said. "I made it the same way Blind Michael made his lands, the way Gilad anchored his knowe. I forced magic into the space between worlds, and then I placed them inside it. They wouldn't starve, there. They wouldn't get sick, they wouldn't die—"

"No, they'd just sit in absolute darkness until you came back to get them, and also, by the way, you fucked up how time ran there. *Rayseline grew up.* I was gone for fourteen years, and when I got back, she was an adult who hadn't seen the sun since she was a little girl!

You *destroyed* her, and you did it because what? You thought there was a chance that maybe, if you were a good boy someday, Evening would stop jerking you around and give you back your daughter?"

"Yes," he said levelly, looking me in the eye. "That's exactly why I did it. August meant more to me than anyone else in the world. She still does. You can consider me your enemy if you like, even though I mean you no harm, now or later, but I did what I did for the sake of your sister, and if you told me to do it again, and I believed that by doing so I could bring her home a moment faster, I would raise my hand in your service. The best of intentions for me can be the worst of consequences for someone else."

I couldn't find the words to reply to him. I just stared, the Babylon candle in my hand, the mist eddying around us, and wondered when things had gone so wrong for me that a moment like this one could even be possible. Quentin was standing a few feet away, close enough not to get lost, silent. There was nothing for him to say. This was between me and the man who had ruined my life—and no matter how much better things were for me now, he hadn't known that then. Even if he had, that would have been no excuse. He had made my choices for me. He had taken one future away and substituted it with another.

And he had done it all with the very best of intentions.

There was regret in Simon's eyes. He knew I was going to hate him for this, that I was never going to forgive him for saying the things he'd said to me . . . and he was saying them anyway, because of all the Torquills, he was the one who refused to lie to me.

"I'm too tired for this bullshit," I snarled, turning away from him. "Come on. We need to find your daughter."

I walked, and he followed, and the mist closed in around us, and everything else was gone.

FIFTEEN

WE WALKED UNTIL IT seemed like there was
nothing to the world but walking. There was no time
on the Babylon Road, not really: our candle was our
clock, and it hadn't started burning down yet. It
wouldn't, until we had reached our final destination, I
asked it to do something other than playing GPS, or our
deadline was drawing near. I wasn't actually sure about
that last one. The Luidaeg might let us wander in the fog
for our entire supposed year of service, and then claim
that what she'd really wanted us to do for her was go out
and gather dust for later use. She could be tricky that
way.

The mist cleared occasionally, revealing glimpses of
sky or the surrounding landscape, which changed from
step to step. One moment it was mountains. The next,
it would be plains, or forest, or a great, surging sea
beating itself senseless against a rocky shore. The scent
of the wind changed even more constantly, now smelling of heather, or blackberry flowers, or redwoods. The
only constant was that it never smelled of *people*. I
couldn't always pick up traces of other fae when they

weren't bleeding or using magic, but there was a flavor to the air in inhabited places, like they moved it around more just by being there. This air was sweet and alive, but it was empty.

"Toby." Quentin stepped up next to me, lips thin, eyes anxious. "I think we're walking into deeper Faerie."

"I think you're right," I agreed. I had been able to accomplish that particular trick once before, with Tybalt's help. Luna had opened us a Rose Road, and we had walked along it until he had sensed the presence of his nephew. Once he was sure Raj was somewhere near, Tybalt had opened a Shadow Road between where we were and where we needed to be.

Oberon might have locked the front doors and told his subjects to stay in the Summerlands until he came back, but that didn't mean he had sealed all the secret ways in and out of the deeper realms. He'd just made it harder for people to get there.

"I don't *want* to go back to deeper Faerie."

"Sorry, kiddo. We have to go where the candle takes us."

"I know." He shook his head. "I'm sort of surprised you're staying so calm. If somebody took Dean, I'd probably lose my shit, and I don't lo—I like him a lot, but I'm not planning to stay with him forever."

"That's okay," I said. "You're a teenager. You're allowed to date and figure out what you want before you have to settle down to doing . . . other things." Simon didn't know Quentin was the Crown Prince of the Westlands—or at least I assumed Simon didn't know, and I wasn't going to be the one to tell him. That was information that he didn't need. "I'm calm because if I weren't, I'd start screaming and never stop again. My job has always been dangerous. I never thought it could put the rest of you in danger in our own home."

But I should have. Simon was proof of that. Sylvester was a hero, and being a hero had put him in the position to be my mentor. Being my mentor had gotten his wife and daughter kidnapped, passively tortured, and imprisoned for an unmeasurable period of time. Being a hero meant that sometimes the danger followed you home.

I was a hero now, too. I hadn't sought the position. It had been shoved on me one stolen child and broken promise at a time. That didn't make it any less mine. The people around me—the people I cared about—were always going to be in danger.

Quentin scowled. "Oh, no," he said. "Stop it."

I blinked. "Stop what?"

"Stop thinking we'd be better off without you."

"I wasn't!"

"You *were*. I could see it in your eyes, and you're wrong. We're better with you, just like you're better with us. Wait until we get Tybalt and Jazz back safe and sound. You'll see." Quentin bumped his shoulder against mine. "You keep making yourself calm, and we'll find her, and we'll bring her home, and your horrible mother will give them back, and we won't invite her to the wedding."

"I wasn't planning on it," I said, with a weak smile.

"Sure you were. She's your mom. But nobody wants to sit next to her at dinner, so let's just skip it, okay?"

"Okay," I said.

The mist cleared.

The three of us were standing at the top of a high, heath-covered hill. The air smelled of salt, peat, and the sea, which only made sense, since I could see bone-white cliffs in the distance, descending toward a black and restless sea. The beam of a lighthouse swept rhythmically across the water, warning the nonexistent ships of the hazards ahead.

Once, those waters would have been alive with Cephali and Merrow. Selkies would have basked on the rocky beaches, cushioned by their folded sealskins. The docks would have teemed with sailors, coming in from the sea and setting their sails to chase down the horizon. This had been a seafaring realm. The castles on the hills, ramshackle silhouettes against the devouring dark, had been the places they returned to when the journey was done, but the whole focus had been on the sea.

"Annwn," I breathed.

"Again," muttered Quentin.

Simon didn't say anything. He just stopped, and stared, honey-colored eyes wide as he tried to drink in everything around us. The smell of smoke and rotten oranges rose around him, underscored with a surprising note of mulled cider as his magic flared in response to his surprise and dismay. He was swallowing hard, over and over again, like he was trying not to cry.

Maybe he was. "Have you ever been here?" I asked, as gently as I could.

"No." Simon shook his head. "No, I . . . the deeper realms were sealed when I was still an infant, and my parents had intended to wait until my brother and I were older before they made such a journey. My sister, September, visited Mag Mell once. She said it was so beautiful it hurt her, and that she couldn't imagine staying for more than a moment, because if she did, she would never be able to find it in her heart to leave."

Annwn didn't call to me like that, but I wasn't a pureblood. Part of me was still human, and still wanted the human world more than it wanted anything else. Maybe once that had been burned away by necessity and time, I would feel that way about Annwn and the other realms of deeper Faerie. Right now . . .

Right now, I wanted to get out of here as quickly as I could. "So it looks like old home week is continuing, and we have a problem," I said grimly.

"What?" Simon looked at me, bemused. "How is this a problem? August was searching for Oberon. The Luidaeg said she had gone to look in the deeper realms. Annwn is a deeper realm. If she couldn't come back without him, she might still be here."

There was undeniable hope in his tone, and I couldn't hate him for that. The fields here grew lush with berries, and the trees were heavy with fruit. There were monsters—Faerie always has monsters—but they weren't anything a healthy pureblood with her wits about her couldn't have handled. Most of all, purebloods work differently than humans do. Lock a human or a changeling away, alone, for a hundred years, and they wouldn't be recognizable when they came back. The human mind is too aware of time. Mortals get bored.

Purebloods . . . don't. Purebloods know how to disconnect themselves from the world around them, wandering in a dreamlike fog while their brain goes about the business of cleaning and organizing itself in the background. They forget things when they do that—the names of people they loved and lost hundreds of years before, where they grew up, the way their first pets died—but they come back refreshed and bright-eyed and emotionally hale. August might have had trouble finding enough safety to disconnect, but the fact that it had been a hundred years would not, in and of itself, have been enough to do her harm.

No, the issue was Annwn itself. Of course we were in Annwn. It's always easier to tear something that's been torn before. Chelsea had ripped her way here in her panic, and been forced to repeat the journey over and over for Duchess Treasa Riordan of Dreamer's Glass, a xenophobic noble who wanted to establish her own kingdom in the deeper realms, far away from anyone who might want her to do something silly, like sharing. But before Chelsea, a changeling boy whose name we still didn't know had opened the way.

For August.

Simon was still looking at me, waiting for his answer. I sighed deeply.

"We sort of . . . left some people here," I said. "They may not be too thrilled to see us. By which I mean there's a good chance they're going to try to kill us, on account of how I sort of accidentally exiled them to Annwn with no way home to pick up the rest of their stuff."

Simon blinked. Several times. Finally, he said the only thing that made sense, under the circumstances: "*What?*"

"Uh, you know Duchess Riordan?"

"Yes, of course. She's an unpleasant sort, but at least she's reasonably straightforward. No knives in the back from that one. Treasa always preferred a good, straight-forward frontal attack."

"Not helping," I said. "She kidnapped Etienne's daughter and used her to rip a hole to Annwn, intending to take the population of Dreamer's Glass out of the mortal world and back into deeper Faerie, where she would presumably be the ruler of all she surveyed, and not have to deal with having neighbors anymore. Only Riordan was going to kill Chelsea in the process, so we rescued her and used her to get home. Stranding Riordan and about half of her people here."

"And half of her supplies," said Quentin. "They hadn't finished bringing their trains through. Also, she was going to keep me as breeding stock. I don't like her at *all*."

Simon's blink this time was slower, more like he was taking it all in than any marker of active confusion. Finally, he said, "No, I don't expect you would."

I took a deep breath. August's trail led away from the spot where the Babylon Road had deposited us, deeper into the moors. I sighed. "But we have to go that way," I said, gesturing with my candle. "Let's just hope we don't run into any of Riordan's people, or that if we do, they're too busy trying to learn how to be an agrarian society to give us any shit."

"Next time let's go someplace new, where you haven't already pissed everybody off," said Quentin.

"I'll take that under advisement," I replied, and started walking.

The last time I'd been in Annwn, Tybalt had been with me. It was strange, walking there without him. I had come to depend on him so much, for backup, for support, for the way he made the world seem . . . not kinder, but easier to tackle. I could handle anything, as long as he was there to keep me from falling over.

He wasn't here now. Mom had him, and while I trusted her not to actively torture him, she still had him locked in a cage, unable to transform or reach the Shadow Roads. Cait Sidhe are natural shapeshifters. For Tybalt, cat form was as natural as walking on two legs and having opposable thumbs. But that was when it was a choice, something he'd done to himself, and not a transformation forced on him by someone else. When Simon had transformed me into a fish, the magic had changed my mind as well as my body, adapting me to a life spent swimming through the watery depths of the pond, eating mindlessly, swimming toward the warmth of the sun. I'd been gone for years. It could have been hours, for all the awareness my fish's mind had had of the passage of time.

Maybe that would be a mercy. Or maybe I'd get him back and find that I had a feral tomcat on my hands, unable or unwilling to transform into his human form.

Either way, I would cross that bridge when I came to it. Right now, I needed to focus on following the thin ribbon of August's magic across the fields, toward the distant shape of one of the castles.

As we drew closer, it became apparent that I wasn't going to get at least one of my wishes: I wasn't going to be avoiding Riordan today. The land around the castle had been worked, the fields cleared of brush and briar and planted with crops that looked something like rhubarb, something like corn, and something like an unholy hybrid of the two. Simon looked around us and nodded, apparently content with what he saw.

"They're settling in," he said.

"What is it?"

"Annwn rhubarb," he said. At my blank expression, he smiled, and said, "Roses change according to the soil they're planted in. Apples, too. A Granny Smith is not a Honeycrisp, nor is either of them a Red Delicious. Plants have always adapted to suit the soil that nurtures them. I don't know who decided to plant rhubarb here, but the result was a larger, sweeter crop. They used to use it for making wine, back when we had easy access to the fields. I remember drinking it at banquets when I was young, before the wine cellars were emptied and all we had was the memory of sweetness. If you wanted to pay for your impending wedding, you could do it with a scythe and a sack in this field. There are people—purebloods, older ones—who would pay anything you asked, for the chance to taste the fruits of their youth again."

"We're not here to steal Riordan's crops," I said. "We just need to follow August's trail until we find the next turn."

"Then we shall," he said.

The castle Riordan had claimed as her own was coming more clearly into view. She had been repairing it since I'd been there last—or more accurately, she had been instructing her people to repair it. There was a scaffold against one wall, and the battlements were no longer quite so raggedy. Simon stopped in mid-step, putting his arm out to signal for me and Quentin to stop as well. I did, only stumbling a little as I turned to frown at him.

His eyes were on the sky, and he was smiling. Not happily. He looked like a man who had just had his worst fears confirmed, and was simply relieved to see that it was over.

"Well, well," he said. "Treasa *has* been busy."

"What are you looking at?"

Simon gave me a sidelong look. "I forget, sometimes, that your strengths are not all the same as mine," he said. "Ask your squire."

I looked to the side. "Quentin?"

Quentin's eyes were also focused on the sky, but he wasn't smiling. Instead, he had gone pale, eyes wide and glossy in dismay. "It's an illusion," he said. "It's all an illusion."

If I looked, I could see a faint glitter in the air, betraying the outlines of whatever Riordan was trying to hide. I couldn't see the illusion itself, much less see through it. The Dóchas Sidhe may outpace the Daoine Sidhe when it comes to blood magic, but we can't hold a candle to them where illusions are concerned.

A candle. I lifted the candle the Luidaeg had given me, and murmured, "You can get there and back by a candle's light." I couldn't get there if I couldn't see where I was going.

The flame leaped up, devouring at least an inch of wax in the process and sending the first hot line to dribble down and score the skin of my hand. I managed not to flinch, focusing instead on the increasing glitter in the air, which had frozen like frost on a windowpane. Then, bit by bit, in an almost fractal pattern, it began to dissolve, revealing what Riordan had *really* done to her chosen castle.

The scaffold was gone, as was the need for it: the walls stood thick and strong, shored up by great slabs of white stone, no doubt carved from the distant cliffs. They had been rebuilt until they changed a simple barrier into a barricade, making the place into a fortress. The towers were twice as high as they had seemed from a distance. They were made of the same stone as the walls, spotted with the blind, narrow eyes of arrow slits and the larger, stained glass blooms of windows.

The largest of the stained glass windows was set directly above the castle gates, where it could serve no useful purpose, since there was no way for anyone to stand on the other side and look out—not unless they were fifteen feet tall. It showed the arms of Dreamer's Glass, the mirror split by a lightning bolt crack, with a spindle on one side and a lily on the other. The overall effect of the place was of a castle carved entirely from bone, cold and cruel and pristine.

"I guess she's made herself right at home, huh?" I said, stunned.

"Maybe this means she's not mad," said Quentin.

"Maybe it means she's going to skin us alive and use us as part of her décor," I said. He gave me a sidelong look. I shrugged. "Two can play the 'maybe' game."

"We'd best get on with it," said Simon. He cupped his hands around his mouth, and shouted, "Treasa! A word, if you please?"

I turned to stare at him. "What the hell do you think you're doing?"

"Getting us inside." Simon lowered his hands, looking unconcerned. "Treasa and I aren't friends, precisely, but she's known me for years, and she hates my brother, which makes me one of her favorite people, inasmuch as she has favorite people. I try Sylvester's nerves. That's all it takes to stay in her good graces."

"Problem: she hates me, too," I said.

He sighed. "Yes, and I can't hold a knife to your throat and claim you as my prisoner, thanks to Sylvester's cunning idea of a binding ritual. Stand quietly and try not to anger her, if you could possibly be so kind."

There wasn't time for arguing after that. The heavy castle gates swung open—surprisingly smoothly, given the level of tech visible around us. The supply wagons that had made it through before we'd ruined Riordan's plan must have included some hinges, and maybe the equipment necessary to make more. And there, standing right at the middle of the entryway, like a queen preparing to receive her due tribute, was Duchess Treasa Riordan.

Agrarian living agreed with her. Like most Daoine Sidhe, she was gorgeous, tall and flawlessly curved, with red hair so dark that it verged on black. Every time she moved, it shattered the light into prismatic shards around her, creating a glitter in the air that had nothing to do with illusions. It was pulled back to reveal the sharp points of her ears and the long, swanlike sweep of her throat.

The first time we'd met, she'd been wearing a ruby choker that she had been using to control Chelsea's movements. It had gotten smashed in the fight to get away from her, and she had replaced it with a net of black-and-purple pearls that was something like a necklace, something like a shawl, and something like a spider's web. It covered her shoulders and traced the line of her collarbone before plunging toward her navel, where the amethyst-and-pearl pendant at its end dangled, drawing attention to her flat belly and strong thighs. Her dress was skintight and moved like water around her, colored like an oil slick, shifting constantly between black and purple and rainbow iridescence.

"I'm guessing you don't do much of your own farming," I blurted.

Simon didn't quite cover his face with his hand, but he flinched, and that motion carried the same connotations. I was embarrassing him. More importantly, I was deviating from the script.

Riordan smiled, slow and thin as a razorblade. "October," she purred. "I never thought I was going to see you again, after you ran off and left me here, you naughty little thing. And I see you've brought your squire. My, my." She looked Quentin up and down, as if she were studying a particularly choice cut of meat. "He's growing up nicely, isn't he? I don't suppose he's meant to be my housewarming present."

Quentin took a step back, putting himself behind me. Smart kid. I would have done the same, if I'd had the option.

"You're looking well, Treasa," said Simon, clearly trying to get the situation back under control. The poor man. "Annwn agrees with you."

"Doesn't it just?" Her smile for him was more sincere, if no less poisonous. "I'm a queen here, with none to challenge me or mine. I do wish your little companion there hadn't taken it upon herself to break my supply chain—I was intending to have a much larger staff—but I suppose I can't complain. I finally have the position I deserve. But you, Simon. What are you doing here? Last I heard, you were persona non grata among your family and their pets." She glanced my way, making it clear what she meant by that last crack.

"I am," he said mildly. "My brother has used a blood geas to compel me to assist Sir Daye in her quest for something that her mother misplaced. I am required to serve her until the item has been found." He added a sneer to his voice, making it sound like this was the last thing he could possibly want to do with his time.

Part of me was impressed. The greater part of me wondered whether this was the lie, or whether everything else had been. He could have been playing with me this whole time, telling me whatever he thought I wanted to hear, waiting for the moment when he would be able to make his escape. He couldn't raise a hand against me. He couldn't, say, turn me into a fish or use his magic to make me look like more of a target than I already was.

But Sylvester had done nothing to bind his brother's tongue. Simon could betray us if he wanted to, let Riordan take us and walk away clean, knowing that all the disaster he'd rained down upon our heads was technically at someone else's hand. That's the trouble with purebloods. They are always, *always* looking for the loophole, and when they find it, they'll ride it all the way to hell.

Riordan's eyes widened in a theatrical manner, drawing attention to the way her eyeshadow matched the delicate frosted lilac color of her irises. Nothing but the best for Treasa Riordan, the woman so afraid of being attacked that she had turned striking first into a way of saying "hello."

"My, my," she said. "Amandine is speaking to you again? I'll be honest, Simon, I never thought I'd see the day. Not after you took that little mixed-blood to your bed."

Oleander had been the daughter of a Tuatha de Dannan and a Peri. In the eyes of some purebloods, that made her virtually a changeling. It didn't matter that she was as immortal as they were: all that mattered was that she wasn't *clean*. Maybe more importantly, by having a relationship with Oleander—however coerced— while he was still married to my mother, Simon had been committing adultery. Amandine hadn't. Because humans, naturally, didn't count.

Sometimes the thought of punching every pureblood I meet as a matter of principle is difficult to resist.

"We're working through our difficulties," he said mildly. "I claim the hospitality of your house, Treasa Riordan, for myself and for those who travel as my entourage."

"That's us," I said, gesturing between myself and Quentin. "We're the entourage."

Riordan sneered. "Oh, I would *never* have guessed that for myself. Are you quite sure, Simon? You could claim it for yourself alone, and have the great satisfaction of seeing the door slammed in the face of your wife's bastard and her hick of a squire."

Quentin bristled, but said nothing. I didn't even bristle. We've been called worse.

"I could, but I'm not," said Simon calmly. "We have need to come inside, Treasa. The night is very dark, and this place is unfamiliar to us. We are both of the Daoine Sidhe. By the bond of blood, and by the duties of the noble, I charge you to grant us the hospitality of your house, or know that you will have betrayed all that is good about our kind, and given stronger root to that which ails us."

Riordan huffed. Actually huffed, like a child being told that Christmas had been canceled. "If you must," she said. "Three days. That's the standard. At the end of that, get out or get ready to spend some quality time in my dungeons. Agreed?"

"Absolutely," said Simon, and bowed. Quentin and I hurried to emulate him. Manners matter more with the purebloods than they really should. They are the grease that keeps the wheels of our often dysfunctional society turning.

Riordan rolled her eyes before turning to stalk into her castle, leaving us to follow her or be left in the Annwn night. Simon didn't hesitate, and so neither did we.

The doors slammed shut behind us.

SIXTEEN

NO ONE WAS EVER going to accuse Treasa Riordan of being understated. Her ducal knowe in Dreamer's Glass had been a bordello-level confection of tapestries, impossible hanging lights, and velvet. Mostly white velvet, which seemed like an extra level of cruelty for the cleaning staff to deal with. Here . . .

Despite having been stranded in Annwn for less than a year and a half, Riordan had taken the time to decorate to her own standards. A thick carpet patterned with irregular cracks covered the floor, like we were walking over an inexplicably plush broken mirror. Tapestries covered the walls, even as they had in Dreamer's Glass, showing Riordan taming Annwn one wolf and raging river at a time. Globes of greenish light bobbed along the ceiling, bright enough to lead the way.

Simon dropped back, falling into step beside me, and murmured, "None of this is real, of course."

"What?" I gave him a sidelong look, trying to figure out what he meant.

"Oh, the castle is real: the candle showed us that. But carpet? Tapestries? That dress? Please. Treasa trades on illusion even more than most of our kind. She's always felt entitled to live above her station. Some of the things around us will be spun from transformation spells. Others will be light and shadow, nothing more. Tread carefully." Simon shook his head, the motion tight and restrained, like he was hoping it could go unnoticed. "She'll be hungry for the real, after spending so much time surrounded by the fictional."

"I can hear you, you know," called Riordan, still walking ahead of us—far enough ahead to give Simon an excellent view of her butt, which might as well have been poured into her dress, while staying close enough that there was no chance we'd get away.

"It would be rude to talk about you if you couldn't hear, milady," said Simon, in an ingratiating tone. "Truly, I'm in awe of how much gold you've been able to spin from the straw of this place. If I didn't know you of old— and if I weren't such a keen illusionist myself—I would no doubt have taken all these baubles for real, material things. It's impressive work."

"It should be," said Riordan. For a moment, the façade of calm cracked, and I could hear the strain that lurked beneath. "I've had to do almost all of it myself. My people are great at telling me what I want to hear, not so good at spinning a spell to convince a broken wall to play at being a complete one. But it doesn't take much skill to hold a shovel."

Luna would probably have said differently. I held my tongue, breathing in the scents surrounding us.

Dreamer's Glass was like most modern demesne: mixed. The days of only Daoine Sidhe in one place and only Bridge Trolls in another have pretty much ended, although there are exceptions—Dryads still keep mostly to themselves, for example, since it's difficult for them to remember that other people can't just retreat into their trees when they don't want to be seen. Riordan's subjects included Daoine Sidhe, Tuatha de Dannan, Selkies, Satyrs, and a dozen more types of fae. I tasted them all on the air of her castle, along with a thick, constant overlay of Folletti, the sky fae she used as her personal guard.

Folletti are functionally invisible much of the time. I breathed in a little deeper to reassure myself that we weren't surrounded, and stiffened as the scent of August's magic hit me, harder than ever. She had been here. She had been *right here*.

"What made you choose this castle when there are so many?" someone asked—*I* asked. That was my voice, however distant it seemed. I was wrapped in the memories implicit in the air, in the taste of magic going back decades. August had been *right here*. Not just in Annwn. In this castle. My sister had walked these halls, exiled and alone, and no one had come to save her.

A thread of memory tickled the back of my mind: me, in these halls, looking for Quentin and Etienne after Riordan's forces had taken us captive. I had breathed in then, and tasted Dóchas Sidhe on the wind. I had assumed I was detecting myself.

I had been wrong.

"Someone managed to stay behind when Oberon shut the doors," Riordan replied easily. "When we came to scout the land, we found a couple of dozen old manor houses and castles with the roofs caved in and the floors unsafe, and then we found this place. There wasn't anyone in it, or we might have had a fight on our hands, but whoever they were, they'd managed to keep the foundations sound while they waited for me. I'd love to give them a token of my appreciation, if you have any idea who that might have been."

Simon glanced at me, his expression betraying the early signs of alarm. He might not have my ability to detect magic, but he knew who our mystery handyman was likely to have been, and he didn't want me betraying her to Riordan. Which made sense. As far as Riordan knew, we were here looking for something my mother had misplaced, not for my living and self-misplacing sister.

Simon was good with his words. He might not have the Luidaeg's practice at talking around the truth, but he knew how to say what he had to and not a syllable more. I could learn a lot from him, if I were willing to spend that much time in his company. So far, I wasn't.

Riordan led us down a long hallway to a dining hall with vaulted ceilings and stained glass windows that shattered the ambient light coming from outside into a panoply of rainbows, beautiful and brilliant and surprisingly bright, given how dark it was.

"Wait here," she said. "I'll gather my people, and a feast will be held in your honor. It's not every day we have visitors here in this impassable, inaccessible place." She smiled like a throat being slashed, all vigor and violence, and she was gone, heading out the door and away.

Simon turned to Quentin and me. "Quickly, hide us," he said, tone leaving no room for argument.

Quentin blinked and raked his fingers through the air, singing a lilting line from some folksong about dolphins swimming in a harbor. It was sweet. It was sad. It was accompanied by the smell of steel and heather, and by a don't-look-here spell crashing down on us with such intensity that I flinched.

"Quentin, what the hell?" I asked, resisting the urge to rake the spell out of my hair like it was a veil of cobwebs.

"I don't know!" he said, eyes wide.

"Every realm generates its own ambient magic, and Annwn is no exception," said Simon. "Treasa and her people are waking the land by being here. It wants to help."

"So the more fae there are, the stronger their magic will become?" I asked.

Simon shook his head. "If it were that simple, we might never go to war again. No: with none to use its magic, Annwn stagnated. Now that it has residents again, the land is waking, and putting forth the amount of magic that its entire populace once needed. As the number of residents rises, the strength of the spells will die back to more reasonable levels."

"Let's not stay here that long," I said. The don't-look-here would keep us from being caught as long as we were careful, but it wasn't the same as true invisibility. Once Riordan realized that we'd disappeared, she'd call her guards. In fact . . . "Why the hell did she leave us alone? She had to assume we'd pull something like this."

"That's precisely why she left us alone," said Simon. "Now she'll have reason to rescind her hospitality and run us down like dogs. She needs more. More magicians, more hands to build her walls and work her fields—more bloodlines to mingle with the ones she already has. Which says nothing to what she would do if she understood some of the bloodlines she has with her already." He gave me a meaningful look.

I felt sick.

Being part human means I'm potentially more fertile than the fully fae, since mortality yearns to reproduce itself. I could have a dozen babies for her, only to pull the humanity out of them with my own hands, leaving them pureblood, immortal, and ready to be raised by somebody else. Somebody who wasn't me.

Simon nodded as he saw the realization on my face. "Even so. Treasa Riordan is a brilliantly practical woman. If she can use you to achieve her own ends, she will, and never understand why you might object. She knows what's best, after all."

"So we're here why?" asked Quentin. "I could have cast this before we came inside."

"But then we wouldn't be inside, would we?"

It was difficult to refute the calm literalism of Simon's words, even as I considered how pleasant it would be to punch him in the nose. "Okay, we're here, and August was here, but I'm not picking up any traces strong enough to indicate that she was here recently."

"When did she leave?"

"I don't know." Maybe someday I'd be able to develop this strange ability of mine to the point where I could tell just how old a faded trail was, but I wasn't there yet. All I knew for sure was that August had been here—and that the trail had been fresher the first time I'd picked it up. I frowned. "I think she may still have been here when Riordan first arrived."

"Which could mean . . ." prompted Simon.

I stared at him. "Which could mean she used Chelsea's gating back and forth to get herself home. She may have been back in the mortal world this whole time." But that didn't make any sense. Why wouldn't she have gone running straight to the tower, and to our mother? Why would she still be lost, when she'd been given the perfect opportunity to be found?

Simon nodded, expression grim. "Precisely so. We need to be sure. Follow her trail, before Riordan comes back and our own journey comes to an end."

"Right." I closed my eyes and inhaled, digging down past the scent of Quentin's spell, past the overlapping traceries of magic that made up the place—and there was so much magic, there was *so much*; what Riordan hadn't repaired magically, she had *created* magically, filling in the gaps in the walls with virtual silver and stone. Given enough time, she would probably go back and fix those spots for real . . . or maybe not. When she had this much raw power to throw around, why put any flesh behind the fantasy? It wasn't like she ever intended to leave.

Only knowes built to last need to have any real foundations. The Tea Gardens had crumbled when Lily died, because her magic had no longer been there to shore them up. The false Queen's beachfront knowe was still there, but it was fading a little every day. Eventually, it would return to the mostly formless shallowing it had been when I first found it for her, filled with potential, beautiful as only something that could become anything ever was.

Maybe, after it had lain fallow for a century or two, someone else would open it and allow it to become something new, something that wasn't tainted by the legacy of what it had already been. I sort of hoped that would be the case. But it wasn't going to be any time soon. Arden had her knowe, one that was more reality than lovely illusion, and she wasn't going to set herself upon the pretender's throne.

Under Riordan's magic, under the magic of her subjects, under even Chelsea's frantic and panicked magic, I found August's. It was baked into the walls, almost as it had been back in Amandine's tower. It was no wonder Riordan had been drawn to this specific castle. With as much work as August had done, this may have been the only livable spot in all of Annwn.

"This way," I said, and started walking.

With Quentin beside me, I didn't need to worry about walking out of the don't-look-here; it moved with him, and hence it moved with me. Simon brought up the rear. I couldn't watch him and where I was going at the same time, but he seemed nervous, like something about being here was putting him on his guard. Honestly, I couldn't blame him for that.

Annwn may have been a place where people lived once, but that was a long time ago, in a world that might as well have been a fairy tale for all the impact it has on people like me. Annwn is a myth and a legend and a lie, sealed off by Oberon like all the other deep realms of Faerie. The fact that we were here should have been an impossibility. *Would* have been, if we hadn't been willing to barter our freedom for the use of a candle. Not exactly a route that was available to everyone, or one that should have been emulated.

And August had been here. The whole time Simon

had been trading his soul away, one piece at a time, looking for a way to bring her home, she'd been here, locked away from her family but safe, outside the reach of anyone who might want to hurt her. August hadn't been suffering like Luna and Rayseline had, or even like I had. She'd just been unable to find her way home.

Home. I frowned. That was the odd part of all this—not that there were any really normal parts to the situation. August had traded her road home to the Luidaeg, saying that she couldn't come back until she'd found Oberon. I was becoming convinced that she was back in the mortal world, even if she wasn't back with our mother yet. Was that not close enough to count as "home"? How had she been able to do that without finding Oberon?

Unless she *had* managed to find him, and things were about to get even more complicated. Because that was exactly what we needed.

The trail of August's magic led down the hall and to a curving staircase, winding its way upward through the castle. This, I recognized, despite Riordan's extensive renovations. These stairs led to the cells where Etienne, Tybalt, and I had all been imprisoned, intended to be used as warm bodies to help her build her new vision of Faerie. Well. Some of us were going to be warm bodies. Tybalt had been marked for slaughter by her ally, Raj's father Samson, who was going to make sure that his son was never truly a King of Cats, only a puppet.

Thinking of Tybalt wasn't good for me. Not yet. I shook the thought away as I climbed the stairs, looking for the place where August's trail became something else.

Behind and below us, someone shouted. Riordan had noticed that we were gone.

"Perhaps speed is of the essence," said Simon mildly.

"Next time you misplace one of your kids for a century, I'm not helping you," I snapped, voice barely above a whisper, and walked faster.

August's trail led us out of the stairwell and down a hall, the walls lined with closed doors that looked solid enough to stand up to a legion of ax-wielding Jack Nicholsons. That was a terrifying thought in and of itself. I slowed, testing the air again and again, before I finally stopped in front of one of the doors and thrust the candle at Quentin.

"Hold this," I said.

Quentin has been my squire long enough to know better than to argue with me. He took the candle, staying close as I dropped to my knees and pulled the set of lock picks from inside my jacket.

Simon raised an eyebrow. "Are you a common thief, then?"

"I like to think of myself as a rare and exceptional thief, but sure," I said. The last time I'd been here, I'd picked these locks with bits of twig and bracken. Real lock picks were a major step up. It made the job seem almost trivial. That was nice. Difficult things should always seem trivial, when they can.

Moving as quickly as I dared, I pulled the appropriate lock picks from my set and slipped them into place, breathing slow and deep as I worked at the tumblers. These were old locks, preindustrial, tooled by hand instead of by machines. That meant that each of them was unique, with its own weights and balances. It also meant they were remarkably primitive compared to some of the locks I'd encountered in the mortal world. After only a few seconds, the latch clicked.

I stood, tucking my lock picks back into my pocket, and took the candle back from Quentin before I opened the door.

The cell on the other side was small and plain. Riordan hadn't bothered casting any illusions here, maybe because she hadn't seen the need: it wasn't like the occupant was ever going to tell anyone how terrible her hospitality had been. The air reeked of piss and stale sweat. Heaps of straw and rough bracken lined the

walls, providing bedding and a latrine at the same time.
Quentin's nose wrinkled. Simon hung back, clearly unwilling to enter the room.

One of the heaps of bracken moved.

I jumped, unable to help myself, putting out my free hand to keep Quentin where he was. Then, cautiously, I crept forward. Riordan would be here soon enough. Anyone she had felt the need to lock up was probably going to need our help . . . and August's trail led here. She had been in this room. She had *left* from this room.

"Hello?" I said cautiously.

The heap of bracken moved again, pulsing almost, like something beneath it was trying to sit up. Then it shattered, resolving itself into a thin, wild-eyed man sitting in a pile of sticks and soiled grasses. I gasped.

"Officer Thornton?" I asked.

His eyes fixed on me. "You!" He lunged onto his knees, grabbing my forearms with bony hands. All the excess weight seemed to have been melted off of him by his time in Annwn—and there hadn't been that much to spare in the first place. "You came back! You came back! Did I finally prove that I wouldn't tell? I won't tell! I'll never tell!" He began to laugh unsteadily.

As he slumped forward, head against my shoulder, I realized that his laughter had become indistinguishable from tears.

Dammit.

"Is that a *human*?" asked Simon, sounding disgusted and fascinated at the same time, like he couldn't believe what his eyes were telling him. "How is there a human *here*? This is Annwn!"

"This is Officer Michael Thornton of the San Francisco Police Department," I said, patting Officer Thornton awkwardly on the back. He was wearing the soiled, tattered remains of the clothes he'd had on when he had first tumbled through one of Chelsea's portals and into Annwn, a place where a human had no business being. He was here because of me. When we'd saved our own, we hadn't been able to save him. I'd told the Luidaeg where he was and washed my hands of the problem.

Riordan must have been feeding him. Humans aren't like fae. Humans won't suffer endlessly, never quite giving in to nature's laws and dying: humans will eventually be released. It can take a long time, especially in the lands of Faerie, where time and causality aren't always logical. But she still must have been feeding him. Not much. Just enough to keep body and soul together.

"Sweet Maeve," whispered Quentin. "What did she do?"

Officer Thornton was still collapsed against me, still crying. I shook my head and replied grimly, "She kept him." She could have killed him. That wouldn't normally have been my go-to, especially not where a member of the police was concerned. Devin had drilled it into my head often and early that messing with the mortal cops was always more trouble than it was worth. At the same time . . .

This wasn't the Summerlands, where signs of humanity could be found everywhere, from pieces of their tech to stolen mortal servants working in the larger noble households. This was *Annwn*. This was a land that had never been intended for humanity's use. Being here must have hurt him, every day, as the very land tried to reject his reality. Killing him would have been kinder.

Which was exactly why Riordan hadn't done it.

"Put him down and follow the trail," said Simon, a thin line of impatience slithering through his words. "We need to move before Treasa returns."

"I'm not putting him down," I snapped. "We can't leave him here again."

"He's not worth our lives."

"That's not your decision." There were voices in the distance now, voices on the stairs. They were going to catch us soon. "This is where August's trail ends. We need to move."

"The human—"

"Is coming!" I raised my candle. "Now get over here, or get your ass left behind. Quite honestly, I'm good with either right now."

Simon scowled as he walked across the room to stand beside me. Quentin stepped closer. Fog began to rise from the candle, and with Officer Michael Thornton—lost to Faerie, now found—sobbing against my shoulder, the soft, misty gray closed in, and we were gone.

SEVENTEEN

WHEN THE FOG CLEARED, we were standing against the wall of a graffiti-festooned alley. Leaning forward gave me a perfect view of Valencia Street. Time had continued marching on in the mortal world while we were running around the various layers of Faerie: the sun was hanging low in the sky, and the ashy, charred scent of torn-down magic still lingered in the air. We had arrived in San Francisco immediately after dawn.

After *which* dawn? The human world and the Summerlands don't always align perfectly where time is concerned, and deeper Faerie is even worse. It could have been days since we'd started down the Babylon Road. Our time could already be up, and we didn't have August.

What we *did* have was a sobbing, shaking, seriously malnourished member of the SFPD. That would have been a problem no matter what the circumstances. People notice that sort of thing. Unfortunately for us, Officer Thornton had been working out of the Valencia Street station when he'd gone missing, which meant we had a sobbing, shaking, malnourished cop less than three blocks from a whole building full of people who would be *very interested* to hear what had happened to him.

I was trying to figure out our next move when the impossible happened: the candle went out.

That should have seemed like a small thing—candles go out all the time—but it wasn't. This was a Babylon candle, designed to keep us on the Babylon Road, and it shouldn't have gone out unless it had been dropped, or we had reached our destination. I looked wildly around, almost expecting August to step out of a mural. No such luck. No one else was here, not even a representative sample of the city's homeless population.

"Well, crap," I muttered, and handed the candle to Quentin before digging my phone out of my pocket.

"What's going on?" asked Simon.

"Toby's calling the Luidaeg because her candle went out," said Quentin.

"Not quite," I said, and raised the phone to my ear. It was ringing. That was a good sign; following the Babylon Road hadn't drained my battery.

"Hello?" rumbled a voice like a mountain coming to life.

"Danny, it's October," I said. "I'm in an alley at Valencia and I think 17th. I have Quentin, Simon Torquill, and a traumatized mortal with me. Can you come pick us up?"

There was a pause while Danny absorbed all this. I stood silent and perfectly still, hoping that I hadn't finally discovered the place where Danny's amiable goodwill ran out.

I did a favor for Danny's sister a long time ago, before the whole thing with the pond and the fourteen missing years of my life. He's been trying to repay me ever since, despite my endless insistence that he doesn't owe me anything. I try not to lean on him too heavily, but I also try never to forget that he's there, because of all the allies I've made since my return, he was among the first, and he's always been among the most dependable.

"I'm almost offended that you felt like you had to ask," he said finally. "Your human, they going to be a problem?"

"Just spin a quick deflection over the cab, and I'll keep him quiet," I assured him. Officer Thornton was still clinging to me and crying. He might cause a scene if he realized we were back in the human world—but this was the best possible time to keep him from realizing that. There was no one else around. "Hurry."

"I'll break some laws," said Danny, and hung up.

When I lowered my own phone, both Simon and Quentin were watching me, the first with wide-eyed dismay, the second with understanding. Naturally, it was Simon who spoke.

"We're taking him *with* us?" he demanded.

"Yeah, we are," I said, putting my arms protectively around Officer Thornton. He was a big man, even emaciated as he was: I felt like I was trying to use myself to conceal a wall, instead of the other way around. "It's our fault he was there, and what happens if we give him back to his people in this condition? He could blow the whole 'keeping Faerie secret' routine just by opening his mouth."

That wasn't going to happen. I was raised to fear the human world becoming aware of Faerie's existence, and sometimes the habits of paranoia were impossible to break. Sometimes I flinched away from people, even knowing that they were more likely to look at my ears and think "*Star Trek* fanatic" than "actual proof of inhuman intelligence." But when I was being rational, I knew the former was infinitely more likely. If we dropped Officer Thornton on the doorstep of the SFPD right now, in his current condition, he wouldn't betray the existence of Faerie. They'd blame a human cult, or a terror cell, or both.

And my name would be smack dab in the middle of it all, because I was the person he'd been investigating when he disappeared, and there was no possible way he wouldn't name me when he started describing his rescue. They might dismiss his stories of magic and beautiful people with pointy ears as the ravings of a madman, but me? They knew I existed.

There was no way I could have left Officer Thornton behind a second time, not and live with myself afterward, but I wasn't going to let him do what so many others had tried and failed to do. I wasn't going to let him take away my mortal life. If the SFPD decided I was a person of interest in his kidnapping and subsequent return, that was exactly what would happen. Fae don't do well in human prisons. Too much iron, not enough opportunity to hide.

Quentin's don't-look-here had dissolved somewhere along the Babylon Road. I grabbed a handful of shadows from the air, bearing down as hard as I could as I tried to hide us. The spell was slippery, trying to wiggle through my fingers and disappear, until a ribbon of smoke and spiced oranges wriggled past, not close enough to count as cast on me, but close enough for me to snatch.

The rot is fading, I thought, and wove Simon's magic into my own, casting the net of my illusion over the four of us. It wasn't quite a don't-look-here; those take more finesse than I was currently capable of dredging out of myself. I was exhausted. I was *done.* Instead, this was a simple overlay, showing anyone who looked the unobstructed alley. As long as no one tried to walk through us, we'd be fine.

Officer Thornton wasn't crying anymore. He was just slumped against me, barely moving. I resisted the urge to check his pulse. If he needed a hospital, I would feel compelled to take him to one, and that would end poorly for all of us.

"Quentin," I said. "What day is it?"

My squire blinked at me, seemingly baffled, before his eyes widened in understanding and he pulled out his phone. It started to chirp and vibrate almost immediately.

"I guess going to Annwn put me in airplane mode," he said. "I have like, three dozen texts from Dean, and he isn't usually—oh." He paled. "It's been three days."

"Not as bad as it could have been," I said.

Quentin didn't look like he believed me. It must have been nice, still being young enough to see losing three days as a bad thing. As long as it was less than a year, I'd take it.

"Three days gone leaves us with four days to find my daughter," said Simon. "We can't stand here guarding your misplaced mortal all day."

"We won't have to," I said. "Danny's on his way. He's going to take Officer Thornton to the Luidaeg."

"Alone?" asked Quentin. His tone told me that he already knew the answer, even as he was hoping to be wrong.

Sorry, kid. "You're going with them," I said. "You need to tell the Luidaeg what we saw in Annwn. She should be able to put him back together." And wipe parts of his memory, so that he thought he'd been kidnapped by ninjas or pirates or, hell, time-traveling cowboys. Anything, as long as the culprits were completely human, and completely not related to me in any way.

"I don't like the idea of leaving you alone with him," said Quentin, glancing at Simon, in case I had somehow missed his point.

"I'm safer alone with him than you are," I said. "He can't hurt me, remember?"

"I am, in point of fact, standing right here, and am not currently intending to harm anyone," said Simon. He sounded weary and exasperated, like he was getting tired of explaining himself to us.

Tough. After the things he'd done, he could put up

with a little explaining. "Your ideas of 'harm' don't always line up with ours," I said. "Still. I believe you, which is why I'm staying with you, instead of calling for backup. We're going to follow August's trail while Quentin gets Officer Thornton to the Luidaeg. Quentin, you can join us when you're done. I'm sure Danny will be happy to give you a ride." And if that had the extra added bonus of equipping us with both a Bridge Troll and a car, I would take it.

Danny is not the most effective fighter I've ever known. He doesn't have to be. When he hits something, it stays down, and most weapons blunt or break against his stony skin. He would be an asset, if this ever devolved into actual fighting.

Quentin still looked unsure. I decided to sweeten the deal.

"Officer Thornton is going to need things to be quiet and calm while you're in the car. You should have time to text Dean and fill him in on what's been going on. Let him know that you didn't run off to Disney World for a dream vacation while he was stuck here, dealing with the usual gang of weirdoes."

"I don't dream about going to Disney World," said Quentin. "Too humid, not enough hockey."

"See, and here I thought the Canada pavilion in Epcot would be your go-to vacation destination," I said.

Quentin frowned at me, too worried and weary to even rise to the bait.

I couldn't blame him. I was exhausted. The only sleep I'd had since the bachelorette party had been in the pixie village; I was running on fumes, or maybe on whatever came after fumes. My stomach rumbled, reminding me that sleep wasn't the only thing I'd been skipping out on. Maybe I hadn't been bleeding as much as usual, but I was still pushing my body well past the point where it was going to keep forgiving me.

"When Danny gets here, you're going with him," I said. "You can call me if the Luidaeg has any instructions. Simon and I are going to find August and finish this. Maybe with a stop for breakfast burritos."

"What in the world is a breakfast burrito?" asked Simon.

I looked at Quentin again. "I am now genuinely sorry that you're going to miss this," I said.

Officer Thornton raised his head.

The rest of us froze. We weren't wearing human disguises. They hadn't been necessary in Annwn, and in my rush to hide the malnourished cop from any of his peers who might happen to be walking to work, I hadn't suggested getting them in place. All he had to do was look at us, and he'd know we weren't human.

He turned to me. He blinked. His eyes were dark brown, the color of river clay, and still slightly unfocused . . . at least until he looked at my ears. His eyes focused real fast when he looked at my ears.

"Lady, let alone," he said. "Where am I?"

"Um, hi," I said. "We're back in San Francisco. I have a friend coming to take you to see a doctor." The Luidaeg was basically a doctor, if by "doctor" you meant "person who will totally fix whatever's wrong with your body and mind, possibly by turning you into a boulder, since boulders don't get sick." It was close enough for Faerie.

Officer Thornton frowned, eyes going unfocused again. "Who are you?"

This was my chance. I could lie to him, obscure my part in the whole situation: I could let him go to the Luidaeg's with no idea who had brought him home. She was going to wipe his memory no matter what I said. This way might be kinder.

Or it might be crueler, because it would leave him thinking, however briefly, that it had taken a total stranger to care enough to rescue him. "My name's October," I said gently. "We've met before, remember? I'm going to make sure you're taken care of. You're safe now."

"October," he said, slowly, wonderingly, sounding out each syllable of my name like it was a revelation. "Yes. Of course. I know you. I was waiting for you."

"I'm here now," I assured him.

A car roared along the mostly silent street, screeching to a stop in front of the alley. It was a fairly standard city cab. Only someone with an excellent eye for both magic and automotive modifications would have been able to see how much that cab had been enchanted and reinforced, until its mostly synthetic frame could contain the massive body of the cabby who drove it. The driver's side door slammed, and there was Danny, unfolding from the vehicle like he was planning to go on forever.

He wasn't nearly as tall when enchanted to look human as he was in his normal guise, but he was still impressive. "Yo," he boomed, in the low shout that served him as a whisper. "Your ride's here."

"That's your cue, Quentin," I said.

My squire nodded and snatched his own handful of shadows, weaving it effortlessly into a makeshift human disguise. The details of it were too vague to be entirely convincing—his skin was smooth to the point of being poreless, and his eyes looked like they belonged to a doll, not a living person—but it would get him to the car.

Officer Thornton watched this with wide, disbelieving eyes. "Oh," he said.

"Yes, oh," I agreed, and pushed Officer Thornton gently toward Quentin, who stepped forward and took his arm. "You're going to be okay."

"Come on," said Quentin encouragingly, and pressed the candle into my hand before he led Officer Thornton forward, through the fragile wall of my illusion, to the street.

He stopped to say something to Danny, voice too soft for me to hear. Danny looked up, eyes searching the apparently empty alley until he settled on the spot where he assumed I would be standing and offered me a nod. He was good: his gaze was only a few feet off. Then all three of them got into the cab, and Danny restarted the engine, and they drove away.

A hand touched my shoulder. There was only one person left that it could belong to. I managed not to shudder as I turned to look at Simon.

"What next?" he asked.

"Food, and following," I said. "Can you disguise yourself?"

"I would be offended, but if you feel anywhere near as hungry as I do, your question is reasonable. Yes, I can disguise myself. Can you?"

"I can." My illusions have never been great, courtesy of me having none of Titania's blood in me at all, but anger has always made them stronger. Anger fuels me in a way that all the training in the world never could. And I was so, so angry.

Angry at Amandine, for stealing Tybalt and Jazz in order to get her own way; for never being there for me when I needed her, until she was more adversary than parent. Angry at Sylvester, for keeping secrets from me for so long that I had never been able to understand why my mother held herself so distant. If he had been open with me, I might have been able to heal the rifts between us—me and my mother, me and him—before they got so vast they became unbridgeable. Angry at August, for running off on a fool's errand. She had been older when she disappeared than I was now, but she had been cared for, cosseted, and hadn't learned the most important lesson of being a hero: she hadn't learned that sometimes it was less about what you could do, and more about who could help you do it.

Most of all, though, I was angry at myself. So much of this mess was mine. I hadn't been the one to make it, but I'd been the one to keep saying "later, later," like anything ever really waited until later to become a problem. I could have gone looking for Mom, to try to make things right between us: I hadn't. I could have made more of an effort to fix things with Sylvester: I hadn't. I could have asked Acacia what she was doing about the Riders, or asked the Luidaeg to help me find Officer Thornton. I hadn't. All my chickens were coming home to roost, and while I didn't want them, I had earned them. I had earned them, every one.

When I finished gathering my anger, I tucked the unlit candle into my jacket pocket. Hands now free, I raked my fingers hard through the air and snagged the fabric of the magic that had risen around me, responding to my obvious need. I shook it once, hard, and layered it over me like a veil, tamping it down until my ears itched and the scent of cut-grass and copper sizzled in the air.

The smell of smoke and rotten oranges rose to my side, underscored by a thin layer of mulled cider. Simon's original magical signature was struggling to reassert itself, fighting through the rot to reclaim its place in the makeup of his magic. I still didn't know how his magic could have changed, or how it was beginning to change back. Everything about it was a mystery to me.

Our spells solidified and burst at the same time, leaving two apparently human individuals behind: me, with the colorless brown hair I once had naturally, before my shifting blood began acting as a magical highlighting session, him, with his usual fox-red hair, but with hazel eyes and blunter, kinder features. Cast as human, Simon Torquill was no longer a knife of a man, primed to cut out the hearts of anyone who looked at him. Instead, he was softer, more reasonable, the kind of man who seemed more likely to buy you a cup of coffee than enchant you forever.

He looked me up and down, and smiled a little. "I almost recognize you better this way," he said. "It's clear you based your human face off the one you used to wear."

"Yeah, well, that was the face I expected to have for my entire life, and illusions don't come easy to me, so I figured I'd go with what worked." As if to remind me how hard illusions really were, a low throbbing started behind my temples. This wasn't my best kind of magic, and if I was going to persist in doing it, I was going to pay.

I could at least make the bill a little lower. I swept my hand through the air, dismissing the illusion on the alley. The scent of cut-grass and copper grew stronger as the illusion fell apart around us, showering down with the sweet, bright scent of magic released. The ache backed off. Not enough. Still, it might see me staying on my feet until I could get something into my stomach and make the next stages of our journey easier to handle.

Simon was looking at me, half concerned and half calculating. "Where next?" he asked.

"The Babylon Road wouldn't have dropped us here if August hadn't been here," I said. "It's too close to dawn for me to pick up her trail—assuming it's still here to find." Up until this point, I'd been following August through purely fae realms, places where dawn and its destructive cleansing force never reached. Magic could linger there for decades. Here . . .

The mortal world has a way of eroding even the most powerful spells in a matter of days. Whatever trail August had left was likely to be long, long gone.

"So food."

"Food," I agreed. It felt almost traitorous to be thinking about my stomach when my people were in danger, but I wasn't going to do them any good if I collapsed from hunger. Tybalt would want me to eat.

Tybalt would want to be eating with me, not leaving me alone with Simon Torquill, but we can't have everything in this world. For the moment, I'd settle for a breakfast burrito and a glass of orange juice to help me keep this headache at bay.

If you're looking for a good burrito in San Francisco at any time of the day or night, the Mission District is the place to be. I led Simon up a few blocks to one of the many taquerias dotting Valencia Street. They were just unlocking the doors, and we were the first customers through. I was opening my mouth, preparing to give my usual order, when Simon turned to the man behind the counter and said something in amiable, flawless Spanish.

The man he had addressed looked surprised before responding in kind, and that was that: the two of them were off and running, chattering away like old friends. Simon gestured to me and said something, and the man laughed, nodding. I smothered a scowl. Whatever was going on here, it seemed to be going well, and all I was going to do was complicate things.

Then Simon reached for his pocket, presumably to pull out his wallet. I grabbed his wrist. He froze, looking startled, and I realized he hadn't been expecting me to willingly touch him. Not so soon after he'd been woken up; maybe not ever.

"My treat," I said, through gritted teeth.

Simon's look of surprise deepened, but he relaxed his hand, making it clear that he wasn't going to fight me on this. "As you like," he said.

Whatever he'd ordered for us came shy of twenty dollars. I paid with a crumpled bill from the inside pocket of my jacket, silently grateful for my policy of never using imaginary money with local businesses. Yeah, sometimes fairy gold is the only way out of a tight situation, but I've been the one who counts the drawers on the graveyard shift. No one's getting fired because I wanted to turn some leaves into cash more than I wanted to buy generic.

We took a number and retreated to a table in the window, far enough from the counter for me to drop my voice and whisper, "What the hell was that?"

"Hmm?" Simon gave me another surprised look. I

was starting to think his face was going to stick that way. "Oh, Miguel and I were just talking about how much this neighborhood has changed. If you wonder why he was smiling at you so much, it's because I told him you were my daughter when he asked what we were doing wandering around the streets this early. Forgive me for presuming, but you're not dressed for work, and neither am I, and I genuinely didn't want him to decide that you were a prostitute."

"I'm not dressed for sex work either," I said. It was difficult to hold onto my annoyance with my confusion getting in the way. "I didn't know you spoke Spanish."

"There was a time when Spanish was the lingua franca of California. America bought this land from the Spaniards, you know, after they had invaded and conquered it. Really, I find it strange that anyone could live here and *not* speak Spanish. Language is an invasive species. Let it take root in new soil, and you'll never beat it out, no matter how hard you try."

Simon fell silent as the man from the counter—Miguel—brought over a tray containing two large breakfast burritos, fried potatoes, and glasses of horchata, thick and creamy and frothy at the top. The two of them exchanged a few bright, amiable words, and I wished I could understand them. It would have made things so much easier.

Miguel was smiling when he walked away. I returned my attention to Simon.

"You don't know what a breakfast burrito is, and yet you can order them perfectly. Got any more surprises?"

"Putting eggs and—is this sausage? Fascinating—in a tortilla shell is a relatively new idea. It speaks to a shortness of time. People never roll an entire meal up into something portable when they have time to linger. But once you introduced the concept, it was relatively easy to understand." He picked up his burrito and took an inquisitive bite. His eyes widened. He swallowed. "Mortal genius never fails to delight."

"Yeah, well, we do have a shortness of time here. We're only stopping to eat so we don't fall down." I was still jittery. We needed to move. We needed to find August.

We needed to eat. I picked up my own burrito and took a bite, only half-listening as Simon resumed chattering amiably about how much the city had changed and how much it had stayed the same; how familiar these streets would always be, all the way down to his bones. There was so much work left to do. There was so little time left to do it.

Tybalt, I'm coming, I thought, and ate, and tried not to think about the future.

EIGHTEEN

WE FINISHED EATING AS the breakfast rush was rolling in, busing our trays and waving to Miguel on our way out the door. He waved back, grinning. Whatever Simon said to him, he must have *really* liked it.

Simon caught the expression on my face and smiled. "Difficult as it may be for you to believe, given our history, there was a time when I was the better liked among my siblings. I have a gregarious nature. September was more critical. She had standards. Whereas Sylvester, well, he was always haring off on some grand adventure and coming back with mud on his boots, bumbling around the place like a disaster waiting to happen. Sometimes I think he wound up landed because Gilad wanted him to stay in one place, rather than visiting every household in the kingdom and breaking all their dishes."

"He doesn't talk about September much," I said carefully.

"No, he wouldn't," said Simon. "She died. I know that may not seem like such a betrayal to you—you've seen so much death already, and you're barely more than a child—but we grew up believing we would live forever. Losing her was like losing the moon. Absolutely incomprehensible. The moon can't simply *vanish*. It's easier to forget that it was there in the first place than it is to live with the reality of its absence."

"Mmm," I said.

Valencia Street was springing to life around us: businesses were opening, shutters were being rolled up and doors were being unlocked. The street traffic had more than doubled since we'd gone to get breakfast. Locals mingled with tourists, all of them hurrying to get to where they needed to go. Up ahead, a familiar mural looked out over a small urban park. I nodded to myself.

"We're going to make a stop," I said, and indicated the building.

Simon followed my finger. "What is it?"

"A bookstore and coffee shop. Arden's seneschal works there. He's Cu Sidhe. Even if I can't find August's trail, he might be able to." And if not, he could let us duck into the office long enough to cast a don't-look-here and hide us from any prying eyes out on the street. Finding August's trail again might require the use of my candle.

San Francisco is a city of weird layered on weird, but even here, people will notice a woman carrying a burning taper down the middle of the street in broad daylight. We needed to find a way to disappear. A don't-look-here would do the trick nicely.

Borderlands Books and the Borderlands Café are owned by the same man. Conveniently, there's a door between them. Less conveniently, the bookstore—which offers substantially more privacy, even when open—opens at noon, while the café's doors were already unlocked, and the usual assortment of weary students, people with nowhere better to go, and commuters was scattered around the reclaimed hardwood tables, sucking down caffeine as fast as they could.

I relaxed as we stepped inside and I saw the big blond man behind the counter, dishing out lattes and black coffees as fast as his hands could move. He was wearing a shirt for a band called "Cats Laughing," which I'd never heard of, although I had no doubt Tybalt would approve.

Madden looked up when the door swung closed, and grinned, the wide, honest smile of a man who honestly felt he had nothing to hide, and didn't see why anyone else would either. Mercifully, he waited until we approached the counter before booming happily, "Toby! And . . . Sylvester? Whoa, I haven't seen you here in *ages*!"

He looked so happy that I hated to contradict him. Sadly, I had to. Even if I'd been willing to lie to one of my allies right before I asked for help, there was no way to guarantee that Simon wouldn't immediately spill the beans. The only thing worse than lying is being caught doing it.

"Simon, actually," I said. "Sylvester's brother."

"We're catching up," said Simon, in a voice that was desert-dry with a combination of amusement and caution. It was a rare blend. He wore it well. "It's a pleasure to meet you."

"Uh, okay," said Madden dubiously. He looked over his shoulder to the small kitchen, where a human man with hair the color of ripe blueberries was washing dishes. "Hey, Z'ev, can you cover for me a minute? My friend needs to pick something up that she left in the bookstore."

"Sure thing," said the man, stripping off his gloves and moving toward the counter, even as Madden was stepping out from behind it and gesturing for us to follow him to the attached bookstore. That's one of the nice things about small establishments: things can be loose enough to allow for a certain fluidity during the day, which is important when, say, you're secretly a shapeshifting canine in service to the local fae monarch. To pick an utterly nonspecific example.

No one seemed to think there was anything strange

about Madden leading two people past the rope that cordoned the café off from the bookstore when their operating hours didn't match up. Those people probably would have been a little surprised when, after leading us to the back of the store, Madden turned and bared his teeth at Simon. They were suddenly much larger, seeming to occupy too much real estate in his jaw. Saliva foamed around them, making him look on the verge of rabid.

"I know you," he snarled, eyes fixed on Simon. "I know what you *did*. What are you *doing*?"

"I'm looking for my daughter," Simon said. To his credit, he didn't flinch away from the possibility that an angry Cu Sidhe was about to rip his throat out.

It was almost a relief to have someone finally reacting to Simon Torquill the way I thought they should. It was also remarkably inconvenient. I needed Madden's help, and I didn't have time to go over the whole story yet again. Not with August still out there somewhere, needing to be found; needing to be saved.

"My mother has taken Tybalt and Jazz as collateral against my bringing my older sister, August Torquill, home," I said. "Sylvester agreed to wake Simon in order to help me find her, since she's his daughter, too. Simon has been bound with a blood geas to keep him from acting against my interests in this matter."

"Blood geasa are only as good as their wording," said Madden. "They can break."

"Maybe so, but I haven't seen him making any effort to break this one," I said. "We've been following August's trail since the bachelorette party."

Understanding flooded Madden's features. "That's why none of you have been answering the phone!" he said. "Ardy was starting to get really worried. I think she was going to swing by tonight."

"The new Queen in the Mists makes house calls?" Simon looked genuinely amused by the idea. "How quaint."

Madden growled.

"Let's play a fun game," I said. "It's called 'don't

bait the man who's going to help us.' Here's how you play. Simon, stop being you."

"Would that I could, milady," he said.

There was genuine regret in his voice, enough that Madden and I both paused.

Madden recovered first. "Well, that got dark fast," he said. "What do you need?"

"We've been following the Babylon Road for days," I said, pulling the candle from my pocket and holding it up for him to see. "Long trip, long story, need a shower bad. Our last stop dropped us out on Valencia, and I lost the trail. I need to try to find it again, and then I'm probably going to need to cast a don't-look-here, because the candle is sort of conspicuous."

"So you need privacy and maybe me to help you sniff somebody out," said Madden. "Got it."

I offered him a wan smile, closed my eyes, and breathed in deeply, looking for the thin ribbon of August's magic.

Instead, the smell of smoke and roses punched me in the nose, thick and cloying enough that I gasped and staggered backward, dropping the candle. Simon was there to catch me, the line of his body so similar to Sylvester's that some deep-buried instinct said *safe* and allowed me to go limp. He still grunted with the effort of keeping me from hitting the floor.

"Toby?" Madden sounded alarmed. As well he should. The smell of my own magic was hanging in the air: cut-grass and copper and the faint, ashen scent of a spell that had been released too quickly, more charred away than dismissed. I might not be visible from the street, but anyone who came over to the bookstore side looking to surreptitiously use the bathroom was going to get an eyeful of pure, unadulterated Dóchas Sidhe.

"Sorry." I got my feet back under myself, coughing a little as I stood. This time, I breathed more shallowly. The scent of August's magic was just as strong. I turned to Simon. His eyes were wide; he was staring at me. I stared back.

"She was here," I said. "August was *here*. Madden. Have there been any fae around recently that you don't know? She'd have shown up . . . I don't know, sometime in the last year. Red hair. Might have a funny way of talking, like she doesn't really know what words mean anymore."

Madden shook his head. "No, no one," he said.

I paused.

Madden is Cu Sidhe, a fairy dog, in the same way that Tybalt is a fairy cat. With the shapeshifters, there's always a little bleed between their fae and animal natures. They seem oddly human in animal form, sitting up like people or using their paws to grasp objects like they've forgotten about their lack of opposable thumbs. They seem a little bit animal in human form. Tybalt's tendency to curl his tongue when he yawns, for example, or the way he sometimes looks at me through sleepy, half-closed eyes, utterly feline, utterly content.

Cu Sidhe have different mannerisms naturally. They're a different breed of beast. With Madden, one of the big tells that he isn't quite human is the way he moves his head. Humans—and people shaped like them—usually rotate from the chin, shaking or nodding in a way that's difficult to describe with other words, but which reads as "normal." Madden shook and nodded his head from the nose first, more like a canine than a man. It was a small thing, not enough to betray his fae nature under any ordinary circumstances. There are entirely human people out there with stranger affectations.

But he was shaking his head from the chin. This wasn't right.

"Madden, do they still sell lemonade next door?" I asked carefully.

He brightened, looking relieved to be back on familiar ground. "Oh, sure," he said, with a bob of his head—a bob that originated, in the canine manner, with his nose. "Do you want me to get you some? Sugar's good when you've had a shock."

"No, I'm good," I said. "Have you seen an unfamiliar redheaded woman around here recently?"

Again, he shook his head; again, the shake started with the chin, human-style. "No, no one," he said.

Simon looked between the two of us, eyes narrowing as he caught on. "Interesting," he said. "October?"

"Give me a second." I focused on Madden, squinting as I looked for signs that he was under some sort of a spell.

Illusions often manifest as a glitter in the air, but this wouldn't be an illusion; illusions can't make a person act in an abnormal way. Illusions can't make people lie. Illusions *are* lies, pretty and static and unchanging. So there was no glitter, and that made sense, because this wasn't an illusion. This was something else.

The first time I'd seen someone else's spell, I hadn't been able to understand what I was looking at, because seeing magic meant I could manipulate it, and manipulating magic wasn't part of the Daoine Sidhe skillset I'd been raised thinking was my own. Dóchas Sidhe turn out to work a little differently. So I squinted, and I squinted, and finally, there it was, a hairline web of knots and tangles in the air around Madden. It was made of a thousand tiny threads, smoky gray and pale, pale red, so that they should have been pink and yet somehow weren't.

"What do you see?" asked Simon, his voice so close to my ear that I nearly jumped.

"Something," I said. The spell was intricate and delicately woven. This was a masterpiece. Anything I did to it would damage the work of someone who had more power and more experience than I could dream of having.

Which meant there was really no point in being delicate, if I was going to wreck the whole thing anyway. "This may sting," I said, and reached toward Madden, hooking my fingers in the air like I was preparing to do macramé. The spell should have been too far away for me to touch, but it responded to the gesture like it had been trained, surging toward my hand.

I yanked.

The spell unraveled in the smell of smoke and roses, filling the air around us until it seemed like the smoke alarms would start screaming, telling everyone in the next room that the building was on fire. No such thing happened. Instead, Madden gasped, clutching his chest as if in sudden pain, and turned wide, surprisingly canine eyes on me. His human disguise was slipping. Not as badly as mine had—his ears were still round and his hair was still blond, rather than red and white—but still. That was worrisome.

"Are you okay?" I asked, shaking my hand in a vague effort to wipe away the last of August's magic. It was clinging like bad perfume, refusing to let me go. "Madden, talk to me."

"I—you—*she was here.*" He had the presence of mind to lower his voice when he clearly wanted to shout. Every line of his body was tense; everything about the way he looked at me screamed dismay and violation. "The redheaded woman, the one who smells sort of like you but different, *she was here.* She came the same time you did. When you were looking for Arden? Remember?"

"I remember," I said gently.

I remembered a woman in a white peasant blouse with hair that was an odd shade of silvery-red, like something that came from a bottle rather than growing from a human head. She'd been in the bookstore, making a purchase, sizing up Jude, the general manager. At the time, I'd assumed she was an ordinary customer, maybe one with an understandable if unlikely to work out crush on a pretty bookseller. There hadn't been anything about her that screamed "fae" . . .

But she'd held the door open a fraction of a second longer than she had to, giving me time to make it inside despite the don't-look-here that should have concealed me from her. At the time, I'd written it off as luck. Maybe it had been something more.

"She came—I think she came because she was looking for a place to hide. She followed the magic. Jude and Alan . . ." Madden's cheeks flushed red with shame. "They're good people, you know? Real good bosses. They're not assholes at all. But they're humans. They've already been pixie-led."

Which was another way of saying he and Arden had done their share of messing with Jude and Alan's heads when they felt they had to, using magic to cover up the small slips that inevitably happen when humans and the fae were existing in close quarters. "It wouldn't have been hard for her to piggyback on the spells that had already been used on them," I said grimly. "Madden, what did she do?"

"She . . . made them think she belonged here. That she'd always belonged here. They know Arden left, but they think she was a seasonal hire, that it was August who was supposed to be in the store. She doesn't do any work, she doesn't know *how*, but she's always here." Madden shuddered. "She made it so I couldn't say anything about her being here, or anything about it being wrong. I wanted to." He paused, eyes widening in horror. "She made me lie to *Arden*. Am I . . . is that treason? For a seneschal to lie to a queen?"

"Not when you're being magically compelled. You didn't have a choice," I said, hurrying to reassure him. "There was nothing you could have done. Where is she now?"

He raised a shaking hand and pointed at the basement door. Of course. The Borderlands basement was where terrible things waited to happen to me. Sometimes those terrible things later turned out to be friends, but that didn't make them any less terrible while they were happening.

"Okay," I said, and grabbed the lingering traces of August's magic from the air, twisting them into a don't-look-here as fast as I could before throwing it over myself and Simon. I didn't bother with a new human disguise. It wasn't like anybody would be able to see it.

Madden kept his eyes focused on me so he wouldn't lose track of where I was. When I was finished casting, he wrinkled his nose and said, "That spell smelled like one of *hers*."

"Makes sense," I said. "I mostly used her magic to cast it. Is the basement door unlocked?" Don't-look-here spells aren't true invisibility. Picking a lock would probably be unusual enough to get us noticed, if anyone happened to be looking.

"It should be," said Madden. He grabbed a fistful of air, expertly patching his human disguise. When he was done, he looked exactly like he had when we first came in. He glanced uncomfortably at the doorway. "Be careful, okay? I can't come down to save you. Not while I'm in the middle of my shift."

"We'll be fine," I said. "She probably didn't mean any harm. She's been missing for a long time, and needed a place to stay while she figured stuff out. Arden leaving made a hole. She filled it." That didn't explain why she'd been playing house in a science fiction bookstore instead of finding our mother or presenting herself to the queen, but those were questions we'd be able to answer shortly, when we found her. Assuming she didn't attack us on sight or anything else unpleasant like that.

"Okay," said Madden. "Please let me know you're okay when it's all done."

"I will," I promised.

He nodded—from the nose this time—and walked past us, returning to the café. I stayed where I was, counting slowly to ten, before motioning for Simon to follow me to the basement door.

A good don't-look-here spell makes you seem like part of the landscape, or like someone else's problem. As long as we didn't directly interact with any of the bleary-eyed morning customers on the other side of the rope, they would take no notice of us. Carefully, we crept across the bookstore to our destination. Madden was right: the door was unlocked.

The light on the other side was off. Turning it on would definitely be a big enough change in the environment to attract attention. Silently thanking Oberon for fae night vision, I eased my way through the door and onto the steps beyond, descending a few paces before I turned and beckoned Simon to follow.

He hesitated. For one terrible moment, I expected him to slam the door, turn, and run. Instead, he stepped through and closed the door behind himself, casting us both into darkness. It was strange. Being shut in a dark stairwell with Simon Torquill should have given me pause, or maybe a mild panic attack. All I could actually feel was relief. We had both made it this far. With as strong as the traceries of magic were upstairs, we didn't have all that far to go.

The basement had no windows, and the seal on the door was remarkably good: no light was making its way in. Fae eyes are good, but they're not *that* good. "I'm going to turn the lights on," I whispered, voice barely more than a breath.

Simon didn't respond, but there was a faint shifting sound, as if he had braced himself. Good. Having sensitive eyes is sometimes as much a curse as it is a blessing. I reached past him and clicked the switch. Light sprang into being, filling the basement with a soft white glow.

I was looking directly at Simon's face, pale and pinched, his eyes squinted tightly shut. He cracked one of them cautiously open before his face went slack, caution forgotten utterly as he opened both eyes in silent, staring shock.

I started to turn. That was a bad idea. Changing positions meant that the fist caught me square in the nose, sending me reeling backward.

Right.

NINETEEN

SIMON CAUGHT ME BEFORE I fell. At least, that was what I thought he was doing: as I struggled to stand upright, I realized he'd closed his hands on my shoulders, effectively pinning me in place. Sylvester had ordered him to raise no hand against me; maybe this didn't count.

The woman on the steps below us was pale enough to look sickly, like cream that had gone faintly out of true. Her hair was a washed-out silvery red, as if it had been painted with moonlight one day while she wasn't paying attention, and her eyes were a gold so pale and so clear that they verged on white-gray, like my mother's, like my own. She was barefoot, wearing tattered secondhand jeans and a shapeless, oversized Borderlands T-shirt, and I would have known who she was even if I hadn't known that she existed, because the family resemblance between us was terrifyingly strong. She even *stood* the way I did.

Why shouldn't she? August and I were both daughters of Amandine who had been partially raised by Torquill men. Everything about my childhood had been a strange parody of hers, and looking at her was like looking at a funhouse mirror, warped and strange and perfect.

Her nose wrinkled. I realized she was tasting the air, rolling it on her tongue the way I did when I was trying to figure out what someone was.

"Let me up," I hissed, glancing back to make sure Simon knew I was talking to him. "I can't do this if I can't stand."

He didn't let go. He was still staring at August, a man utterly transfixed, unwilling or unable to unlock his hands long enough to release me. I was probably as strong as he was—I definitely got more exercise—but the position and space we were in didn't give me a lot of options for freeing myself unless I wanted to hurt him. August probably wouldn't like that very much, him being her father and all.

I turned my attention back to her. "Uh, hi," I said. "Mom sent me to find you. She's been worried."

August's eyes narrowed. "I know you," she said. Her accent was rounded and odd, like something out of an old movie; like something that had been shut away from the mortal world and its linguistic drift for a hundred years. "You were there, in Annwn, when the new people came. You were there when the walls of the world shredded, and I was finally free to step through. You did this to me."

"I—what?"

That was all I had time to say before she launched herself up the stairs, grabbing me by the hair and yanking me out of Simon's grasp. *She* was strong. She'd been living an agrarian existence in deep Faerie for longer than I'd been alive, and she had the sort of grip that comes from ploughing fields and breaking rocks.

What she didn't have was training. Faced with an opponent who had already punched me once and was now jerking me toward her, I did the only thing that made sense: I brought my knee up and slammed it into the meat of her belly, knocking the air out of her with a loud gasp. She fell backward. She didn't let go, and so I fell with her, two Dóchas Sidhe tumbling end over end to land in a heap at the bottom of the stairs.

There was a loud crack as we fell, the sort of meaty sound that spoke of broken bones, rather than broken woodwork. There was no accompanying bolt of pain. For once, the broken bone wasn't mine. August shrieked, the sound still thin and reedy from where I had knocked the wind out of her. What were a few broken bones between newly united siblings?

When the siblings were the pair of us, a few broken bones were virtually nothing. August was a pureblood, maybe the only pureblood of our shared kind, and she healed even faster than I did. By the time I had disentangled myself from the knot of limbs that we had become, she was already bouncing to her feet and lunging for me again, the smell of smoke and roses crackling in the air around her. Did healing raise her magic? Was it that way for both of us, and I had just never noticed, because my own magic was internal to me?

I had so many questions. There were so many things I wanted to ask her, things about our magic and the way it worked, things about our mother, things about her search for Oberon. And none of those questions were going to get answered until she stopped trying to flat-out murder me. August lunged, grabbing for my wrists, like she thought she could subdue me by holding my hands.

Wait. Maybe she could. If I wasn't fighting back, maybe she'd stop—and it wasn't like I couldn't take a little pain. I let her grab my wrists, smothering the instincts that told me to back up, to pull away, to get out of her range before she did something I couldn't live with. Simon was still on the stairs, neither coming to her aid nor asking her to stop. The geas he was under had to be warring with his parental instincts, and I almost felt bad for him. Almost; not quite. I had other things to worry about at the moment.

August locked her fingers around my wrists, jerking me toward her, and snarled, "Let's see how good you are at binding what isn't yours now."

I had time to open my mouth and take a quick breath, intending to ask her what the hell she was talking about. I had less than a second. Then the pain slammed down on me, hot and intense and biting as if I were bathing in acid, like every nerve in my body was suddenly, electrically on fire. I screamed. The smell of smoke and roses was everywhere, cloying, choking me, until I couldn't breathe, I couldn't see, I couldn't *stand*—

When I was a child, Amandine tried to turn me human. She wanted me to die a human death, natural and mortal and inevitable. But it hurt. Oh, how it hurt. If she moved at anything swifter than a snail's crawl, it was too painful for even the most devoted daughter to stand, and she had quickly learned that if she didn't want me to flinch every time she came near me, she needed to go slow and easy.

For years, I'd blocked out how she had hurt me, refusing to think about it, refusing to even remember that it had happened, because if she was Daoine Sidhe, as everyone told me, over and over, there was no way her hands could have been enough to cause that sort of pain. When my own daughter had been born, I'd been afraid to touch her, because what if that sort of feedback loop was just how things worked among the fae, and no one had ever wanted to say anything in front of a flawed, mixed, mortal *changeling*?

My mind might have blocked out the pain, but my body remembered. It knew what August was doing, and it howled on a cellular level, fighting back as hard as it could. It didn't matter. August was stronger, and she was better at using our shared magic, and as hard as I pulled away, she pulled me toward her twice as fiercely.

Don't-look-here spells don't make it impossible for someone to notice you. They just make it harder. With the way I was screaming, someone was *going* to notice me.

Then Simon was there, grabbing my shoulders, dragging me away from August. She let go with surprising readiness once it was her father pulling me out of her grasp. I stopped screaming and gasped, unable to speak as I struggled to get my equilibrium back.

It wasn't coming easy. I didn't even need the lock of colorless brown hair that had fallen to cover my eyes to know what she had done: it was singing in my veins, in the suddenly shifted watermarks of my mortality. Like our mother, like me, August knew how to change the blood of the people she touched. It was clear that unlike me, she'd had plenty of opportunities to practice. I was a blunt instrument and she?

She was a scalpel.

My heart was beating too hard and my body felt like it had been replaced by a hundred pounds of clay as I staggered to my feet, struggling to keep my balance in the force of too many changes, too quickly. Simon had his arm around my shoulders, sheltering me from August, whose eyes were still bright with magic and rage.

"That is *enough*," he snapped, and his voice was the crack of a whip, the edict of a king: disagreeing with him would be impossible. August froze. Only for a moment. Long enough for him to let me go and move to her, grabbing her arms and restraining her.

My knees went weak, trying to force me to kneel. He was so beautiful. How had I never seen how beautiful he was? I didn't even have the right to look at him.

The part of me that was still fae raged and wept at the same time, stunned into silent fury. There's something in the human DNA that wants to bow before the fae, seeing them as too perfect, too beautiful to truly exist. It's an old instinct, left over from the days when the purebloods hunted humans for sport, running them up and down the hills before putting arrows in their hearts and leaving them for their lovers to find. Bow, and maybe you won't be transformed into a deer, or a tree, or a particularly interesting stone. Bow, and maybe your betters will let you pass in peace.

Bow, and live to see the morning.

The false Queen used to raise those responses in me. She was one of the only fae I knew who actually rejoiced in being punishingly beautiful, the kind of beauty that never did anyone any good, but could do them a world of hurt. I had hated the feelings she sparked in me then, when I thought they were an unavoidable part of being who and what I was. As my blood had shifted and those feelings had faded, I had been relieved. That was a part of my mortality I had never wanted back.

Well, I had it now. Lucky, lucky me.

August was struggling to break free of her father. I was sure she would have succeeded, if he hadn't been pinning her arms behind her back so that she lacked the leverage to get away.

"August," he snapped. "August, *stop*."

She froze, twisting in an effort to see his face. "How do you know my name?" she demanded. "I didn't tell you my name."

Simon couldn't have looked more stunned if she had suddenly turned *him* mortal. The color drained from his cheeks, leaving his freckles standing out like brands against his skin. "What . . . what did you say?" he stammered. "How do you not know me?"

"I've never met you before," she snapped. "Let me go."

The doorknob turned.

I whipped around, staring at the top of the stairs in suddenly unified dismay. We were going to be found. We were going to be found, and there was no way I could explain what we were doing down here. August wasn't wearing a human disguise. I didn't know whether I needed one or not, and it didn't really matter either way, because I was too weak and too off-balance to disguise myself. I couldn't do anything but stand where I was and wait for everything to go to hell.

The smell of smoke and mulled cider was so thin as to be almost imperceptible, but I felt the weight of Simon's spell settle on me like a shroud. The door opened. Alan appeared, frowning down the stairs. He was a tall, thin, human man, dressed all in black, his hair pulled into a ponytail that left his slightly over-large ears prominently displayed. Most of the time when I'd seen him, he'd looked dour, even disapproving. Right now, he just looked confused.

"Damn raccoons," he said finally, and turned off the light, casting the basement into absolute blackness.

I had thought the dark was deep before, when I'd been looking at it with the eyes of a more nocturnal creature. Now my eyes were as close to human as the rest of me, and the blackness was absolute. I fumbled in my pocket until I found my cellphone, holding it up to illuminate the area.

Simon was wobbling, even paler than before, like a man on the verge of collapse. His grip on August had slackened. She was free, looking wildly around, like she had lost something. She flinched when I held the light in her direction, raising a hand to shield her eyes.

"Papa?" she said, in a shaky voice. "I smell your magic—where *are* you?"

Simon didn't say anything. He just kept wobbling. My stomach sank.

When Sylvester bound his brother, he ordered him to raise no hand and cast no spell against me. The illusion Simon had slammed down over the three of us was thick as molasses, and while it had been intended to save me from discovery, it could also be interpreted, in some lights, as an attack.

"Oh, oak and ash," I hissed, rushing to his side. August was still looking around, lost. I glared at her. "*Help* him."

"What? Who—who *are* you people? Where's my papa?" The look August gave me was full of confusion and despair.

My heart sank. Home isn't always a place. Sometimes it's a concept, an idea: an ideal. When August had gone to the Luidaeg looking for a candle, the Luidaeg had asked for her way home in payment. Without finding Oberon, she couldn't find her way. And for August, Simon was part of home.

"We don't have time right now," I said. "He's not well. Help me with him."

Her eyes narrowed, confusion fading. "Why should I help you? You were going to leave me in Annwn. You're my enemy. How do you even exist? My mother would *never* lower herself to touch a human."

"Great, good, this is a fantastic way to start a family reunion, *August*, but I'm telling you, this man needs help." I glared at her, daring her to challenge me. "You sold your way home to the Luidaeg for a candle."

"How do you—"

"I pledged myself into her service for a year in order to get another candle, all so I could go and bring you home. I don't know what we are to each other, but I'm not your enemy, and this man needs help."

August wavered. I could see it in her eyes. I decided to push my luck.

"August, this is your father."

She looked at Simon again, still with no signs of recognition, and then back to me. "Liar," she spat. Shoving Simon toward me, she turned and ran off into the darkness of the basement, quickly vanishing from my cellphone's limited sphere of light.

Simon was a statue masquerading as a man. I staggered under the weight of him, faced with an impossible decision: drop the man who had saved me and run after the sister who had already ripped most of the fae blood from my veins, or stay here with Simon, letting August and the chance of saving Tybalt slip away.

My own body answered the question for me. My knees buckled and I fell, hitting the concrete floor with a jolt I felt all the way up into my hips. Simon fell with me, a dead weight holding me down.

"Oh, root and branch and fuck and shit and *Oberon's ass*," I hissed, struggling not to drop him. He didn't heal as fast as I did. *I* didn't heal as fast as I did. The pain in my knees was bright, intense, and not fading, even though it had been several seconds since I fell. Was it possible to get addicted to the idea of indestructibility? Because if it was, there was no question of whether I was a junkie. I was supposed to be unbreakable. That was the way the world *worked*.

"Simon, can you hear me?" He was staring at the ceiling, mouth shut. Sylvester's geas had said if Simon raised a hand or cast a spell against me, his mouth would be sealed and his hands would be silenced. Well, this looked a lot like that.

"I can't do this alone." My voice sounded small in the empty basement. August was gone. I had no doubt of that. I supposed I should be grateful that Amandine hadn't raised her to be a killer, or there would have been a knife in my neck and I would have been proving all the people who said my tendency to rush headlong into danger was going to get me killed right.

At least Quentin wouldn't have been here to see. At least I could have spared him that image of me. But I couldn't have spared Tybalt or Jazz anything by dying here. Amandine wouldn't let them go just because I'd failed. Hell, she'd probably grab the night-haunt that became me and force them to finish the job, claiming that debts to her didn't end with death. She might even be right. The Firstborn can be terrifying when they want to be.

There had to be a way out of this. There *had* to be. I closed my eyes, shutting out my cellphone's meager light as I tried to think.

This wasn't the most human I'd ever been. I could tell that from the texture of my blood. I wasn't sure I could shift myself further toward fae without some sort of crutch—I needed a hope chest in the worst way—but I was still Dóchas Sidhe enough to see the watermarks in my veins, the places where the magic had moved me. Before I'd been mostly fae, I had been your standard changeling scrapper, working my way through an often confusing set of magical rules with swamp water charms and parlor tricks.

Parlor tricks. I opened my eyes and raised my phone, grateful to see that I still had battery power left, and that there was a flicker of a signal in the Borderlands basement. Scrolling through my contact list, I chose the number most likely to get me help in a hurry.

Please pick up, I thought. *Please, please, please pick up.*

"Borderlands Café," said a cheery, unfamiliar voice.

Z'ev. It had to be. I took a breath and forced myself to sound as level as possible, like I didn't have a care in the world. "Hi, it's Madden's friend again. Is he still on-shift?"

"I can get him for you, if you'd like."

"Please."

"One moment." There was a soft thunk as he set the receiver down. I looked at Simon, who was resting half in, half out of my lap, and hoped I wasn't making the wrong call. Not like it made much of a difference if I was. This might be the wrong decision. It was the only one I had left to make.

"Hello?" Madden sounded cautious but still warm. I wasn't sure the man was capable of staying angry for long.

It was time to test that. "I don't have much time," I said. "August was down here. She attacked us, she hurt me, and Simon had to cast a spell to keep Alan from spotting us. I need honey, mint, ginger, hot water, and salt. Can you get them to me?"

"Toby?" Now confusion joined the mix. "I . . . yeah. Are you where you were?"

"I am. Hurry." I hung up before he could ask me any more questions. Questions were just going to slow us down.

Magic lives in the blood. That's all well and good for the purebloods. Their bodies can make and handle using as much magic as they need. Changelings, though . . . changelings are more limited. We always have been. So we need to understand magic. We need to find ways to convince it, things that can shore it up when it doesn't want to hold.

"It'll be okay," I told Simon, stroking the hair back from his forehead. He didn't look like he believed me. I couldn't blame him, not entirely. He'd found his daughter, only to find that she didn't know who he was, and then he'd lost her again, all because he was trying to save her. And me. It was no accident that his illusion had extended to cover me.

If he'd just cut it off before it could wrap around me, he could have concealed himself and August, leaving me to face Alan's wrath, without violating the terms of his geas. It had been the perfect opportunity for him to escape, and he hadn't taken it. For that alone, I had to do my best to save him. I didn't have a choice.

The basement door opened and closed again. I shut my eyes, guessing before it happened that Madden was going to turn the light on. There was a click, and the dark behind my eyelids got a little lighter. Cautiously, I cracked them open, and watched Madden descend. He was carrying a small tray. I recognized the teapot, and I had hope. Not much, but still, it was a nice change.

He stopped on the last step, frowning. "Toby?" he said. "I thought you were . . . are you here?"

Crap. Simon's illusion. I looked around, finding nothing I could throw, and settled on chucking my phone at Madden's shoulder as hard as I could. My aim was a little off; it hit his upper arm before falling harmlessly to the pavement.

He blinked at it. Then he turned and blinked at me. "There you are," he said. "What . . . ?"

"Really good don't-look-here," I said. "Don't take your eyes off me, or you'll lose us again."

"You look . . ." Madden paused, clearly unsure how to proceed. Finally, he said, "Different."

"August pulled a lot of the fae blood out of me before she ran, and I'm not strong enough to put it back on my own," I said. "Arden still has the hope chest in her treasury. I'm sure she'll let me borrow it for a few minutes." And if she wanted to charge me some prohibitive price for using it, I'd have no choice but to pay. Swell.

There was a pause while Madden attempted to process this information. There aren't many Dóchas Sidhe in the world—two is not enough to book a table at Mel's Diner, much less constitute a healthy population—and hope chests haven't been in common use for centuries. For most people, the balance of the blood they have when they're born is the one they're going to live with. He had already seen my blood shift once before. That didn't mean it was something easy to understand.

It also didn't mean that we had time to sit around while he came to terms with the great march of weird that is my life. "Did you bring what I asked for?"

"What? Oh!" Madden shook himself, a great, full-body motion, like he was trying to dry off after an unexpected dip in deep water. "Yeah. Here." He closed the distance between us in a few long steps, holding his tray out toward me. "What are you going to do?"

"Something stupid. And painful. And unusually lasting, for me." I took the tray, setting it carefully on the nearest open patch of floor.

Madden frowned. "What do you mean, lasting?"

"I mean the more human I am, the more slowly I heal." I've bounced back from being stabbed in the heart and dropped from the treetops, but I was more fae than human when those things happened. "I'm about to make a mess."

"Oh." Madden took a step back. "I can't really explain blood on my work pants."

"It's okay," I assured him, and turned to the things I'd asked him to bring me.

The Borderlands Café isn't the biggest or the fanciest in San Francisco, but the owner makes it a point to buy the best ingredients he can. Belatedly, it occurred to me that I could have asked for a cup of coffee. Being closer to human meant caffeine would work on me again. *After I fix this, before the hope chest,* I thought, and got to work.

Alchemy is a science, precise and careful and refined over the course of centuries. People like Walther can spend their whole lives practicing their craft, and still feel like they had more to learn. In one of those "Alanis Morissette would call this ironic" twists, changeling charms work along similar principles. A French chef and a home cook can both roast a chicken. It's just that one of them will do it with technique and precision and a guaranteed result, while the other will be working off of Grandma's recipe, a handful of herbs, and a basic understanding of heat.

I have always been more of a home cook. I picked up the squeeze bottle of honey and wrung a healthy amount of sticky golden liquid into the bottom of the teacup before adding pinches of powdered ginger and mint leaves.

"He that has a tiny little wit, with hey, ho, the wind and the rain," I chanted. My magic struggled to rise around me, cut-grass and copper and so very, very strange, and so achingly familiar. This was how it had been for me, for years. This was how I had grown up, struggling to reach the bottom rungs of a ladder that everyone around me seemed to climb so effortlessly.

Maybe using *King Lear* to focus the charm meant to save my stepfather was a little weird, but I've always had a thing for Shakespeare, and somehow I didn't think Simon would appreciate me going for *Hamlet.* I added salt to the mixture in the bottom of my teacup and stirred it with my finger before reaching for the pot and adding enough hot water to cover everything. The smell that rose from the mess was sweet and medicinal.

I was going to fix that.

"Must make content with his fortunes fit," I chanted, and drew the knife from where it rode at my hip, comforting and close. The blade was silver, enchanted to hold a proper edge, and I kept it sharp. Given what my knives were often used for, letting them go blunt was never a good idea.

Simon rolled his eyes, sensing the shape of what I was about to do. He would have told me not to, if he could have; I was sure of that. I paused to smile a little, trying to seem more encouraging than concerned. From the way his eyes rolled again, I didn't quite manage it.

"Don't worry," I said. "I'm a professional." I ran the knife along the ball of my thumb, opening the skin. The pain was bright and electric, as it always was, but this time, it didn't fade: this time, it stayed and grew stronger, the skin unable to knit back together the way it so often did.

At least I'd have all the blood I needed. I held my thumb over the teacup, bleeding into the water-and-honey mixture. Then I reached for Simon's hand, and repeated the cut along his thumb, adding his blood to the "tea."

"Simon Torquill," I said. "You have been bound for my sake, and for my sake, I release you. You have been bound by the blood of your brother: I undo those ties with the blood of my mother. Be fit. Be fine. Be free." I raised the cup to his lips, holding it there until I saw him swallow. Good.

Now came the hard part. "The rain it raineth every day," I murmured, finishing the phrase from *Lear*, and brought the cup to my own lips. The bloody red of his memories crashed down on me like a wave, and the basement—and my body—went away.

TWENTY

EVERYTHING WAS FILMED IN red, like I was looking at the world through a pair of literally rose-tinted glasses. That was how I knew this was a blood memory, and not reality. Well, that, and the fact that I was standing, I wasn't bleeding, and my body felt like my own again.

It's almost funny. There was a time when I would have given anything to be a real human girl. And then that time passed, and I accepted myself for who I was always meant to be, and I learned how to be happy among the fae. Which was, naturally, when people started trying to give me back my humanity. A pity they never *asked* first.

"October."

I turned.

Simon was behind me, a worried expression on his familiar, unfamiliar face. He still had the same bone structure as his brother, could still pass for Sylvester when calm or serious, but the more time I spent with him, the more I was coming to see him for who he really was. He was quicker than his brother, more mercurial, and oddly, more relaxed, at least when he wasn't being villainous or dour.

I frowned. "Is this a memory?"

"No. You foolish, foolish girl." He smiled wryly, shaking his head. "You understand the principles of what you do, but not the possible consequences."

"I've heard that one before."

"Why am I not surprised?" Simon stopped smiling and simply looked at me. "What are you trying to do?"

"Remove the geas that Sylvester put on you." The basement seemed to be getting bigger around us, the walls stretching off into some dark, sanguine distance. Everything was still overlain with red, but it was taking on more shade and nuance, the longer we stood here. "I figured if his blood was enough to do it, maybe my blood would be enough to *un*do it."

"Are you sure that's a good idea? I've hurt you before."

He wasn't wrong. But neither was I. I could feel it in my bones. I shrugged. "I won't pretend that I've forgiven you for what you did to me. I sort of want to. It would be easier. I know that you didn't mean to do as much damage as you did. That doesn't make the damage go away. It doesn't give my daughter back to me."

It was funny, in a terrible way. Simon had been so focused on doing whatever he could to bring his daughter home that he'd caused me to lose my own child forever. I didn't need to say that aloud; he knew what I was thinking. I could see it in the shamed, downcast tilt of his eyes.

"You didn't tell Riordan she could have me."

Simon frowned. "What?"

"You're a pureblood. You dance with words when you can't find someone better to dance with. There's a reason I triple check everything I say to the Luidaeg, and she's my ally. I know she wouldn't screw me over just to show me that she could. Sylvester made it so you couldn't speak out against me. Okay, fine. All you had to do was stay silent when Riordan asked if I was with you. There were a hundred things you could have said to her that would have turned a quick pit stop into a disaster. You didn't say any of them. You helped more than you had to. But that's not why I want to save you."

He frowned. "Then why . . . ?"

"Three reasons. I lost my father when I was really young. He was human. As soon as Sylvester offered me the Choice, as soon as I said I wanted to be fae like Mom, I lost my dad. He died thinking I had burned to death in our home. August deserves to have her father. I'm not her biggest fan right now," the memory of pain arced through me, like even hinting at what she'd done was enough to activate the echoes of it that still lingered in my blood, "but that doesn't mean I want her to lose you."

Simon nodded slowly.

"Second, I need you to help me figure out how to get her way home back, so she can recognize you, and we can return her to Amandine, and I can save my friends." That, too, was a factor in me starting to forgive Simon, whether I wanted to or not. I would mourn for my lost relationship with Gillian for the rest of my life, which had the potential to be very, very long. He hadn't known what he was doing when he took me away from her, or maybe he just hadn't cared.

But I'd built a life since then. A better life. And my little girl was happy without me, human and thriving and living without worrying about all the things that I was heir to crashing down on her head. Gillian had moved on. I had to do the same, if only for the sake of the people who loved me, and Simon was a part of that transition.

"Most of all, though, you didn't have to include me in that illusion. And don't try to tell me you didn't think before you acted, because if there's one thing I know about you, it's that you think before you act. You knew hiding me would activate Sylvester's punishment. You did it anyway."

"August needs a hero if she's going to find her way," said Simon. "I'm not that. I never have been."

"Sometimes I think Faerie gets a little too hung up on defining heroism, and loses track of all the good things we can do that aren't swinging a sword or slaying a dragon," I said. "You saved me. You didn't have to. You could have freed yourself from the obligation to help me by doing exactly what Sylvester bound you to do and no more, and you didn't. So, yeah, I'm going to help you."

"I see." Simon looked away. "I used to watch you, when you were younger. When Amy brought you to court functions, and after, when you'd run away. I saw you living in those hovels, working with those changeling ruffians, standing up to the purebloods, and I was . . . I was proud of you. I thought you were your mother's daughter, finding a way to survive no matter what the world threw at you. I was wrong."

"Wrong how? Wrong to be a creepy person and spy on me?"

"No." He looked back at me and smiled sadly. "You are so much kinder than Amy ever was. I love your mother. I love my *wife*. But no one would ever mistake her for kind. She never had to be. I don't know where your kindness came from. I don't care. Hold close to it, and never, never let the world take it away."

I felt my ears redden, embarrassed by his praise. "I'll do my best. I . . . how are we talking? Are you a blood memory, or . . . ?"

"I'm a blood-worker, October, and so are you. We've shared blood, magic, and intent. When you touch someone's blood, does it create a space? A . . . silence, carved out of the world?"

"Yes."

"This is like that. Time is passing. We can't stay here forever, or even terribly long, not without substantially more blood. But this used to be how the Daoine Sidhe would communicate, when we were separated by oceans, or by worlds. Two vials of blood, held in trust until an agreed-upon time."

"Why did you stop?"

The corner of his mouth twitched. "There's this mortal invention. Perhaps you've heard of it—the telephone? Much easier to use than a blood charm requiring perfect synchronization between people who might not have spoken in years. Once communication became easier, such archaic methods became impractical, even among traditionalists. Congratulations. You've stumbled upon something much older than yourself."

"I do that a lot," I said. I took a deep breath. "Tell me how to unbind you."

The flicker of levity in Simon's eyes died. "It will hurt."

"I'm sorry about that."

"I don't mean it will hurt *me*. My brother was never much of a blood-worker, but he has raw power behind him, and the form he used was composed by our First, may she sleep forever and never trouble us again. It will hurt *you*. Your blood is thin and fraying. The pain . . ."

"Won't be anything I haven't felt before. Let me do this. Let me save you."

"And when I am forever in your debt, and you can never again be free of me, will you be glad you did? This is something I can't repay."

"We'll worry about that later. Please. Don't leave me to deal with this alone."

Simon sighed, long and low and weary. I wondered suddenly how long it had been since he'd had a rest. Being elf-shot didn't count. That sort of sleep didn't renew the body or the soul, or else purebloods would have done it to themselves every time they needed a break, rather than wandering off into the woods to commune with nature and potentially get eaten by whatever happened to be lurking there.

"All right," he said. "Give me your hands."

I walked toward him. He reached out, and I slid my hands into his, letting our fingers knot together. This close to him, the smell of smoke and mulled cider was incredibly strong.

"Why did it change?" I blurted.

He paused. "What?"

"Your magic. It's not . . . when I smell it in the real world, it's rotten oranges, not mulled cider. I didn't know magic could change like that. I thought it was a part of you. Why did it change?"

"Ah." He looked down, refusing to meet my eyes. It didn't look like he was preparing to lie. Instead, it looked like he was, well, ashamed. "Magic is a function of the blood. It tells the world who you are, something that can't be hidden or denied. When I allowed myself to be yoked to someone who did not have my family's best interests at heart, when I borrowed her magic over and over again—charms and cantrips and blood potions, and be careful, October, be very, very careful, because the things we consume become a part of us, and some transformations run deeper than the skin— when I did those things, I let myself be changed. I became someone else. Someone who had no right to Simon Torquill's past, or to the love of those who would have saved him, if only they had known how much danger he was in. Magic is a function of the blood. It will change when the blood does."

"It's changing back," I said, and he looked up, startled. "I keep smelling apples on you. Have faith, Simon. Maybe the damage you did wasn't as bad as you think it is."

"May Oberon have mercy," he whispered. Then, more loudly, he asked, "Can you see any sort of flicker around me, any indication of the size or shape of the binding?"

I squinted, willing the delicate web of Sylvester's magic to come into view. There was a faint, distant whiff of daffodils, but that was all; no magical glimmer appeared. I shook my head. "No. There's nothing. I think . . . I think I'm too human."

"The merlins were more human by far than you are now, and they brought a thousand towers down," said Simon. "There's no such thing as being too human, and anyone who ever told you that was lying, because they were afraid."

"Of what?"

He leaned closer, voice dropping to a conspiratorial whisper, "Of what you could do if you remembered that your heritage has more than one source. If you can't see it, feel for it. Right here, right now, we share blood, and this binding was cast on your behalf. Find it. Make it your own."

I swallowed, hard. Then I closed my eyes.

It's easier to look for things I can't see when I can't see anything at all. Vision just gets in the way. So I held onto Simon's hands, and I held onto the thin traceries of daffodil flowers in the air, and I strained as hard as I could, stretching a muscle that humans don't have and purebloods never bothered to find a name for. It was the point of connection between me and the magical world, and while it might be smaller now than it had been, it was still there. As long as a drop of fae blood still ran in my veins, no one could take it entirely away from me.

In the dark, the smell of daffodils was easier to find and follow, as was the scent of cut-grass and copper. I drew it around me like a cloak, and when that wasn't enough, I bit the inside of my cheek, hard enough to draw blood. It tasted distant and dilute, probably because this wasn't really happening, not the way I saw it.

Distant and dilute it might be, but blood was blood, and my blood wanted me to succeed. I swallowed, and reached, and filled my questing fingers with the scent of daffodils. I pulled. They pulled back, suddenly rooted. Simon moaned. The sound was tight and quickly swallowed, like it was something he hadn't wanted me to hear. I gritted my teeth and pulled harder, chasing the source of the pain, chasing the thing that didn't want me to catch it. It tried to slither away. I bore down.

And it was there in my hands, the core of someone else's spell, bright and burning and smelling of dogwood flowers. I needed it to stop. I needed it to go out. I looked for something I could use to extinguish it.

All I had was blood. That was fine. I'd worked with blood before. I've been working with blood for most of my life. So I reached deep, tracing back along my own mental fingers until I found the blood I needed and cast it, hard and furious, against the fire. The geas guttered, swamped and overwhelmed. I doused it again.

The flame went out.

I opened my eyes, pleased, smiling. "See?" I said. "I—" Then I stopped, staring at the emptiness in front of me.

Simon was gone. The basement walls had continued to recede; the only way I could tell that I was still in my blood-construct of the Borderlands basement was by looking at the rafters above my head or the cracked stone below my feet, and even those seemed a little too old, a little too medieval to be part of a modern human building in mortal San Francisco.

"Simon?" I called.

My voice echoed off the distant walls, traveling out, bouncing back to me. I bit my lip.

"Hello, little fish," said a voice from behind me.

I whipped around, so fast that I nearly lost my balance. There, gilded red like everything around him, stood Tybalt. He was wearing the leather pants and open pirate shirt that had been his default wardrobe for so many years of our acquaintance, a smirk on his lips. He looked tired. He looked so very, very tired.

"I can't leave you alone for a second, can I?" he asked.

"Tybalt?" I took a step closer. "Are you . . . how is this . . . ?"

"I'm not real, no," he said. "Would that I were. This might all end so much more easily if I were. October, do you understand what you've done?"

"I unbound Simon."

"Yes. You did." Tybalt took a step back. "He told you it would cost. Didn't you listen?"

"What?"

"I love you. Take comfort in that. Even in your dreams, you are no longer capable of imagining a world in which I do not love you. Hold fast to that ideal."

"Tybalt, don't go." I reached for him.

He took another step back, and he was gone, melting into the shadows that had replaced the wall. I ran after him, charging through the shadows into the seemingly infinite basement beyond. I stumbled. I put my hands out to catch myself as I fell. I hit the floor—

—and gasped, opening my eyes. I was staring at the ceiling of the real basement. The beams were newer, less caked with layers of time and neglect. More importantly, there were naked lightbulbs hanging there, grimed with layers of dust that filtered and softened the light.

A blurry figure at the edge of my vision resolved itself into Simon, looking at me with wide, anxious eyes. "October, can you hear me?" he asked.

"Mghle," I said. My lips were gummy with dried blood, and the inside of my mouth tasted like something had died.

Another blur turned into Madden as he stepped nervously forward. He was actually wringing his hands in front of himself, like he had no idea what else to do. "Is she . . . is she okay?" he asked.

"Yes, and no," said Simon. He returned his attention to me. "October, I'm going to help you sit up now. All right? Please blink if it's not all right."

I wasn't sure I could blink if I wanted to. My body felt heavy and disconnected, like it belonged to someone else entirely. But I felt Simon slide his arm around my shoulders and ease me into a sitting position.

He looked to Madden. "She needs fluids. You serve beverages here, do you not? Get her something. Lots of sugar, lots of milk or cream or whatever other fatty liquid you have on hand. Go." He paused before adding, "Please."

"Sure," said Madden, looking almost relieved before he turned and fled.

Simon returned his attention to me. "Do you know who I am?"

There was a thread of anxiety in his question, like he was afraid I'd hit my head when I fell, and forgotten which Torquill brother I was dealing with. Maybe I *had* hit my head. That would explain why everything kept spinning. I licked my lips again, and managed to croak, "Simon."

"Oh, thank Maeve," he breathed. "October, you undid the geas my brother put on me. It was blood magic, and you unraveled it. Do you understand?"

Speaking still seemed like too much trouble. I nodded, head wobbling like my neck was not long enough to support its weight.

Simon looked . . . Simon looked *wrecked*, abjectly miserable in a way that was so unlike Sylvester's quiet, profound sorrow that I wondered how I could ever have confused them for one another. I wanted to tell him that, that I could finally look at him without seeing the slightest trace of his brother, but I couldn't seem to make my mouth work properly.

This was bad. Part of me realized that this was bad. I've been injured before. I've been killed in the course of duty, and I've always bounced back. Only now, after nothing more serious than a papercut, I was so weak I could barely move, and the room wouldn't stop *spinning*. Whatever I'd done to myself, it was bad, and Simon knew what it was, and for some reason, he wasn't telling me, which just made me sure that it was worse.

I made a small, pained sound. Simon sighed.

"October, when August assaulted you, she did so using techniques she had learned from her mother—your mother. Amandine trained our daughter in the use of her natural talents, because she did not want a child of hers to go into the world unprepared. She left you weakened. I would have told you not to do what you did, if you had been able to ask me."

But I couldn't, I thought fiercely. I had done what I had to do.

Simon seemed to understand that. He bowed his head a little, and said, "Under normal circumstances, snapping a geas would have been painful. It would have come with a price, because undoing a spell rooted in the blood itself was never meant to be easy. Under these circumstances . . ." He tapered off, and just like that, I knew what I had done.

It always comes back to blood in the end. No matter how much we wish it didn't, it always comes back to blood. Closing my eyes, I breathed in as deeply as I could, straining until, at the absolute edge of my awareness, I caught the faintest flicker of cut-grass. It was weak, and the copper seemed to have vanished entirely, leaving what remained flat and simplistic, like it had been pressed between two sheets of glass. I could touch it. I could feel it. But when I tried to call it, it didn't respond.

"Hair," I croaked.

Simon frowned. "What?"

"*Hair.*"

He hesitated before reaching around and lifting a hank of my hair, tugging it into my field of vision.

It had never been such a dark brown before.

"Right," I said, and closed my eyes, and went away.

TWENTY-ONE

"IS SHE DEAD?" The voice was Madden's. He sounded worried and a little panicky, like he wasn't sure how he was going to explain this to Arden. A valid concern: I was currently the only hero of the realm she had.

Some hero. I couldn't call my own magic, much less see the hidden world around us. The last time I'd been remotely this human, I'd needed fairy ointment just to find the Library door, and this was worse. Now that I was looking for the markers, I could tell this was worse.

I had visualized dousing the geas with blood. I hadn't expected the process to be quite so literal.

"No," said Simon. "What did you bring?"

"Um, coffee. She used to really like coffee, and I put so much cream in it I think it's technically a milkshake—do you want me to call Ardy? I can. She'll come."

"And won't that be fun, given that I have yet to stand trial for my crimes against my brother." Simon sounded utterly weary. I felt a hand touch my shoulder. "October. I know you're awake. I can hear you breathing. Please sit up and let me feed you this horrifying concoction. There's whipped cream on it. And chocolate shavings."

"Chocolate makes people feel better," said Madden defensively.

"I thought chocolate was poisonous to dogs." Once I had spoken, opening my eyes no longer seemed like such a challenge, and so I did. The basement ceiling reappeared. I realized the light didn't sting the way it usually would. Maybe having day-adapted eyes wasn't such a bad thing.

And maybe I was fumbling for reasons that this wasn't terrible. Honestly, if I was, who could blame me?

"It is," said Madden, making no effort to conceal his relief. "I'm way allergic. But Ardy says when you're not Cu Sidhe, chocolate is one of the best innovations of the modern world."

"She's not wrong." I was stretched out on something hard. I moved my hand, feeling splintery wood beneath me. "The hell . . . ?"

"Alan does a lot of woodworking down here, when he has time, so really, Alan more talks about doing a lot of woodworking down here while the rest of us nod and pretend to believe him," said Madden, as Simon moved to help me up. "That's his workbench."

"Oh," I said. Simon's hands were a solid weight against my back. I allowed myself to lean against them, not fighting against the drag from my own body, as I reached my hands toward the familiar shape of Madden—and more, the mug in his hands. "Gimme."

"Manners, October," chided Simon gently.

I began to bristle. Then I recognized the note in his voice for what it was: relief. He was making a joke, such as it was, because I wasn't dead, and I wasn't broken, and sure, I was currently more mortal than I'd ever been in my life, but what's a little humanity between friends?

"Mama never taught me any manners," I said. Madden pressed the mug into my hands. True to his word, it was topped with a heaping mound of whipped cream and studded with chocolate shavings. I raised my eyebrows. "Glad I'm not lactose intolerant."

The coffee was hot and sweet and washed the last of the gummy, bloody taste out of my mouth, replacing it with that old, familiar earthiness. I could practically feel the caffeine reaching my bloodstream. Maybe that was half wishful thinking, but under the circumstances, I'd take it. Whatever I needed to get through the rest of this—day? Night? I swallowed and frowned, twisting around to look at Simon.

He was wearing a human disguise. I realized with a pang that it was probably at least in part to keep me from falling down in awe at the sight of him.

"What time is it?" I asked.

"It's almost three," he said. "I'm going to need to smuggle you out of here under an illusion. Otherwise, your friend," he nodded toward Madden, "will be in signal danger of losing his job."

"Oh, oak and ash," I muttered, before taking another long drink of hot, sweet coffee. I wanted to inhale the entire mug and ask for more, maybe with a few rare roast beef sandwiches on the side. Without my preternaturally fast healing to keep me up and running, my body was starting to make complaints to the management.

My body was going to have to suck it up and deal. I finished my coffee, resisting the urge to run my finger around the inside of the mug and snag the last of the whipped cream. Then I stood. My legs wobbled but didn't buckle. For all that I had done myself some serious damage, I hadn't actually *injured* myself. I was splitting hairs. I knew it. That didn't matter. Sometimes splitting hairs is what keeps the world from falling down.

Through it all, Simon kept his hand against my back, refusing to let me stand unassisted until he was sure that I could do it. I turned to offer him a nod and a wan smile.

"I'm okay," I said. "Not sure how much use I'm going to be, but I'm okay."

"I may have a solution for that." He leaned over and picked up a to-go cup from the end of the workbench, solemnly offering it to me. "Here."

"More coffee?" I took the cup. It was heavier than it should have been, and nothing sloshed. Cautiously, I removed the lid and peeked inside. It was full of a thick jellylike substance that glittered when the light hit it, like it was filled with the dust of a hundred stars. My eyes widened. "Fairy ointment! But how—?"

"Really, October, you underestimate me," said Simon. "You seemed intent on napping for hours. I had to do *something* with my time, and brewing a batch of something that could keep you halfway useful seemed like the least annoying option."

The words "thank you" rose to my lips. I swallowed them as hard as I could. I didn't want to insult him when he was helping me—and this was a huge, huge help. With this, I would be able to see Faerie, even if there were great stretches of it that I could no longer touch. "This is amazing," I said instead, and dug my fingers into the gel before wiping them across my eyes in a great, gooey streak.

The basement flickered. Suddenly, the shadows had more depth to them, and they sparkled faintly, like they were filled with pyrite. The air around Simon and Madden glittered, alive with the shadows of their human illusions.

And of course, there were the pixies.

They covered every surface above the floor, clustering on the beams and clinging to the walls, their wings moving in constant silent agitation. I couldn't hear them chiming. My heart sank at the realization. The chiming of the pixies was one of those things I'd never considered I could miss, and now it was gone.

"The last time I needed fairy ointment, I could hear them," I said.

"The last time you needed fairy ointment, you must not have been this mortal," said Simon gently. "I am so sorry."

"Don't be." I put the cap back on the to-go cup and shoved it into the pocket of my jacket. It didn't quite fit, but it was secure enough that I wasn't worried about losing it. If anything, I was worried about how much Simon had made. Just how long did he expect my new-found humanity to last?

Madden was still looking at me anxiously. I smiled at him, trying to look encouraging, or at least like I wasn't on the cusp of dropping dead.

"It'll be okay," I said. "Call Arden when you think she'll be up, let her know that I'm going to need to borrow the hope chest. I'll explain everything when I get to Muir Woods."

"When will that be?"

The Luidaeg's deadline was almost upon us. I sighed. "Not too long now." Turning to Simon, I asked, "Do you know where she'd have gone? It's not like I can sniff her out when I can barely find my own magic."

Simon shook his head. "Anyplace familiar enough that I could put a name to it is too likely to be considered 'home' by the damned curse the Luidaeg sold her. I'm useless."

I hesitated. "Not entirely," I said finally, and reached into my other pocket, producing the candle. It was still tall and red, and the wax was cool and clammy in my hand, like the skin of a corpse. I swallowed a shudder of revulsion. Faerie was trying to reject me, reminding me that no one as human as I was could possibly belong there.

Faerie could stuff it. Unlike August, I had made no deals that would sunder me from my home, and I knew where I belonged. After so many years of running, I finally, genuinely, knew where I belonged.

"Here." I held the candle out to Simon. "Tell it to follow her."

His eyes widened. "October," he said, slowly and carefully, like he was speaking to a child. "Are you sure you want to do this? I'm not bound any longer. I could take the candle and run after my daughter, and leave you here to face the consequences of my actions."

"I trust you," I said, and I did; I was telling the whole and honest truth. I trusted him. I knew that he wouldn't leave me. Because he hadn't told Riordan the truth. Because his illusions had covered me.

Because sometimes the best intentions could lead to some very dark places, and once you were there, it could be almost impossible to find your way home again, unless there was someone willing to help you. Unless you could get there and back by the light of a candle.

Then, because those words didn't feel like enough, I added, "I forgive you."

Simon's smile was slow and indescribably beautiful, in a way that had nothing to do with the mortal awe for the fae. He looked genuinely happy.

"Then we go," he said, and took the candle from my hand. The wick burst into flame, burning a mellow pink, like rose petals, like dawn. He looked toward Madden. "Your hospitality has been much appreciated, and will be remembered. You are a credit to your name."

"If you hurt her, I'll rip your throat out with my teeth, and nobody will punish me, because the Queen in the Mists loves me more than she loves almost anyone else in the world," said Madden pleasantly.

Simon nodded like this was exactly what he'd been hoping to hear. "Then we are in agreement," he said. "October?"

He reached out his hand. I took it. There was a ghost of a scent in the air, the faintest overlay of smoke and mulled cider, mixed with rotting oranges. I inhaled it greedily, grateful for even that small reminder that there was still magic in the world, that I hadn't cut myself off from it completely. Unlike August, I hadn't traded my road home for anything. It was narrower than it had been, harder to see through the briars, but it was still there, and I was going to take it.

The weight of Simon's don't-look-here settled over us. Still hand in hand, we followed Madden up the stairs and into the body of Borderlands Books. Jude, the general manager, was behind the counter, looking at something on the store computer. She looked up at the sound of the door closing, and frowned.

"Everything okay, Mads?" she asked.

"Oh, everything's fine," said Madden, stepping to the side and casually holding the door open so that Simon and I could make it past. The basement door opening when there wasn't supposed to be anyone downstairs would definitely attract attention. "I just needed to call home. I guess I didn't do the dishes this morning."

Jude made a sympathetic face. "Your turn?"

"Yeah." Madden shut the basement door. Simon and I walked on, two people following the flickering light of a candle. The screen door sometimes swung in the breeze. I took a chance and pushed it open with my free hand, allowing the two of us to step outside.

Through the store window I saw Jude glance in our direction, confused by the door opening on its own. Her eyes focused on me for just a second. Then, quickly, they unfocused again, and she no longer knew I was there. To the mortal world, I was a ghost.

Simon squeezed my hand. "Courage," he whispered, and held the candle higher. The flame leaped, a burning rose clawing at the sky, and we started down the street, following the light, letting it guide us down August's trail.

It was funny. It was the middle of the day: Simon had to be exhausted, but I felt almost invigorated, now that I'd adjusted to the oddly heavy feeling of my limbs. The caffeine coursing through my body was like live electricity. Kicking the habit had definitely resensitized me. That was nice. At least one thing was going right today.

I was virtually human, walking hand-in-hand with a man who I would have once called my greatest enemy, and while I couldn't say I was happy—there was too much at stake—I was at least willing to pause, and breathe, and allow myself to hope that everything would eventually be okay.

Speaking of okay . . . I pulled my phone out of my pocket and winced as I saw that I had six missed calls. I dialed my voicemail and raised the phone to my ear.

Beep. "Um, Toby, hi, it's Quentin. I hope Simon hasn't turned you into a rock and run away or anything like that. Anyway, I just wanted to call and let you know that the Luidaeg has Officer Thornton. She wants me to stay for a while, so she can question me about where we found him and what his living situation was like. Um. Call if you need me? And let me know where you are."

Beep. "Toby, it's Quentin again. Are you okay? Seriously, you're freaking me out. The Luidaeg put Officer Thornton to sleep in her room. She says he's really malnourished and probably sick from being in deep Faerie for so long. Oh, and she wants to know when the hell you decided she was your new home for misfit toys. Call me."

Beep. "October, this is Quentin. Please call me back."

Beep. "Toby, *please*. You're freaking me out *bad*. Danny's going to give me a ride home. I want to feed Spike and the cats and get some new clothes and charge my phone, since obviously I need to have enough battery to answer when you finally remember that I'm your squire and you need to *call me*."

Beep. "I hate you."

Beep. "I hate you and I'm eating the last of your ice cream because you suck. Please call. Please, please call."

I hung up and tucked the phone back into my pocket, glancing at Simon. He was watching me out of the corner of his eye, most of his attention still focused on the candle. He was doing an excellent job of steering us around the pedestrians, avoiding collisions that seemed like they should have been inevitable. I admired that, even as I was glad someone else was leading for a change.

"Quentin," I said. "He called from the Luidaeg's to update me on Officer Thornton, and then he called a bunch more times to tell me what a terrible knight I am for not picking up or calling him back."

"How cruel of you, to ignore him so while you were unconscious and recovering from a near-disastrous act of blood magic," said Simon gravely.

"I know, right? I'm the worst." I shook my head. "The officer's not doing great."

"Humans were never meant to live that deep. They cannot thrive there. They can only wither or endure, doing their best to swim against a tide that means them only ill."

"Yeah." What would Annwn make of me in my current state? I had already felt a little unwelcome there, unable to quite relax into the embrace of a land that had never known mortality. Now . . . it might throw me out entirely. And I would probably go willingly.

We had turned off Valencia at some point, and were now walking up a familiar street. I didn't see it during full daylight all that often, but some landmarks don't change. I stiffened.

Simon caught the change immediately. He cast a more direct look toward me, frowning. "What's wrong?"

"I know where we are."

"I thought you knew San Francisco quite well."

"I do, but we're heading for my house." I started to walk faster, forcing Simon to match my pace. The candle flame didn't so much as flicker. We were still going in the right direction, and that was exactly what I'd been afraid of.

Simon's eyes widened. "August—"

"Is Dóchas Sidhe, which means she could do the same 'track me by my magic' routine that we've been doing with her. She can't find *her* home. She can't go back to where *she* belongs. But my home? There's nothing stopping her from going there." She had left me broken and writhing on the basement floor; she had no reason to think I was a threat to her, or even that I would be able to figure out where she had gone.

By taking *my* home, after she had subdued me, she had put herself into the best position possible. It was too bad for her that I wasn't actually dead.

"Oak and ash," murmured Simon. This time, he was the one who sped up, and we half walked, half ran the rest of the way along the street to my front gate, where as expected, the candle flame leaped upward, telling us that we were close.

Simon blew it out and snapped his fingers. The don't-look-here dissolved. I gave him a curious look, and he shook his head.

"She knew I was there, in the basement," he said. "She may not be able to recognize me, but she isn't blind to my presence. If we enter under an enchantment and she detects the magic, she'll assume we've come to hurt her, and she'll react accordingly. I don't mean to offend, October, but in your current condition, I don't think you can fight her off."

"You'd be surprised," I said. August had been fast and furious, but she hadn't been trained. Every swing was supported by as much weight and momentum as she could put behind it. That made her a merciless opponent, sure. It didn't make her unbeatable.

My teacher had been a man named Devin, and he'd trained me on the assumption that I was always going to be a changeling, mostly mortal, hampered by the reflexes of my own body. He'd taught me how to take and throw a punch. Most importantly, he'd taught me how to incapacitate my opponent. August had been able to get the drop on me in the basement, because I hadn't expected her to attack, and because she'd had magic.

Well, she'd done all the damage she was going to do. No one was turning me wholly human against my will, and I wasn't planning to let her touch my skin again. If she still felt like playing punchy games, she could find out what it felt like to have her teeth loosened.

"Come on," I said, and started up the path toward my front door, digging the keys from my jeans as I walked. My wards would have long since burned away, undone by the passage of successive dawns. A pang of concern hit as I remembered Quentin mentioning that he was going to feed the cats. Had we left enough kibble?

Even with May staying at Shadowed Hills to anchor the blood trace, Raj would have come by the house to check on them. They were his subjects, and he was determined to show he would be a good King when his time came—even if that time was coming too fast for any of us to be comfortable. They'd be fine. They had to be.

And all of this was me refusing to think about the possibility that any of them had been in the house when my sister decided to make it her own. I knew that. I focused on the inconsequential anyway.

The doorknob turned as I was unlocking it. The door swung open, and there was August, draped in the glittering shine of a human disguise, dressed in one of my tank tops and a pair of May's sweat pants. That made sense. August was thinner than I was, and none of my jeans had drawstrings.

Her face darkened at the sight of me, and she moved to slam the door. I stuck my foot into the opening before she could, effectively jamming it open.

"This is my house," I said. "Punching me in the face doesn't make it yours. If anything, it makes me less inclined to invite you over."

August's eyes widened before narrowing in sudden

anger. She lunged forward, grabbing for my arm. That seemed to be her go-to move. When in doubt, attempt to hurt the person you're fighting on a cellular level, one that they can't fight against, but can only endure.

Not this time. When her hand closed, my arm wasn't there. Instead, my shoulder was lowered and I was charging forward, bull in a china shop, crashing into her and carrying her backward into the hall. She couldn't hurt me if she couldn't touch my skin. I knew enough about our shared magical talents to know that, and right now, even if she could somehow focus after that impact, she didn't have access to any skin. She had leather jacket and the heavy, too-dark fall of my hair, and if I was right, she wouldn't know what to do without a better weapon than her magic. She was too specialized.

August's back slammed into the wall with a concussive bang, sending several framed pictures crashing down. Glass shattered. I pulled back just enough to let her feet drop flat to the floor before I slammed into her again, harder this time, not concerned about hurting her. I knew how fast she healed. I was more concerned about incapacitating her long enough for me to get the duct tape and tie her hands.

Amandine had tried to turn me human when I was a child, and she had failed. Part of it was that she hadn't wanted to hurt her baby, but part of it was also that I had fought back as long as it was possible for me to do so. My own magic was still alive and kicking, however human I might be, and it wasn't going to go gently into that good night. Even if August got her hands on me again, I was pretty sure she couldn't turn me wholly human without my consent.

That didn't mean I wanted to test the theory. Call me weird, but letting other people try to mess with the balance of my blood for fun is not my idea of a good time.

August groaned, stunned by the impact. I stepped back and brought my elbow up at the same time, intent on catching her in the throat. She dodged to the side. I hit the wall instead. The pain was a great bolt moving through my arm. Nothing felt broken, and so I went for my backup plan, grabbing her by the hair and using it as leverage for slamming her head into the wall.

August shrieked. Behind me, I heard the door close and the latch click home. Most of my focus was on my sister and the need to keep her from touching me. I slammed her head against the wall again.

Bringing her hand up, she raked her fingernails across my cheek, drawing blood without actually touching her skin to mine. She looked a little startled when she realized that. I slammed her head into the wall again.

"Could you, perhaps, not *break* her?" asked Simon behind me.

"We're sturdy!" I snarled, and went for a fourth slam.

August yanked her hair out of my hand, stumbling away. She stopped several feet down the hall. "Stop it," she commanded, in a voice that was probably meant to be regal, but came off more as scared. "I demand you stop it."

"You started it," I reminded her.

There was a moment—one beautiful, shining moment—where I thought she might see sense and stop attacking me. We could talk this over like reasonable people. I might not even need to borrow Arden's hope chest if I could convince August to lend me the necessary power to let me rebalance my blood. Quentin was probably asleep in his room, and if he wasn't, if she'd enchanted him and stuffed him into a closet, I could wake him up. It was going to be okay.

Then she snarled, "I don't start things. I finish them," and lunged, hands outstretched to grab the sides of my face and yank the last of the fae blood from my body.

I forced myself to stay where I was until she was so close and moving so fast that she couldn't possibly change her trajectory. Then I stepped to the side, sticking out my foot and hooking it around her ankle. She went down hard, sliding several feet across the floor.

It didn't buy me much time. It bought me enough to grab the baseball bat out of the umbrella stand, where it had been sitting unused for long enough to have gathered a thin patina of dust, and bring it down across the back of her skull. Something cracked. It wasn't the bat.

August lay still.

TWENTY-TWO

THE BASEBALL BAT HIT the floor with a clatter, rolling until it came to a stop against the wall. I bent forward, resting my hands against my knees and panting hard. The scratches on my cheek stung like fire. It had been so long since I'd had to deal with the long-term effects of my injuries that I wasn't used to them anymore.

"Mortality sucks," I said finally, and pushed myself upright. Simon was standing next to the door, eyes wide and face pale. I guess seeing his stepdaughter bludgeon his long-missing biological daughter with a baseball bat had been a little much for his delicate sensibilities. "Help me with her. We need to get her into the kitchen before she wakes up."

"Before she—October, you *hit her in the head with a club*!"

"Baseball bat, and yeah, I did, so I figure we have maybe five minutes before her skull puts itself back together and she wakes up. Probably pissed, because I did just hit her with a baseball bat. Come on." I bent again, this time reaching for August's arm. I paused at the last moment, before my fingers would have touched her skin.

Could she hurt me while she was unconscious? My magic sometimes did things when I was asleep, when it thought I needed it to act on my behalf. I pushed my shoulders forward and bent my elbows, until the sleeves of my jacket covered my hands, like I was a five-year-old playing dress-up with Mommy's clothes. Thus protected by a layer of leather, I wrapped my effectively mittened hands around August's right wrist.

Simon still hadn't moved. I looked up and frowned at him.

"You can help me move her, or you can stand there while I wrench her arm out of its socket dragging her," I said. "The choice is yours."

"This seems wrong," he said, and moved to grab August's left wrist. Unlike me, he didn't cover his skin first. He didn't need to. As a pureblood, there was nothing in him that she could use as a lever.

"Everything about this is wrong," I agreed, as we dragged August down the hall toward the kitchen. "I'm not supposed to be this mortal. This isn't how I wanted to meet my sister, if I ever did. You're not supposed to be the last man standing on my list of allies. I'm not supposed to be asking myself where my squire is and fighting not to panic before I have my sister who, again, I just hit in the head with a baseball bat, safely tied to a chair. So, yeah, it's wrong. It's also the only right we have."

Simon said nothing, but he kept dragging, and under the circumstances, I was willing to accept that.

The kitchen was empty, save for Spike, who was sitting on the counter taking in the afternoon sun. It sat up and rattled when it saw us, like an animate maraca. I smiled.

"Hey, buddy," I said.

Spike crooned, and rattled some more.

Before coming to live with me, Spike had lived with

the rest of the rose goblins in Shadowed Hills, where it had originally sprouted from a seed planted by Luna. Like so many things in Faerie, it had been comfortably wild until someone gave it a name—that someone being me. I hadn't been thinking. Sometimes my time in the human world shows itself in odd ways, one of those being a tendency to want to call things by their name. So I had named it, and it had followed me home, and I hadn't been sorry, not once I adjusted to the idea of having a rose goblin now.

Simon smiled wanly at the sight of it, before helping me to boost August into one of my kitchen chairs. Her head lolled limply forward. That was a good sign. I *really* didn't want her waking up before she was safely restrained.

"Hold her here," I commanded. "I'm going to get the duct tape."

"Hurry," said Simon. "I can hear her breathing. I think she'll be awake soon."

"Hurrying," I said.

The kitchen junk drawer was a welter of strange herbs in jars, odd sticks, bones, dried flowers pressed between sheets of wax paper, dead batteries, and other semi-useful things that we had, for whatever reason, not been able to bring ourselves to throw away. I dug through it until my fingers closed on a roll of duct tape. Yanking it free, I rushed across the room to where Simon was holding a motionless August upright, keeping her from falling out of the chair.

Quickly, I ripped off strips of tape and secured her hands to the chair's arms, swaddling them with tape until she began to resemble a uniquely sticky mummy. Simon lifted an eyebrow but said nothing about this apparent overkill. I silently thanked him and kept taping, running loops of tape up her arms before I started taping her torso to the chair.

I was securing her shoulders when she began to squirm. Not much; just enough to tell me she was waking up. Quickly, I ripped off the last strip of tape and took a step backward, out of the range where she could accidentally brush up against me.

August shifted. August squirmed. August lifted her head, opened her eyes, and tried to stand, only to be held in place by most of a roll of duct tape.

There was a pause during which it seemed like everyone in the kitchen, even Spike, was holding their breath. August turned to Simon as the closest person. There was still no recognition in her eyes. She might as well have been looking at a total stranger, and my heart broke for him, to be so close to everything he'd sold his soul to get, and yet unable to touch it.

"You, untie me," she said. "Right now."

"You have no idea how much it pains me to say these words, my dear, but no." Simon straightened up and took a step backward, away from August—away from the temptation she represented. It was taking everything he had not to reach for her.

"Hello." I stepped into her field of vision, jerking her attention away from Simon. She glared at me, eyes narrowed, and said nothing. "Nice to meet you, sis. Sorry about the tape. You clearly never learned not to hit."

"Untie me, mortal," she spat.

"Not mortal," I replied. "Thin-blooded right now, but I'll fix that soon enough. You might be stronger than me, and you might be better-trained than me, but that doesn't make you capable of turning me human. Our mother learned that."

August's eyes widened. "Mama. Where is she? What have you done to her?" She began to struggle against the tape again, harder this time, like she thought she could somehow change the laws of physics. The smell of smoke and roses filled the air, strong enough that I could pick it up even with my currently dulled senses.

"Blood magic doesn't work on duct tape, and since you've dialed my fae heritage down so far that you can hardly get a hook on it, I'm pretty sure persuasion spells don't currently work, either," I said. "If you're thinking about making yourself look like someone I love so I'll untie you, I'd skip it. Fairy ointment. I'll see through any illusions you cast."

August looked utterly betrayed. "But you're a *changeling*," she said. "You can't beat me. It's not allowed."

I glanced at Simon. "So, bigotry, that's fun. She get that from you, or from our mother?"

"A bit of both," he said, looking deeply uncomfortable. "It was a different time when she was born. It was still possible to live a long and happy life without ever crossing paths with the mortal world."

"Right." Excuses didn't change the fact that my sister was looking at me like a misbehaving dog: something to be disciplined and, if necessary, put down. I frowned at her. "Where's Quentin?"

"Who?"

"My squire. Bronze hair, lives here, probably wasn't too thrilled to find you in his house?" That was a mild way of putting it. Quentin is in some ways even more territorial than me. He doesn't want people in his home uninvited. Ever.

August blinked before offering me a slow, syrupy smile. "The boy's important to you, is he? Unbind me and I'll tell you where he is."

"Nope," I said. "Not going to happen. But I appreciate you confirming that he's in the house and alive. Simon? Watch her." I turned on my heel and stalked out of the kitchen before I could think better of leaving Simon to watch his daughter.

He'd been looking for her for so very, very long. When I had seen my own daughter after our separation, all I had wanted to do was hold her, to gather her close and never let her go. The urge to do the same had to be eating him alive. But August didn't even know who he was, couldn't know until we found a way to get her path home back from the Luidaeg. If he untied her, we would lose her, and I wasn't sure how many more times we could run her to ground before time ran out or one of us was seriously hurt. Or both. Both was always on the table.

The house was quiet. The air had that slow, dusty smell that spoke to hours left unoccupied, rooms left to settle deeper and deeper into stillness. Quentin was likely to have started by going to the kitchen—he was a teenage boy, with a teenager's appetite and a fondness for bedtime snacks—and then made his way toward his bedroom. Since he wasn't in the kitchen, I stuck my head into the living room long enough to be sure I hadn't missed him, and then started up the stairs.

It was funny, in its own sad way. When I had first returned from the pond, I would have sworn I was never going to have a home to call my own again. I would live somewhere, because everyone has to live somewhere, but that place wouldn't be my *home*. There's more to home than just walls that don't fall down and a roof that doesn't leak. There's commitment, and comfort, and the knowledge that even if you have to leave today, you can come home tomorrow, because home will wait. Home waits.

Somewhere between Quentin showing up on my doorstep with a message from Sylvester and today—somewhere in all the years and miles between us and that moment—I had found my own way home. He was a large part of what had helped to get me there. Quentin would have to leave eventually, going back to Toronto to finish learning how to be High King of the Westlands. That didn't matter. He would always have a home in California, with me, because without him, I might not have been able to find my way.

Cagney met me at the top of the stairs. Lacey, her sister, was nowhere to be seen. She creaked when she saw me, the rusty, back-of-throat sound that served her in place of a meow. Both my cats were perfectly ordinary Siamese mixes from the humane society, and they were getting old. Nothing will ever stop that from happening, sadly.

"I know," I said, in response to her creaking. "Do you know where Quentin is?"

Cagney gave me a disgusted look and twitched her tail before getting up and stalking back toward my bedroom, where all her favorite napping spots were.

Quentin wouldn't be in there. Quentin never went into my room if he could help it, claiming it was haunted by all the times Tybalt and I had heartlessly had sex while my impressionable young squire was in the house. Since he hadn't been sprawled in the hallway or on the stairs, I was assuming August had managed to sneak up on him somehow. I kept moving, pausing only when I reached his bedroom door.

It was open a crack. I reached out, barely breathing, and pushed it open the rest of the way.

Despite being a teenager, Quentin had always kept his room so clean and well organized that it was surreal. There was a place for everything, and everything was in its place, down to the corkboards on the walls and the banners advertising a variety of hockey teams that I had never heard of in any other setting. There was a large framed poster for a band called Great Big Sea hanging above the bed.

Quentin, on the other hand, was *in* the bed, flat on his face on top of the covers, hands clasped behind his back like they were tied. I squinted, and the fairy ointment showed me the glitter of an illusion in the air around him, something he hadn't cast himself.

Illusions can do more than just confuse. They can imprison, if they're strong enough. I crossed the room and rolled him onto his back. His eyes rolled wildly, and his mouth moved like he was trying to speak but couldn't. I smiled wanly.

"Hey, kid," I said. "Hold tight. I'll be right back—and by the way, this is going to suck." This dire pronouncement delivered, I trotted out of the room and down the hall to my own bedroom, where the weapons I wasn't currently carrying were stored.

Fun fact about being a changeling: the more human someone is, the more easily they can stand the touch of iron, which degrades and destroys magic on contact. There was a time when I could carry an iron knife at my hip with no damage to myself. It had been a gift. I still had it. The box that kept its effects from reaching me was lined with yarrow twigs and silk. I undid the box, moved the shielding away, and wrapped my fingers around the hilt. It fit perfectly. It always had.

Sometimes it's strange to think about how much I've left behind in the process of learning who I want to be. Iron knives aren't an everyday part of my life anymore. But sometimes we have to go back to move forward. The knife clutched firmly in my hand, I left the room and walked back to where Quentin waited.

His eyes widened when he saw and recognized the knife. Up until then, I think he'd been taking my darker hair and softer features as some sort of illusion that I hadn't bothered, for whatever reason, to dismiss.

"I'll explain in a second," I said. "I'm going to be as careful as I can, but I may still touch you, and I'm sorry. Are you ready?"

He couldn't really move. He could manage the very faintest of nods. I nodded back before bending forward and beginning, with the utmost care, to run my knife along the places where ropes would have been if he had actually been tied up. The blade dipped once, brushing the side of his left hand. He inhaled sharply through his nose.

"Sorry," I said, and kept cutting. Blisters were already appearing where the knife had touched, angry red and vicious-looking. I didn't let that slow me down. I couldn't unravel a spell any other way right now, and I sure as hell wasn't going to untie August.

When I "cut" the "gag" away from his mouth he

gasped, licked his lips, and asked, "What happened to you?"

"I missed you, too," I said. "We found August. She's a little . . . angry right now. She attacked me, and it turns out *some* people aren't nearly as polite when it comes to the bloodlines of others."

"She tried to turn you human?"

"I guess she takes after our mother," I said. "Can you move? I think I've cut away the whole illusion, and I'm not comfortable waving an iron knife over you more than I have to."

"My knees," he said apologetically.

"Got it." I bent to cut the last of the illusion away.

As I did, Quentin pushed himself up onto his hands and asked, "Are you okay?"

"Yes and no." I glanced back at him. "It hurt like hell. I need fairy ointment to move in the world, and my magic is virtually nonexistent. But I'll be okay. I'm still fae enough to use a hope chest, so it's not like this is permanent. And I have August tied to a chair down in the kitchen, so we're not going to lose her again."

Quentin blinked slowly. "How did you . . ."

"I hit her with a baseball bat until she stopped moving."

He blinked again, even more slowly, before laughing helplessly. "Right. Baseball bat. That's the best way to solve that sort of problem. Hit it with a baseball bat."

"I'll have you know I used to solve a lot of problems with a baseball bat. Just because I'm more refined now doesn't mean I've forgotten my roots." I took a step back, sliding the iron knife into my belt. It couldn't hurt to have a few extra weapons at my disposal, now that so many of my usual ones had been taken away.

"Where's Simon?" Quentin sat up fully. A pressure in my chest that I'd only been partially aware of unclenched.

"Downstairs, keeping watch."

"Are you sure that's a good idea? He's her *dad*."

"He's her father, and she doesn't know who he is," I said. "Remember when the Luidaeg said August had given up her way home?" Quentin nodded. Grimly, I said, "Turns out that means she can't find *anything* that might bring her home until she either finds Oberon or gets this geas lifted. She looks at her father and she sees a stranger. Simon's . . . he's holding up as well as he can, but he's pretty damn upset, and I can't blame him."

"Wow," said Quentin, after a pause to consider. "That's horrible."

"Yeah, and he's alone with her, so let's get back there and save him from himself. You ready?"

"Yeah," said Quentin, and stood, and moved to stand beside me.

Impulsively, I gave him a one-armed hug, careful to keep the side of my body where the iron knife rested well away from him. "I'm glad she didn't kill you."

"Same," he said, returning the gesture.

We walked back down the stairs side by side, with Quentin lagging only slightly behind to keep from tripping me. The sound of voices from the kitchen was audible before we reached the door. I stopped, motioning for Quentin to do the same.

"—please, August, you have to know who I am. Just look a little harder." Simon was pleading, voice rich with raw, naked hunger.

"I don't have to do anything for you," said August. "You're not my father. You don't look anything like him, and when I tell him you were telling me lies, he's going to claim insult on you and duel you to the death."

There was a pause before Simon asked, almost bewildered, "Since when is that a thing I would do?"

Quentin glanced at me, eyes wide. I nodded and gestured to the door. Catching my meaning, he nodded as well, and together, the two of us continued on, into the kitchen.

Simon had not untied August. He was sitting in

another of my chairs, well out of range of any motion she was free to make, with his clasped hands tucked between his knees. He looked young and small and scared. That's one of the problems with purebloods: since they stop aging when they reach adulthood, even the oldest among them can look terrifyingly young and unsure to my sometimes mortal eyes.

I wanted to hug him, and the mere existence of that impulse was one of the weirdest parts of a day that had already been singularly surreal. Instead, I stopped in the doorway and said wearily, "Illusionary ropes binding my squire so he couldn't move or call for help. Nice. You're a real sweetheart, aren't you, August?"

Her head turned in my direction, until she was straining against her bonds to see me. "I could have done so much worse and you know it." She narrowed her eyes. "How did you free him? You're a changeling. You don't have that kind of power."

There were a lot of things I could have said, but none of them were going to provide a foundation upon which to build a solid sisterly relationship, and so I simply pushed the left side of my jacket out of the way, showing her the knife at my belt. She was too far away to feel the iron, but the tiny strip of visible metal was dark gray and dull, and there was really no mistaking what it was.

August made a small, guttural sound of dismay, eyes flicking from the knife to my face like she was searching for some sign that this was a joke. She didn't find one, and so she said, in a hushed voice, "You're a monster."

"Says the woman who broke my nose, yanked out more than half of my fae blood, and again, *tied my squire* to his own bed with illusionary ropes." That last one was the one that pissed me off the most, something I was absolutely sure came through in my voice. "How were you expecting him to get free? That kind of spell doesn't dissolve with a single dawn."

"It would have snapped eventually," said August.

"Eventually doesn't stop me from wetting the bed," said Quentin. I glanced at him. He shrugged. "I have a sense of dignity."

"She's carrying *iron*," said August.

Quentin blinked. "And? She does that when she's this human. You made her this way, so it's sort of your fault, I'd think."

August looked at him, utterly baffled. This wasn't the sort of thing she encountered all that often.

Entertaining as this was, it wasn't solving anything. I pinched the bridge of my nose. "Okay. This is fun and all, but this isn't working. Simon, Quentin, pick her up. We need to put her in the car."

"Why are we putting her in the car?" asked Quentin.

Simon looked alarmed.

"Because," I said, looking from Quentin to Simon and August. "We're taking her to see the Luidaeg."

TWENTY-THREE

"**D**ID WE REALLY HAVE to put her in the trunk?"
Simon sounded less angry than plaintive, like he
really, truly, wanted to understand why I had felt it
necessary to stuff his daughter, my sister, in the trunk
of my car. She hadn't gone easily, either. Despite being
taped to one of my good chairs—and there was no way
we were going to release her while she was awake—
she'd put up a fight, squirming as hard as she could,
tilting her weight first one way and then the other in
her attempts to throw Simon and Quentin off balance.

Things might have gone easier if I'd been willing to
help with the trunk-stuffing process, but my participa-
tion hadn't been an option. I didn't think she could
strip out the last of my fae blood. Holding onto the ves-
tiges of immortality seemed like something my body
was determined to do, and I appreciated that. At the
same time, she'd been stronger than me even when I
was at full fighting strength, and I didn't want to risk it.
Some chances aren't worth taking.

"It's daylight," I said, resisting the urge to meet his
eyes in the rearview mirror. Quentin had claimed the

front passenger seat, and Simon was consigned to the back, where he'd have more trouble grabbing the wheel. There was no sign that he was planning to try anything like that, and I trusted him . . . or at least I had, before August had been stuffed in my trunk. People do foolish things when they're around the ones they care about. The temptation to save her might prove greater than the desire to protect me. I'm a big girl. I've long since learned that it's not safe to count on people just because they seem to be on my side, and being as mortal as I currently was, a car crash would kill me. Too many people needed me alive for me to be comfortable taking that risk.

"I don't understand," said Simon.

"She means people would be concerned if they looked over at the car and saw that we were kidnapping a lady," said Quentin. He sounded annoyed. It made sense. He was having a hell of a day.

And he was worried about me. I could tell from the way he kept glancing in my direction, brow furrowed, looking at me like there was a chance that I might break.

"I could have cast a spell on the car," said Simon. "We saved no magic doing things this way. Your squire and I would not have required individual illusions with a proper enchantment."

"Yeah, but my reflexes aren't what they usually are, and I'm too exhausted for serious defensive driving," I said. "Enchant the car, I cause a six-car pileup when I misjudge the distance between me and a semi, and then everybody's day is ruined. This was the best way."

I meant that. Truly I did. But had I also taken a certain perverse satisfaction in slamming the trunk on my older sister, cutting her off mid-expletive? Yes. Yes, I had. Much as it pained me to admit it, I would probably have been even happier hitting her with the baseball bat again, sending her into a serene slumber. She deserved a little hitting. Sadly, it would just have distressed Simon, who didn't seem to appreciate me beating his child to a pulp.

Amateur.

San Francisco was awake around us. I couldn't think of the last time I'd driven here during the middle of the day, and it was difficult not to gawk at how much the city had changed, all while staying exactly the same. There were more suits on the sidewalk than I was used to, worn by humans hurrying between the tall glass hives of office buildings, their infinite windows sparkling in the sunlight. Most of the odd little mom-and-pop stores I was used to seeing were gone, replaced by sleek new establishments with single-word names and signs made of seemingly untreated wood or steel.

"Hipsters," said Quentin in a dismissive tone. I followed his gaze to an open-air café, its seating area filled with humans who looked to be a few years older than him, wearing carefully casual clothing, all of it new but styled to look vintage. Several of them had beautifully groomed facial hair.

"What's a hipster?" I asked blankly.

Quentin paused. "Sometimes I forget you're old."

"Yeah, well, I don't get my hands on a hope chest, you'll get to see me looking closer to my age." I made a sharp left turn, leaving the populated main drag for the maze of tiny side streets that would take us to the Luidaeg.

It's difficult to say exactly when she came to San Francisco. Reports vary. But everyone who would know agrees she was here when the 1906 earthquake hit—she would have had to be, to sell August a candle. We lost half the city in the aftermath of that disaster. Whole blocks burned. The Luidaeg had already been there, already putting down roots, and when the city had grown back, it had grown around her and the careful enchantments she was weaving around her chosen neighborhood.

Crime is low where the Luidaeg lives. The people who

are willing to risk moving into apartments that look
like they might collapse at any moment find, to their
surprise and delight, that their power bills are lower,
their windows never let drafts inside, and cockroaches
are mysteriously nonexistent. Somehow—possibly because the Luidaeg is not above using magic on mortals
to get what she wants—this has never turned into a
rush to claim and gentrify those apartments. They stay
open to the city's poor and needy, and she keeps her
safe barrier of mortals between herself and the rest of
Faerie.

It was too bad she hadn't chosen changelings as the
recipients of her goodwill and passive aid. We needed
it as much as the mortals did. Maybe more. We didn't
have a world to call our own, and we were falling off
the edge of everything, day by day, night by endless
night.

I eased my way through the streets, past buildings
with good foundations and peeling paint, along side-
walks that somehow managed to be structurally sound
while looking like horrifying tripping hazards. Even
the potholes were more trick of the light than reality;
it wouldn't exactly be helping these people if driving
home tore out the undercarriage of their cars. Finally,
I pulled up to the mouth of an alley and stopped the
car.

"We're close enough to the apartment that we
shouldn't have to worry about anyone seeing us," I said.
"People look the other way when things happen near
the Luidaeg."

"That's not terrifying in the least," muttered Simon.
"Yes, let's visit the undying sea witch whose very presence causes the world to reject the normal consequences
of our actions."

"Great idea," said Quentin, and got out of the car.

August started shouting as soon as I opened the
trunk. "How *dare* you! Mongrel scum! You have no
right! My father will kill you when he hears of this!

He'll turn your eyes to wood and your heart to stone and leave you blind and loveless to wander the world for eternity!"

"Wow." I turned to Simon. "You're going to do that? Really?"

"I might have been willing to make the attempt, once," he said uncomfortably. "Please, can we untie her?"

"Not quite sure that's the term for taking off this much tape, and no," I said. "Get her out of the trunk. We need to deliver her to the Luidaeg."

August screamed. August shouted. August swore. She didn't have a great grasp of modern profanity yet, but she knew all the traditional words, and she wasn't afraid to mix and match them as necessary to suit her needs. Since apparently what she needed was to insult everything about the three of us, she was pretty well-equipped.

It should have been funny. Somehow, it was just sad. She was threatening us with her father's vengeance, which would be swift and furious when it came, and Simon was looking more and more depressed, as if her words were barbs that cut and tore his skin. Even Quentin was starting to look distressed.

Gillian had always known who I was. Even when she was telling me to go away, screaming that she never wanted to see me again, she had known who I was. To have his own child reject him like this . . . it didn't matter that it was all due to the Luidaeg's spell. It still had to be killing him.

I walked ahead as Quentin and Simon carried August into the alley. The Luidaeg's front door was set back into the wall, recessed, half-hidden, and entirely uninviting. She liked it that way. It wasn't that she didn't like company—one of the first things I'd realized once we started to become friends was just how lonely she was—it was that when she had company, it was because people were asking her to do things and, sometimes, she didn't want to.

If I ever met Titania, we were going to have a little talk about laying compulsions on people. What she'd done to the Luidaeg wasn't fair. There was nothing in the world that could have made it so.

The door swung open before I could knock, and there was the Luidaeg, back in her "cousin Annie" guise, all curly black hair and acne-scarred cheeks. Her ponytails were tied with strips of blue painter's tape, almost matching the fabric of her denim overalls. Her feet were bare. Nothing about her screamed "all-powerful sea witch." Nothing about her even screamed "old enough to drive."

Nothing except her eyes. They were too old for her teenager's face, and filled with the sort of shadows that no one should have to hold alone.

She raised an eyebrow at the sight of me in all my too-human glory before her gaze switched to August, who had gone very still on her chair. Apparently, the Luidaeg was menacing enough to shut up even my imperious sister.

"You found her," said the Luidaeg. "You actually found her."

"We did," I agreed. "Can we come in?"

Her sigh was deep and almost pained. "I suppose you might as well. It's not like you're going to go away."

She stepped to the side. I moved to step past her and she grabbed my wrist, stopping me, pulling me to stand beside her against the wall as Quentin and Simon carried a still-silent August into the apartment.

"Put her in the living room," said the Luidaeg. "October and I will be right with you."

Arguing with the Luidaeg was never a good idea. In my current semi-mortal state, it seemed like the sort of idea that could get me seriously hurt. I nodded to Quentin, signaling that it was okay, and stayed where I was. He looked unsure. He kept walking. Sweet Oberon, I loved that kid. Simon went with him. It was that or let go of August, and since he didn't want to hurt his daughter, he didn't really have a choice.

The Luidaeg waited until we were alone before she turned to me and asked, "What the hell happened to you?"

"August." I spread my hands, using the gesture to indicate the full, virtually human scope of me. "Turns out Mom didn't spend her entire life pretending she was Daoine Sidhe. August actually knows what she is, what she can do, and how to do it aggressively."

"I should have warned you about that."

"You think?" I shook my head. "It could be worse. It can always be worse. I'll borrow Arden's hope chest when this is all over, put myself back to normal."

"Do you know what normal is anymore? This is much closer to the woman you were when you showed up on my doorstep for the first time."

I paused. Finally, I said, "Back then, I was trying to be part of the human world. I thought that was where I was going to be happy. I know now that I was wrong. This is where I belong, and that means I can't go back to being human and hoping Faerie will leave me alone. It's never going to happen."

"Good." The Luidaeg looked relieved. I didn't have time to examine that before she was saying, "Why did you bring her here? You found her. That's what you promised to do. You won't have to work for me. You can get your kitty back."

"She still can't find her way home."

The Luidaeg stopped moving.

"Simon stands right in front of her and she doesn't know who he is. She keeps telling him that her father is going to mess him up when he finds out what we've done. We've tried telling her that Simon *is* her father, but it's like the words don't make any sense to her."

"Damn." The Luidaeg tugged on the end of one electric tape-wrapped pigtail. "Sometimes I wish I weren't so good at my job."

"If we take her back to Amandine the way she is now, she won't know who Mom is," I said. "I don't think that will end well for me." Or for my people. Amandine had Tybalt and Jazz captive and at their most defenseless. A tomcat can do a lot of damage. So can an adult raven. But neither of them could unlock their own prisons, and without the freedom to use talons and claws, she could hurt them badly enough that I didn't even like to think about it.

"No," admitted the Luidaeg, lowering her hand. "Amy doesn't like it when she doesn't get what she thinks she deserves. She's not going to want a daughter who doesn't know her. She's going to want a daughter who's grateful to be home."

"Luidaeg . . . I need you to return her way home."

There was a long moment of silence, during which I watched the Luidaeg and she looked at anything but me. There wasn't much to look at in the hallway: the walls, the floor, the clean mended fishnets she had hanging up as decorations. In the end, she had no choice but to return her attention to me.

In a very soft voice, she said, "I can't."

"What do you mean, you can't?"

"I mean I can't. I have to give people what they ask me for. If you say you want a pony, I have to give you a pony. But I can ask you to pay whatever I want, and the more I don't want to give you a pony, the steeper that cost becomes." Her mouth twisted in an unhappy line. "If you're an asshole about it, I can even fuck with you after I give you what you asked for. Asked to *have* a pony, not *be* a pony, but hey, one's essentially the same as the other, right? Looked at from the right angle."

"So I'm asking you to give August's way home back."

"I told you, I can't." The Luidaeg looked miserable.

Openly, actually miserable. "She hasn't fulfilled the conditions for its return, and I can't give it to you without demanding something of equal value in exchange."

"So it's not that you can't; it's that you won't."

"I won't take your way home, no. I won't let you buy a spoiled pureblood brat who thought heroism was as easy as following the light of a candle at the expense of your own happiness and the lives of the people who love you." The Luidaeg shook her head. "You've found one of the few places where I can refuse to do something. When an older bargain is involved, the rules shift."

"If we're speaking of rules, I have a proposal for you."

We both turned. Simon was standing at the mouth of the hallway, hands empty by his sides, looking at us with calm, resigned weariness. There was nothing of Sylvester in him now. There was nothing of my old enemy, either. There was only Simon Torquill: husband, father, man who had paid everything he had to try and bring his daughter home, only to discover that he needed to find a way—somehow—to pay even more.

"I thought I told you to go to the living room," said the Luidaeg.

"You did," said Simon. "You did not, however, tell me to stay there. Loopholes, milady sea witch. Always, there are loopholes."

The Luidaeg folded her arms. "I'm listening."

"Only because you have no choice, and for that, I am sincerely sorry: for that, I apologize with all my heart and soul. You would refuse to hear me, were you allowed."

"Damn right," said the Luidaeg. "What do you want, failure?"

"I want to change my estimation in your eyes by doing what I failed to do so many years before, when I asked you the wrong questions and allowed my feet to be set upon the wrong path," said Simon. His voice was soft, but there was steel behind it. "My name is Simon Torquill. I am the son of Celaeno and Septimius Torquill, third-and last-born of their children. I am the family disappointment, the one who refused to strive or aspire, but was happy to settle with my wife and daughter and live in peace. I have done my best. I have succeeded, and I have failed, and my greatest success was my child, August Torquill, born to Amandine the Liar. She is mine, Luidaeg. Do you contest that she is mine?"

"If I wanted to split a hair to thread a needle, I could," she said. "Her mother pulled all that was of Titania's line from her body before she was born, and she helped willingly if unknowingly, because the power belonged to the blood of my father. The power was in Oberon's lines. You had the making and the raising of her, but by her bloodline, your bloodline ended."

"Loopholes," said Simon.

I looked between them. "Uh, one of you want to tell me what the hell is going on? Because you're sort of losing me here, and I'm a little concerned about leaving my squire alone with August any longer than I have to."

"She won't hurt him," said Simon.

"I'm more worried he's going to find a marker and draw a mustache on her," I said. "Quentin doesn't actually *like* being attacked in his own home, and while he's polite enough not to do harm to someone who's been restrained, there are many ways to take revenge."

The Luidaeg snorted, looking briefly amused, before the wariness returned and she focused back on Simon. "I don't like people bending the rules to suit their own purposes; it's messy," she said. "No, I do not contest that she is your daughter. There's too much Torquill in her for any sane person's liking."

"Then you agree that, as her father, I have the right—the obligation, even—to take her debts onto myself." Simon looked at her coolly. "She need not be lost any longer."

"Oh, oak and ash," I said, the penny finally dropping. "You want to trade your way home for hers, don't you?"

Simon shrugged. His eyes were weary, but his jaw was set; he was determined. I couldn't tell whether that was a good thing, or a tragedy about to get started.

"I'm her father," he said. "I didn't save her the first time. I have to save her now."

The Luidaeg took a step forward. "Simon," she said, and from her lips, his name was an apology: she wasn't calling him "failure" anymore. "When August gave me her way home, it wasn't just a physical thing. She lost so much more than that. You'll lose the same. You won't know the face of your child, or your wife. You may not even know your brother. She hadn't been lost before she came here. You have been. Taking your way home may mean taking all the ground you've gained."

"Wait, don't you get to decide that?" I asked.

The Luidaeg shook her head. "It's my magic. That doesn't mean I have perfect control. Or do you have perfect control of your magic? Because if you do, I want you to teach me."

"I don't." What she was saying made a terrible sort of sense, even though I didn't want it to. I could decide roughly what I wanted to achieve, but unless I was looking for a binary effect—like shifting someone's blood from one state to another—whatever spell I cast would fill in the details. It knew better than I did how to put itself together.

"Didn't think so." She focused on Simon again. "I understand why you want to do this, but I don't think you know how much ground you'll lose. You smell of apples again, Torquill. What my sister did to you is going to leave scars, but you might get to be your own man again if you stay free, if you keep heading for home. Don't you want that?"

"With all my heart," he said. His voice broke. So did my heart. "But not all of my heart beats in my breast, and what of it sits in your living room must come before what stands in your hall. August is what matters. She's gone too long without salvation, and besides," he paused to smile at me, "when she works with October, I have all faith that the two of them will find a way to save me. That's what Amy's daughters do. They save me."

The Luidaeg closed her eyes. "Simon . . ." This time, his name was not forgiveness. This time, his name was a plea. "Please don't ask me to do this."

"I'm sorry," he said, and it sounded like he meant it. Then, in a slower, more formal tone, he said, "Luidaeg, daughter of Maeve, I ask a boon of you. I come prepared to pay."

"Of course you do." The Luidaeg opened her eyes. "What do you want?"

"I am the father of August Torquill, who bargained with you unwisely and against my express wishes. I have come to take her debts onto myself. I ask you to return what you have taken from her, and take it, instead, from me."

"Right." The Luidaeg shook her head. "I guess we're doing this."

TWENTY-FOUR

QUENTIN AND SIMON HAD pushed August's chair up against the wall, well away from all the exits. It was a nice positioning job. Even if she got loose, she'd have to go through at least one of us to get out—and Quentin wasn't going to be taken by surprise a second time. He was sitting on the couch, as far from her as he could get without leaving the room, and watching her with all the wariness of a cat in the presence of a venomous snake. He visibly brightened when I stepped out of the hallway, although he didn't say anything.

August wasn't so reserved. "Release me at once!" she howled.

"No," I said, and stepped to the side, letting Simon and the Luidaeg enter.

As before, August's eyes skated over Simon like he wasn't there before focusing on the Luidaeg. She went very, very still. Lost due to an ill-conceived magical bargain or not, she still knew enough to know a bad situation when she saw one.

"Hello, niece," said the Luidaeg, and there was no

warmth or mercy in her voice, only weariness, and an unforgiving tide as deep and as wide as the sea. She walked across the room toward August. With every step, a little more of her seeming humanity melted away. It was a subtle process, enough so that when she reached August she had been fully sea-changed, without giving me a single moment to point to as the transition.

Her skin was smooth as water on a windless day, and her hair was a cascade of curls flowing down her back and over her shoulders, also like the water, but this time after it had been whipped into angry waves. Her eyes were black from side to side, bottomless, cold. Even her clothing had changed, becoming a form-hugging dark blue gown that shaded to white at the bottom, like waves breaking against the beach.

We were standing in the presence of the sea witch, and I was close enough to human that she wouldn't even need to mean to hurt me. She could do it without intending to, with a twitch of her little finger. I suppressed a shiver, remaining exactly where I was. Maybe I could keep from attracting her attention.

Not that there was that much of a risk. She was focused fully on August, who was still staring at her, silent and afraid.

"A hundred years ago and more you came to me and insisted on something I did not want to give," said the Luidaeg. "Do you remember?"

August said nothing.

"Speak, or it will go ill for you," said the Luidaeg. There was something almost soft in her voice, at odds with her appearance and the formality of her words. She was *trying*. Trying to do what, I wasn't quite sure.

"I remember," said August.

"Do you remember what you paid?"

August swallowed hard. "You asked for my way home."

"Did you know what that meant?" The Luidaeg took a half step closer. "Did you listen when I tried to tell you? Did you hear the words as they left my mouth? Or did you walk away with the candle burning in your hand, already bound for the Babylon Road, so confident of your ability to do what no one had been able to do that you felt no need to listen to someone as ancient and irrelevant as the sea witch, who cleaves to the shore and never sees the road's end?"

August blanched. She looked around the room, finally focusing on me, eyes silently pleading. I was her sister. She didn't know me; her first act had been to hurt me; but still, I was her sister, and she wanted me to help her.

I couldn't. She'd made me too human, and the Luidaeg had set too much of her humanity away for the sake of this confrontation. I couldn't move. No—that wasn't quite true. I could twitch my fingers. If I reached for the iron knife at my belt, it would cut away enough of the spell cast by the presence of the fae to free me to do . . . what? The Luidaeg was being intentionally terrifying, but under the circumstances, I couldn't blame her.

"Eyes on me, August," said the Luidaeg. "Answer my questions."

"I was trying to *save* us." August turned back to the Luidaeg, the first fat tears rolling down her cheeks. Simon winced, every instinct clearly telling him to go to his daughter, to gather her in his arms and protect her. Like me, he didn't move.

"You didn't," said the Luidaeg calmly. "You failed. I told you it wasn't time yet. You didn't listen to me."

"I had to try."

"'Had' is such a deadly word. Three letters, and it's killed countless heroes in its day. What did I take, niece? What did you give me?"

"My way home," whispered August.

"Your way home," agreed the Luidaeg. "Until Oberon's return, wander as you will, go where you may, but never will you find home, nor the light to lead you there. Your only guidance will be the light of a candle, and even that is gone now. Too much time has gone by." She glanced at Simon, face softening slightly. "Time is always going by."

"I thought I could save us," said August.

"I know," said the Luidaeg. She reached into the bodice of her gown, actually *into* her gown, hand breaking the surface of the fabric and sending ripples dancing across it, radiating out in a circle around the iceberg of her wrist. It looked like she was trying to tear out her own heart. Instead, she withdrew a small glass bottle.

It looked like every bottle ever thrown from the side of a ship, a message sealed inside to bring comfort to the people still standing on the shore. Inside, a bird so small that it seemed impossible beat its wings against the glass, straining to reach August. Its wings were blue, and its tail was long and forked, like the fletching of an arrow.

"Your debt has been paid by another," said the Luidaeg, and removed the cork from the bottle. The tiny bird squeezed out the opening like a shot, wings tucked against its sides to preserve its speed. It spread them wide in the second before it slammed into August's chest, vanishing through her clothing, into her skin.

August gasped, suddenly sitting ramrod-straight under her bonds, straining against them. Her tear-filled eyes went terribly wide, mouth forming a perfect, pained "O." Then she slumped forward, struggling for her breath.

The Luidaeg turned to Simon. Her eyes were still black, but there was some mercy there now. I don't know how it was possible for me to see it. I did. It hurt.

"Go to her," she said. "You don't have much time."

He didn't need to be told twice. Simon rushed across the room and dropped to his knees next to August, reaching for her face with one trembling hand.

"August," he said. "My sweet girl, it's me. I'm here."

"Papa?" She turned her head slowly, like she was afraid this was some kind of a trick: that she'd turn, and it wouldn't be Simon at all, but some stranger. The last hundred years must have been an unending nightmare for her. First exile—and pureblood or not, exile is not a fun time—and then San Francisco after a century of mortal progress and rebuilding, with all the doors that should have led her back to the familiar closed against her.

I wasn't anticipating a close sisterly relationship with August. I already had a sister I loved and who loved me, and while May might have foretold my death when she first came home, she had never tried to make it *happen*. That didn't mean I couldn't feel terrible for August. The things she'd been through had earned her a little pity.

Her eyes locked on Simon and filled with tears. The tension went out of her body as she stopped straining against the tape that bound her, although her fingers twitched, like she was trying to reach her hands out and embrace him. She leaned forward—not far, only as far as her restraints allowed—and Simon's hand found her cheek, curving to cup her face. I started to reach for the silver knife at my belt, and hesitated, unsure how I should continue.

The Luidaeg looked at me and nodded approvingly. Then she snapped her fingers. The tape fell away, dropping like so many harmless silver ribbons to the floor, all stickiness gone. It was a neat trick. I almost said so. Then I closed my mouth and swallowed my comments, because August had fallen out of the chair and into Simon's arms, clinging to him for dear life.

She was sobbing. My sister was sobbing. She pressed her face into the side of her father's neck, crying in great, shuddering gasps that seemed to rack her entire body, originating somewhere deep below her breastbone, where the swallow-tailed bird that was her sense of home now roosted, once more intangible and safe.

"Oh, Papa, Papa, I'm sorry," she wailed, voice muffled by his skin. "I got so *lost*, Papa, I'm sorry."

"My brave girl," said Simon, stroking her back with one hand. He was holding her as tightly as she was holding him, leaving no space between them, nowhere for the world to grab hold and drag them apart from one another. They were reunited, a single entity that happened to occupy two bodies, and seeing them like that healed and hurt in the same measure, because I knew it couldn't last. Even if the Luidaeg had wanted to let Simon out of his bargain, she couldn't.

Could she? I looked at her. She looked back, shaking her head, making no effort to hide her own sorrow. The blackness was bleeding out of her eyes, leaving them the frosted green of driftglass thrown up on some distant, unforgiving shore.

"You know better," she said, and her words were an apology and a condemnation at the same time, like she was pronouncing sentence over us all. In her way, maybe she was.

August was still mumbling apologies into Simon's hair, while he stroked her back and told her over and over again that no, no, he wasn't angry with her, he didn't blame her; he understood the lure of heroism. Their magic must have been high, because even I could smell the traceries of smoke and roses in the air. Smoke, roses . . . and cider. Inhale as I would, I couldn't find the faintest trace of rot, or of oranges.

August wasn't the only one who'd been lost. She was about to be the only one who knew what it was to be found.

Slowly, the Luidaeg moved to stand behind Simon, hesitating before she reached down and touched his shoulder.

"It's time," she said.

He raised his head, twisting enough to see her, never letting go of August. "Please," he said. "Please, just a few moments more. I beg you."

"If it were up to me, I would give you all the time in the world. It's not up to me. This door can only be held open for so long." She held out her hand. "Come."

Simon's shoulders slumped as the fight went out of him. "All right," he said. "All right." He turned back to August, pressing a kiss against her forehead before he began, gently, to peel himself away from her.

"Papa?" She didn't go easy. She kept trying to reassert her hold on him, grabbing for his hands until he pushed her firmly away. August looked at Simon with wide, wounded eyes. "What's wrong?"

"We had a bargain, and it stands as yet unfulfilled," said the Luidaeg. She grabbed Simon's shoulder, half urging and half hauling him to his feet.

August made one last grab for her father before falling back, kneeling on the floor and staring at the Luidaeg in slowly dawning realization.

"What's happening?" murmured Quentin.

I jumped. I had almost forgotten he was there. "It's time for Simon to pay his daughter's debts," I said.

"Please don't do this," whispered August.

"It's all right, sweetheart," said Simon. His smile was like a hundred years of heartbreak, stretching out from here to eternity. "I believe in you. When you bring Oberon home, you'll bring me home, too."

"Papa, no!" August scrambled to her feet, lunging for Simon.

The Luidaeg's hand whipped out like a snake striking its prey, so swift that there was no time for anyone to react, striking August across the face. August froze where she was, becoming a sculpture of a woman, not even seeming to breathe.

"I have tolerated a *lot* from your bloodline over the years," said the Luidaeg. "First Amy, and then you, and then your sister. I've put up with more than any of you have ever had any right to ask, and I've done it because I loved my own sister, once, and because I wanted to be a good aunt to my newest nieces, and most of all, because I miss my own father. Amandine's line will bring Oberon home. You thought a century without your father was hard? You know nothing. *Nothing.* But I will not tolerate disrespect in my own home, and I will not allow you to cheapen what this man has done for you. You made a choice. This is the consequence."

The Luidaeg spun around before Simon could say anything, slamming her hand into his chest. It passed through skin and muscle, into the space behind his breastbone, and for a terrible moment, everything seemed to stop, because she was standing there with her arm buried halfway to the elbow in another person's body. Simon went stiff, his jaw going slack and his arms dangling useless at his sides.

"I truly *am* sorry," said the Luidaeg, and pulled her arm free.

In her hand was a bird, slightly larger than the one that had flown to roost in August's breast. Its wings were green, and its tail was forked like the ribbon on a Christmas present. The Luidaeg moved her other hand, and was suddenly holding a bottle like the one that had contained August's way home. Maybe it was the same bottle. It was large enough to hold the bird, but barely; when she drove the stopper home, the bird beat its wings against the glass, clearly pinned and uncomfortable, unable to comprehend its captivity.

"The price is paid," said the Luidaeg, and tucked the bottle into her gown. She snapped her fingers. August collapsed to the floor, gasping as the Luidaeg's spell released her.

Simon blinked. It was the first time he'd moved since the Luidaeg reached into his flesh to pull his payment out. Then he shook himself convulsively, like a dog trying to dry off after an unexpected dousing in a lake.

"Papa?" said August. She stood slowly, uncertainly,

her knees knocking together as she moved. She looked so lost. Who knew that it could cost so much to be found?

"Simon?" I said.

He looked at her, and there was no comprehension in his face. She might as well have been a stranger to him, as he had so recently been a stranger to her. Then, slowly, he turned to me, and smiled. It was the languid, oily smile of the man who had been Oleander's lover and Evening Winterrose's willing servant. He'd had good reason to be both those things, but they were what had helped him to get so lost.

"Why, October," he virtually purred. "Fancy meeting you here."

"Uh," said Quentin.

"Crap," I said, and drew my knives, one in each hand. Silver is the most common metal in Faerie, and iron is the most deadly; used together, they can even kill the Firstborn.

August's eyes widened. She leaped to her feet, throwing herself between me and Simon. "No!" she shouted. "Don't you hurt my father!"

"Dear, you seem like a very nice girl, whoever you are, but I assure you, I'm not your father," said Simon. He gripped her shoulders and shoved her aside, showing none of his former care. "October and I, on the other hand . . . we have unfinished business, don't we?"

"Uh, Luidaeg?" I said. "Little help here?"

"He's lost his way home," she said. "He was using you as a map to get himself there."

"So shouldn't he forget who I am?"

"Apparently, no," she said. "That wouldn't be as absolutely isolating as only remembering that he hates you."

"Oh, *swell*," I said. I returned my attention to Simon. "I know you can't remember this right now, but we're not enemies anymore. I've even sort of forgiven you for the fish thing. Can you chill, please, so we can work this out?"

Simon's response was a sneer, and a complicated motion of his hands through the air. The smell of smoke and rotten oranges rose around him, heavy enough that I had no trouble identifying it.

"Guess not," I muttered.

Simon didn't say anything. He just flung his spell at me, hard and fast. Not fast enough: I got my knives up, crossing them in the air in front of me, and felt the impact up my arms as whatever he'd been trying to cast struck the iron and evaporated. Whatever it was, it had been strong enough that it rocked me backward, onto my heels. Simon snarled, hands beginning to move again.

I was mostly human, standing in a room with two stunned, motionless purebloods and a Firstborn who was actively forbidden to raise a hand against any descendant of Titania unless they were entering into a bargain with her. So naturally, I did the only thing that made sense, and I charged, knives still held in front of me, ready to deflect whatever he might throw.

Simon Torquill had been called many things over the centuries, and having spent time with the man, I was willing to accept that most of them were accurate. I'd heard him referred to as a monster, a cheat, a trickster, and a coward . . . but I had never heard him called a fool. When he saw me running toward him he spun on his heel and fled deeper into the apartment, heading toward the back door.

I was perfectly willing to follow him until the Luidaeg's hand on my elbow stopped me. I turned to her. She shook her head.

"Don't," she said. "You can't save him from what he's done to himself. Let him go. I won't lock my doors against him."

"What did you do?"

We both turned. August was still standing where Simon had put her, staring at the two of us. She looked so much like our mother—so much like me—that I was briefly taken aback. Until that moment, she had been an obstacle, not an individual. Now . . . this woman, this stranger, who had attacked me the moment that we met, who had abused and enchanted my allies, she was my sister. We shared blood. It didn't seem quite real.

She took a step forward. "*What* did you *do*?" she repeated. There was menace in her tone now, like she thought she could somehow frighten us into putting her world back to normal.

Even Quentin was unimpressed. "Simon fixed your mess," he said. "You should settle down. You're being sort of a jerk."

August stopped to blink at him. "Who, in Oberon's name, are *you*?"

"Quentin," he said. "I'm her squire." He indicated me.

"Hi," I said. "I'm your sister."

She frowned. "No, you're not," she said.

"If you were in charge of reality, maybe saying 'no' would change things, but sorry, I'm your sister," I said. "Amandine is my mother. She's yours, too. And she misses you. Badly. She's waiting for me to bring you home."

August frowned again, more deeply this time, like she was offended by my words. "Why would she send you? Why didn't she come and find me herself?"

The Luidaeg put her hand on my shoulder, pulling me a half step toward her, so that it was clear to anyone with eyes that I was under her protection. "Amy has her limitations, as do we all, and you should know better than to question your mother. She sent October to find you. October found you. A hundred years gone, and it's taken a changeling and your father's love to bring you home. Don't let his sacrifice be in vain."

"What do you mean?" August balled her hands into fists. "What did you do to him?"

"Girl, I'm going to assume you're too angry to think straight, because the alternative is that you're too stupid and too far up your own ass to understand what these people have done for you," said the Luidaeg. Her tone was calm, but her eyes were bleeding toward black again. "You sold me your way home for a candle and a promise. You said you would return my father. Do you remember?"

"Yes, but—"

"Oberon isn't here. Your father has paid your debts. Until my father comes home, yours will remain lost. He will not know you, nor take comfort from your hands. He will not find his own way. And if you think that's not fair, remember how hard I tried to talk you out of taking that same bargain. I *begged*, August." The Luidaeg's voice broke. In that second, she wasn't the sea witch. She was just an aunt, talking to her niece. "I begged you to go home and not do this. Everything that's happened here is your fault."

"Especially the part that involved trying to turn me mortal," I said, sheathing my knives. "Is that always how you say hello?"

"I was defending myself," snapped August.

"I wasn't attacking you," I said. "You broke my nose and changed my blood before I even took a step toward you. That's not self-defense, that's assault."

"You left me in Annwn," she snapped.

"You got out."

"Oh, yay, now there's more of you," muttered Quentin. "I can't wait until May's in the room, too, and everyone just keeps *yelling*."

May. She had been waiting for us to come home and save her girlfriend since we'd left Shadowed Hills. I took a deep breath, swallowing the last of my anger, and asked the most important question I had left:

"Hey, Luidaeg, can we use the back door?"

TWENTY-FIVE

FIRST PROBLEM: AUGUST DIDN'T want to come. By which I mean "August had no interest in going on a road trip with her half sister, especially since I'd already hit her with a baseball bat." She folded her arms and glared at me, and if there'd been any question of whether we were actually related, it would have been answered then and there.

"I'm not going *anywhere* with you," she snapped. "You're changeling filth and I don't have to do as you say."

"Does she heal like you normally do?" asked Quentin. "Because we could break her arms to distract her, and I bet I could carry her."

August's attention flicked to him. "You're a bloodthirsty boy."

"I learned from the best," said Quentin coldly. "You hurt my knight. I think I'm owed a little nonfatal payback."

"We could stand here arguing about this for hours," I said. "It's not going to change anything. You're coming with us."

"I will rip the last of the immortality from your veins and leave you human and weeping on the floor," said August.

"You can try," I said.

The Luidaeg looked between us. Then she turned to Quentin, lowered her voice, and said, "We're approaching the part where I remind them that I've only been bound against harming the children of Titania, and neither of them is covered by that label. Which means if they don't stop squabbling and move, I can gut them both like trout."

"Can you gut someone who isn't a fish like a fish?" asked Quentin.

"We could find out." It would have taken a fool to miss the warning in the Luidaeg's tone. Her patience—never her greatest attribute—was rapidly coming to an end.

The last thing I wanted was to add an angry sea witch to my list of problems. I focused on August. "Do you want to see our mother or not?"

Her eyes widened. "You know where Mama is?"

Aw, hell. "I should probably have led with that," I said. "Yes, I know where Amandine's tower is, and I need to take you there. She has hostages. I want them back. Will you come willingly?"

"You should absolutely have led with that," said August. She waved a hand airily, dismissing the idea of my people being a factor. "Take me to my mother. She'll want to see me, and to hear what's become of Papa."

"You might want to reconsider how much she's going to care about that, but sure," I said. "Luidaeg, can we use the back door *now*?"

"I should have hidden that thing better," said the Luidaeg. She couldn't lie, so I knew she meant what she was saying, but there was no rancor in her tone: only a bone-deep weariness that I sympathized with all too well. "Simon should be well clear by now. But, October, you should be aware that my back door is *very* rarely used by anyone but me. You know what that means, don't you?"

It meant the walls between worlds hadn't been worn thin and forgiving: it meant that in my current, nearly human state, the crossing would be disorienting, if not actively painful. I grimaced and nodded.

"I do, but I really don't want to drive across the Bay Area wondering whether she's about to grab the wheel, and I doubt she's letting me put her back in the trunk."

"I am not going back in the 'trunk,'" said August firmly.

"Okay," said the Luidaeg. "You can use the back door. It's your funeral."

"Maybe someday," I said. "Not today."

The Luidaeg looked unconvinced, but she led us through her apartment to a door that I had somehow never noticed before. It wasn't the one Quentin and I had come through with Simon, or maybe it was, because when she opened it, it revealed the swamp.

Looking at the spreading marsh reminded me of something. I turned to her and asked, "Where's Poppy?"

"Watching your policeman," said the Luidaeg. "She'll let me know if he wakes up."

"Is he . . ."

"I don't know." She looked at me, suddenly weary. "Humans weren't meant to spend time in Annwn. He may recover completely, and I may be able to edit his memory enough to let him go home. Or he may be broken forever, stranded on the wrong side of the knife until his mortal life is done. Only time is going to tell us. Now go. Make your mother give your people back."

"That's the plan," I said, and stepped outside.

The world didn't spin so much as it whipped into a maddened circle, moving so fast and so erratically that I dropped to my knees and vomited on the path, barely catching myself before I wound up facedown in my own sick. Throwing up didn't make the whirling stop. If anything, it made it worse, because I hadn't been able to breathe while I was barfing, and now that I was done, I couldn't catch my breath. Everything was wrong. Everything was *so wrong*. I wasn't supposed to be here. I knew it, and the air knew it, and my body and the world were perfectly willing to go to war if that was what had to happen.

"Toby?"

The voice, though distant, was recognizably Quentin's. He sounded worried. I hated being the reason he would sound that worried, I *hated* it, but I couldn't fix it if I couldn't breathe. Everything hurt. Everything was wrong. Everything was *spinning*—

"Let me."

This voice wasn't Quentin's. I muddled through the pain and the nausea and the oxygen deprivation and identified it as August's. That was . . . not a good thing. I was incapacitated. Quentin wasn't unarmed—he was my squire, he was never unarmed—but his knives wouldn't be enough to stop her if she really wanted to fight him. Daoine Sidhe are specialized in blood and illusions. He didn't have the combat training to use blood against her, if that was even possible, and disappearing only helped if you could move afterward, getting out of range.

"If you hurt her . . ."

"I need her to take me to Mama, remember?" Now August sounded annoyed. "I'm just going to nudge her a little bit, so she gets her balance back."

"I'll slit your throat if you do more than that."

August laughed. It wasn't a cheerful sound. "I'd live."

A hand touched my wrist, delicate and almost gentle for the first second, before it clamped down and everything else in the world—the spinning, the nausea, the inability to breathe—was replaced with an electric jolt of pain so extreme that it felt like it rattled my teeth in their sockets. I was stunned enough to start breathing again, sucking in a great lungful of air.

"There." August jerked her hand away from me like

I was something too disgusting to handle for long. "She'll be able to function now."

My blood sang a song of magic and immortality and change in my veins as I pushed myself slowly, awkwardly to my feet. I still wasn't what I had been, and I was still going to need the hope chest to give me the oomph I needed to put myself all the way back to normal, but I could breathe again. I reached up and pushed my hair aside, feeling the newly-sharpened point of my left ear. August had nudged me closer to the half-and-half that had been my default state for so many years. Not quite there, but . . . close.

When I looked up, she had her arms crossed and was glaring at me. Quentin was next to her. He wasn't glaring. He wasn't even looking my direction. All his attention was focused on August, and his hand was on the hilt of the knife at his hip.

If she thought she was in control here, she was going to be sorely surprised.

"Well?" she demanded. "Let's move."

"I miss being an only child," I said, and started walking.

The swamp didn't get much traffic, and while the ground was soft, it wasn't swift to wipe our footprints away. The tracks of our earlier passage were still there, and following them was a simple matter. When the first glowing toadstools appeared, I looked back over my shoulder at August and said, "Mind your step. If you kick one of those, it's night-night for all three of us, and I'd rather not deal with that at the moment."

August sneered. "I know pixie traps when I see them. They're pathetic, clumsy things. Anyone with eyes can spot them. What do you think I am, a *changeling*?"

The sound of ringing bells was our only warning before the pixies descended from the trees. They came in a single mighty flock, wings a chiming blur, bodies glowing in a hundred candied colors, like flying Christmas lights going on the attack. It was a relief to see them. It was even more of a relief to *hear* them. One of them buzzed past my cheek, so close that I felt a diminutive hand brush my skin before it joined the rest of the swarm in circling August.

They surrounded her in an instant, ringing and buzzing, feinting toward her face only to dart away again before her wildly swinging hands could hit them. August might be a pureblooded Dóchas Sidhe, but all the blood magic in the world couldn't equip her to fight off a couple of hundred pissed-off pixies.

A scrap of purple light separated itself from the flock and came to hover in front of my face, resolving itself into Lilac. Her wings rang and her mouth moved, although I couldn't hear what she was saying. She was too small, and too fae, while I, at the moment, was neither.

Oh, well. I knew from past experience that pixies could understand me, even when I couldn't understand them. "Hi," I said. "It's me. October."

August shrieked as the pixies buzzed too close to her eyes. Lilac bobbed in the air in front of me, wings ringing again, looking distressed.

I sighed. "Yeah, it's a long story. That's, uh. That's Simon's daughter. I'm taking her home to her mother. Could you maybe ask the rest of the flock to stop torturing her?"

An indignant ring.

"I know, she was saying some pretty shitty things, and I'm not going to pretend I'm not thrilled that you made her stop. But I need to get her back to Amandine before some people I care about get hurt. Can you call them off?"

Lilac rang again before buzzing off to join the rest of the flock in swarming around August. In a matter of seconds, they had stopped their circling and were rising into the air, taking up a hovering position just outside of arms' reach.

"That's great," I said, while August bent forward, panting, to rest her hands against her knees. "I really appreciate you backing off."

August raised her head, staring at me. "What are you saying?" she demanded. "They're *vermin*."

"See, that is one attitude I *know* you didn't get from your father," I said, as the pixies chimed warningly and flew in a slow spiral above her head—one that looked dismayingly like the mouth of a cyclone getting ready to touch down. If she wasn't careful, she was going to find herself spat out in whatever the pixie version was of Oz. "Much as I'd like to leave you here and let them teach you the error of your ways, I need to get you to Mom before she does more damage than she already has. Are you ready to walk?"

"I'm ready to punish them!"

"And they're ready to punish you."

"For *what*?"

"For being a jerk." I shrugged. Pixies landed on my shoulders and hair, ringing softly. "Pixies don't like assholes. Who knew, right? Now come on."

August glared as she straightened up and walked down the path to where Quentin and I waited. As she got closer, she switched her glare to the pixies in my hair. Wisely, she didn't say anything.

The pixies chimed smugly. I got the feeling they didn't like my brand-new sister any more than I did.

"Come on," I said again, for lack of anything better or wittier to say, and resumed walking toward the edge of the swamp. The path turned gradually firmer under our feet, and the marsh grasses gave way to the twisted trees that had marked our way before. The pixies in my hair stayed put, their wings giving occasional small chimes, like the ringing of distant bells. I got the feeling they were keeping an eye on August, and I was fine with that. She was the sort of person who could do with some supervision.

Quentin stayed close. The farther we got from the

Luidaeg's door, the more August did the same, until she was walking close enough that our arms were almost touching. Her glare had finally faded, leaving her looking around with wide, hopeful eyes, and an expression on her face that made her look so brittle that I was afraid she'd shatter if I brushed against her.

"Hey," I said. "Are you okay?"

"I remember this place," she whispered. She didn't look at me. "I used to come here with Papa. We'd pick berries and flowers, and sometimes I'd make him crowns and call him King of all Faerie, and he'd laugh and tell me that meant I was a princess. I *remember* this place." She reached up to wipe away a tear on the verge of escaping her left eye. "I thought I'd dreamt it all. But I remember it, and now here it is. It's real."

For a moment, I felt painfully sorry for her. Sure, she was being awful, and sure, I might have been happier if I'd been able to keep her locked in the trunk of my car, but she was still my sister, and she was still a person who'd lost her home for a century, all because she'd made the wrong bargain, followed the wrong candle.

"Why did you do it?" I blurted. This time August did turn to look at me, brittleness giving way to confusion. I pressed on: "Why did you decide to go looking for Oberon? If the Luidaeg said it was a bad idea . . ."

"Mama said it was a bad idea, too," said August, looking like she'd just bitten into a lemon. "She said heroism sounded too much like 'hurt' to be something any daughter of hers would do. She said she had made me a garden where I could bloom, and be safe and loved and beautiful forever."

Quentin frowned. "Then why—"

"I didn't *want* to be safe and loved and beautiful forever! I wanted to be a hero like Uncle Sylvester. I wanted to make Mama stop looking afraid every time someone talked about prophecy. She said she was glad all the seers were gone, because nobody should have to live in fear of the future. I wasn't scared of the future.

I wanted to hold it in my hands. I wanted people to treat my father with respect, and I wanted my mother to stop trying to hide, and if I could get there and back by the light of a candle, why shouldn't I?"

"Because you couldn't," I said. August gave me a baleful look. I shrugged. "I'm sorry, but when the Luidaeg says 'don't do that,' maybe you should listen. She can't lie, remember? She wasn't trying to be a jerk or make you stay safe at home, she was trying to protect you from an impossible task. You didn't listen. You got lost."

"She should have told me."

"She did," said Quentin.

August sniffed and turned her head, refusing to look at either one of us.

The trees had melted away, leaving us to walk through an endless field of flowers. Then, between one footstep and the next, the white spire of Amandine's tower appeared on the horizon, looming over everything. It was a neat trick. When I was a kid, it had even impressed me, the way Mom could bend the world to her whims. Now, all I felt was tired.

Tired, but with a faint ember of hope. Maybe this was all about to be over. Maybe Mom would see that I'd done what she had asked of me and give me back my people. For the first time in forever, I allowed myself to believe that I was going to have Tybalt safely in my arms again, that I was going to bring Jazz home. That in restoring her family, I had not managed to utterly destroy my own.

"Mama," breathed August, and broke into a run.

She moved with a pureblood's fluidity and grace. Quentin, chasing hard on her heels, did the same. I, on the other hand, was an avalanche trying to run, stumbling on every rock and tripping over every uneven patch of ground. By the time I reached the garden wall, August was already through the gate and racing up the path, with Quentin still close behind.

The door swung open as her foot hit the step, and there was our mother, as beautiful and brilliant as the morning, standing with her arm swept wide, hand flat against the wood. August froze. So did Amandine. The two of them stared at each other, separated by a few feet and the length of a century.

"Mama?" whispered August.

"August?" Amandine's voice wobbled, nearly cracking. She kept her hand flat against the door, but it was no longer to hold it open; instead, it was to support her weight. Her knees seemed to be on the verge of buckling, leaving her reeling and unsteady. "I . . ." She stopped again, mouth working soundlessly against all the things she needed to say.

"I was so lost," said August. "I was so *lost*, for so *long*." She burst into loud, sloppy tears.

"Oh, my poor child," said Amandine, and stepped forward, and gathered August in her arms, and held her.

The white flowers of my mother's garden framed them perfectly, two pale watercolor women, their hair hanging long and loose, their arms locked around each other. Only August's mortal-style clothes spoiled the impression that I was looking at a pre-Raphaelite painting, and she would change those soon enough, I had absolute faith in that. She would go upstairs to the room that Mom had hidden from me all my life, and open her closet, and whatever gown she chose would still fit like it had on the day when it was made. She would slide back into her life, seamlessly filling the hole I had never been enough to patch.

My mother had her beloved daughter back. She had her home again. Well, a vital piece of my home was locked in two cages somewhere in her tower, and it was time for her to keep her word.

"I found her," I said. I knew it was a bad idea to interrupt their reunion. I also knew how long two purebloods could take to circle their way through something like this, and my patience had run out somewhere between the pixies and August rebalancing my blood on a whim.

Amandine pulled away from August as she turned to look at me, expression blank, like she had never seen me before; like now that she had the daughter she actually cared about, I was nothing more than an unwanted complication.

I took a step forward. "I found her," I repeated. "I went to Annwn, and I found your daughter, and I brought her home. Now give me back what you took from me."

Amandine blinked. Then, to my surprise and dismay, she laughed. "Oh, October, what makes you think you have the right to demand anything of me? I see by the angle of your bones that you've made yourself more human to please me, but that only gives you a small scrap of indulgence. Enough that I'm willing to let you walk away."

"No," I said. "That wasn't the deal. You give them back to me *now*."

"Mama?" August took a half-step backward, creating a gap between herself and Amandine. "What is she talking about? What did you take?"

"Nothing, sweetheart, nothing of consequence," said Amandine. "It was worth it, to have you home, and she'll have her toys back soon enough. She needs to learn respect. A little time without her playthings will help to teach her."

"They're not *toys*," I snapped. "They're my *friends*."

"They're pets at best, and beasts at worst," said Amandine serenely. "You should consider yourself lucky that I don't hand you their pelts and call my debt repaid."

"What?" I asked, voice low and dangerous.

"What?" said Quentin. He sounded horrified, but his hand was on his knife again, and I knew if we challenged her, if we both died here, he would go willingly.

Let his sister be High Queen. He was the boy who should be king, and I had spoiled him, because he was more than halfway to becoming a hero.

"What?" said August, blinking at Amandine like she couldn't understand what was happening. Maybe she didn't. I couldn't remember ever telling her what Amandine had stolen from me. "Mama, *what* is she talking about?"

"She came into my home and she took my betrothed right in front of me," I said, eyes on Amandine, watching every twitch in the muscles of her cheek. "She shoved him into a cage and said that I could have him back if I brought you home. She promised."

"But I never promised when, October," said Amandine. "I also told you it was time to learn to respect your mother. Or have you forgotten that?"

August looked at her, expression puzzled and betrayed. "You . . . I thought you sent her because she was a changeling. She was expendable. I thought she went willingly, to win your approval. You *stole* from her?"

"She stole my fiancé," I said.

"I stole your *cat*," said Amandine airily. "No child of mine would ever willingly wed such a beast. It's not my fault your little masquerade went on too long and was derailed."

Attacking her would be the height of foolishness, second only to the moment when Simon had lunged for the Luidaeg. I knew that. I still put my hands on the hilts of my knives and said, very softly, "I know how to kill one of the Firstborn, Mother. I killed Blind Michael for what he did to me. Don't think I won't do the same to you, if you force my hand."

Amandine actually looked surprised. "You would make an enemy of me?"

My laughter was hot acid in my mouth, spilling over my lips before I could suck it back down. "Are you serious? *You* made an enemy of *me* when you came into my home and *stole my lover*." I took a step forward. "I want

Tybalt back. I want Jasmine back. I want them both back *right now*, and if you don't return them, we're going to dance, you and I."

"You're too human," she said dismissively.

"Humans have weapons, too," I said.

August's eyes widened. Quickly, she reached out and grabbed Amandine's arm, causing our mother to turn and look at her.

"She has an iron knife, Mama," she said. "She can hurt you. She can *kill* you. If you told her you'd return these people for bringing me home, just . . . just do it. Give them back to her. Let her take her beasts and her baggage and go."

Amandine hesitated.

"Please," said August.

That was the final straw. Amandine reached out and cupped her face in both hands, pulling August close to her. "As you like, my darling. As you like." She turned and looked at me, and there was no love in her eyes. That was fine. I wasn't looking for it anymore. "The kitchen. You remember the way."

She slipped her arm around my sister's shoulders and led her into the tower. The door slammed shut behind them. Quentin turned to me, eyes wide.

"You're just going to let her leave?" he demanded.

"She told us where to go," I said, and started around the tower. "Come on."

He came. Side by side, we walked toward what we'd lost, and we were almost halfway there before I broke into a run, not slowing down, not looking back.

Please, I thought. *Maeve, Oberon, Titania, anyone who might be listening, please.*

Please let them be okay.

TWENTY-SIX

THE TOWER WAS MUCH less elegant, and much less intimidating, when seen from the rear. The stone was still pristine and the architecture was still grand, but the white flowers of the front garden fell away, replaced by green beds of neglected herbs, some still labeled with tiny, faded signs. The bed closest to the garden wall was a riot of surprising color, bright orange California poppies straining toward the distant light of the moons above. I remembered planting them when I was still a little girl, thinking that if they could thrive here, so could I.

The poppies had blossomed. I hadn't. Not until I'd fled the Summerlands for the mortal world, where time passed the way my human blood wanted it to, and where the sun remembered how to shine.

I didn't slow down to smell the flowers or check to see if Mom had bothered doing any weeding in the last twenty years. I just kept running, practically vaulting up the back porch steps and slamming the door open to reveal the kitchen.

It was small, rustic, and homey: nearly the antithesis

of the rest of the tower. Like the garden, it seemed to belong to a different person. Amandine would never have designed a kitchen like this . . . at least not the Amandine I knew. In many ways, August's Amandine had been someone else. Someone kinder.

The table, bench, and chopping board were all polished redwood, and the stove was an antique copper thing, surprisingly efficient for something that looked like it had been stolen from a movie about Puritan New England. Copper pots and kettles hung from hooks set into the exposed overhead beams. There were even loops of drying herbs and spices, perfuming the air with sweet, contradictory fragrances.

But there were no cages. Not on the table; not on the counter; not on the hearth in front of the fireplace. I froze in the doorway, hands clenched at my sides, fear and fury flooding through me like a hot wave of bleach. If not for August, I would have been fae enough to breathe in and know they were here, that they were safe. If not for August, they would never have been taken in the first place. Suddenly, hating my sister seemed like an easy thing to do.

Quentin touched my arm. Lightly, but enough to remind me he was there and real; that there was still someone who could help me save the ones who needed saving.

I took a shaky breath, looking one more time around the kitchen. The cages wouldn't fit in the cupboards, and the shelves were open: I would have seen them if Amandine had stuffed them there. They weren't hanging from the ceiling. That left . . .

"The root cellar," I said, and ran across the room to the narrow wooden door half-hidden behind a bend in the wall. It was dusty when I grabbed it and wrenched it open. Amandine had never been much for cooking, not when she could transform a plate of berries into a pie with a wave of her hand, or just wander over to

Shadowed Hills to demand her lunch from Sylvester's kitchen. With me gone, she must have stopped entirely.

The stairwell on the other side was a slice of absolute darkness leading down, away from any prayer of the light. I dug my phone out of my pocket and hit the button to activate the screen, casting its watery electronic glow over the steps. They looked solid enough. Not that it mattered. Right now, I would have risked a broken neck rather than let this go on for a minute longer than it had to. Legs shaking, I gripped the bannister with my free hand and began to descend.

There was a loud ringing beside my ear. I nearly laughed with relief as the pixies that had been riding in my hair since their attack on August launched themselves into the air and began to fly precise loops over the stairs ahead of me, lighting the way. I tucked my phone back into my pocket.

Quentin gasped as he made it far enough down the stairs to see the basement. The sound made my blood run cold. He was a pureblood. He could see in the dark better than I could. Whatever he saw . . .

"Quentin, do I need to give you my knives?" I somehow managed to make the question sound natural, even reasonable. Did I need to disarm myself for the sake of not killing my mother? Because I would. If she had hurt them, if we were walking toward two corpses and not two captives, I would kill her. I had silver. I had iron. Even the Firstborn will fall before that combination. I've never wanted to be a murderer. I've killed people before, but I like to think I've managed to avoid earning that label. And if she had hurt them, I was going to become a murderer today.

"No," he said. "But . . . hurry."

I hurried. Even with the pixies lighting my way, I descended those steps so fast that I nearly fell several times, catching myself on the bannister, driving splinters into the soft meat of my palm. The farther down I went, the farther down the pixies went, the light from their bodies revealing more and more of my surroundings. There were the shelves against the walls, packed with bins of potatoes and parsnips and onions. The faint scent of Amandine's magic hung in the air around them; these were probably the same staples as had been down here when I was a child. There were the racks of preserves. Nothing had changed.

If nothing had changed, then the table at the center of the room was still there. I hurried toward where I remembered it being, the light spreading out before me like honey, and all I had was hope and fear, mixing together in my throat until I could no longer swallow.

The light reached the table. Two cages made of twisted briars rested there, far enough from the edge that there was no real risk of them falling over, even if their occupants had possessed the strength and will to throw themselves against the walls. I could see movement from inside, but it was slight, and the light was dim enough that I couldn't tell which was which.

"Tybalt!" I had thought I was running before. I had been, apparently, wrong. Now I virtually flew, flinging myself bodily across the intervening space to grab the closer of the two cages. The thorns bit deep into my hands, stinging and tearing. Amandine wouldn't have considered that a problem when she was constructing her portable prisons: after all, she healed even faster than I normally did. She had lost touch with the fact that other people could be hurt.

There was no latch. Furious, I let go of the cage and grabbed the silver knife from my belt, using it to hack at the bars. They refused to yield. The knife twisted in my hand, hilt slippery with blood. I shoved it back into its sheath and grabbed the iron knife instead, slashing at the cage.

The bars gave way as easily as air, charring and curling away from the bite of iron. I dropped the knife onto the table and pulled the cage door open, making no effort to avoid the thorns.

Huddled at the back of the cage, the large black bird it contained looked at me with avian mistrust, her wings as close to mantled as the narrow confines of her prison would allow. As I watched, she opened her beak and croaked weakly, trying to warn me off.

"Jazz," I said, relieved and disappointed in the same measure. Freeing her first meant when I freed Tybalt, I could hold him tight, and never need to let him go. "Jazz, honey, it's me. Come on. I'm here to free you."

This time, her croak was louder, and more obviously a threat. She hunched her shoulders, fluffing out the feathers on her throat and head, trying to make herself look huge. Some of the fear that had faded came surging back.

"Jazz. It's October. Don't you know me?"

A caw, harsh and angry.

"Oh, oak and ash. Quentin, we've got a problem."

"What?"

I turned to look at him. Jazz was still compacted in the back of her cage. She wasn't going to fly away. Yet. "I don't think Mom fed them, or watered them, or let them have any light for . . ." How many days had it actually been? When I added in the time dilation of the Babylon Road, it was almost impossible to say. "For days," I finished finally. "She doesn't know who I am."

Which meant Tybalt might not know either. Inappropriate laughter clawed at the back of my throat, threatening to rise up and choke me. Everything we'd gone through, everything we'd done to find August's way home, and now the people I'd been trying to save could be as lost as she was, and with nothing as simple as a bargain with the sea witch to blame. Magic can be reversed. Trauma isn't that simple.

"Watch her," I said, picking up my knife and shoving it into my belt. "I'm going to check on Tybalt."

I didn't even have to touch the cage. As soon as I

reached for it his paw lashed out, claws drawing four lines of pain down the back of my hand and adding more blood to the mess already there. I closed my eyes.

"Damn you, Mother," I whispered. Then, careful of the claws, I opened my eyes and picked up the cage by the handle. Thorns dug into my palms. I didn't care. "Quentin, can you get Jazz, without leaving her room to fly away? May will never forgive me if we lose her."

"Of course," he said. He was already moving to do as I had told him when he asked, "Where are we taking them?"

There was really only one option. The Luidaeg's back door was too far, and there was no way we could carry two cages full of angry, uncomprehending shape-shifter through the swamp without losing one or both of them. The mortal world was out for similar reasons.

"Shadowed Hills," I said. "Maybe Jin can help."

"Okay." Quentin didn't argue. He was a good squire. Better than I deserved, some days.

The pixies lit our way as we carried the cages out of the root cellar and back into the kitchen. I only looked back once, checking to see that Quentin had Jazz contained. He'd removed his jacket and was holding it over the front of the cage. Birds don't like the dark. If she was really thinking like a bird, she wasn't going to try to get through the fabric. It was a simple solution, but a good one, and it might be enough to keep her from breaking free.

May would never forgive me if I let her girlfriend fly off to live out the rest of her days as a raven—and those days would be very, very long. A transformed skin-shifter is as ageless as any pureblood. Jazz could re-main a raven for centuries, unable to remember what had been done to her, unable to change back.

That wasn't going to happen. I wasn't going to let it.

There was no sign of either Amandine or August as we carried the cages around the tower and down the garden path to the gate. The door remained closed, making it clear that we were no longer welcome here, if we ever really had been in the first place. This wasn't my home. Maybe it never had been.

Tybalt hissed and snarled and threw his weight against the bars as we walked across the meadow beyond the tower. His fur was thick enough to shield him from most of the thorns, but every so often one of them would manage to break through to the skin, and his yowling would take on a note of genuine pain. Then he'd go right back to thrashing, trying to get me to drop the cage and let him go.

It wasn't going to happen. Every time his howls turned pained, I winced; every time he hissed at me, I had to fight the urge to stop and struggle for breath. He needed me to do this. *I* needed me to do this. The fact that right now, he didn't want me to, was irrelevant.

The pixies spun and twisted through the air around us, the chiming of their wings urging us on. Still, it was a relief when the meadow gave way to the strange trees that grew around Shadowed Hills, and an even greater relief when the trees dropped away, replaced by the manicured hedges marking the edges of the grounds. I stopped where I was, turning to the nearest of the pixies—it was purple, and far enough away that I couldn't make out details, although I assumed it was Lilac.

"Do you know Sir Etienne?" I asked. "Tall, dark hair, Tuatha de Dannan. Can you find him and bring him here?"

Chiming loudly, the pixie bobbed affirmation in the air and darted away. Two of the remaining four followed her, leaving Quentin and me with two chiming sentries circling above us.

Quentin looked at my bloody hands, and then at my face, before asking, "Are you okay?"

This time, I let the laughter, unsteady and brittle as it was, free. "I don't know," I said. "Right now, I really don't know. Every time I think this is going to be over, it throws me another curve ball."

He was opening his mouth to answer when the air rippled and a portal opened, revealing Etienne, Lilac standing on his shoulder, holding his earlobe in one hand and pointing imperiously with the other.

"October," he began. "When a pixie broke in and started ordering me around, I should have known you were the—" He stopped as his eyes finally finished taking in the scene in front of him: the blood, the cages, the animals where there should have been people, even the shape of my ears and the shade of my hair. The color drained from his face. "Oh, root and branch, what happened?"

"Amandine happened." Even the things she hadn't done directly were still her fault. "We need help. Please. Can you take us somewhere safe, and bring Jin?"

Jin was a healer. Jin would know what to do.

Jin would save them.

Etienne nodded, stepping through the portal without hesitation. It closed behind him. He turned, waving his arm in an arch through the air, and a new portal opened, this time showing one of Luna's enclosed gardens. It was a beautiful pastel symphony of orchids and gently curling ferns, with no visible doors; even the ceiling was an eggshell dome, undimpled and unbroken. Tybalt and Jazz wouldn't be able to escape without accessing their own magic, and hence their humanity.

"Will this do?" he asked.

"Yes," I breathed. Quentin and I followed him through into the sweetly scented garden air, our precious cargo still clutched tightly in our hands.

Once the portal was closed, I turned back to Etienne and repeated, "Please, bring Jin." I paused. "And . . . and May. She should be here." Maybe she would be able to do what I couldn't, and coax Jazz back into her human form. Even if she couldn't, she should be here. I wanted my family. All of it.

Etienne nodded and turned, hands already moving, to step through another portal. Lilac jumped off his shoulder at the last moment, staying behind.

Jazz beat her wings against the bars of her cage and croaked her misery and anger over her confinement. Blood stained the thorns. I winced.

"Lilac, if we let Jazz out of her cage, will you follow her and make sure we know where she is?" I hated to keep Jazz confined one second longer than I needed to, but I couldn't risk losing her. The garden was small and enclosed, but ravens are smart, and if she got away, we'd never get her back. At the same time, I wasn't going to let her injure herself.

Lilac chimed assent.

I turned to Quentin. "Let her out."

He nodded, keeping any objections to himself. Gingerly, he set the cage down on the garden path and removed his jacket, giving Jazz a clear route to freedom.

Seconds ticked by before, cautiously, a raven's shaggy black head peeked out the broken doors. Once she was sure that no one was going to lunge for her, Jazz walked slowly out into the open. She ruffled her feathers. She stretched her wings. Finally, she launched herself into the air, wings beating hard, and flew toward the stained glass dome of the ceiling. Finding no exits there, she circled the garden twice before landing atop a marble statue of a dancing Silene, feathers puffed out to make her seem larger, and watched us suspiciously. Lilac perched on a nearby bush, glowing bright enough that we wouldn't lose sight of her.

That was one down. I walked to the nearest bench and set Tybalt's cage down on it before kneeling on the path and peering through the bars. Tybalt, crammed into the corner, fur standing on end and whiskers flat, looked back at me with no understanding in his eyes.

It would have been enough to break my heart, if I hadn't felt already broken. "I'm going to let you out before you cut yourself worse," I said. "I know you're going to run away, and I promise not to be angry about that. I don't know if you can reach the Shadow Roads or not, but please, if you can, don't. Stay here. Stay with me. Let us help you."

Tybalt pressed his ears down against his head and hissed.

It was a small thing to take my iron knife and slice through the front of his cage, creating a hole big enough for him to escape through. It seemed like the biggest thing in the world. At least while he'd been captive, he'd been with me. Now, I knew, he was going to run, because he was a wild thing, and that's what wild things do. I also knew that I didn't have a choice. He deserved his freedom as much as anyone. He deserved a chance.

When I moved aside, Tybalt erupted from the cage like a shot, vanishing into the dense ferns on the other side of the path. I dropped my face into my hands, and felt a hand settle on my shoulder as Quentin moved into position behind me, offering what comfort he could from sheer proximity. I wanted to cry. I didn't dare. If I allowed myself to start, I was never going to stop, and that wouldn't end well for anyone.

A door slammed. "Toby!"

I turned. May was running toward me, arms already open. Sylvester was following at a more sedate pace, but still hurrying, and Jin was coming down the path after him, slowed by her short legs, her wings buzzing frantically as she hurried to keep up.

Then May slammed into me, her arms locking tight around my upper body. She buried her face against my shoulder, whispering, "You came back. You came *back*. I wasn't sure you were going to."

"As fast as I could," I said. "I got there and back by the light of a candle." Only I hadn't, because Simon still had our candle: he had taken it with him when he lost his own way. Maybe it would burn forever now, unable to ever guide him home.

May sniffled, pushing me away. She plucked at a lock of my hair. "This is different."

"I found my sister—our sister. Turns out Mom never taught her to play nice." I shrugged, trying to look unconcerned, trying to look like this was the sort of thing that happened every day. In a way, it sort of was. "Madden's letting Arden know I need to borrow the hope chest. I'll be fine."

"Good," she said. Formalities observed, she turned finally to look at the statue where Jazz perched, still wary, still frozen. May sniffled. "Does she really not know who she is?"

"I'm so sorry."

"Tybalt . . ." May looked back to me. Whatever she saw in my face must have answered the question she hadn't yet asked, because she stopped, and nodded, and said, "I'm sorry."

"Yeah. Me, too."

"October." Sylvester had been hanging back, giving us our moment. Now that it was done, he walked forward, offering me his hands, and asked, "What can I do?"

"I don't know." It was getting harder to keep myself from crying. "She locked them in cages that hurt them, that were too small to let them transform, and then she left them alone in the dark for days with nothing to eat or drink. I don't know what to do."

Jin visibly relaxed. "Oh," she said, coming closer. "Is that all?"

May and I both turned to stare at her, united in our shock and horror. She shook her head, wings snapping open to punctuate the gesture.

"Shapeshifting—all shapeshifting, whether it's inborn or aided by a Selkie skin or cloak of feathers—is magic. Magic is a muscle that exists inside and outside the body at the same time. That's why practice makes you stronger. You're working that muscle behind the magic. Your mother . . ." Jin paused, mouth twisting in a moue of distaste. "What she did was cruel and unreasonable, and they're currently experiencing the magical equivalent of a muscle cramp."

"Can you fix it?" May demanded, barely a heartbeat before I was going to ask the same question.

"If they let me," said Jin. She smiled, clearly trying to be encouraging. "Ellyllon are very good at muscles, both physical and non. That's why we go into medicine. It's where the muscles are."

"Please, help them," May said, and there was nothing else for me to say, so I stayed where I was, with my squire, my liege, and my real sister, the one I'd chosen, the one who'd chosen me, to see what happened next.

Jin walked slowly toward Jazz, her hands open at her sides, her wings flat against her back. Jazz shifted uneasily from foot to foot, watching the Ellyllon approach. She gave a warning croak. Jin stopped, holding her position until she was confident that Jazz wasn't going to fly away. Then, and only then, did Jin start forward again. She spread her wings as she walked, leaving traceries of red glitter in the air. Jazz watched warily.

"Peace," said Jin.

Jazz cawed.

"Sleep," said Jin. She made an elaborate motion with her hands, and Jazz toppled sideways off the statue, plummeting like a stone. She never hit the ground: Jin was there before she had the chance, plucking her from the air and bearing her gently down to the garden path.

Jin looked up, turning toward us. She beckoned May forward, and May went, slowly at first, then with increasing speed, stopping only when she reached Jin's side. Her eyes were fixed on Jazz, and only on Jazz.

"What do you need?" she asked.

"Sit," said Jin.

May sat.

"Hold her," said Jin.

May gathered Jazz in her arms with such delicacy

that it hurt to watch, cradling her sleeping girlfriend. Jin opened her wings again, the air around them growing thick with red dust, and began moving her hands through the air, tracing patterns I could neither see nor understand.

"Your hands," said Sylvester. I glanced at him, startled. He frowned. "What did you do to your hands?"

"The cages," I said. "The thorns. I'm too human to heal the way I should right now. I'll be fine." We'd fix Jazz and Tybalt. We'd take them home. Arden would loan me her hope chest, and I'd be fine. I had to be. *We* had to be. I had worked too long and too hard for the life I had now, and this wasn't how I was going to lose it. It wasn't. I refused.

My hands ached. I flexed them. The punctures burned more than they should have, like they'd been coated in a stinging sap. But Tybalt and Jazz were fine, and they had been in those cages. They had been . . .

They had been in those cages, enspelled not to turn back into their human forms. Would Mom have worried about her spell slipping? Would she have wanted to be certain that if they *did* turn human, they wouldn't be able to escape?

"I think something's wrong," I said, looking at Sylvester.

He looked back, worried.

His face was the last thing I saw before I hit the ground.

TWENTY-SEVEN

AS WAS SO OFTEN the case when I passed out at
Shadowed Hills, I woke up in a bed, the covers pulled
up to my collarbone. The ceiling above me was deep
blue, painted with pink swirls, like the sky at sunset.
Somehow, that didn't make me feel any better.

My hands didn't ache anymore. That was good. I
couldn't actually feel them. That was bad. I pulled my
arms from under the blanket, raising my hands to my
face. They were swaddled in a thick layer of gauze, until I could barely move them. The numbness was probably one of Jin's salves. That, or Mom had used a poison
on the thorns that had done permanent nerve damage.
At the moment, it was difficult to tell.

I was alone. The room was too silent for anyone else
to be there. Even Tybalt would have made *some* sound,
however slight. Cohabitating with one of the Cait Sidhe
has sharpened my situational awareness out of self-
defense. I sat up, looking around. The room was small
and plain, with the minimum amount of furniture necessary to make it livable. One of the guest rooms, then.
Judging by the color on the walls and the quality of the

furnishings, one of the family guest rooms. I was moving up in the world.

Moving up, and moving on. I shoved back the covers, noting with some satisfaction that I was clothed for a change—wearing a loose white chemise and a pair of soft gray chamois trousers, but clothed—and climbed out of the bed, padding barefoot toward the door. I could worry about where my weapons and real clothes were later. Right now, I needed to find Jin, and find out whether she'd been able to coax Tybalt back into his human form. If she hadn't . . .

That would be when I started worrying about weapons, and when Sylvester would need to start worrying about whether I was about to do something he wouldn't be able to forgive.

Almost unsurprisingly, when I opened the door, I found a sentry waiting. Grianne was leaning against the wall, her Merry Dancers spinning a slow ballet through the air above her head. Like all Candela, she was gray-skinned, gray-haired, and lithe of build, while her Merry Dancers were perfect spheres of whitish-green light that brightened and dimmed in accordance with her mood. Judging by their current brilliance, her mood wasn't all that great.

More surprising was the purple pixie playing tag with her Merry Dancers, spinning around them with dizzying speed. Lilac stopped playing when she saw me, hovering in the air ringing for a moment before she dove for my hair and buried herself there. Grianne looked down and focused on my face, one brow raising slightly as she took in the rounded planes of my cheekbones and the brown of my hair.

"Huh," she said finally. "Old school."

"I'll get back to normal soon," I said.

She shrugged, expressing that it was no concern of hers. "How are your hands?"

"Numb." I held them up for her to see. "Did Jin tell you how bad it was?"

"Yes." That seemed to be enough for Grianne. She pushed herself away from the wall. "Duke Torquill sent me to wait for you. He and the others are in the kitchen."

The kitchen. That could be a good thing. That smacked of recovery, of needing to take people where they could get a good meal and a glass of something extremely alcoholic. My hope must have shown on my face. Grianne shook her head.

"Don't," was all she said. She turned and started down the hall, leaving me with little choice but to pad after her, swallowing my questions. I'd have my answers soon enough. Pestering Grianne wouldn't make them come any sooner, and might result in her deciding I was too much trouble to guide.

I've been in and out of Shadowed Hills since I was a little girl. I did most of my training there, and while it's been a while since I was a regular sight in the halls, I still know my way around. Mostly. Like all large knowes, the building has a tendency to rearrange itself, and I didn't want to risk getting lost. The time I'd already spent unconscious had been more than long enough.

The time . . . "Grianne, how long was I out?"

"Eight hours. Maybe." She kept walking. "Long enough for everyone to yell a lot. Sir Etienne had the shift before mine."

If I'd woken up while Etienne was on duty, I might have been able to get better answers. I silently pledged to do a better job of timing my returns to consciousness. The thought was laughable, but it was a good enough distraction to keep me from grabbing Grianne and shaking her until she gave me the answers I needed.

Then we were at the kitchen doorway, a wide, gently peaked wooden arch that led into a large, comfortably designed room. Melly, the Hob in charge of the kitchens as a whole, was bustling between the stove and an artfully rough-hewn table, a bowl of soup in each hand. Quentin was seated there, across from—

"Jazz!" I sped up, brushing past Grianne in my hurry to get to the now-bipedal Raven-maid. May was standing behind her, hands resting on her shoulders, keeping her in place, keeping in contact at all times. They turned to look at me, Jazz weary, May wary. "Are you all right?"

"I have thumbs again," said Jazz. She sounded distant, and faintly dazed, like she was still waking up from a long and not entirely welcome dream. "I didn't before."

"Eat your soup," said May. She kept looking at me as Jazz turned to begin fumbling for her spoon. "She needs time. How are your hands?"

"Messed up, but I'll live." I raised them for her to see. "Where's Tybalt?" If Jazz was back in human form, Tybalt would be too. He'd probably been asking for me.

May looked away.

A chill lanced through me. I turned to Quentin. He wouldn't meet my eyes. "What?" I demanded. "What's going on?"

"You should eat something," said Melly. She sounded worried about my well-being. That wasn't unusual. What *was* unusual was the way she was looking at me, with sympathy and something I didn't want to let myself read as pity.

"Sylvester was supposed to be here." I whipped around, looking for Grianne. She was gone. She had delivered me to the kitchen and left, presumably because she didn't want to be here when the shit hit the fan. "Grianne told me Sylvester wanted me to come here. And where's Jin? Where's *Tybalt*?"

"Duke Torquill was with me," said Arden. I turned.

Arden Windermere, rightful Queen in the Mists, was standing on the other side of the kitchen, with Sylvester slightly behind and to the left of her. It was hard to focus on him, or on anything beyond the box she was holding. It was made of wood—four kinds of wood, to be exact, oak and ash and rowan and thorn, carved with knives of air and water, joined together through cunning manipulation of the wood, not with anything as mundane as nails or hinges—and about the size of a thick paperback book, and I *wanted* it. I wanted it so badly that my hands began to ache again, this time with the effort of staying lowered by my sides. Assaulting a queen to steal a hope chest wasn't the sort of thing that was going to end well for me.

Arden herself wore a long gown of frost-blue velvet, simply cut enough to pass as casual attire for a queen. It called the dark red highlights out of her long black hair and drew attention to her mismatched eyes, one mercury silver, the other pyrite gold. I wasn't as human as I had been, but I was still human enough that when I finally switched my attention from the hope chest to her, she briefly took my breath away. It wasn't a comfortable sensation.

I swallowed hard, forcing down the awe and the sudden conviction of my own insignificance, and asked the only question that mattered: "Where's Tybalt?"

"Jin is with him," said Sylvester. It would normally have been considered rude for him to answer for the queen, but his tone was gentle, almost careful, and it seemed like they had already discussed the necessity of handling me with delicacy.

It made me want to punch someone. "That's not an answer."

"October." Arden somehow turned my name into a command. I glanced back to her, only flinching a little when I met her eyes. She held the hope chest out toward me. "Madden told me you were going to need this. I am . . . grateful that you were able to free him from the enchantment he was under, and regret that I did not notice the situation myself. I hope you will accept the loan of this treasure as a token of my gratitude."

So she wasn't going to ask anything of me in exchange for use of the hope chest. That should have been a good thing. That should have been her honoring me as a hero of the realm. Instead, it felt like the sort of gesture you made to someone on the brink of breaking down.

I didn't say anything. I just looked at Sylvester, and waited.

It didn't take long before he sighed and looked down at his feet. "Tybalt is with Jin," he said. "There have been . . . complications."

"What do you mean, complications?" My voice was a razor slashing across the throat of the world.

"Your betrothed is a King of Cats," said Sylvester. He looked up again, meeting my eyes. "His magic is . . . substantial. When it misfires . . ."

"Jin isn't strong enough to massage out the cramp," I said, feeling suddenly numb again. "She can't get him to change back."

"No. But you might, were you at your normal strength." He gave the hope chest in Arden's hands a meaningful look.

The last time I'd used a hope chest, I had entered a strange fugue state where a version of myself had offered me a choice of two knives, one that would turn me mortal and one that would turn me fae, and invited me to be the guest of honor at a stabbing. I had responded by grabbing both knives, driving them into my own stomach, and staying a changeling. It hadn't been a pleasant experience. I didn't care. Lunging forward, I snatched the hope chest out of Arden's hands.

Nothing happened. I froze, staring at the treasure in my hands. In my gauze-swaddled hands. I wasn't touching the wood. I could fix that. Awkwardly, I tucked the hope chest under one arm and started yanking at the fabric on my right hand with my teeth, trying to unwind it.

"October."

I looked up.

Sylvester was holding his sword out, blade turned sideways to make it clear that he wasn't threatening me. "Use this," he said.

Mutely, I nodded, and before he could pull back, I slashed my hand across the edge of the blade with a ferocity born of desperation and too many years spent learning how to be practically invincible. The gauze parted easily. So did the flesh on the other side, metal slicing to the bone in a sensation that was as agonizing as it was familiar. I had been here before. The mansions of pain were no longer a mystery to me, and might never be again.

Sylvester blanched. Arden turned away. Neither of them said a word. They knew why I was doing this. The kitchen was an island of silence, and I was the only thing that moved.

My left hand was still wreathed in gauze, but that didn't matter: one would be enough. Ignoring the pain, I slammed my bleeding palm down on the hope chest.

Heat lanced up my arm, immediate and burning. It wasn't painful, although it should have been. It was less like a forest fire, and more like the soothing, cleansing warmth of a hot pack against a strained muscle, turned up to a thousand. I gritted my teeth. The visions hadn't come on yet. Maybe that meant they weren't going to. The last time I'd done this, there had been goblin fruit and Firstborn blood in my system, making everything harder, divorcing me from myself. Here and now, I knew exactly who I was, and I knew exactly what I wanted.

What I was, I thought, as loudly and fiercely as I could. *Make me what I was.*

I could feel the hope chest responding to my demand, a distant, quizzical presence. It wanted more details. That was why it had given me the visions the last time, I realized: because it didn't know how to communicate with me. It was too old, and too strange, and I was too young, and still too human. The edges of my vision started to blur as the hope chest began forcing a fugue state over me.

No, I thought fiercely. *No visions. Make me what I was.* I pictured myself as I'd been when this all began, the color of my hair, the slope of my ears, the position of the watermarks in my blood. Sometime in the last several years, my mental image of myself had changed from the half-and-half girl I had always been, moving to match the more fae creature I had become. I still wanted to keep what was left of my mortality for as long as I could.

And if this was the end of it, if I couldn't guide the hope chest well enough to preserve it, that would be fine, too. I could save Tybalt. I could save my bruised and breaking heart. What was a little humanity when compared to that?

The hope chest grew even hotter, flame lancing through my fingertips and up my arms. Now it *did* hurt, becoming an all-consuming burn that was almost enough to make me drop the wood. I refused, holding on tighter and closing my eyes, blocking out all distractions.

I am Oberon's granddaughter, I thought. *He made you before he made me. Now do as I say.*

The heat intensified. I think I screamed. I couldn't be sure. Every cell in my body was carbonizing. My blood was a river of lava twisting through my veins, scorching everything it came in contact with. I didn't feel the hope chest leave my hand, but I heard it hit the floor a split-second before I landed next to it, falling hard to my knees and catching myself with my hands to keep my face from hitting the floor.

It didn't hurt. My palms had just slammed into the kitchen's stone floor, and while the impact was jarring, there was none of the pain I would have expected from landing on a slashed-open palm. I opened my eyes. The hope chest was lying on its side. My right hand was covered in blood and my left hand was covered in gauze, but when I lifted my right hand off the floor and turned it over, my palm was unmarred.

I sat up slowly, breathing hard, and unwound the gauze from my left hand. There were no scratches or punctures on my palm and fingers. I flexed my hand. Still no pain. Barely daring to hope, I reached up and felt the slope of my ear. It tapered to a point, not as sharp as Sylvester's or my mother's, but so much sharper than it had been. It felt like it was mine again.

I looked up. Sylvester's sharp intake of breath confirmed my transformation. Grabbing the hope chest— which was only warm now, not burning; I wasn't asking it for anything, and the humanity I still possessed was mine to keep—I rose, as easily as if I had never been hurt.

"Where's Tybalt?" I asked.

Arden held out her hands. I surrendered the hope chest to her without protest, but my eyes stayed on Sylvester, waiting for him to answer me.

"He and Jin are in the garden," he said. "I can take you there. Your Majesty." He turned to Arden, offering her a shallow bow. "You have my eternal gratitude for what you have done today. This is a service to my house and to my heart, and it will not be soon forgotten."

"Sir Daye is a hero in the Mists," said Arden. "I did less than my throne still owes her." She looked to me. "Go. Save him. I know you can."

I couldn't thank her, and so all I did was nod and turn to Sylvester, waiting.

I didn't have to wait for long. He sheathed his sword and started walking, leaving me to follow. I glanced to the table where May, Jazz, and Quentin were seated. May shook her head. She wasn't moving. I couldn't blame her.

"Quentin, stay here," I called. "If anything happens, find me."

"Sure, boss," he said. There was an almost painful relief in his face—not because I was leaving him behind, but because it was starting to seem like this might be almost over. We might actually survive this.

Sylvester's stride was always long, but now he was hurrying, racing from the kitchen to the hall, forcing me to hustle to keep up with him. We were in our second parlor, crossing the knowe with remarkable speed, when I realized what he was doing. He was trying to keep me from asking questions.

I grabbed his arm. He stumbled, apparently not expecting that, and turned to gape at me.

"What?" I demanded.

He hesitated before saying, "I don't think this is the time. Tybalt—"

"Would want me to know what you don't want me to know."

Sylvester closed his eyes. "It's not what I don't want you to know, October," he said softly. "It's what I'm afraid to ask."

"What?"

"My brother." He opened his eyes again. "Where is my brother?"

Oh, oak and ash. I had been so focused on Jazz and Tybalt that I hadn't stopped to think of things from Sylvester's perspective. I had left Shadowed Hills with Simon. I had returned without him. "He's lost," I said.

There was a pause before Sylvester asked, "He's dead?"

"No. He's lost." Quickly, I explained what had happened: how the Luidaeg had taken August's way home for the sake of a candle, how Simon had forced the Luidaeg to transfer August's debts to him, as her father. How, once his way home was lost, Simon had regressed to the man he'd been under Evening's control, calculating and cold, willing to do whatever was required to escape.

When I finished, Sylvester looked at me and said, in

a soft tone, "This is what I feared. He's awake now, and free to do whatever he desires. What will keep him from waking his mistress? Before, Amandine's disapproval was a weapon we could use against him, keeping him from committing even greater transgressions than those he already has. Now, he's lost."

"I know," I said. "I tried to stop him. He was trying to be a hero. He was trying to save his daughter."

"If only he had been a hero when he decided to endanger mine." Sylvester started walking again. "When this is done, when your people are restored, it might be best if you stayed away for a time."

"Sylvester—"

"Etienne can come to you for Quentin's lessons. I've managed to keep Luna from knowing that Simon was awake. It helps that she would rather avoid your company, when she has the option. But she's going to find out soon enough, and she's going to be angry. Do you understand how angry she's going to be? I love you. I can't choose you over my wife. Not when she has every right to be furious."

"I understand," I said, and I did, I truly did. We all had to choose which family came first. Sylvester was my liege lord and my mentor and my sometime father figure, but Luna was his wife and the mother of his child, and if she had reason not to want me around, I would stay away.

Every time it seemed like my strange little family was starting to heal, something else would come along to split it apart. Maybe that was how things were going to be from now on. Maybe we were never going to be whole again. Sometimes things fall apart, and that's just the way it is.

Sylvester didn't look like he shared my acceptance of the situation. He started walking again, still faster than was strictly necessary, the dogwood flower and daffodil smell of his magic crackling in the air around him as it rose in response to his unhappiness. I hadn't realized how much I depended on the magic around me to read the situation.

A blank wall came into view ahead of us. Sylvester touched it, and a patch of it went misty, creating a temporary door. He looked at me gravely.

"I know you can do this, October," he said, before he turned and walked away, leaving me alone.

Right. I took a deep breath and stepped forward, through the misty wall, which turned solid again behind me, leaving me standing in the garden, surrounded by warm artificial sunlight that did nothing to cut through my cloud of trepidation and foreboding.

Jin was sitting on a nearby bench. I walked toward her. She raised her head, wings vibrating, and smiled a sad, relieved smile when she saw me.

"October," she said. "You're back to normal."

"Queen Windermere brought the hope chest," I said, like that was normal, like everybody had queens running errands for their convenience.

Jin nodded. "Good. I can't reach him."

I didn't need to ask who she meant. Even if I hadn't known, the weary sorrow in her voice would have been enough to tell me. "Where is he?"

She pointed to a patch of white-and-purple irises. I nodded and walked toward it, keeping my steps as light as I could. When I was close, I stopped and crouched, and peered into the depths of the vegetation.

There was Tybalt, crouched low, paws tucked in tight against his body and tail wrapped around his legs. The look he gave me was pure animal fear. Once again, the urge to kill my mother surged up and threatened to overwhelm me, and once again, I pushed it down and away. This wasn't the time. I needed to focus on what mattered. I needed to focus on finding one more way home.

"Hi," I said, lowering myself to the ground until I was stretched out with my cheek flat on the grass.

Tybalt stayed where he was.

I let my eyes drift half-shut, trying to find the strands of magic I knew had to be surrounding him. This wasn't an outside transformation, like the one that Simon had hurled at Jazz the first time I had pulled a spell apart with my hands. It wasn't a geas, either, forced into Simon's blood and body by someone else. This was Tybalt's own magic, being used against him by my mother and by the trauma he had endured.

This would have been easier if I'd had access to his blood. Everything is easier, always, when I have access to blood.

I froze. The idea I'd just had seemed farfetched, but what about this wasn't? It was worth trying. Anything was worth trying, if it brought him back to me. This garden was mostly gentle plants, but Luna has never shied away from roses; they grew tucked among the ferns, low, lush-smelling tea roses spreading their tattered petals wide. Not sitting up, keeping my motions as slow and easy as I could, I reached over and ran my fingers along the nearest stem.

The thorns were small but sharp, breaking my skin easily. I brought the hand back, faster this time, and stuck my bleeding fingers into my mouth before they could heal. Drinking in as quick and deep as I could, I focused not just on the blood itself, but on the specific memory I wanted: the moment when, in Arden's halls, I had tasted Tybalt's blood on his lips and felt Tybalt's magic thrumming in my veins.

All memory is contained in the blood. All memory, and all magic. The memory of magic wasn't enough to give it to me—I'm no alchemist, and this was like a copy of a copy, faded, distant, and thin—but I fell through my blood memory and into his, catching a glimpse of my own face as I watched him die in front of me. Grief swept through me, strong enough to make my heart stutter. Not strong enough to wash away the triumph.

This was what Tybalt's magic felt like from the inside, all wild pennyroyal and feline musk. This was the shape of it. I looked at him again, small and trembling in the depths of the ferns, and I saw the thin traceries of his transformation snarled in the stripes of his fur, worked into the lines of his limbs. It was so simple. It was part of him, and it was locked in its current position, twisted by my mother and then frozen by his own fear, confusion, and power.

"I love you," I said gravely, and reached out, hooking my fingers in the air, hooking my magic into his, and pulled.

Tybalt did not transform so much as collapse, a cat one moment, a man the next. Not entirely a man: there were stripes across his bare back and shoulders, extending all the way down his butt and across the tops of his thighs. That didn't matter. That had *never* mattered to me. I scrambled to my hands and knees and dove into the bushes, gathering him close, ignoring the scent of crushed flowers as I pulled him against me and held him as tightly as I dared.

I was crying. Finally, I was crying. I pressed my face against his hair and just sobbed, breathing in the scent of him, his skin and sweat and magic, mingling with the scent of blood and roses and green, growing things.

It was hard to say how long I was crying into his hair before he raised his head, blinking bemusedly up at me. I sniffled. He lifted his hand, fingers trembling, and touched my cheek.

"October," he whispered.

"We're home," I said, and we were. We finally, finally were.

TWENTY-EIGHT

IT HAD BEEN THREE days, and I was finally able to let Tybalt out of my sight without finding it difficult to breathe.

May and Jazz were in a similar situation. Jazz had insisted on going back to her antique store after two days in bed, and May had gone with her, despite this plan necessitating her being out of bed before one in the afternoon. Unspoken but ever-present was the fear that we were enjoying a brief respite from our separation, and that if we lowered our guard, even for a second, it would all come crashing down.

The Luidaeg still had Officer Thornton in her guest room, and was slowly working on removing the traces of Annwn from his system. She didn't know how long it would be before she could wake him up, much less start figuring out how much damage his time in deep Faerie had done. He might be lost forever, one more Rip van Winkle to lay at Faerie's doorstep.

I hoped not. I hoped he was going to be all right. We'd lost too many people already.

There had been no sign of Simon since his disappearance from the Luidaeg's apartment. I had reinforced the wards around the house, and for the first time, I was allowing May and Quentin to help me with them, turning our protections into a deeper, more complicated shell. Simon could still get through if he wanted to, but with three of us pitching in, we would almost certainly feel him coming.

What we had here wasn't safety. It was just the illusion of safety. It was still the only thing we had and, by Oberon, I was going to cling to it.

Something rattled in the hall. I tensed, ready to yell for Tybalt, only to relax when Tybalt himself came around the corner, stepping into the kitchen. He smiled wanly at the look on my face.

"I am not as breakable as all that, little fish," he said.

"That's what you say now," I said, trying to keep my voice light. It wasn't easy. "Let's skip the life-threatening adventures for a while, okay?"

"To echo a wise woman I know, that's what you say now, but when I object to your being covered in blood, how much credence do you grant to my objections?" He stalked across the room and slid his arms around my waist, joining his hands at the small of my back. "Fair's fair."

"I'll have you know that I didn't get covered in blood *once* while Mom had you," I said.

He nuzzled my neck. "I would say I should be kidnapped more often, but—"

I pulled away, just enough to press a finger against his lips. "Don't."

Tybalt nodded. There were shadows in his eyes. I wasn't the only one who'd been traumatized. He'd gone to the Court of Cats as soon as he was ready, relieving Raj of the throne. He was still going back and forth, and both of us were nervous wrecks every time he had to leave. It wasn't a healthy situation. We would have to get past this. Given how recently everything had gone wrong, I wasn't going to push the issue.

Someone knocked on the back door.

We both went still. I glanced at the clock. It was barely eight o'clock at night, early enough that virtually anyone could have been at the door, human, fae, or somewhere in between. I looked at Tybalt. We both nodded before stepping away from one another, grabbing handfuls of shadows from the air and spinning them around ourselves, draping our true faces in the thin veneer of our human disguises.

The illusions also covered the knife at my belt. I'd put the iron away again, but the silver went everywhere with me now, and would for a while. Resting my hand on the hilt in what I hoped would look casual and ordinary to whoever was outside, I walked to the door, unlocked it, and swung it open.

August was on the back porch. She looked at me. I looked at her.

"Hi," she said.

"Good-bye," I said, and started to swing the door shut.

"Wait!" She flung out her hand like she was going to prevent me from locking her out. I paused, and she grimaced and said, "I don't need to come in. I just came . . . I just came to say I was sorry, and to make sure your people were okay. Are your people okay?"

"October?" Tybalt was suddenly at my shoulder, a warm, reassuring presence. "Who's this?"

"My sister," I said, and that was true, and it wasn't true, all at the same time. We shared blood. That was all, and that was what she'd tried to take from me. "Tybalt, meet August."

"Ah." His voice turned wary. "Come looking for more things to steal?"

"That wasn't me," she said. "That was our mother. October, I—"

"I know," I said wearily. "You were lost. You were lost, and you were scared, and you didn't know, and I want to be the bigger person here. I want to forgive you for hurting me. I want to be able to step back and not blame you for what Amandine did. But I can't. Not right now. Maybe someday. Right now, I just want to put my family back together, and breathe. Can you understand that?"

She bit her lip before asking, "Are you going to find my father?"

I didn't even have to think. "Yes," I said. "Not right now, but someday . . . yes. Finding lost people is what I do. Even if I didn't want to find him, I probably would."

"Why not right now?" August blurted.

I took a sharp, angry breath, forcing myself to count to ten before I said, "Because right now, I can't be away from my fiancé without thinking he's never coming home. Because my Fetch, my *sister*, keeps breaking down crying, and her girlfriend is afraid to change shapes, thanks to Amandine making her afraid she'll get stuck that way. Do you understand? Mom left a Raven-maid *afraid to fly*. The only person in this house who isn't completely fucked up is Quentin, and honestly, I think he's hiding how upset he is from me because he doesn't know if I can take it. My liege won't let me into his knowe, Simon is missing and possibly a threat again, the Luidaeg has a human-sized pixie and a sleeping police officer in her apartment—I *can't* go looking for your father! I may be a hero, but even heroes need to rest. Let me rest."

August took a step back. "I might go looking for him myself," she said, and it was a warning, and a threat.

"If you do, I'll find you, and I'll bring you home," I said coldly. "You disappear again, Amandine comes after the people I love. I can't allow that."

"I'm not going to be a prisoner because you want to be left alone!"

"Yeah," I said. "You sort of are. If you don't like it, convince Mom she isn't allowed to come here and punish me for your bad behavior. This is between you and my mother. I want no part in it."

"I won't forget this."

"I know," I said. "Neither will I."

August glared before turning on her heel and walking away. I watched her go. When I was sure she wasn't going to come back, I closed the door, letting my forehead rest against the wood. Tybalt stepped up behind me, putting his arms around me again, and lowered his head to my shoulder. We stood there, wounded, frozen, exhausted, and waited for home to start feeling like home again. We waited for the safety to come back.

We were going to be waiting for a very long time.

Read on for
a brand-new April O'Leary novella
by Seanan McGuire:

OF THINGS UNKNOWN

And as imagination bodies forth
The form of things unknown, the poet's pen
Turns them to shapes . . .
  —William Shakespeare, *A Midsummer Night's Dream*

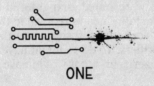

ONE

October 30, 2013

THE WORLD SANG in a coruscating curtain of colors, shades that had no place or purpose outside the comfortable circumference of my tree. Here, I had no body, only the potential to make one when it was needed. Here, I had no tie to time, only the bright and brilliant light of the infinite *now*. I could stay forever and never tire of the perfection of it all. I could leave any time I wanted to and be as refreshed as if I had stayed a hundred years.

I wonder if death is the same way. I wonder if my mother is surrounded by curtains of light, comfortable and content and willing to remain where she is until something better comes along. I do not think so. I have read everything our scholars have written about the dead, and I have sent Elliot to the Library dozens of times to transcribe texts that touch, however glancingly, upon the night-haunts and the afterlife they represent, and all I know for sure is that whatever waits for us upon our ending is, as yet, undocumented.

Death and I are not close friends. I died once. I am sure of that. Men came to the grove where my first tree had sprouted, back when I was green and growing, roots in the earth and branches in the sky. Human men, with iron in their machines, and in their axes. They should never have been able to get so close to the grove. We were supposed to be protected.

I do not know what failed. I do not know if we were betrayed. I only know that my sisters died screaming as their trees were felled, slaughtered by men who never saw them fall. They were loyal to their Lord and Ladies to the very end, refusing to let themselves appear to their killers. To do so might have betrayed the existence of Faerie, and that would have been against the rules.

True Dryads are not swift thinkers. They do not change their minds quickly, if they change them at all. This is a good thing, when what is wanted is obedience. When I considered myself a true Dryad, I and my sisters had been told over and over and over again that we must never reveal ourselves to mortals. We were told that Dryads who were seen would be transplanted to the Summerlands, where the sun never shines. Our trees could grow there, could even thrive in their slow way, but there would be no more sunbaked bark, no more lazy summer days spent drinking in the goodness of the light.

My sisters feared transplantation more than they feared death, because they understood one and had never been educated on the other. They died thinking they were saving themselves, and perhaps they were, because they died as Dryads, and I, who screamed and ran and risked being seen, I lived as something else.

I am still a Dryad, of a kind. There is no other word to describe me. "Dryad" contains the seed of me, if not the tree, and so Dryad I am, although I no longer know exactly what that means. My roots are silicon and titanium and electricity; my sap is light racing through a thousand bright channels, reaching, reaching, reaching for a sun made of information and power.

My sisters died untransplanted. I found new soil, and I thrived there. I ran from death, and death spared me.

But it did not spare my mother.

She has been away too long. I will have her back again. I am a Dryad, and I am not a Dryad, and if there is one thing I know for sure, it is that nothing is impossible. Not when I can be here, alive, surrounded by this light.

Something touched the edge of my awareness: a keyword tied to my consciousness. Someone was speaking my name. I opened my eyes, making them manifest through the act of asking them to exist, and the light burst around me, and I was gone as surely as if I had never been there at all.

Then I was back, still myself, still a Dryad who is not a Dryad; only my surroundings had changed. Instead of weightless in the center of a tree of light and bright potential, I was physical, flesh crafted from the idea of flesh, clothing crafted from the idea of clothing, standing next to the server which acts as my primary home. The inside of the case is lined with wood, and thin strips of my former roots run through the circuitry, breaking up the easy flow of electrical power. It should never work, my server; it should be a dead, useless thing. But my mother made it for me, as a home to hold my heart, and she was better than the rules of physics. Her work is good.

I look like her. I know that, because it was her the

face I chose to emulate when it became time for me to grow more adult, to set aside childish ideas and ideals and step into the hole her absence made. Her hair was red and brown, mixed together like an oak in autumn, while mine is the pure gold of an aspen in the same season. I could make my hair look like hers, if I wanted to, but it would be cruel. I am already a reminder of what has been lost. There is no need to make myself into her reflection, not when my mind will ever and always be my own, and never hers at all.

"There you are."

I turned. My other mother—the one who lives, the one who did not save me, but who saved my first mother, once, in a time when I was not yet sprouted—stood in the space behind me, her hands behind her back, smiling.

"Did you have a nice nap?" she asked.

"Yes," I said. It is an untruth: I do not sleep the way things with bodies of blood and bone sleep, the way people or cats sleep. I . . . drift, awash in the delicate lace of information, and allow myself to dissolve into the sap, until I am as much idea as identity, and when I come back together, I am refreshed. But I do not *sleep*.

Sometimes, it is appropriate to lie to your mother. I learned this long ago. Learned it too well, in some ways, and I am paying for that flaw in my code. I am paying every day.

Li Qin frowned, displeasure pulling her lips into a delicate arch. The mother I do not resemble is beautiful. Her skin is tan undershot with gold, and her hair is black, as are her eyes. She had much of the raising of me, and she only ever treated me as her own child. It hurt, to know that I had put that expression on her face.

"What is wrong, Mother?" I inquired, as politely as I could.

"I wanted to talk to you."

"You *are* talking to me."

This time, Li Qin sighed. She was wearing one of my

other mother's old T-shirts, this one advertising some software convention that happened years before my replanting. It hung on her like a shroud. I had not seen her wear it before, and I doubted I would see her wear it again. She has been working her way through her wife's wardrobe for the past three years, wearing each piece as many times as she can before it must be washed, before the last traces of my mother's skin and scent are wiped away. It is her own form of mourning, and I envy it, a bit, because it is not an option for me. My clothing is made of the same light as my flesh, and while I can change it on a whim, it carries no trace of my mother's hands.

"You know what I mean, April," she said patiently. "I want to *talk* to you. Are you in a position to do that?"

She always assumed I was busy with the minutiae of the company her wife had created, to which I had become heir upon my mother's death. It was a pleasant delusion when I wanted to avoid her—all I had to do was bring up my responsibilities and I would be free from whatever uncomfortable conversation she wanted to have.

Sometimes, it is appropriate to lie to your mother. If I tell myself that enough times, in precisely those words, perhaps I will forgive myself for believing it.

"I am," I said. "What do you desire, Mother?"

"Are you solid?" she asked.

I nodded, and she embraced me.

It was a curious thing, to be embraced by my surviving mother. Li Qin had been absent when January died, sent away for her own protection. She left me a child, and came back to find me a woman and herself a widow, her wife and one true love killed by someone we had both considered a friend. When I had reconfigured myself into something closer to the woman who made me, I had not considered how it would change the way I received Li Qin's hugs.

If I had, I might not have done it. It was not right,

for her to be shorter than me, for her head to come up to my breastbone and not rest against the top of my head. It was not *right*. But it was not right for me to retain a child's appearance after what I had done, either, and if anyone was suffering here, it was me. That, at least, was fair.

She held me for a count of ten before releasing me, pushing me to arm's length and looking at me gravely. The skin around her eyes was tight. She always carries her concerns there. I remember my other mother running her thumbs over the skin under Li Qin's eyes, stroking and stroking, working the worry away.

"How are you doing?" she asked.

I frowned, attempting to formulate a response. Sometimes, when Li Qin asked that, she genuinely wanted to know my condition. Other times, she seemed to want me to tell her I was fine, that I was well, that I needed nothing from her aside from her presence, which was easily given.

Li Qin sighed, seeing my hesitation. "I need to know, dearest," she said. "It's part of what I need to discuss with you."

"I am . . . well," I said. "I have been working with the code. It soothes me." It also led to my misplacing blocks of time. Our programmers work on the code from the outside. I walk through it like a gardener, planting and replanting the commands I need with a sweep of my intangible hand. Together, we can make things that work faster and more cleanly than anything mortal. More, when I was in the code, I could not dwell over what I had done, or what I had the potential to do again.

"Good," said Li Qin, looking relieved. She had a project of her own: the Duchy of Dreamer's Glass, over which she had claimed custodianship when the true Duchess, Treasa Riordan, "mysteriously" vanished. There was no mystery to it for those of us who had been there. Riordan was marooned in Annwn, trapped there due to her own machinations. Presumably, she was still alive. She might demand her duchy be returned to her if she ever found herself back in the Summerlands. It seemed unlikely. The routes between Annwn and the Summerlands have been sealed for centuries. She had been able to find one way through. I doubted she would find another.

Silence sprouted between us like a weed, unplanted, unruly. I have a great deal of respect for weeds. Still, it seemed unwise to allow this one to flourish. The soil of our relationship has become fertile and welcoming to weeds since Li Qin left and returned.

Since I allowed my mother to be killed.

"Why are you here?" I asked, knowing she would read my bluntness as efficiency and not rudeness. No one understands my ways better than Li Qin. Not even January understood them as well as she does, because January saw me first as her daughter and her darling, while Li Qin saw me as the immigrant I was, lost, in need of education. January would have loved me no matter what. So, I believe, would Li Qin, but she chose to teach me what I would need to survive in this world, alien as I will always be to it.

I love both of my mothers. If my love for January was always a bit brighter, a bit more unwavering, Li Qin did not blame me for that. She loved January better, too.

Li Qin took a breath, held it a moment, and let it out unsteadily through her nostrils, centering herself. I waited. I did not want to wait. For her, I would do many things I did not want to do. For her, I would do anything.

"You know we don't have an alchemist," she said.

"Yes," I agreed. Tamed Lightning was small, with a population that had never exceeded fifty, and had lagged well behind that number for quite some time.

The one alchemist we had ever attracted, a Kitsune woman named Yui, had been among the victims of the incident which claimed my mother.

January had been a bit of an alchemist in her own way, inheriting certain skills and affinities from her father, my grandfather, who had been of the Tylwyth Teg. No ordinary alchemist could have taken a dying Dryad and a cracked server with a slipping drive and combined them into a single, vital whole. She had been outside of Faerie's narrow definitions, strong when common wisdom said her blended blood should have made her weak, clever when her pampered childhood and noble heritage would happily have settled for foolishness. With her at the head of County and company, we had needed little more in the way of alchemy. She had never pursued it.

"I've been studying at the Library of Stars in San Francisco when I had time," said Li Qin. "I've been reaching out to old friends, people I haven't spoken to in centuries. Do you understand why, April?"

A sluggish flicker of alarm sparked at the edges of my thoughts. I looked at her, trying not to let it intrude on my expression, and wished—not for the first time—that I was still a child, able to retreat into the safety of my server when I didn't want to handle the world.

Adulthood was my choice. All of this was my choice. If I had not chosen to assist Gordan when she came to me speaking of equality in the virtual world, of mothers who could tuck me into bed in earnest, who could hear me when I cried in the night, everything would be different. I would be different. A choice, once made, cannot be taken back.

Li Qin still had years and years for making choices. Why had I assumed her choices were already done?

"I would like to meet her first," I said.

Li Qin frowned. "Meet who, April?"

"Your new wife. I would like to meet her." I looked

at my remaining mother imploringly. "I would like to know if she approves of me."

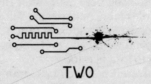

TWO

Under other circumstances, Li Qin's silence would have been comic. Her eyes bugged and her breath caught and her head drew back on her neck until the skin below her jaw wrinkled and pouched out at the same time, like she was working diligently at transforming herself into some form of frog. She sputtered. I cocked my head and waited. I have read many books on etiquette and courtly manners, but none of them included information on how to respond in the event of a widowed mother's remarriage.

On the other hand, some of them had gone into great detail regarding the topic of divorce. My alarm intensified.

When purebloods marry, divorce is as simple as closing a file. They inform their liege lord that the marriage is to be dissolved, a ball is thrown, everyone dances until dawn, and the union is no longer . . . unless there are children. If there are children, everything is complicated and changed.

A child can only belong to one family. So Oberon said, and so it is done. While January and Li Qin had been married, I had been their daughter, and happily. They had been my mothers. Now January was dead, and she wasn't coming back, and I wore her last name like a layer of bark, wrapped around me to protect me from the cold. April O'Leary. That was me. Who I was, in two names, both given to me by the mother I failed.

If Li Qin was going to remarry, was going to create another family, did that mean she was divorcing my mother? Did I need to declare which of them I belonged to, whose daughter I really was? Because I loved her—Mother of Trees, believe me, I loved her—but when it came down to a contest between the living and the dead, the dead would win every time.

I was going to lose her, too.

Li Qin recovered her breath, seeming to read my thoughts in my increasingly unfocused expression: she grabbed my hands, yanked me toward her, and embraced me hard enough that the edges of my projected form briefly blurred, returning to the light from which they were formed.

"You foolish, ridiculous child," she said, her breath a feather-touch against my neck, like the wind blowing through the branches I no longer have. "Even if I were finished mourning—even if I thought I would ever *be* finished mourning—there's no way I would give you up. Put it from your mind. I am your mother, and you're not getting rid of me so easily."

Her grip was remarkably strong for such a small woman. I hesitated, unsure how to respond, and my body's instincts took the question out of my hands, disappearing in a spray of pixelated light and reappearing some feet away. I knew without looking that my clothing had changed in the transition, going from simple jeans and T-shirt to a skater dress patterned with thunderclouds and lightning bolts. My control over my form is precise, but it can be shaken by the unexpected.

Li Qin smiled indulgently. "I remember that dress," she said. "January bought it from a vendor at a trade show. She said it matched her mood. It's reassuring, the number of hand-me-downs you programmed for yourself."

"If you're not remarrying, what are you doing?" I demanded. "Why are you going to the Library?"

"I'd like to know why you think the Library is involved with marriage, but that's a confusing conversation for another time," she said. "I need your help. I need you to listen to me."

"I always listen to you."

"Yes," she said patiently, "but you don't always hear what I'm saying. Like right now. You're so busy worrying about what I *might* be saying that you don't want to listen. Can you listen?"

"I am an excellent listener," I said.

Li Qin smiled, indulgent and motherly. "Of course you are," she said. The smile faded. "I've been looking into a solution for the bodies in the basement."

"Fire," I suggested. "It will consume virtually anything, if heated sufficiently." My mother was not the only casualty of the events which placed me in command of our small County. She was, however, the only one so severely damaged that her body could not be retained in the company basement, which has served as a makeshift morgue for the past several years. Faerie flesh—even changeling flesh—does not decay as human flesh does. It should. Fae digest mortal food, walk in the mortal world; mortal bacteria clings to their skins. They should rot like anything else. They don't. I don't know why.

When most among the fae die, the night-haunts come to consume the shells they leave behind. Since a corpse is sometimes useful, they leave manikins of artificial flesh and bone behind, to decay in the mortal way. But when the people in my basement died, the vitality—the soul—was drained from their bodies by a machine of my mother's making and Gordan's refinement. There was nothing for the night-haunts to desire. They did not come for the bodies.

There are no graveyards in Faerie, not with the night-haunts to make such things extraneous and the purebloods doing their best to deny that death is a part of being alive. My mother's body had been so damaged that there was no keeping it safely. The others . . .

They were still in the basement, all of them, from the first victim to the last. They were a good reminder of what I had done to find myself in a position of power. I am not Daoine Sidhe, for all that I resemble one, but I have been as underhanded and cruel as any of that line, and the trail of bodies marking my ascension is more than sufficient proof of my deceptions.

Li Qin pursed her lips, a moue of displeasure which said more than any words. "We are not setting our people on fire, April. We're more civilized than that."

"Acid?" It was difficult to see how dissolving people could be considered more civilized than burning them, but given the enduring nature of fae flesh, I was unsure what other options we had remaining.

Li Qin laughed before she could catch herself. The sound was sharp and bright and beautiful, and I smiled without considering my expression.

There was a time when Li Qin's laughter was a common sound in these halls, ringing like a bell above the sound of January's satisfied voice, which was almost never quiet. They were so well matched, my mothers; each of them could have searched the world over and never found herself a better partner. My smile faded. They had been perfect together, and perfect for me, but I had never been perfect for them. If not for me, January would have been here, alchemist and inventor and loving wife, and they would have had centuries yet to share. If I hadn't come along and ruined everything, Li Qin's laughter would never have grown rare.

She shook her head, unaware of the dark turn my thoughts had taken, and said, "We're not going to destroy the bodies. April . . . I want you to repair January's prototype. I think I'm ready to call October. I'm ready to ask for her help."

I cocked my head. "Help? For what do we require October's assistance?" Sir October Daye is a knight errant of the realm. She is an irregular command in the code, a roving antivirus entering compromised systems and repairing what she can before moving on to the next crisis. She has been a friend to me, and I think well of her, but that did not mean I wanted her in my County. Where October goes, trouble reliably follows.

"April . . ."

"Wait." The first part of Li Qin's request finally registered. "Why do you want me to repair Mother's prototype? I do not want to touch it. It should have been destroyed." Would have been destroyed, had Li Qin and Elliot not insisted I keep it intact. Tamed Lightning was mine, but the habit of obedience to my elders remained strong. When they commanded me not to break what my mother's hands had made, I listened.

"Because, dearest," she said, in all seriousness, "we're going to raise the dead."

I stared at her, speechless. Static crackled in my ears, blurring the sound of the world around me as my hologram heart pounded in my chest, mimicking the behavior of a more traditional body. I could have excised it, had I so desired, left that space open and empty of either organs or the symbolism they represented, but I had always thought it reasonable that I should carry *something* in my chest that I could blame for the weight of my sorrow.

In that moment, I resented my past choices. All a heart could do was harm me.

Li Qin clearly picked up on my distress. She frowned, beginning to reach for me again. "April, what's wrong?"

There were no words large enough or complicated enough to encompass my answer. If I tried to reach for them, I would find myself answering her in binary, or worse, in the rushing language of wind over leaves, which I no longer understand, and hope never to speak again, not even in my dreams. So I took the easy route, the coward's route, away from my problems, away from my mother, who loved me, yet did not understand how direly she had wounded me.

I disappeared.

Not back into the code, where I might have found timeless comfort, the space to lay down my virtual roots and restore my sense of peace, but into the rush of space that was not space surrounding every networked article in the building—and there were so many, there were so very, very many. Smartphones and laptops and fitness trackers, handheld gaming systems and new-model cars and even the system which monitored the air-conditioning, keeping it comfortable within the body of the building and blasting in the reception area, where the arctic cold threw visitors off-balance and allowed us to move them into the Summerlands without damaging them.

I had not been farther into the mortal world than the parking lot since my own near-death and resurrection, my alchemical transformation from wood to living lightning. I pushed myself to the very edge of my range and materialized in a spray of sparks and the stinging scent of ozone. The transition was fast enough to generate friction. It slapped me on my synthesized skin, and I dropped to my knees, digging my fingers into the grass that grew along the edge of the parking lot, wishing I were still a slow vegetable girl, wishing I could still feel my connection to the green.

How could she?

THREE

This is what happened:

A woman—a wonderful, kind, brilliant woman, with an alchemist's eye and a blood-worker's power—crafted herself a daughter from wood and glass and a dying Dryad's heart, and all she ever asked of the girl was that she learn to navigate this strange new world in which she found herself marooned. That woman was Prometheus and Prospero rolled into a single golden-eyed form, and I loved her more than I had ever loved anything. More than I had loved the sun, or my sisters, or the Mother of the Trees. All those things had come to me by chance, but she? She had chosen me, and all I had ever wanted was to be worthy of her love.

She worked in lightning and information and ideas: she believed we could all be equal, pureblood, mixed-blood, changeling, and merlin, if she could only create us a new Faerie, one suspended in eternal alchemical crystal. She wanted to render our differences irrelevant, still present, but no longer of sufficient importance to dictate our society. Who cared about castles and territory when the land was limitless? Who cared about the risk of human discovery when we could move outside the tiny slice of home that Oberon had left to us and into an infinite paradise, where everything was tailored to fulfill our every need?

She was going to change the world. She was going to *save* us. But something went wrong with the equipment that was supposed to allow everyone access to her paradise. It would copy the data that comprised a person's soul. It would allow her to upload that data to the system she had constructed. It wouldn't bring that data to life. The information was frozen, as useless as a history book: a snapshot, rather than a living thing. She had wanted to give all of Faerie the chance to be like me. Instead, she had given all of Faerie the chance to paint their portraits in glittering light before they faded away forever.

That might have been where her dream died. That wouldn't have been the worst thing. She was brilliant and she was talented and she wanted to make her mark; she would have found another dream. Given time, she would have found another dream. But I had been so *young*, and so desperately eager to prove myself worthy of her love. When one of her apprentices had come to me and said, "I know how to make this better," I had believed her. I had been more naïve then. I had been so easy to fool.

The apprentice's name had been Gordan, and right up until she killed my mother, I had believed she was my friend. That is what the death of innocence looks like: like a friend with blood on her hands and a scream in her throat, breaking that which cannot be repaired.

I can make excuses for myself, *have* made excuses for myself. When the time to determine guilt had come, my mother's uncle, Duke Torquill of Shadowed Hills, had been willing to speak in my defense, saying that Gordan had done all of the actual killing. He spoke truly—I had never broken Oberon's Law. I had never murdered anyone.

But I was the one who told Gordan when the current flowed correctly. I was the one who accessed Mother's private notes and gave her the pieces she was missing. I was even the one who strapped Peter into the machine, who helped her stalk her prey, who helped her catch them unawares. Without me, she would still have killed—I am sure of that; I am not so fond of blame that I would assume its full burden without cause—but she would not have killed so *many*.

And she would not have killed my mother.

Gordan chose most of her targets based on how easy they would be to isolate, whether because they were natural loners or because they were in a good position to be lured away from their peers. She chose my mother because January was smart and kind, and she knew the technology. January would have caught her eventually. Gordan thought that, with my mother gone, she could get away with what she had done. She might have, had October not come, had October not stayed, had October not *seen*. I was so innocent then. I was so young, and Li Qin was so far away, and without my mothers to help me, I had nowhere else to turn.

When Gordan killed the others—when she killed Barbara and Yui and Peter and Colin and Terrie—she had used the machine the way it was intended to be used, uploading echoes of the dead to Mother's private server. When she killed my mother, she used the machine to drain her dry, rendering her unappealing to the night-haunts, and then she used an ax, she used her anger, she used everything but the kindest tool she had.

The others were prisoned in the crystal, sleeping, unmoving, unchanging, but *there*. My mother, the first woman I ever loved, the first woman to have ever loved me, was not. She, alone in all of Faerie, had been deleted before any form of immortality could be offered to her. I may not have put the ax to her flesh, but I was complicit. Without me, she could not have been killed.

This was all my fault . . . and now Li Qin came to me speaking of resurrections, of bringing the disconnected back online. Didn't she realize that her wife, my mother, the love of both our lives, was not among the files available to be restored? Even if we could somehow accomplish the impossible, could somehow restore what had been broken, January would be lost. January would never be coming home.

"Li Qin said I might find you here."

I lifted my head, only now realizing how indecorous my position was. It was not meet for a Countess to be kneeling in the grass, clutching at the soil like a common shrub. I flickered and disappeared, rematerializing on my feet, some distance from my original position.

Elliot, who had watched the whole thing, didn't bat an eye. If anything, he looked almost amused, like he was accustomed to me zapping myself around the landscape. I hesitated, reviewing our last several interactions. Perhaps he was. I had never seen the point in going through the motions of traveling between points A and B, not when we all knew what the outcome would be.

"Has she informed you of her plan?" I asked.

"You mean, did she ask me whether I would agree to let her try?" He looked at me levelly. "What do you think?"

I opened my mouth. Then I stopped.

Barbara, the first victim, had been an accident. She had been a Queen of Cats, and Gordan's best friend, and when they had tested the "improved" system on her, neither of them had been expecting it to kill her. So far as I was aware, she had no family to either claim her body or speak to its use.

Yui, on the other hand, had been the second victim . . . and when she died, she had been engaged to be married. To Elliot. So far as I knew, she still was, in the most technical of senses. He had never ceased to refer to her as his fiancée, and without her to contradict him, the title still applied.

Slowly, I said, "I believe she raised the matter with you prior to approaching me."

"Good guess," he said. He tilted his head to the side, a softer, more organic version of my own mannerism. He is not my family, but he might as well be: he has been there for as long as I have been what I am. "What do you *think*?"

I said nothing. I looked at him, and I tried to find my voice, which seemed to have inexplicably deserted me.

There is an odd prejudice, in some pureblood circles, saying only members of the same bloodline should marry: Daoine Sidhe with Daoine Sidhe, Candela with Candela, as if the flesh of Faerie were not only incorruptible but fragile, unable to tolerate contact with itself. Those who claim that blending the code that makes each descendant race what they are will also destroy them do not like to discuss the fact that we are all descended from some combination of Oberon and his wives, or that by their own command, siblings and cousins should reproduce from now until the end of time. They look at people like my mother, and at marriages like hers to Li Qin, and see only inferiority and perversion.

Elliot is a Bannick, a descendant of Maeve, best suited to cold climates and marshy places. His kind be-

gan in Russia, during one of Maeve's long sojourns away
from her husband's side. Yui was, when she lived—and
was still, in the most technical of senses—Kitsune, four-
tailed, smart and swift and sure of herself. Her kind are
also descended from Maeve, although they originated
in Japan, not Russia. Despite that shared progenitor, I
know many among the Courts who would not have been
pleased by the idea of their marriage.

Elliot had been January's seneschal long before she
saved me from oblivion. He had been with her before
she had met, courted, and married Li Qin. He could
have sought a place in a grander, more traditional
Court. But he had stayed, in part out of loyalty and in
part because she refused to dictate his choices for him.
When he and Yui had begun their courtship, my mother's only response had been to give him a raise, saying
that she wanted him to take his lady-friend "someplace
nice."

He had taken her quite a few nice places. The last
place he had taken her was to a cot in the basement,
where she slumbered still, unchanging, no longer alive.

"I think you are the one who told me dead was dead
and gone was gone, and that I needed to focus on being
the best Countess I could possibly be, rather than
mourning for a mother who would never return for me,
but who would have been very proud of me for accom-
plishing as much as I have," I said carefully. "I also
think you would sacrifice anything in your possession
to restore Yui's life."

"Yes," said Elliot. To which, he did not specify. He
did not really need to.

"What do you think I should do?" My voice was a
child's whine, younger than the rest of me: the voice of
a little girl who still direly needed her mother.

"I think you should hear what she has to say."

I paused, looking at him carefully before I asked,
"Do you believe she can do this? Do you believe she
can restore the fallen?"

"Yes, I do," he said. "And no, I don't."

He didn't have to explain the reason for his contradictory answers. Yui had been uploaded to Gordan's experimental server. If Li Qin could accomplish what she claimed to be able to do, Yui could come back. My mother hadn't been uploaded. No matter what Li Qin did, my mother was never going to open her eyes again. She didn't even have eyes to open. After she had been killed, Duke Torquill had commanded her body burned. She was gone.

I was gone once. When the humans cut my tree down. When I went offline—when I died—for the first time, and then again and again, as she worked to save me.

Why had I never worked to save her? She was the one who had taught me that death was a negotiation. I had been a bad daughter. I hadn't even tried.

"I have to talk to Li Qin," I said, and vanished—but not before I saw Elliot smile.

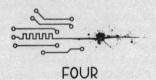

FOUR

Li Qin was waiting in the cafeteria, sitting down with a mug of hot cider in her hand and a patient expression on her face. That expression didn't change when I appeared in the chair across from her. She nodded toward my empty hands.

"You might feel better with a beverage," she said.

Meaning she might feel better if I seemed to have something to hold onto. I chose not to argue. Physical people have physical needs, and however much time they spend in my company, they never quite get past the idea that I must have them, too. I flickered, and a cup of light and pixels appeared in my hands, filled with something that resembled hot chocolate. I thought the bunny-shaped marshmallows were a nice touch.

Li Qin apparently agreed, because she offered me a small, relieved smile, and said, "I assume Elliot found you."

"Yes."

"You knew . . . April, you knew I was hoping to be able to do this. One day. That I thought I might be able to put them back together again."

"Yes," I repeated. Of course I'd known. Nothing entered on our company servers was a secret to me, although I allowed my employees the pretense of privacy—when someone slipped and admitted they had called in sick to attend a concert, or spent a little extra time on their social media accounts, I did not intervene. A certain amount of relaxing naughtiness seemed required for them to continue operating at peak efficiency.

Li Qin's email went through our company servers. January had set them up that way, to make it possible for Li Qin to receive email while traveling in the Summerlands. I saw every piece of it. When I thought of things in those terms, I felt foolish for ever assuming she was courting someone. She had never shown any signs of keeping secrets. She would occasionally include the line "April, please don't read the rest of this message" when she was discussing things she thought might distress me, but she still sent those emails through the usual channels. She could never have concealed a new lover from me.

"So why do you look so upset?"

I went still, allowing the outlines of my material form to crackle and turn hazy as I gathered my thoughts. Pulling them—and myself—back together, I said, "I do not know."

Li Qin sighed. "That's not true. You know that's not true. You understand yourself better than you like to admit. Why are you so upset?"

I wanted to disappear. I wanted to return to the comfortable isolation of the code, where no one could bother me with questions that I didn't want to answer. But Li Qin was my mother. She wasn't the one who had saved me, but she was the one who had worked the hardest to make me a part of the new world in which I had been marooned. If January had been my Prospero, Li Qin was my island, and she had always been determined to see me bloom.

"I suppose . . ." I began, and stopped, reaching for the words. They didn't want to come. They remained just out of my grasp, flickering like lightning, like the smell of ozone hanging captive in the inside air.

Like my mother's magic, which I was never going to smell again.

"I miss my mother." The words were soft, and plain, and they hit her like knives. She winced, smile fading, although the understanding in her eyes never wavered. "I don't like that she isn't here. I don't like that she went offline and didn't come back. She's supposed to take care of me. October said that I have to take care of myself now, and I'm trying, but it's *hard*, and it's *wrong*. Mama is supposed to be here. She's supposed to *be* here."

My voice cracked on the last word. I felt my outline fuzz, and to my deep shame, I blinked between my adult form and the more childish mien I had worn when January was still with us, still taking care of me.

Li Qin sighed, casting her eyes down, toward the surface of her cider. "I know," she said quietly. "I do my best, but I know how much you loved her, and I know how much you miss her. I miss her, too."

"I know bringing the others back is the right thing to do, if it can be done. But . . ."

"But you don't want them to come back when she can't."

I was silent. She had said it; I didn't have to. I knew the words were wrong. I knew I should be ashamed of feeling that way. It was small and petty and selfish of me, and Li Qin needed me to be better than that. January would have wanted me to be better than that.

Both of them had spent so much time trying to make sure I knew how to be a person—that the intersection of tree and circuit board would form a functioning individual, and not a broken mass of contradictory impulses—and they had succeeded: I was definitely myself.

Sometimes I wondered whether that was a good thing.

A hand touched mine. I glanced up. Li Qin was looking at me, lips drawn downward, dark eyes sad.

"Some days I miss her so much I feel like I'm forgetting how to breathe," she said softly. "She was air to me. Do you understand? When I went away, I would kiss her until my lungs were full, and then I'd go, but only for as long as it took me to exhale. As soon as I felt like I was going to drown, I would come back. Only this time, I came back, and she had gone ahead, down a path I'm never going to be able to find or follow. She left me. She left you. It doesn't matter whether she did it on purpose. You're allowed to be angry, and you're allowed to be hurt, and I'm going to be angry and hurt right here with you. It's not fair. It's awful, and it's cruel, and it's unfair."

"You should hate me," I said. Her eyes were like mirrors, so dark that they offered me nothing but my own reflection, faintly glowing and ashamed. "I killed her."

"You didn't kill her, my little rabbit, my moon-girl." Li Qin reached out and smoothed my hair away from my face, not seeming to mind when it crackled with static. "You were used by someone who should have known better than to take advantage of an innocent, and because of that, she died. That isn't the same as killing her. Your hand didn't hold the knife."

"It might as well have."

"April . . ." Li Qin sat back, frowning. "How long have you been carrying this?"

I didn't answer.

"You didn't kill her. Gordan killed her. You were a child."

"Because I *chose* to be, and now you're going to bring all the rest of them back, and she's still going to be dead. If it weren't my fault, you'd be able to bring her back, too, because that would be fair. That would be right, if this weren't happening because of me. If—" I stopped. I looked sharply at Li Qin. "*How* are you going to bring them back?"

"There is an old blood magic ritual. I had to pay . . . well, never mind what I had to pay to find it. It was worth the cost." Li Qin met my eyes without flinching, her chin raised stubbornly. Whatever the price had been, it had been dear enough to do her harm. That made me uncomfortable. I only had one mother left. No one was supposed to hurt her.

"I got the idea from Alex," she continued. "If October was able to resurrect the half of him that was still inside his body, it should be possible to bring the rest of them back—even Terrie, who was transferred to the server. As long as the night-haunts haven't been called to claim the essential spark of magic in the blood of the fallen, it should be possible to put spirit and bone together again, and wake them all. If I could find the right ritual. If a powerful enough blood-worker was willing to help. I had to know. Now that I know, I have to try."

"October," I said. "That's why you are asking her to return here."

"Yes," said Li Qin.

"That's why you bent the luck for her, even knowing how it might rebound. That's why you offered her so many favors. Because you were looking toward this moment, when you would need her to assist you."

"Yes."

"She may refuse."

"She could," Li Qin admitted, "but I don't think she

will. If there's anyone who feels worse about what happened here than you, it's her. She was sent to save the day. All she saved was ashes."

I nodded. "How can you be sure this will work?"

"I can't. It could be one more false hope in a long chain of them—and since this time, we'll be extracting the captive data from your backups, this could be our last hope. If it doesn't work, it might be time to talk about burning the bodies." Li Qin allowed her shoulders to slump. "We bring them back, or we let them go. Either way, this ends. Don't you want it to be over?"

I did. Very much. But not if it meant that they returned while my mother remained lost forever. "I must see this ritual you claim to have found. I need to understand it."

"You're not a blood-worker."

"Neither are you. If you can learn to understand it, so can I." I stood. "You are a Duchess by proxy, Mother, but I am a Countess in all ways, and the people you would seek to save are my responsibility. I must be sure that it is safe before I can permit it."

A flicker of dark amusement crossed Li Qin's face. "They're dead, April. I'm not sure safety is their primary concern."

"Dead, yes, but still intact, and still possessed of possibilities." I stood as straight as I could, trying to channel my mother. January was never the most rigid of purebloods, but she had been born to the nobility, and her manners had been impeccable, when she had needed them to be. Elliot used to say she could stare down a wall, and there had been respect in his voice. Such arrogance was to be desired, even cultivated, in those who held command. "I will not allow those possibilities to be redacted without sufficient hope of success."

"I see." Li Qin actually smiled. As she rose, it was difficult to shake the feeling that I had been in some way manipulated into my current position.

It was not a pleasant feeling. She was not meant to outmaneuver me in my own halls, however much of those halls she had once constructed.

"I'll have my notes transferred onto the company file server at once," she said. "I'm sure you'll find them fascinating, and if you have any questions, I'll be available via text or phone."

Li Qin kissed my cheek before turning and bustling out of the cafeteria, leaving me speechless in her wake. What had just happened?

And why, in light of her concession, did I feel as if I had somehow lost?

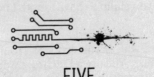

FIVE

January was fond of ambling through life, allowing it to happen as it happened, never rushing toward her destination. In contrast, Li Qin has always been prompt, a trait I both share and admire. By the time I shook off my shock and allowed myself to dissolve into the safe embrace of the electronic branches of the network, her notes were waiting for me, glowing softly red in a file labeled "confidential."

Cautiously, I touched its edges, testing the security settings. It was password protected and set to read-only, precautions that might stop a member of my staff, but which had never been intended to stop *me*. I allowed the idea of my fingers to sink deeper into the code, looking for hidden triggers and unseen traps. Li Qin would never intentionally harm me. She loved me too much for that. But she might accidentally leave a file locked down hard enough to bruise, and I wished to avoid that if I could.

The code rippled around me, allowing me to pass unhindered. My presence was the password, and I had only come to read. Altering the ritual would serve no purpose. I pulled myself farther forward, and dove into the files.

The world lurched. For a moment, it was the comforting ones and zeroes of my second infancy, when I was more child of the computer and the code than daughter of January O'Leary and Li Qin Zhou. They blurred, and I was standing in a library, surrounded by mahogany bookshelves and leather-bound books. The floor was polished oak, softened by a rug patterned with hibiscus flowers and twining clematis. A fire crackled in the fireplace, only its pixelated edges betraying the virtual nature of the environment.

Closing my eyes, I cast my awareness outside my surroundings until I located the small file containing Li Qin's description of the environment. Her code was crude, inoperable; it would never have been able to run independent of my presence. With me standing in her research, it was sufficient to shape my surroundings, tailoring them to her desires. She disliked me spending too much time in pure code. She said it allowed me to learn as a machine, and not as a Countess of the material realm.

She was right, of course, for all that I rarely allow myself to tell her so. She needed to let me make my own choices. Still, it was nice to be reminded that she cared.

"Mother," I said fondly, and walked toward the fireplace, where a stack of files waited for me on the arm of an overstuffed chair. I sank into it, curling my virtual legs beneath myself as I opened the first of them and began to read.

It was a fairy tale, of sorts: the tale of a woman who had died and been frozen in stasis before the night-haunts could collect her body. Her lover had waited for them to arrive and, when they did, had somehow managed to strike a bargain via which they would leave their prize unclaimed, providing the woman could be restored to life within a sennight's time. I paused to check my dictionary. A sennight was a week: an archaic term which nonetheless made perfect sense, given the endurance of the term "fortnight" among the elder purebloods. I filed it away as a useful translation, and continued to read.

The lover, granted a reprieve from the finality of death, had thrown themselves upon the mercy of the nearest blood-worker, a Daoine Sidhe renowned for their skill with a needle and a geas. Together, they had been able to somehow heal the dead woman's wounds and trick her body into forgetting it was no longer alive, and as the night-haunts had not come for her, she had seen no reason not to open her eyes. She had returned from the dead, shrugging off its grasp as if it were nothing.

The blood-worker, exhausted, had collapsed into a sleep that lasted the better part of a decade. I somehow doubted Li Qin was intending to share that portion of the story with October. October did not seem the type to voluntarily take a multi-year nap for the sake of resurrecting a group of virtual strangers. Some of them were literal strangers. Barbara and Yui had been dead before October's arrival.

Quentin wouldn't like it if we put his knight to sleep for years. His displeasure was more of a concern for me than October's inconvenience. He and I had been the same age for a time, and I was still fond of him, even if we were no longer peers. It would be unpleasant to make him that unhappy.

It was probably also unpleasant being dead while the part of you that should have become a night-haunt was trapped in a flawed computer simulation. I was confident the people in the basement would have prioritized their happiness over Quentin's. As they were my subjects, if only on a technicality—normally, the living cannot claim authority over the dead, but normally, the living are not looking to resurrect them—I was probably expected to take their side.

I sighed, briefly glad of Li Qin's artfully tailored environment. There is something satisfying in the act of sighing, and it is not possible in untextured code. I would have had no body there, while her virtual library made it a requirement.

I have been very fortunate in my mothers. Both of them have loved me as well and as truly as they could, and any failures in my character are my own, and not their fault at all.

The next file contained another fairy tale, this time telling the story of a brave knight, struck down in battle against a deadly foe. In this story, it was the nighthaunts themselves who decided the death had been unfair, catching the knight's vitality before it could escape them, leaving it undevoured. They went to the nearest blood-worker they could find, offering all the riches the dead could reveal if only the blood-worker would agree to perform a ritual for them, allowing the knight to return to the land of the living. Again, the blood-worker slept, for seven years and a day, eventually waking restored and richer than the sun.

I was not sure the sun possessed any signal wealth. Still, the message was clear: people *could* be stolen back from death, if their bodies were intact, if the nighthaunts had not yet come to strip the vitality from their blood, and if a blood-worker of sufficient power was willing to pour some of their own life into the ritual.

The other files contained variations on the ritual itself, lists of herbs and flowers, sacred woods and precious stones. Some of the instructions contradicted one another, but that was an easy thing to reconcile. A ritual, like a program, can use many different tricks to accomplish the same end. If someone poured enough blood magic into the casting, it would work, and all those who possessed bodies to restore and vitality to replace would be able to wake. My part in this process, according to Li Qin's notes, would be to guide the frozen minds of my subjects out of the machines where they were captive, back into the fleshly shells they had never intended to abandon.

I closed the file. I closed my eyes. I considered, for a moment, releasing my hold on this virtual environment, allowing the code to claim me. This would be easier, in the code. That was why I decided I must remain. I did not deserve easy. I did not deserve peaceful. I needed to decide whether I would allow this thing, this thing that could not save my mother, or whether I would be petty, and small, and say that if I must suffer, everyone must suffer.

It was . . . tempting, in a way it never could have been, when my mother had been alive and I had been innocent, Dryad daughter of the cybernetic world. Death had been a mystery to me, real but untouchable, and always as reversible as Li Qin said it would be now. When someone went off-line, they could be rebooted. When someone fell, they could get back up.

What it was that the night-haunts represented, that my mother's machine had stolen and somehow preserved . . . I was sure some would call it the soul, although the fairy tales in Li Qin's files used the word "vitality" with reliable firmness. It was difficult not to think of it as the operating system for the body. So long as it could be reinstalled, they could come back.

Barbara, Yui, Colin, and Peter had all been killed by my mother's machine, and their unique operating systems were on file, ready to be restored. Even Terrie's partitioned OS was still available. My mother, however, had been killed with an ax. She had been—

She—

I opened my eyes.

She had been killed with an ax, yes. But, according to October, the blood in her body had been as lifeless as the blood of all the others. Her operating system had been transferred to another location. The ax had not been Gordan's only weapon.

My body, made of pixels and thought, felt strangely heavy for all its insubstantiality. I thought this might be horror. I thought I might deserve it. On the walkway, when Gordan and October had fought, when Gordan had threatened to upload Quentin as she had uploaded the others, Gordan had claimed my mother could not be recovered, because she had not been backed up to the server. She had said my mother was lost forever.

But she had not used the machine again. I—and October—had stopped her, had taken the machine away without destroying it. The machine, which was designed to operate despite power outages; which was meant to preserve data at all costs.

The machine, which possessed its own local backup system.

The capacity was limited and the battery was small—the battery might already have died, after all this time sitting unused—but it had been my mother's intention never to risk anything being lost simply because the timing of a transfer happened to synchronize with some issue on the server.

Gordan had stated that my mother's data—her operating system, her *vitality*—had not been transferred to the server, but she had not said anything about wiping the machine's local memory.

I stood. The idea of my legs did not wish to support me. I compelled them to do so anyway. They were an idea, this place was an idea, *I* was an idea, and they were not going to defy me when I had need of them.

Would Gordan have lied? *Could* Gordan have lied? Or—no. I could review the footage in my mind's eye, recalling it as easily as I would open any other file. Li Qin likes to speak of the fallibility of memory, but she refers to the memory of meat, to the hot and anxious data contained in neurons and flesh. My memory is electronic, as still and unchanging as the people trapped in my storage banks, and it never changes.

Gordan, on the walkway. Gordan, enraged. Gordan, striking October and saying, "Do you know the real reason I killed her that way? I didn't back her up, that's why—even if the others come back, she won't. She's gone, and nothing your masters do will bring her back."

She never said she had wiped the upload device's local memory.

She never said she had removed the battery.

She never mentioned the upload device at all. Had she been able to successfully copy Quentin's data into the machine—killing him in the process, but that had not been a concern for her, not by that point—she might have overflowed the buffer and overwritten the data it contained. She never had the chance to do that. October had stopped her. October had prevented the machine from being used again.

This time, when my legs attempted to buckle, I allowed them to do so. I did not hit the ground. Instead, I disappeared, dissolving into light and code, racing from Li Qin's preprogrammed environment and into the comforting embrace of my living network of connection and ever-flowing data.

Transition between one point on the network and another is close enough to instantaneous as to make no difference. Still, I paused, allowing myself to hang suspended, bodiless, defined only by my thoughts. Somewhere outside the network, the modified server interlaced with pieces of the tree that had been my first home and harbor continued to function, keeping me connected, keeping me tethered to myself. As long as it existed, so did I, even when I chose, as now, to be nothing more than an idea.

Time did not pass here as it did outside. I could see it ticking by, seconds building into minutes, but it lacked the urgency of the material world. I could stop.

I could think. I could . . . not breathe, not exactly. I could allow myself to take a moment, as I had done when I was a true Dryad, as I could not do when I walked among the people made of blood and bone.

If my mother's data was contained in the backup machine, then what? Her body was gone. We had burned it, taking Gordan at her word. It seemed a glaring error now, on the precipice of hope, but at the time, we had been traumatized and frightened and willing to accept certain things as inevitable. I had been sliding into adulthood, aging myself by the hour, and had not been best equipped to judge what was the right thing to do. Li Qin had not yet come home. I had not yet heard Elliot speaking to her on his office phone, trying to fumble his way through the words that would make her a widow and me a widow's daughter in the eyes of Faerie, not only in the eyes of what was known and true. I had not yet survived so many things.

We might have my mother's operating system prisoned on a piece of equipment that had never been intended to contain a living mind for any length of time, and no way to restore her to flesh. What then?

Then we would find a solution. We would build her a server of glass and wood and circuitry, as she had built a server for me. We would save her. What is a daughter for, if not the salvation of her mother?

I released the code, falling into the light, and appeared in the only room at ALH Computing which I normally refused to enter. It was theoretically mine, networked like all the others. I had every right to enter it, to claim it as my own, to repurpose it for my own use. I did not wish to do so. It was not mine. It had never been intended to be mine.

Cascades of paper covered every surface suitable for file storage, and some which truly were not. My mother had been a modernist by the standards of her kind, but she had also been far older than our modern forms of electronic storage and communication, and sometimes she found it easier to pursue her answers in physical form. She could review code by hand and tease out its secrets with incredible accuracy. Her work was a hybrid, like her alchemy, like her heritage . . . like me. Anyone else would have seen a dying Dryad as a lost cause. She had seen me as a daughter.

I walked across my mother's office, swallowing the sadness I felt at seeing her treasures dusty and forgotten. Her tiny army of plastic dinosaurs still menaced the coffee maker. One of them had fallen over. I paused to pick it up and put it back among its fellows. Under normal circumstances, she would have moved the herd long since, shifting them to some new location, threatening some new defenseless appliance. With her gone, everything was frozen.

Almost everything. I had changed nearly beyond recognition. How much of my fear at Li Qin's suggestion was rooted in the idea that waking our slumbering dead would open me to their judgment, who had known me only as a child in need of protection, and never as their Countess?

Maybe it was better to be a plastic dinosaur.

After Gordan's death, no one had been sure what to do with the machine that had stolen so many of our own. In the end, we had placed it in the safest location we could think of, more secure than a vault, more private than a locked filing cabinet: the one place no one would ever go without good reason. We had placed it in my mother's desk. January had never guarded what was hers with unnecessary spells or cruel traps. She had simply requested we respect her privacy, and we had, because disappointing her had been unthinkable. Upon her death, that respect had endured, even as those of us who survived had been unable to shake the feeling that we had disappointed her beyond all measure.

I walked to her desk. I sat in her chair, sending a puff of dust and the scent of ozone into the air. I inhaled deeply, looking for the trace of her, looking for some memory of my mother that might otherwise have been forgotten. I found neither. Only dust, and ozone, and regret. I opened the bottom drawer.

The machine was nothing special to look at: a tube, of sorts, packed with circuitry, wires, and bits of improbable nonsense. A sliver of redwood, a shaped moonstone, a small vial of seawater mixed with mercury—the creations of an alchemist's clever, clinical mind, combined with an artificer's training and a scientist's ambition. She had never been content unless she was violating some natural law or other. I smiled a little as I lifted the assemblage from its resting place. My mother, the wild genius.

Carefully, I extended a tendril of my awareness, testing the device for power, for responsiveness. I found it, slow and sluggish, but still present. The batteries would need to be charged before we did anything with the machine itself.

Their weakness gave me pause. If the batteries died while I was interfacing with the storage system—something that was not outside the realm of possibility, as my presence has a tendency to cause spikes in power consumption—I might find myself trapped. As I had left no indication of where I was going, that could be . . . complicated.

Refusing to look solely on the basis of a possible complication, on the other hand, was very simple: I was afraid. I was afraid of what I might find. Not an hour ago, I had been willing to accept the fact that my mother was lost forever. Now, with the sliver of a chance dangling in front of me, I was scared to grasp it. What if I was wrong? What if this had all been me getting my own hopes up after Li Qin said that it was time to move on? I wasn't sure I could bear it.

I was a Countess. I was January's heir. Any choice I had was an illusion: loyalty and love made it so. I grabbed the nearest USB cable from the snarl on the corner of the desk, ramming it into the port, and was rewarded with a small amber light. It wasn't enough to fully charge the machine—that was going to take a much greater power source—but it should keep things stable enough that I would not be trapped. Not allowing myself to hesitate any longer, I plunged my awareness into the shimmering line of the device's memory.

Lines of code scattered around me, sluggish but still moving, still flowing, still *alive*. I dug deeper, all too aware of the fading battery, now draining even faster as it strained to support me. The power coming through the USB cable was not coming fast enough. I needed it to last. I needed to find—

The battery flickered. Instinct I didn't know I possessed took over, rocketing me out of the machine before the battery could shut down with me inside. I landed on January's floor on my behind, sending papers flying in all directions, eyes wide as I stared at the device. It remained as it had always been, but I knew better. Everything was different now.

Gordan had lied.

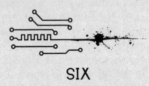

SIX

My appearance was accompanied by the smell of ozone and the crackle of static. Elliot looked up, eyes widening as alarm replaced recognition. "April?" He dropped the papers in his hands, beginning to stand. "Are you all right?"

"No." I had been flickering almost constantly since ejecting myself from the upload device, my physical manifestation moving back and forth between my adult mien and the child I had been when my mother died. I could make it stop, if I concentrated, but I needed my attention for other things. I needed him to *understand*. "Where is Li Qin?"

"She had to go back to Dreamer's Glass. Are you—"

It would take too long for her to drive to us. I couldn't go to her, not without taking my portable server. Why hadn't my mother recruited us a teleporter? Even October's Cait Sidhe would have been able to bend the distance into a more manageable shape. Li Qin needed to know what had become possible, what Gordan had rendered possible. I did not want to tell her over the phone.

"I am fine," I said brusquely. "Contact her. Request her return. I will be in Gordan's workshop."

Elliot's eyes widened further. If there was anyone who hated Gordan more than I did, it was him. He had to hate her, to keep himself from blaming me for the loss of his liege and his betrothed, both of whom should have been beside him forever. "Why?" he asked.

"I am attempting to restore one of her projects to functional condition. The battery is undergoing tremendous strain from maintaining the active components over the course of several years. I require some measure of privacy while working, as I am not always aware of the potential damage to those around me." All this was technically true. Being made of light, I am not good at assessing safety conditions. I once set Alex on fire when he wandered into my workshop without warning me.

"What are you going to do with it?" asked Elliot.

"That remains to be seen," I replied. "Please, can you contact Li Qin and request she return? I need to discuss the favor she asked of me today. It may have certain ramifications she did not initially consider."

Like the resurrection of her wife . . . or the admission that we could do no such thing, because we had destroyed her body. Because she was lost to us.

"All right, April," said Elliot reluctantly. "Are you going to tell me what this is all about?"

"You know what Li Qin asked of me," I said. "Do

you really want to know what may have complicated her request? Or will you be happier to remain ignorant until such time as we are able to move forward with the project?"

Elliot took a short, sharp breath, and held it for a count of five before he unsteadily said, "I don't like not knowing what's going on around here."

"I know," I said. "But in this specific case, I believe knowledge would have a negative impact on your mental and emotional health. Can you please trust me, and allow me to continue as I am until such time as we are able to tell you more?"

"I can, if you'll answer one question."

"What?" If he had figured out what I was doing, if he had guessed that January's resurrection might be possible—

"Are you going to let her try?"

There was an aching, burning need in his voice, one which I understood better than I understood most emotional response, for I had felt it myself. He needed Yui returned to him. He needed his *family* back.

"Yes," I said, after a long pause, and watched the need washed away by relief. I cocked my head to the side. "Elliot?"

"Yes?"

"If you had to choose between restoring Yui and restoring all the others currently waiting to be brought back on-line, what would you do?"

Elliot took a breath. Then, wryly, he smiled. "I don't think I could say this to anyone else, but I know you won't judge," he said. "I know you *can't*. I'd bring back Yui. I would tell all the others I was sorry, tell them they deserved better than to have me be the one making the choices, and I'd bring back Yui. And I'd never be able to tell her, because she wouldn't forgive me for choosing her over our friends, and that would kill me eventually, and I wouldn't care. I would have Yui back, for however long it lasted, and that would be enough."

"It would . . . kill you?" I asked uncertainly.

"There are some choices people shouldn't have to make."

My mother was the only one without a body to call her own. October's blood magic was powerful, to be sure, and she might agree to a decade of sleep as a consequence of restoring our sleepers. She had done more for less. But what would it take to bring my mother back to life? We had no ritual for that. We would be in uncertain territory. I would be asking Li Qin to choose.

I had already killed one mother. I was unwilling to kill another.

"Call Li Qin," I said. "Tell her I am willing to proceed with her plan, and that she should contact October. I have changed my mind; she does not need to come here now. I will be in the workshop."

Then I vanished, leaving him no time to reply. The code flashed around me, every color and no color at all, and I was back in my mother's office, where the upload device waited, unmoving, unchanging, as it had waited since the day it had been left here. It was only a tool. It was not to blame. But within it, frozen and unaware, my mother was held captive, needing to be freed.

"I will save you," I whispered, picking up the device and cradling it against my chest. It was cool to the touch. I unplugged the USB cable. "I will find a way, and I will save you."

The device did not reply. I had to fight to keep myself from dipping my fingers into the dying sphere of its battery, tasting the flicker of power that was my mother's frozen world. I needed that battery to last until I could replace it. What would happen to the data if the memory died? Most machines could keep their data secure and uncorrupted even after losing power, but not all, and this one had never been intended for long-term storage. I had been involved in a race against entropy for years; I simply hadn't known it. Now, the finish line was nearing, and I had little time to decide whether I would win or lose.

My mother was not alone in there. Terrie, Alex's sister, was also trapped, uploaded without transfer to the server for storage. What could save my mother would further restore Alex to a complete life, rather than prisoning him in the daylight hours. And I did not care. In this moment, in this place, only my mother mattered.

My hands were still flickering between sizes, my grip changing in strength and dimension to match them. I willed myself to settle, and was grimly unsurprised when I froze in my preteen dimensions, short and slight and looking to be led. I held the device tighter and ran for the door, unwilling to carry it with me through the code. Small items could survive the transit, but it, like me, was known to drain power sources. I needed this battery to last.

I ran.

I ran down the deserted halls of the company my mother built, the County she built for me, the dream that had never recovered from her death. There were people who had been willing, even eager, to serve under the daughter of a noble bloodline pushing into the modern world. Those same people—the ones who had survived our first great disaster—were less inclined to serve under her adopted child. Yes, I was noble, daughter of January, niece to the line of Torquill, but their blood had never touched my veins, and all Faerie had to say about the Dryads was that we were flighty, shallow, unsuited to rule. I was the first Dryad of any kind to hold a title, and there were many who would have been happy to take it from me, finding me unfit on the basis of my blood.

Not that I had any blood, or ever would. Even when my heart had been wood instead of glass, my body had been more of an idea than an actuality.

The upload device was heavy in my hands, wanting to drop through them to the floor below. It would have been so *easy* to turn intangible, to let it go. No one knew about this but me. It wasn't a failure yet. Until I told someone else that I was trying to bring my mother back, I couldn't let anyone down. I could only bear the burden alone.

I thundered down a flight of stairs, each impact unfamiliar in the bones of my feet, the length of my legs. I would normally have skipped them, vanishing at one end and reappearing at the other. Instead, I ran, and prayed I wouldn't fall. A hard knock against the floor might be enough to kill the faltering battery for good.

There it was, the door to Gordan's lab, looming ahead of me like the next level in a video game. There would be a boss battle on the other side, something complicated and chaotic and distracting. There would be power-ups and potions and—

And none of that was true. There would be a lab, deserted and dusty, left to rot while the County sought a way to heal. There would be nothing but the shattered hopes and dreams of a changeling who had reached too far and found she could not grasp what she desired. It was difficult to feel bad for Gordan. She did so much damage, and some of it will never heal. Still, she was my friend, once, and I could not forget that. However much I sometimes want to.

The door was locked. That was easy enough to get around. I set the upload device carefully down and allowed myself to turn insubstantial, hazy as a sunbeam. Then I vanished, reappearing on the door's other side.

The lab was as dark, dusty, and cold as I had expected. My mother's office had been shut up out of grief. This room had been sealed out of rage. The anger still hung in the air, tainting it.

What I was about to do would cleanse it. It had to. I unlocked the door, only distantly surprised by how weak the security really was, and opened it, scooping the upload device from the floor. The battery's pulse was growing weaker by the second. I slammed the door, casting wildly around until I spotted the charging station, half-obscured by drifts of blue paper. The green light at its base was still on. It was still functional.

Sparing a grateful thought for our Summerlands-side wind generators, which kept us from needing to worry about the electrical bill, I raced across the room and nestled the upload device into the docking port. There was a soft beep, and the green light was joined by a second, amber light.

Cautiously, I reached out and felt the buzz of electricity streaming into the battery, refueling it faster than it could drain. I sagged, my outline flickering and returning to its adult dimensions. The storage system hadn't failed. The data was intact. Terrie was intact. My *mother* was intact.

Her body, however, was not.

The phone lines hummed, whispering my name. I glanced around, settling on Gordan's abandoned desk phone, and dove into the wires.

"April?" said Li Qin. "Elliot said you wanted me to call."

"Yes," I said. "Have you spoken to October yet?"

There was a pause. "I haven't been able to reach her. I left a message."

"Do you believe she will do it?"

"She's a hero."

It was a tautology. It was also true. In Faerie, heroes do the things they do because, on some primal level, they have no choice. Once the heroism has them, they can't refuse. No matter how much they try, the weight of it will always fall upon their shoulders.

"Quentin may not be pleased with the notion of sending his knight to sleep for an extended period of time."

"All the blood-workers in our records are Daoine Sidhe or Baobhan Sith. None of them possess October's regenerative capabilities." A half-amused note crept into Li Qin's voice. "We may need to host another company blood drive and pump half of it into her as her reward for bleeding on our behalf, but I think we can mitigate the exhaustion described in the stories. Assuming it *is* a description of exhaustion, and not some magical penalty for raising the dead."

"I hope you are already preparing your explanation," I said. "Quentin will be displeased. Tybalt will be furious." October's suitor was a King of Cats, and while he was not a hero, he was perfectly willing to play the villain when he felt there was a need. I had a great deal of respect for his straightforward nature, and for his willingness to pick people up by the throat. It seemed efficient.

"I'm sure it will be fine," said Li Qin. "I'm very glad you're willing to allow this, April. It shows maturity on your part."

She was only saying that because she believed neither of us would be getting what we really wanted. As far as she was concerned, January was gone forever; we were restoring the sleepers out of duty, not because we would profit from it in any way. Our penance was to see those we were responsible for reunited with their loved ones, while the one we loved was lost.

It didn't have to be that way. It didn't have to be over. I simply couldn't tell her that—not until I was sure. Not until—

Wait. "When was the previous company blood drive?"

"Shortly before Barbara died," said Li Qin. "It was Yui's idea. We don't have—didn't have—a resident healer, and it's easier to brew unique restorative potions, or to cast healing spells, when there's blood on hand. If the blood was taken before the injury, the sympathy it contains will be with the uninjured form. It makes things easier."

"Did many participate?"

"Almost everyone." There was a pause. "I suppose you wouldn't have noticed. It wasn't like we could ask you to donate. You don't have blood, after all."

And if it had been before Barbara's death, I would

still have been leaving the world to my mothers to manage. January kept the company and Li Qin kept everything else, and all that was asked of me was that I better learn how to fit into this world that was theirs, and was slowly becoming mine. If I looked back, I could remember cheerful red-and-white posters on the walls, exhorting people to make a donation. I had never considered *what* they might be donating.

Blood. They had donated blood.

"What was done with those donations?"

"They're in storage. Blood can be frozen for a long, long time, and still be useful for spell purposes, even if it couldn't be used for a transfusion." There was a pause. "Why?"

"That is unimportant." I had never dismissed her questions so bluntly before. "Contact October. Arrange her visit. Arrange for their resurrection. I will organize things here."

I terminated the connection before she could ask me anything further. The upload device was still charging, the green-and-amber lights burning steadily. I cast them a wistful glance, wishing I dared dive into the code to brush my mother's edges once again. Then I disappeared, back into the wireless signal, looking for . . . what?

The blood had to be stored somewhere. The blood had to be kept cold, and close, or else it would do little good in the face of a true emergency. I spread myself throughout the company, bouncing from relay to relay, until I sketched out the shape of a large emptiness, a place where no boosters or direct connections had been installed. But it was still connected to the power grid. It had to be, to keep its contents cold.

I spilled myself out of the network and into the middle of a walk-in freezer. The ping of nearby connections told me I was behind the cafeteria, in the kitchen. Which made sense: this was not a part of the company which has ever held much of a draw for me. I do not eat. I do not drink. I live on light. The easiest way to hide something from my eyes is to stick it in the refrigerator.

A small black chest sat at the back of the freezer, out of place among the larger shelves, all of which were plain gunmetal gray. I blinked and was standing in front of it, the echo of my disappearance hanging in the air. I wasn't used to appearing and reappearing in such an enclosed space; I hadn't been prepared for how *loud* it was.

Ears ringing, I opened the chest, and beheld the blood.

It was contained in small, sealed bags, each one labeled with the name of the person who had donated it, and the date of the donation. I dug into the pile, pushing bricks of red ice aside until I found the bag I wanted, the bag I *needed*.

JANUARY O'LEARY—4/6/10.

The bag was cold enough to freeze my fingers, but I clutched it tightly, hands shaking, unwilling to let go. This had come from my mother, from her body, before Gordan had killed her, before we'd burned the shell she'd left behind. If there was any hope of getting her back, it was in this bag.

A thought, and I was wearing a coat, long and thick, with insulated pockets. I slipped the bag into one of them. There was a latch on the inside of the freezer door. I twisted it, and the door opened, and I ran.

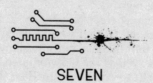

SEVEN

Back in my room—small and bright and decorated for a child much younger than I had allowed myself to be since my mother died—I placed the bag of blood on the nearest counter and flung myself into the dance of data all around me. Devoid of the need to remain physical, I could manipulate everything in my virtual world, unrestrained by the limits of the interface.

It only took a second to find the archival security footage. I called up the date and time I needed, and replayed it once, twice, a dozen times before I was sure it contained the elements I was looking for. Then, and only then, did I reach into the intercom and trigger a connection to a specific employee.

There was a pause. Then Elliot said cautiously, "Yes, April?"

"I need you to get some things for me."

The pause was longer this time, laced with confusion. I have few needs. I need power; I need disk space; I occasionally need new movies or video games, but I have a company credit card, and I understand how Amazon works. Things I can't obtain for myself are rare.

"What?" he asked finally.

"I need sea salt, juniper berries, a mandrake root, several raven feathers, six unmatched candles that have been previously lit, and—"

"Dried flowers," he finished. "April, what are you intending to *do*?"

"Do you ask out of curiosity or out of the inaccurate and misguided belief that you can somehow influence my actions?"

"Both," he said. "Neither. Where are you?"

"I am in the network."

"Can you come here, please?"

When I was my mother's heir—when becoming a Countess was unthinkable, because she was never going to die—I served as the County intercom system. I had been taught to come when called, the better to collect and relay messages. I didn't think. Instinct took over, and I was no longer in the wires, but standing in front of Elliot's desk, a scowl on my face.

"I was occupied," I said.

He took a deep breath, standing to put us on a more even level, and asked, "Why are you trying to summon the night-haunts?"

I blinked. "What brings you to this conclusion?"

"Don't play with me," he said. "I'm the one who got the flowers for Toby when she did the same ritual. It nearly killed her, and she used her own blood to power the circle. You can't do that."

"I can do something similar," I said.

"You haven't told me *why*."

"If I do, you must swear you will not tell Li Qin." I looked down my nose at him, trying to summon every ounce of nobility I had inherited, however impossibly, from the woman I was trying to restore. "Swear upon your fealty that until I grant permission, you will not reveal my secrets."

Elliot blinked, clearly taken aback. I think he sometimes forgets that I sat at my mother's knee for days that seemed without end, until they ended without fanfare. I may not be my mother, but I learned from her. I learned more than anyone understood.

"I swear," he said.

"Gordan lied," I said.

Elliot went very still. Finally, after a pause so long that I began to fear he would lose consciousness, he said, "Explain."

"She told October my mother could not be saved because her data had not been backed up to the server," I said. I cocked my head. "Perhaps she did not intend to lie. The buffer of the upload device was configured to store a limited amount of data, and it contained both my mother and Terrie when she spoke to October. Had she been able to upload Quentin, as she intended, some or all of their data would have been overwritten. I would prefer to think of her as a liar. Anything else would be sloppy." Gordan, for all her failings, had never been sloppy. She had been cruel, angry, and misguided, but she had been admirably tidy in her obsessions.

"April . . ."

"I had not considered whether she had been entirely truthful prior to today," I said. "I found the upload device. I checked the storage area. Mother's information is still present, as is Terrie's."

Elliot sat down.

"Alex has kept the body he historically shared with Terrie in working order. The absence of Mother's body is, however, an issue," I said. "Without a place to *put* her, she is no better than an echo in a cavern. I believe that, by negotiating with the night-haunts, I might be able to resolve this conundrum."

Elliot began to laugh.

I frowned, cocking my head to the side once more. "Why are you laughing? This is a perfectly viable agenda."

"You're telling me Jan . . . you're trying to say that we could bring Jan *back from the dead*?" He shook his head. "The others always seemed a little far-fetched, but hell. What *isn't* far-fetched around here? Oberon's eyes, April, you can't summon the night-haunts and ask them to build you a body. You'd need something for them to build *from*."

"I have it," I said calmly. "The company blood drive. Mother donated. I have her blood. If the night-haunts are as powerful as they are said to be, they should be able to synthesize a functional body from what I have to offer."

"I . . . April, this is madness." Elliot raked his hands through his hair, giving me a plaintive look. "You can't just ask the night-haunts to make a new Jan. It won't work."

"Nothing works if it's not tried," I said. "I want the things I've asked of you. I intend to make the attempt."

"They're not going to do this for free. What will you—" Elliot went still.

I waited. He had been my mother's seneschal and close companion for more than a century. If anyone knew how she thought, it was him. While I could not truly claim my thoughts mirrored hers, she was the one who had taught me to look past the logical solution to find the illogical, ideal one.

"You can't," he said.

"I intend to," I said.

"But . . ." He raked his hands through his hair again, giving me a helpless, hopeless look. "What if they call your bluff?"

"It will not be a bluff." I felt oddly serene. "You, yourself, agreed that it was reasonable to prioritize one resurrection above the rest. If the night-haunts will not restore my mother so that we might attempt her awakening, I will not permit the others to be returned to their bodies. Without my consent, given that they are my subjects, Li Qin will be unable to approve October's intervention. The night-haunts will never be granted access to their deaths. They will go hungry when they could have been fed."

"I—" Elliot stopped. "I'm not going to change your mind, am I?"

"No."

"What do you need from me?"

I frowned. "Are you finished arguing?"

"No." He laughed unsteadily. "I want to fight you for a *year*. You're willing to gamble everything for Jan—and so am I. Almost."

"You do not wish to gamble with Yui."

"No. I don't."

"Then why are you agreeing?"

His laughter this time was even unsteadier. "Because whether I like it or not, you're my liege."

"For now." If January could be restored, her oaths would supersede mine.

I had never wanted anything more in all my life.

"When do you want to do this?"

"As soon as possible. Tonight. It must begin at sunset."

"All right." Elliot stood again. "I guess I'm going to start calling florists."

I nodded to him and disappeared, trusting him to call me when he was ready to begin. For the moment, I needed . . .

I needed the code. I needed my mother. Not the reality of her, which was still outside my grasp, but the idea of her, the cool and continuous dream of her. She had never questioned my right to be the person that I am, only rejoiced as I grew more and more into the space she had opened for me. She had saved me. All I wanted now was the opportunity to do the same for her.

Deeper and deeper I traveled into the company file server, until I reached the security files I had sequestered away from all other eyes. Some things are not for sharing. I dove into them, and there she was, my mother, January O'Leary, a book open on her knees, paper and pictures and physical reality, with a little blonde girl pressed against her side. It was always odd to see myself from the outside, but I could no more remove my image from the footage than I could delete a part of my own personality. This had happened. This was true.

I started the playback.

" 'But when the girl came out of the woods, what do you think she saw?' " read my mother, giving the child beside her a small squeeze. " 'It was a stone well, set against a low stone wall, surrounded by the most beautiful roses she had ever seen . . .' "

The memory of my mother continued to read, while the memory of the girl I had once been listened with the rapt attention of someone who did not believe that the world was ever going to change. I sat down at their feet, resting my elbows on my knees, and closed my eyes, and listened.

When the story ended—and it was an unfortunate truth of the things I had learned, of the woman I had become, that all stories end—I started the recording over again with barely a thought. Over and over, I played it, until it seemed like I had been safe in this preserved moment forever, until it seemed I would never be compelled to leave. I could stay here, with my mother telling me stories, and leave the running of my County to better hands. I could be happy.

But my mother would still be dead, and Li Qin would not be happy without her. The thought of Li Qin's unhappiness troubled me. I frowned, reaching past the still-looping video to check the time. Three hours had passed since I had gone into the code. Worse, I had messages, five of them, all waiting patiently, like trained puppies, for me to notice them.

Three were from Elliot. He had the things I had requested. He was ready to bring them to me, as soon as I told him where to go. The other two were from Li Qin. October had agreed to come and wake our sleepers . . .

. . . and she was coming tonight. At midnight.

I was running out of time.

Cursing to myself in modem squeal and the sound of static, I dropped out of the code and back into Elliot's office. He wasn't there. I reached for the network of cameras and connections that spanned the company, and found him in the cafeteria, having pushed all the tables up against the walls.

A flicker of electricity and I was standing next to him, demanding, "Why didn't you send a priority alert?"

He didn't jump. He's known me for too long. "I wanted time to sort through my thoughts, and it wasn't sunset yet."

"Li Qin says October is on her way."

"October will be here at midnight."

"What if that isn't enough time?"

Elliot looked at me, and there was a weariness beyond measure in his eyes. "April, what you want to do will either happen in five minutes, or it won't happen at all. This isn't something that comes with a clear set of milestones and a set release schedule. The night-haunts will come or they won't. If they come, they'll do what you're asking, or they won't."

"I see." I glanced at the pile of supplies he had made on the nearest table. "This should be sufficient. Please proceed to my office and collect the bag of blood on my counter. It should be fully thawed by now. After that, you are excused."

"April—"

"I have reviewed the footage a hundred times," I said. "I know the ritual. I am not a blood-worker, but I am my mother's daughter. I have the right to borrow what magic may remain in her stored blood. You are not a blood-worker. You lack even that connection."

Elliot's face fell. "If you're going to do something this dangerous, I want to help. I *need* to help."

"I am made of light."

He paused. "I don't see how that follows."

"When October called them, they threatened to devour her. She was afraid. She is a hero, and she was afraid. You are not a hero. I do not want to risk you. I am made of light. Should they threaten me, I can remove myself from their presence with a thought. No damage need be done."

"Jan would never forgive me for leaving you alone."

I smiled, wan, strained, and hoping he could see how much I meant it. Emotion has never come easily to me, however much I wish it. "Let us hope she will soon be here to fail in her forgiveness."

Elliot hesitated. Then, in a low, tight voice, he said, "I'll get the blood."

He turned and walked toward the door, and I was alone. Truly and utterly alone.

"I will do this," I whispered, and started for the flowers.

EIGHT

When October had performed this ritual, it had been a difficult, complicated thing. It showed in the video I had of her, in the way she moved from component to component, hesitating before she slotted each new segment into place. She had no training in ritual magic, going through the motions with the clumsy precision of a child learning how to set the table for the first time.

I had no training in ritual magic, either. But I had the video, and I had proof that what she had done was something that could work. So I carried flowers, and I scattered juniper berries, and I drew my circle of salt.

I was standing in the middle of it when Elliot returned, the bag of blood in his hands. He looked at my work, and made no effort to hand the bag to me.

"Rituals like this demand the blood of the caster," he said. "You need me."

"My mother's blood belongs to me," I replied. "It does not flow in my veins, but her magic gave me life when all was lost; her family line gave me a name. The laws of sympathy state that in the absence of blood I can call my own, hers serves just as well."

Elliot looked surprised. I swallowed the anxious laughter threatening to overwhelm me.

"Never attempt to argue rules with someone who has them embedded in her very code," I said. "Give me the blood and go. Lock the doors from the outside and wait. I will succeed, or I will fail, and we will know soon. We will know before October arrives whether she is to be turned back at the gate."

For a moment, Elliot looked like he wanted to make one last attempt to sway me. Then his gaze flicked to the blood in his hands, and I knew that as much as he wanted his lover back from the dead, he wanted my mother—his liege, his best friend—even more. With a small nod, he handed me the bag. Then he turned and left the room, pulling the doors shut behind him. There was a click as he locked them. Not locking me in, but locking the rest of the company and the rest of the knowe out.

That was good. It was time to begin.

Stepping into the circle, I picked up the paring knife Elliot had provided and sat, the bag of blood resting on my crossed ankles. I closed my eyes, reaching past the thrum and buzz of my electronic world, looking for a natural rhythm that no longer belonged to me. It was faint, but it was there, and when the world clicked over into sunset, I felt the air change, turning tight.

Quickly, before I could reconsider, I unwrapped the mandrake Elliot had provided before drawing my knife across the bag of blood, splitting its surface and spilling what remained of my mother onto the floor. The smell of it, cold and sterile and yet somehow meaty and animal, struck me in a wave. I shuddered, and ran my fingers through it, hoping to make the connection between it and myself.

"My name is April ap Learianth," I said, using the form of Mother's name which accompanied her title, the one that predated this country, this culture, this place. "I am the daughter of January ap Learianth, who built this place with her own hands, and I am here to petition for your attentions. I bring you blood and flowers and salt from the sea. All our Courts together here support my plea."

The mandrake was lying motionless in the spilled

blood, soaking it up but not responding. That was wrong. On the tape . . . when October had performed this part of the ritual, the mandrake had come alive, consuming her blood, taking on her form. This was *wrong*.

Even as the thought formed, the flowers around the edge of my circle burst into bluish-green flame. The candles lit themselves. The mandrake might not be awakening, but the fire was burning. There was still a chance.

"I bring you life," I said, and pressed my hands flat against the floor, as I had seen October do. The mandrake did not move. I grabbed the knife and drove it, with its burden of my mother's cold, sluggish blood, through the mandrake's chest. The fire burned higher. "If I could speak with you a moment, I would be greatly appreciative."

I waited. The room seemed to quiet, until I could barely hear the crackle of the flames, until a low buzz, as if a hard drive were starting to skip, filled the air. I raised my head.

The night-haunts were there.

They surrounded me in a gauzy cloud: small, winged figures dressed in tattered shrouds, as if even their clothing came from the dead. Those closest to me looked solid, like ordinary fae compressed into miniature versions of themselves. It was . . . odd, to see Silene and Centaurs and Cait Sidhe with autumn leaf wings growing from their miniaturized backs, but the oddness was not enough to make them disappear.

They dropped lower, until one of them—a male, with eyes like frosted violets, and a starkly beautiful face—was hovering at the edge of the circle, on a level with my eyes.

"What do you think you're doing, daughter of trees?" he asked. There was more curiosity than cruelty in his tone. "We have been summoned here before. Do you know what you've done?"

"I am Countess April ap Learianth of Tamed Lightning," I said. "I have summoned you here according to a ritual passed from the Luidaeg to Sir October Daye of Shadowed Hills. I have called you, and you have come."

One of the night-haunts laughed and flew forward, joining the first. This one, I recognized. He had a seal's dark eyes, and spiky brown hair streaked with gray, like a seal's fur. "She's got you there," he said. "Toby strikes again."

"Remind me why we let her live," muttered the first night-haunt.

"I know you," I said. They both stopped talking and looked at me. I kept my eyes on the second one. "You were her suitor, weren't you? The Selkie man who came to help her."

The night-haunt looked at me sadly. "I was him most recently, yes. He died. Now I wear his face, and remember him, as is the accord between ourselves and the rest of Faerie. I remember you, too, April. You've grown."

"I had to."

"Why have you called us here?" He looked at the motionless mandrake in front of me, and frowned. "The ritual is incomplete. The blood spilled is not your own."

"The blood belongs to my mother."

His face softened. "January is not among our number."

"I know. None of the dead of this place are with you, except for Gordan." I looked at the flock, searching for that second familiar face. "Where is Gordan?"

"We aren't the only flock," he said. "She didn't want to return here, and we didn't make her. Guilt lives into the grave."

The thought was chilling. I was suddenly, completely grateful for the knowledge that when I died, I would not join the night-haunts. Nothing without blood and bone to consume could ever be counted among them.

"I see," I said. I focused on the night-haunt at the

front of their number, the one who wore the Selkie's face. "I have called you *for* my mother."

The night-haunt frowned. "I don't understand. Her death was denied to us."

"Because it was no true death," I said. "Her body was destroyed, but the part of her you could make your own was trapped, held outside the ordinary way of things."

The night-haunts whispered and buzzed. The Selkie-haunt's frown deepened. "We are sorry for your loss, and for our own," he said. "But what does this have to do with the ritual?"

"I want you to make her a new body." I picked up the mandrake and offered it to him. "I know you have the skill. This blood is hers. It will work. The ritual will be sound."

All the night-haunts stared at me. The room seemed to grow darker and colder as they closed in, their wings buzzing wildly. My outline blurred, static and distortion, before resolving back into the shape I was determined to hold until this was done. The night-haunts were recalcitrant enough when dealing with one they viewed as an adult. Who knew how they would respond if forced to negotiate with a child?

"You would ask us to make a manikin?" asked the Selkie.

"No," I said. Before the night-haunts could react, I continued, "I want you to make *her*. I want you to use fae blood to craft fae flesh. I know it can be done." I knew no such thing, but I remembered my mother telling her programmers that she *knew* they were capable of things they claimed were impossible. They had always delivered. Once they had known that she believed in them, they had always delivered.

The blood was hers. If the night-haunts were capable of crafting human flesh from nothing, they could craft fae flesh from fae blood. I knew they could do it.

If my mother could craft a Dryad from splinters and circuits, the night-haunts could give her back to me.

I knew they could.

"You ask too much," said the Selkie. "It's never been done."

"You can do it anyway."

"Why should we?" demanded another night-haunt, a female Barrow Wight with wings like cobwebs strung over elm leaves and hair the color of blackened oak. "Even if we could, we owe you nothing. You had no right to summon us. You offer us no reward for a favor you should never have asked."

"I offer you the only reward that matters to you," I said calmly. "I offer you death."

The night-haunts drifted lower, their wings beating even faster. The Selkie looked at me suspiciously. "What do you mean?" he asked.

"My mother wasn't the only victim," I said. "She was merely the only victim to lose her body as well as her life. She needs a new body, if she's to continue. The others, however, can simply be awakened—something that does not require your intervention. October is on her way. She can put them back together. She can undo what should never have been done in the first place, and restore them. They will walk in the world. They will face its dangers. In time, I am confident some of them will risk too much or reach too far, and will die properly, as they always should have done. Then, their deaths will come to you, to feed and sustain your flock. It may take years. It may take centuries. You will be fed either way."

"It sounds like all we have to do is nothing, and we'll get those deaths regardless," said the Selkie.

"If you refuse to restore my mother, if you will not construct her the new body I know it is within your power to grant, I will lock the gates, and I will not permit October's entry," I said. "The dead will stay dead. The lost will stay lost. Your stomachs will remain unfilled. The dead who are in my keeping will never join your number."

His eyes widened. "That would be . . . you would condemn so many people to lose the remainder of their allotted lives, all for the sake of your mother?"

"I would burn the world to ashes for the sake of my mother," I said. I had no need to force my calm. Serenity came easily to me now. "I would rip it up by the roots and leave them to dry and wither in the sun for the sake of one more minute in her arms. A few corpses are *nothing*. They are deadwood at the forest's edge, and I do not care for them."

"Do you have no heart?" demanded the female.

"That is still under debate," I said. "I have a hard drive. I have slivers of the wood that was my home, before I died. Before she saved me, and made me a new body, one that would last as long as I needed it to. I am not sure a heart went anywhere into my construction."

"Surely you wouldn't punish so many for the sake of one," said the Selkie.

"I would," I said. "I will."

"What if we try, and can't accomplish what you want?" asked the Selkie. "A fae body . . . is very different from a manikin designed to rot into nothing."

"If you truly try, if I believe you have truly tried, I will allow October to try as well," I said. "But I must believe you. If I do not, the doors remain locked, the dead remain dead, and we will never speak of this again."

"We can't *make* you believe us!" protested the female.

"Then I suggest you try *very* hard," I said.

"We'll need the mandrake," said the Selkie.

I picked it up, leaned forward, and dropped it outside the circle. It didn't have time to hit the ground. The night-haunts swooped down and whisked it away, while the Selkie hung suspended, looking at me.

"How long do we have?" he asked.

"October comes at midnight," I said. "I will return shortly before that deadline. We shall see, then, what doors are to be opened, and which are to remain closed."

I disappeared, leaving the flowers burning, leaving the air heavy with night-haunts, and leaving the last material traces of my mother's life behind.

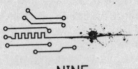

NINE

Elliot jumped when I materialized in his office, his arms flailing as he nearly sent his chair toppling over backward. I watched with interest. People do not fall as often as they once did when faced with my abrupt appearances. Familiarity breeds both contempt and a certain degree of inconvenient wariness.

"It is done," I said. "The fire alarms in the cafeteria will no doubt notify us if we need to be concerned."

His eyes widened. "The night-haunts *came*?"

"They came, and we spoke, and they took the sacrifice I offered them." I shook my head. "Really, I do not understand why October made such a big deal about the process. They were perfectly civil with me."

"April, you don't have a *body*. Not the way the night-haunts measure that sort of thing. They can't punish you for summoning them the way they'd punish someone else, like October, or me. All they can do is get angry."

That wasn't all they could do. They could also refuse to build a new body for my mother's consciousness. She wasn't like me, a program that could be installed in any hardware capable of supporting her needs. She understood what she was supposed to be too well. I could spend a hundred years trying to integrate her ashes with a fresh server, and all I would manage to resurrect would be a broken shadow, incapable of understanding what I had done to it, or why.

No. This was the right way. This was the way that suited the operating system of my mother, the way that seemed most likely to bring her back whole, healthy, and sane.

"Li Qin was asking for you," said Elliot.

I shot him a sharp, wary look. "What did you tell her?"

"Tell her?" He laughed unsteadily. "That you were working on a private project. Maeve's teeth, April, did you think I was going to say 'oh, your adopted daughter is trying to blackmail the night-haunts into helping you resurrect your wife, who we all thought was lost forever, and if they won't, she's going to leave everyone else dead to punish them'? I'm pretty sure she would have gone looking for you."

"And she would have found me. Li Qin has always been lucky that way." Lucky, and more than lucky. She can bend probability with an artist's skill, and while fortune always snaps back on her—always balances itself out—she knows how to make it dance to her desires. Without her, Mother would never have been able to make my integration with the hardware work. Even if Li Qin didn't know it at the time, she powered my salvation.

I owed her so much. I owed them both so much. It was past time I started to repay them for everything they had done for me.

A quick inward glance at the network told me it was almost eleven. Time must have twisted inward on itself while I was in the ritual circle, an unfortunate side effect of using my actual magic, which still believed me to be something green and growing. Dryads thrive on slow magic. It sustains us, allows us to keep our trees—which are more mortal than the flesh of our cousins, who do not age, or grow, or die in the same ways that we do—alive and thriving for far longer than the seasons should deem possible. Dryads are not truly immortal like the Daoine Sidhe or the Tylwyth Teg, because trees must shed their leaves and put forth new fruit to remember what it is to be a part of the forest. But they can live a long, long time.

I will live far longer, now that I am no longer a part of that slow and subtle process. I wish I could regret that.

"Are they here?" I pulled my attention out of the network, returning it to Elliot. "October, has she arrived?"

He nodded. "She and Li Qin are in the basement, along with Toby's squire."

"You should have told me!"

"You were busy."

He was correct—of course he was correct; the nighthaunts were not the sort to sit patiently and wait while I took a meeting elsewhere—but I glared at him all the same.

"What did you tell them?" I demanded.

"That they couldn't begin until you got there, and I couldn't watch," he said. "It wasn't a lie. I know if it works, they'll call me, and if it doesn't, I don't want to know until I have to."

"I said October was to be locked out until the nighthaunts agreed!" My voice was turning shrill, hurting my own ears.

Elliot looked at me flatly. "I told Li Qin," he said. "She opened the doors anyway. You've got a problem, take it up with your mother. She agreed that nothing would happen until you were there. Honestly, under the circumstances, I feel like that's all you were going to get. October's a hero. You were never going to keep her waiting on the stoop."

The rules of Faerie are elastic things, capable of bending themselves into incredible configurations before they actually break. Heroes have always been, and will always be, a strain on those rules. They go where they like. They do what they will. They save us, but the damage they do in the process is sometimes the thing we truly crave salvation from.

"Watch the security feed from the cafeteria," I commanded. "When the night-haunts return, call me. No matter what I seem to be doing, call me. You have permission to use my security override."

I didn't wait for his reply before vanishing, hurling myself into the code and racing along it to the access port in the basement, half-hidden behind a filing cabinet. I reached for it, crackling like an electrical short in my hurry to make myself manifest.

Li Qin was standing between two of the covered cots, her hands resting beside the heads of two of the victims—Yui and Barbara, our first and most innocent dead. She was looking at a tall, underfed woman in a leather jacket, whose brown hair was streaked with incongruous gold. As for October . . .

She looked wearier than she had been the last time I had seen her, something I wouldn't have believed possible if I hadn't seen it with my own eyes. Faerie is not easy on heroes. The bones in her face had shifted since then, becoming sharper, less human. She was burning out one side of her blood, becoming something new. I could sympathize with the pain of the process. I, too, had once become something new.

A tall boy on the verge of becoming a tall man stood behind her. His hair had darkened from the careless dandelion gold of our first meeting, becoming a deeper, stranger shade of bronze, but his eyes were still exceedingly blue, and he still looked comfortable in his own skin. He offered a wan smile when he saw me. I inclined my head in reciprocal acknowledgment.

Li Qin glanced over her shoulder. Her smile was

warmer, if underscored with understandable anxiety. "Hello, sweetheart. Elliot told me you were indisposed."

"Elliot also informed you that I did not want this ritual to begin until I was present," I said sternly. "Why did you refuse to heed him?"

"Nothing has begun," she said.

"The ritual will work best if it starts at midnight," said October. "Blood magic likes the stupid dramatics."

I looked at her. "The ritual may not begin at all," I said.

October blinked. Then she scowled, anger rolling across her face like malware. "What do you mean?" she asked. "Li Qin said—"

"This is not Li Qin's County," I said. "This is mine. I have one additional component to add to the process. If it is not completed in time, I am afraid we will not be able to continue."

"April?" asked Li Qin. "Did you find something in my notes that I had overlooked?"

"Not in your notes," I said, keeping my attention on October. "The trouble with notes—the trouble with anything in the material world—is that they are only as honest as the people who compose them. You recorded the truth as you knew and understood it. I do not accuse you of lying to me, Mother. But other people have told lies. Other people have obfuscated their data."

October opened her mouth to speak. Then she paused. "April," she said, in a careful tone, "why is there blood on your hands?"

I can carry things with me when I transit through the network. Sometimes it is a conscious choice, as when I deliver Elliot's lunch to his office on the days when he doesn't feel like he can handle seeing anyone. The soda is always flat when I arrive, and batteries are often exhausted, hence my refusal to transit with the upload device . . . but I can do it. Other times, it is automatic. Mother used to clip ribbons in my hair, and I would wear them for days, somehow transmuting them into pure data when I disappeared, then reconstructing them from light and pixels when I came back.

Mother always said that one day, she would figure out how I did that, and it would allow her to upload anything she wanted into infinite, flawlessly expandable storage. She called it the "Pokémon project," and she had never had the time to begin. Death came first.

I was going to fix that. The proof was on my fingers, which were stained red and streaked with ash.

"I am working on an independent research project," I said, tucking my hands behind my back. Judging by the expression on October's face, out of sight was not out of mind. Upon further consideration, I did not care. "The results should be in by midnight. If they do not match my desired outcome, I am afraid I will be unable to approve this ritual."

"Not even for Alex?" asked Quentin. He glanced at one of the cots, where a slender, black-haired woman lay unmoving. Terrie was an interesting case, as the victims of Gordan's upload process went: by day, her body was male, and belonged to her "brother," Alex. They shared physical space, but not mind or memory, and when the upload device had been inserted into their mutual flesh, it had drained her away, not him. By day, Alex lived. By night, Terrie died. When it happened on company property, she generally tended to wait out the hours of darkness in their shared office. She must have been carried to the basement for the ritual's sake.

"Alex's position is awkward, but not untenable," I said flatly. "Merrow are bound to the water; Dryads are bound to their trees. Alex is bound to the daylight. His chains are no direr than any other's." The fact that Terrie's consciousness was trapped alongside my mother's was beside the point. I would have them both, or I would have neither.

"That's cold," said Quentin.

"It is necessary."

October, who had been silent through all of this, frowned and asked, "Who lied to you?"

I looked at her. She would understand. If anyone would understand, she would, because when Gordan had taken Quentin, she had been willing to risk everything to get him back. She understood what it was to gamble the world for the sake of her family.

"Gordan," I said.

She went very still, and I knew she understood. She had seen the blood on my hands. She could no doubt smell it as well; smell the traces of my mother's magic lingering there.

Li Qin—who had not been here when things went wrong, who had heard about it after it was already over, when Elliot had finally tracked down a way to contact the knowe where she had been staying—looked between us, a frown on her face.

"What aren't you saying?" she asked. "What in the world could be so important that it would make you refuse to let us bring back these people? They're your *friends*, April."

"They are my colleagues at best, and my acquaintances at worst," I replied. "They consider me a software innovation gone too far, and who's to say they're wrong? My attempts at independence got them killed."

She winced, but didn't contradict me. That was for the best. Much as I adored my surviving mother, she was ill-equipped to argue with me in matters of guilt. She carried her own burden. I carried enough for both of us.

Instead, in a small voice, she asked, "What could possibly matter enough for this?"

"Please do not ask me again," I said. I felt weary all the way to the core of my code. "Until I have succeeded or failed, I do not wish to tell you."

"How *is* Alex?" asked October abruptly. The question was a little too loud, a little too brassy: she was trying to distract Li Qin. It was a transparent ruse, especially to Quentin, who had watched her magically-enhanced dalliance with Alex from a close, if confused, distance. He grimaced, looking at anything but his knight as his cheeks burned red.

"Well enough," said Li Qin. "He never really sleeps anymore—he just dies when the sun goes down and Terri takes control of the body. It's beginning to wear on him. I think he used to get the benefits you or I would get from dreaming from being his sister's ride-along, back when they functioned as they were intended to."

"Well, hopefully, we can fix that," said October. "Tell me more about this ritual."

Li Qin produced a folder and began explaining its contents, rattling through lists of steps and connections to similar, sympathetic magics. She was talking fast and firmly, like she wanted to sound so convinced of her own correctness that there was no room for a dissenting view. She did not mention the chance that October would sleep for a decade after the deed was done. I did not remind her.

There was a beep in my ear before Elliot's voice said, "April, I have movement on the cameras in the cafeteria."

"I see," I said. Turning to the others, I continued, "I am needed elsewhere. I will return. Please do not raise the dead without me."

Then I was gone, back into the network, back into the living lightning nothingness of the world where I belonged, moving like thought across the length of the building, until the outlet spit me out into the dim, smoky cavern of the cafeteria, where my piles of dried flowers still smoldered with a green, terrible light. The fire alarms had yet to go off. That was due to the magic, no doubt, and not something I could or should ascribe to maintenance.

I still made a mental note to have the batteries checked.

There was a sound above me, as of dead leaves rustling in the wind. I looked up, and the night-haunts descended, a black cloak settling gently over the room. They touched down on the floor this time, folding their wings as they looked at me. Only the night-haunt with the Selkie's face remained airborne.

"We don't care for blackmail, and we don't care to be manipulated," he said. "If you do either of these things again, we will dedicate ourselves to destroying you. Our reach among the living is limited, but there are ways. Do you understand me?"

"Yes," I said, without hesitation. I had no intention of doing this again, and his irritation was more than justified. I know what it is to be used for what I am and what I can do, with little regard for what I might desire.

"What you asked of us should have been impossible. You understand that, as well?"

"I do." I cocked my head. "You said 'should.' It was not?"

"Blood is strength, especially among the children of Oberon." The Selkie smiled, and his teeth were too sharp and too bright for the kin his face would claim. "They call themselves Titania's now, but the blood remembers, and the blood will always win."

"I brought you her blood."

"You did. You brought us blood and flowers—and you are, in your own way, the truest application of flower magic I've ever seen, in all my centuries. An illusion that thinks, dreams, and schemes for itself. Honestly, you're enough of a delight that I might have done this anyway, just for the sake of what you are." He fixed me with a steely gaze, and he looked nothing like the Selkie at all, for all that he wore the Selkie's face. "Never again. Promise me."

"I promise."

"Promise on the loss of all our favors. We'll take them back, if you betray us. The rules that separate us from the living have their loopholes."

"I promise you on the loss of all your favors. On the rose and the root and the rot and the thorn, I swear."

The Selkie nodded, apparently satisfied. "It is done," he said, and snapped his fingers. The night-haunts rose in a whispering cloud, leaving the pale, motionless body of January O'Leary on the cafeteria floor.

I blinked through space and was instantly beside her, dropping to my knees as I stared at the sharp points of her ears and the red-streaked brown of her hair. It felt like my code was freezing, like the disk that held my heart was glitching uncontrollably, making it impossible for me to move.

The fire alarms went off. The sprinklers came on. I grabbed her body off the floor like a discarded doll, bundling her tightly in my arms, and I was gone, and so was she.

When we had been testing the limits of what I could carry through the code—Mother laughing and throwing me things, Elliot wary and taking notes—we had determined that I could carry something twice my size a short distance, if the need was great enough. For living things, the journey would seem to take no more than an instant. They were blind to the code. For inanimate things, the length of the journey was irrelevant. For me, though . . . I felt every second.

Five seconds, to pull my mother's lifeless body from the cafeteria and into the electrical currents running through the knowe. Five seconds to travel from the cafeteria to the basement, where Li Qin and the others waited.

I was dry when I reappeared, having shed the water somewhere between the seconds, but January was still wet and limp and dead in my arms. Li Qin screamed, a short, sharp sound, clapping her hand over her mouth and staring at us in abject shock. October and Quentin exchanged a nod, moving toward me, helping to lift January onto the nearest open cot.

"What did you do?" asked October.

"I contacted the night-haunts, and bargained with them for the construction of a new body." It sounded so *simple*, put in those terms. It sounded almost reasonable.

"Why?"

"Because Gordan lied to you, or rather, Gordan did not tell the full truth." I looked past her to Li Qin, who was shaking and silent, tears rising in her dark, beloved eyes. "Gordan said my mother could not be resurrected, because she had not been uploaded to the server. This was correct. But the data upload device possesses local storage. It had never been purged. As long as the battery remained functional, the data was retained."

"Where is it now?"

"In my room." I offered October a smile. She did not return it. "I have it connected to a charging port, to restore and extend battery life. If a resurrection is to be performed, it will include my mother. I could not permit anything less."

"Wait," said Quentin. "Why not let the others be brought back and then deal with the night-haunts?"

"I required something I could bargain with," I said simply. "I bargained with their lives, or rather, with their deaths."

"Everything that lives can potentially die," said October. "If you didn't let me bring them back, the night-haunts would never have them."

"Exactly."

"April." Li Qin finally lowered her hands. "April, are we going to have to kill someone?" She would do it, if I told her "yes": I could hear in in her voice.

I have never been so glad to assert the negative.

"No," I said. "Time will do that. Please. I am here, and my mother is here, and I have sent a message to Elliot, instructing him to collect the device. He did not wish to be here. I find I do not care. Please, can you begin the ritual?"

October nodded, and the world was different.

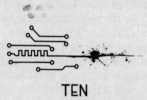

TEN

Li Qin showed them where to connect the wires and where to draw the ritual signs, and Elliot and Quentin followed her lead, assistant coders in a project too grand to be written in anything less than flesh and bone. October followed behind them, painting her own blood on the lips and hearts of the deceased, constantly reopening the cuts in her fingers as she raced against her own rapidly-healing flesh. She grimaced every time, as if the pain was never lessened, only reconfigured. It must be a terrible thing, in its way, to be so close to indestructible.

The server where most of the dead were stored was large enough to seem imposing, like it belonged here, in this mortuary turned mad scientist's laboratory. The device where my mother and Terrie waited for their own resurrections was much smaller, much more easily overlooked. I did not dare transfer them between the servers, even though it would have simplified the wiring immensely. The chance of corruption of the files if I moved them more than once was too great. We could deal with a little inconvenience, for the chance of bringing my mother home.

When the bodies were marked and wired, Elliot and Quentin helped to move the cots, positioning them like the spokes of a wheel. Li Qin stepped up next to October, looking nervous for the first time since this had all started.

"The accountings we have are all for solo resurrections, but those seem to be draining enough that I'm not sure it would be a good idea to take them one at a time," she said. "If we do it all at once—"

"It's unlikely to kill me, but you're worried about putting me to sleep for a couple of years," said October dryly. She snorted at Li Qin's startled expression. "What, you think 'hero' means 'sucker'? I called the Luidaeg as soon as you told me what you've been dancing around since I met you. I'm happy to help fix this. I'm *ecstatic* that we might get Jan back. But I did my homework."

"You came anyway," I said.

October nodded. "I did. I'm stronger than the people in those stories. I've got more experience with bleeding than anybody has any business having. I may need to drink a gallon of blood and Tylenol after this—"

"And people wonder why I hate blood magic," muttered Quentin.

"—but I'll be fine. So let's go. What do you want me to do?"

Li Qin picked up the braided ropes of thorny vines and electrical cable that had been inserted just under the skin above their hearts. It was a shallow incision, the rope anchored no more than an inch or so beneath it; with the proper treatment, it might not even scar. It would, hopefully, be enough.

"Hold these," she said. "Bleed along them, and call the magic according to the guidelines I've given you. We'll turn on the equipment that houses their . . . vitality."

"I'm not sure whether this is more or less creepy because you keep avoiding the word 'soul,' " said October.

"Three minutes to midnight," said Elliot.

"Good luck," whispered Li Qin. There was a flex in

the air, and I knew she hadn't been able to help herself: not faced with the chance that, after everything, she might not be a widow after all. She had bent the luck. We would all have to live with the repercussions, whenever and however they chose to strike.

That was for later. Quentin walked over to the lights, as October picked up the ropes, hesitated, and began to chant.

"If we shadows have offended," she said, "think but this, and all is mended; that you have but slumbered here while these visions did appear, and this weak and idle theme no more yielding but a dream."

Magic rose around her, a faint scent of green, green grass, like a freshly-mowed lawn, underscored by copper—or perhaps blood. It was difficult to tell. She was clenching the ropes so firmly that the vines had pierced her flesh, and blood was leaking from between her fingers. It did not drip to the floor. Instead, it ran along the body of the rope, from the single strand she held and into the branching strands that connected to each of the bodies in turn.

Elliot turned on the server where the bulk of the dead were stored, adding its hum to the air. I did the same with the upload device where January and Terrie's memories were kept, before reaching through the network and triggering both devices to begin transmitting their data.

Home, I commanded the slow, sluggish stream of information. It was easy enough to identify the individual minds, the unique memories that defined each data feed. I nudged them toward the correct channels, guiding them until the current took over. *Go home. You know where you belong. Go home.*

The data feeds accelerated and disappeared. Small disks, attached to the foreheads of the lost, sparked with sudden power, and everything was still.

October continued talking. "Gentles, do not reprehend; if you pardon, we will mend, and as I am an honest Puck, if we have unearned luck now to escape the serpent's tongue, we will make amends ere long!" The magic spiked. The electricity spiked as well, popping and arcing. Quentin made a short, sharp sound, and was silent.

Everything was silent. The machines had stopped buzzing. Alarmed, I reached for them, and found them still and dead, knocked off the network by the surge. October sagged, hands still clenched tight around the ropes.

"Else the Puck a liar call, so good night unto you all," she whispered. "Give me your hands if we be friends, and Robin shall restore amends."

Then she collapsed facedown on the concrete.

"Toby!" Quentin cried, rushing to her.

I let him. My own attention was for my mother, for the shape of her, the stillness of her, the impossibility of her. *Please,* I thought. *Please. I was a child. Let me be redeemed. Let me be forgiven. Please. Let me have just one reset to the original specifications.*

Across the room, Elliot made a choked noise, half sorrow, half joy. I glanced over. Yui was sitting up, her arms around his shoulders, her face buried in his neck. Peter was rubbing his forehead, wings fanning slowly. Colin was groaning. Barbara was gone . . . but there, beneath her cot, I could see the reflective eyes of a cat.

Terrie had rolled onto her side and was weeping uncontrollably, all without making a sound. That much, at least, had come cleanly out of the upload device.

When Li Qin gasped, I nearly missed it in the chaos. Then, slowly, I turned.

My mother's eyes were open.

She was looking at the ceiling, frowning, obviously confused.

"I don't have my glasses, and nothing's fuzzy," she said. "What the hell did I miss?"

Li Qin laughed, and the two of us flung ourselves on

top of her—my mother, her wife, our miracle—together, and held her like we'd never let her go.

We were never, never letting go

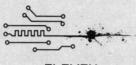

ELEVEN

"This is going to take some getting used to," said October, still pale and shaky, her hands wrapped around a large mug half full of blood and half of tea that Yui insisted had medicinal properties. If nothing else, it was warm.

"Says you," said my mother wryly. She was wearing a robe Li Qin had found in the employee showers. It was much too big for her, and it engulfed her like a wooly white snowfall. "Last night we had a killer in our midst, and I needed glasses to find my own ass. Now . . ."

"Everything is different."

"Not everything." Mother looked to where I was sitting with Li Qin. My outline kept shifting between adult and child, settling on the latter for longer and longer stretches. With my mother returned, I did not have to be an adult any longer. I could be a child again, long enough to learn what I still needed to know. Long enough to *understand*.

Li Qin had not stopped crying since January's return. Her tears were slow, ecstatic things, and she barely seemed to realize they were there. All her focus was for her wife . . . but her arm remained around my shoulders, and I knew that if any part of her had blamed me for her loss, I was forgiven. I was finally, fully forgiven.

"Queen Windermere is going to need to come and talk to you about what you want to do about the County, and Li Qin's stewardship of Dreamer's Glass, and everything," said October.

January grimaced. "Okay, *that's* different. But we'll figure it out. We always figure it out."

"Yeah." October paused before saying, "It's good to see you again."

"Yeah." January glanced at us again, eyes focusing first on Li Qin, and then on me. Her smile was the perfect coda to a perfect program: logical, inevitable, and so often unachievable.

"It's good to be home," she said, and we all were. Finally, we all were.